For Dottie —
All best
Stan Potter

Once A Warrior

Once A Warrior

a novel by

FRAN BAKER

DELPHI BOOKS
Lee's Summit, Missouri

Copyright © 1998 by Fran Baker

ISBN: 0-9663397-0-3

Library of Congress Catalog Number: 98-92659

First Delphi Books printing November 1998

Manufactured in the United States of America

Cover and book design by
Out on a Limb Publishing,
1810 East 51st Street
Tulsa, Oklahoma 74105
Phone: (918) 743-4408
Fax: (918) 743-5374

Quantity discounts are available on bulk purchases of this book.
For information contact
DELPHI BOOKS
P.O. Box 6435
Lee's Summit, MO 64064.

ALSO BY FRAN BAKER

When Last We Loved
Love In The China Sea
On Love's Own Terms
Seeing Stars
The Widow and The Wildcatter
King Of The Mountain
San Antonio Rose
The Lady and The Champ

For Vincent, for believing,
For Shane, for being Shane,

and

In loving memory of
Lieutenant Edmund Francis McCoy
Lieutenant Vincent de Paul McCoy
Sergeant Emeran Albert McCoy

Requiescant in pace.

Prologue

DOVER AIR FORCE BASE, DELAWARE; 1998

After thirty years, Johnny Brown was finally coming home.

Cat had dressed warmly this morning as the first breath of winter had blown in during the night, dropping the temperature below the freezing point but leaving the sky a brilliant, cloudless blue. Now she was all bundled up in a black coat, boots and gloves. A wide-brimmed hat shielded her face as much from the cameras as from the cold gold of the November sun.

And yet she shivered as she scanned the sky, watching for the transport plane that was bringing Johnny back to the world and thinking that he would have been the first to say it was a perfect day for flying.

"You okay?"

She glanced sideways at the question, asked in an undertone that was dense with concern. Only someone who knew her inside and out would have noticed the slight tremor that had just passed through her. That someone was the same man whom she had once branded a traitor and claimed to despise. A man whose "badge of honor" served as a daily reminder of how wrong she had been.

"Yes." She let out a breath she hadn't been aware of holding, then searched the angles and planes of his strong, scarred face. "And you?"

A trenchant smile twisted his lips as he turned his head, first to the right, then hard to the left, surveying the crowd that was milling about them in the shadows of the hangar. With a twinge of sadness, she wondered if he was reliving his own, very different homecoming. Recalling, perhaps, the way protesters had sneered at him and jeered at him and scorned him as a "baby-killer."

"Surprised," he said quietly.

But Cat heard him loud and clear because she hadn't known what to expect herself. The Vietnam War had ended more than a quarter of a century ago, and Americans now seemed to view it as ancient, albeit painful, history. So at the most, she had anticipated a private gathering of family and friends and a swift procession to the cemetery. Maybe someone from the Pentagon, maybe not, but no ruffles and flourishes and no one who really ranked.

Instead, there was a full honor guard, a military band and enough brass to launch a major offensive or quell a minor rebellion.

The human-interest angle of the story had drawn the press as well. Still photographers checked their camera lenses. Print reporters surrounded both the American Ambassador to Vietnam and the Chairman of the Joint Chiefs of Staff. A video crew from one of the networks' nightly newscasts made final preparations to film the upcoming ceremony, clips of which would soon be aired in a Veteran's Day segment.

There was a time when Cat would have jumped at the chance to generate this kind of publicity. But that was yesterday. Today she had a different agenda. She had come to bury Johnny at long last. To complete her role in his life by seeing to it that he received the respect and the recognition he'd earned from a country which had finally learned to distinguish between the war and the warrior. And she was grateful, more grateful than words could say, that she wouldn't have to do it alone.

She didn't need to turn around to know that her stalwart old soldier of a father was standing right behind her. Or that her mother, who'd died as gallantly as she had lived, was there in spirit. Even her brother and sister had set aside their radical differences to lend her their support.

Cat's eyes grew misty when she looked at her four children—her oldest son, who bore such a haunting resemblance to his father in those dress blues and spit-shined shoes; her "twins," who'd been born five months and a world apart; her daughter, whose delicate beauty was already turning heads—and the reminder of just how much Johnny had missed threatened to overwhelm her.

She shifted her gaze before she lost her composure and saw, like paired mirrors reflecting her own blurred tears, the poignantly familiar faces of a couple who had lost almost everything they held dear but had found a precious freedom in their adopted homeland.

Heedless then of the curiosity seekers and the cold, she took off her hat and rested her head on the shoulder of the man who had made this mission of closure possible for them all. He responded by putting his arm around her and pressing a kiss into the soft, silvering tangle of her hair. And she knew she was right where she belonged, where she had always belonged, within the shelter of his embrace.

"He's here." That deeply beloved voice vibrated in her ear as the big gray C-17 dropped, thundering, out of the sunlit sky and descended steadily toward the tarmac.

Yes, it really was a perfect day, Cat decided. Not just for flying, or even for meeting Johnny's long-delayed plane. But also for remembering those who had gone before . . .

PART ONE

Tiger Lily

Chapter One

STE. GENVIÈVE, FRANCE; 1944

"Bonjour, Monsieur." Anne-Marie Gérard spoke calmly even as her heart did a frantic pirouette inside her chest. She had just sat down to lunch with her grandfather when she heard the knock. Thinking it might be one of his patients with an emergency that couldn't wait, or maybe even her cousin, Henriette, with a special treat to spice up their tasteless meal, she had excused herself from the table and rushed to answer the front door.

Now terror whipped into the vestibule on the raw January wind. It curled around her stockinged ankles and clawed its way up her shaking legs. Her palms slickened with sweat, her breath sliced at her throat, and her face grew taut with the dread expectation suddenly coursing through her.

Nearly four years under the Nazi boot had taught her well. The short, stocky man in the pin-dotted overcoat and green fedora standing on the snow-covered step was her worst nightmare come true.

He was Gestapo.

What did he know and how did he know it? Anne-Marie gripped the edge of the door with icy fingers. Had some Judas of a collaborator denounced her? Were the agent's henchmen waiting around the corner to search the house? Or worse, the garage?

The thought of who they would find out there made her ill with fright. Until she reminded herself that the Gestapo didn't normally knock *on* doors. They knocked them down.

As her panic faded, she found her wits. It was better to show no fear or hesitation. That much she had learned in her dealings with the German patrols that routinely stopped civilians and demanded to see their papers. Even a moment's delay in producing one's identity card with its photograph and official stamps could result in a brutal beating. What happened to those who'd either left theirs at home or were caught with forged ones was too horrible to dwell on.

"How may I help you?" Keeping her expression as serene as possible, she opened the door a little wider to prove she had nothing to hide.

"Who are you?" The agent's small round eyes focused on her intently as he grunted his demand in atrocious French. His mouth was thin, his cheeks fat, and his ears came to porcine points at the top. Redness from the cold mottled his pallid skin.

Anne-Marie met his gaze unflinchingly. She refused to cower before this *cochon*. He and the others of his ilk—sons of sows, every one of them—had dismembered her family, deported her best friend and defeated her beloved France. Someday he would pay for what he had done, she vowed to herself, but not nearly as dearly as he deserved.

"I'm Dr. Gérard's granddaughter." She was proud of the composed sound of her voice. "And since he has no nurse to work with him, I'm also his medical assistant."

He continued to stare at her, his piglet eyes gleaming beneath the brim of his hat, and she found it amazing that he could go so long without blinking. At the curb behind him idled a sinister black Citron *traction avant*—the Gestapo's favorite kind of car. The driver, sporting SS tabs on his collar and a swastika armband, kept watch on the road through rimless glasses.

"I want to see the doctor." The agent's hands remained at his sides, hidden in the folds of his overcoat, but his burly shoulders moved menacingly under the heavy wool.

"My grandfather is having lunch, but I'll certainly tell him you're here." She stepped back on legs that were rubbery despite her resolve. "Would you like to wait in the clinic?"

He nodded curtly and pushed past her, into the dimly lit vestibule. His arrogance was such that he didn't even bother to stamp the snow off his feet. He seemed to assume she had nothing better to do than to clean up after him.

Anne-Marie shut the biting wind outside and grabbed her sweater off the corner coatrack. The brown wool cardigan had belonged to her grandmother and had been mended in a dozen places. The new holes in the elbows aside, it helped to ward off the sudden chill that permeated her grandfather's home.

"Which way?" he demanded.

She indicated the door on his right. The one to the left led to the living area she shared with her grandfather. Only when the agent rudely gestured that she should open the door to the clinic for him did she notice that he carried a full bottle of Rémy Martin cognac.

"For the pain," he said in response to her raised eyebrow.

"The pain?" she repeated in a strained voice.

"I have an infected tooth." Not seeming to notice her agitation, he eyed her accusingly across the narrow entrance hall. "And your village has no dentist."

Anne-Marie judiciously refrained from pointing out that that was because the dentist and his family had recently been "resettled" in Germany and their house confiscated by the government to pay the "special assessment taxes" levied against all Jews.

The fate of the dentist's daughter haunted her to this day. She could still see Miriam Blum, with her shiny black curls, ripe-olive eyes and that horrid yellow star she'd been forced to wear on her clothing. And she remembered with fondness all the nights that they had slept over at each other's house, closeting themselves in the privacy of one or the other's bedroom to giggle and to gossip and to plan their futures.

But if the rumors about the death camps proved to be true, poor Miriam no longer had a future.

Anne-Marie couldn't look at the man she held partially responsible for that because she was certain that he would see the hatred in her eyes. Instead, she bowed her head in what she hoped he would interpret as submission and, with an after-you gesture, ushered him into the anteroom. It was empty, as it always was in the early afternoon, so he had his pick of chairs.

"Please, sit."

"I prefer to stand."

Seeing him with his back to the wall and his eyes trained on the window that faced the street, she realized that the agent didn't feel safe from sabotage even in a doctor's office. Yesterday's derailment of that train carrying reinforcements into lower Normandy, which had left three German soldiers dead and a number of others severely injured, must have hit close to home for him. What she felt wasn't triumph, not yet, but simply anticipation of the day when *les boches* were driven out of her homeland and into the bowels of hell, where they belonged.

"As you wish." Her wartime wooden soles clunked on the bare floor as she crossed to the door. She left it open in case another patient should arrive before she returned. "I'll get my grandfather."

"Tell him to hurry," Piggy directed. "I have a meeting to go to."

Her ears perked up at that. "I'm sure he can see you right away."

In the combination sitting-dining room across the vestibule, Dr. Henri Gérard had just finished his simple lunch of watery bean soup and stale bread and was reaching for his customary demitasse.

The wind rattled the open-shuttered windows, making Anne-Marie grateful for the fire in the hearth that helped to offset the effects of the increasingly severe gas cuts imposed by the Germans. Sick of living in the dark, she had drawn back the silk damask draperies and raised the blackout shade that morning. Then almost wished she hadn't when she saw the dust that felted the furniture and the lint that covered the fading carpet.

Now, as her grandfather looked up from the medical journal he'd been perusing in the gray light, the shame she'd managed to hold at bay came rolling back.

When his wife was alive, Henri had been as nattily groomed as a

Parisian *boulevardier*. A petite woman with the figure of a pouter pigeon and the fussy energy of a mother hen, Yvonne Gérard had sponged and pressed her husband's suit every morning, trimmed his snowy hair once a week, and turned his shirt collars whenever they began to look worn. And after his nurse unexpectedly eloped, she'd rolled up her sleeves and added those duties to the cooking and cleaning chores she had taken such pride in performing herself.

Even a long bout with breast cancer hadn't slowed her down. At least not in the beginning. When the disease finally caught up with her, she fired three maids before finding one who was malleable enough to let her continue ruling the roost from her sickbed.

Her death had so devastated her widower that he scarcely noticed the Germans' lightning-quick strike against France some three months later. When Anne-Marie first came to live with her grandfather, shortly after the *blitzkrieg*, she'd been shocked to see that his hair had grown shaggy, his collar frayed, and his suit looking like a remnant of the Hundred Years' War. Most distressing of all, however, was the resignation—almost a sense of impending doom—which dwelled in his rheumy eyes.

It was no better now. Henri was still a shadow of his formerly impeccable self. The maid, after sweeping the dirt under the rug and setting an overcooked meal on the table, had quit. And Anne-Marie lived with the guilty knowledge that she had failed to meet Yvonnne's exacting standards.

"*Merde*," her grandfather cursed after drinking from the small cup. "This exotic 'coffee' the Germans are sending us tastes more like one of Hitler's stupid chemistry experiments every day."

Giving silent thanks that she had managed to close the living room door before his words took wing and settled in the wrong ears, Anne-Marie walked purposefully to the lace-covered table. "You have a patient."

"Already?" His bristly gray brows drew together in a confused frown as he glanced at the mantle clock above the blue-and-white tiled fireplace. "Can't a man even be allowed—"

"May I clear the table now?"

Something in her sharp tone of voice must have alerted him to the fact that this was no ordinary patient. He nodded and sat back in his chair, the nasty demitasse all but forgotten. Seeing the soup stains on his tie, she reminded herself to spot-clean it before he returned to the office.

"Gestapo." She deliberately clattered the china as she whispered the word.

"Here?" he hissed, his voice filled with dark history.

"In the anteroom."

"But . . . why?"

"He has a bad tooth." Ignoring her own growling stomach, she tucked the piece of bread she hadn't eaten into her skirt pocket for the wounded Royal Air Force pilot whom she was hiding with neither her grandfather's knowledge nor permission in the garage. "And extremely bad manners."

"Anne-Marie . . ." Bony fingers which had once been steady enough to perform the most delicate of surgeries but which now trembled with age and fear clasped her wrist with surprising tenacity. "You weren't rude to him?"

"Of course not."

When he nodded in relief, she felt a sharp twinge of remorse. Her grandfather had lost so much—even his *raison d'être*, it seemed—that it was only natural he was afraid. Not for himself, of course, but for her and for the rest of his family.

And perhaps of what was yet to come.

It was common knowledge that the Allies, led by the Americans, were going to invade Europe sometime this coming spring. Summer at the latest. The question was, where would the invasion begin? Convinced that it would come at the narrowest point of the English Channel, the Germans were now concentrating panzer and infantry divisions at the Pas-de-Calais.

But Anne-Marie believed that the *débarquement* might well come elsewhere. She had already learned the code name of the operation, Overlord, from the forbidden British radio broadcasts she listened to in the attic late at night. And the pinprick sabotage pattern by French resisters against German communication and transportation systems, while not yet of a scale to unduly alarm them, made her think that the Allies were planning to attack the coastal batteries behind the beaches at Normandy and move inland from there.

Which could eventually place Ste. Geneviéve in the path of their advance, if not in the thick of battle.

"You mustn't keep your new patient waiting, *Grand-père.*" She gently extricated her wrist from his grip. "He has a meeting to attend."

And if she was lucky, she thought, he might just have some important information to impart under the influence of that expensive cognac.

Anne-Marie pulled down the blackout shade on the winter-white moonlight flooding into her drafty bedroom, then turned to her cousin with a preoccupied smile. "I'm sorry, Henriette, I didn't hear what you said."

From her kneeling position on the double bed that they were sharing tonight, Henriette Bohec's eyes glittered excitedly in the chamberstick's flame that had lit their way up the dark staircase. "I said, I'm going to kiss the first American soldier I see!"

The thunderous snores emanating from their grandfather's room, directly across the hall, precluded an immediate response on Anne-Marie's part.

Cupping a protective hand around the flickering candle flame, she crossed to the door her cousin had carelessly left open and shut it with a silence born of practice. At twenty, she was only four years older than the giddy Henriette. Given the danger she'd faced of late, however, she sometimes felt one hundred and four years older.

Tonight was one of those times.

Satisfied that they wouldn't wake their grandfather, she leaned back against the doorframe with a heavy sigh. After scrubbing the office and washing the dinner dishes with the gritty gray soap that was going to be the ruin of her hands, she had dusted and swept the living area and banked the fire for tomorrow. That she had hours to go before she slept only added to her exhaustion.

Absorbed in her own thoughts, Anne-Marie didn't realize that Henriette was still waiting for a reply to her earlier statement until she caught the girl's expectant gaze in the wavering candlelight.

Straightening, she said the first thing that came to mind. "And if the soldier kisses you back?"

"Sticks his tongue in my mouth, you mean?" Henriette's horrified tone said that she hadn't thought before she spoke.

"That's usually how it happens." Even though Anne-Marie's own experience with kissing was rather limited, her "advanced" age gave her voice the ring of authority.

Henriette mulled that over for a moment before declaring indignantly, "If he uses his tongue, I'll slap his face!"

"That hardly seems fair." Anne-Marie realized she was sweating in spite of the cold that permeated her room. Both she and Henriette wore knitted shawls over and ribbed stockings under the voluminous, high-necked night-gowns they'd taken turns donning in the small bathroom next to their grand-father's office. Unbeknownst to her cousin, however, Anne-Marie had kept on the skirt and blouse and wool sweater she'd worn today. "First to kiss your liberator and then to slap him."

Henriette yawned, too tired to argue the point, then scrambled beneath the feather coverlet. She had bicycled the five frigid kilometers from her parents' farm to the village earlier that evening and was planning to go home tomorrow morning. But not before consuming her share of the eggs she had packed in straw and smuggled in her saddlebags to supplement the Gérards' usually meager breakfast of bitter ersatz coffee and tough, gray bread.

Candlelight projected Anne-Marie's well-padded shadow onto the whitewashed wall as she followed her cousin to bed.

To look at them lying side by side, one would never guess they were the daughters of siblings—sister and brother, in fact—because they were polar opposites.

Where Henriette's dark coloring reflected their Breton heritage, Anne-

Marie's Alsatian roots on her mother's side had lightened her hair to the shade of wild honey and her eyes to clear amber. Their lack of resemblance didn't end there. Henriette was short and top-heavy, partly due to nature and partly due to a lifelong diet of cream and butter and cheese, while Anne-Marie had been able to eat from morning till night before the strict wartime rationing set in without gaining an ounce on her taller, more slender frame.

"I think I'll offer the American a glass of Papa's Calvados instead of a kiss," Henriette said in a sleepy voice.

"That certainly sounds less troublesome." Anne-Marie blew out the candle, plunging the room into complete darkness, then crossed herself and clasped her hands together.

"What are you doing?"

"Praying."

Henriette chuckled drowsily. "For Guy Compain, I presume."

Anne-Marie's blood froze in her veins. "What makes you say that?"

"Papa told me that he saw you two coming out of the woods near the lake yesterday."

"Did he seem to think we were doing something wrong?" she asked in a careful voice that betrayed none of her sudden anxiety.

"He said you appeared to be arguing." Henriette took most of the coverlet with her when she turned onto her side, giving Anne-Marie her back. "A lover's quarrel, perhaps?"

Anne-Marie repressed a shudder of revulsion at the very idea of sleeping with Guy Compain. He was brave and uncompromising, she would grant him that, but he was also short and pimply and gauche. The fact that he was one of the few men over the age of eighteen still living in the village instead of doing forced labor in Germany made him, she supposed, a logical paramour in Henriette's innocent eyes.

"Actually, we were discussing Descartes." She affected a reflective tone as she rolled onto her opposite side so that she was lying—literally and figuratively—with her face to the wall.

"Who?" Sixteen-year-old Henriette was more interested in getting her hands on the latest issue of *Pour Elle* than she was in reading the words of some long-dead philosopher.

"'*Cogito, ergo sum*'," Anne-Marie prompted.

"You know I failed my Latin examination."

"'I think, therefore I am.'"

"Oh."

Enjoying herself at Henriette's expense was cruel, but Anne-Marie continued, embroidering a tale that rivaled the Bayeux Tapestry for complexity. If nothing else, she decided she would bore her cousin to sleep. "And then, of course, there's the whole question of mind over matter."

"What?"

"Do you believe the world exists, or is it only an illusion of our senses?"

"I didn't realize Guy was so serious," Henriette admitted after a moment's pause.

He wasn't. At least not about things like philosophy. In fact, he'd hated school and often bragged that he'd been expelled for writing BBC messages from the exiled General Charles de Gaulle on the blackboard during lunch break. Far be it from Anne-Marie, though, to correct Henriette's erroneous impression.

Besides, her real concern was her uncle. She didn't trust him. And with good reason. Not only did Henriette's father drink too much, but when the Calvados—the potent apple-pulp brandy he brewed from the trees on his farm—had finished dulling his senses, he talked too much.

"Did your father say anything else about Guy and me?" she inquired casually.

"Only that your mama and papa would roll over in their graves at such a liaison," Henriette mumbled into her pillow.

Tears stung Anne-Marie's eyes at the mention of her parents, who'd been killed during the June 1940 invasion. One day while she was shopping with a girlfriend near Rouen's Place du Vieux Marché, the square where Jeanne d'Arc had bravely died at the stake, a German bomb had hit their home and it had burned to the ground. Cringing in a doorway across town as the sirens wailed and the Stukas swept down, she hadn't known that it was already too late for her mother and father and a younger brother who'd been confined to bed with a touch of flu. Her dear, sweet Pap had come home from his law office for lunch and to check on him.

By nightfall, she'd been both an orphan and a refugee in a world turned upside down. Her immediate family was dead, the old Norman house of her birth had been flattened, and longtime neighbors were preparing to live without any sanitary facilities in cellars and in hovels made from blackened beams and planks. The next day she'd fled the rubble of Rouen with only the clothes on her back, joining the long line of defeated people plodding south, bypassing numerous other burned-out villages and praying that her father's younger sister would take her in.

But her aunt was a farmer's wife with four sons and a daughter of her own to feed. And her uncle, who had just received notice that the Germans were requisitioning his wheat harvest, had emphatically said "No more!" Her grief-stricken grandfather, however, had gladly welcomed his son's only surviving child into his home. Anne-Marie had lived with him ever since, earning her certificate from the local *lycée* and her keep by helping around the house and assisting him in his office.

It was the perfect "cover" for her Resistance work.

Resisting the Germans was, in fact, a family tradition. When the Prussians invaded Alsace in 1870, her maternal grandparents, who were determined to remain French, had moved to Caen, where her mother was born. And when the "war to end all wars" broke out in 1914 and France found herself crossing swords with Germany yet again, her father, a law clerk in Rouen, had sallied forth.

Now it was her generation's turn to answer the bugles of patriotism resounding across the land, and Anne-Marie was proud to be one of the partisans who'd rallied to the call.

She'd been careful to keep her grandfather in the dark about her activities with the local Resistance. What he didn't know, after all, wouldn't hurt him. But by agreeing to serve just this once as a *passeur*—one of the people who moved downed Allied pilots and Jewish refugees across occupied territories to safety—she had put him in jeopardy as well.

Still, she had decided it was a risk worth taking. Because if she'd known then what she knew now, she might have been able to help Miriam Blum.

Anne-Marie crossed herself again and said a silent "Amen." Outside, that bright bomber's moon shone down upon a village where all but one slept under a patchwork quilt of snow. Inside, Henriette's soft, steady snores and their grandfather's louder ones echoing from across the hall told her that her prayers had been answered.

"Ssh!"

"What's the matter?"

Shivering as much from nerves as from the bitter cold, Anne-Marie turned to the wounded RAF pilot crouching in the ditch beside her. After checking to be sure that both Henriette and her grandfather were sound asleep, she'd sneaked down the stairs and out the door of the house. Her "lodger," whom she'd alerted when she slipped into the garage while gathering wood for tomorrow's fire, had been lying in wait in the loft above her grandfather's coupe.

"I hear something," she whispered now in the English she'd learned at school.

"The German patrol?" he asked on a cloud of breath.

"They're not due back for twenty minutes." She'd managed to glean the timing of their new schedule while the Gestapo agent's bad tooth was being pulled. While she was at it, she'd filched a small glass of the cognac he'd anesthetized himself with before submitting to the painful extraction. She'd poured some of it into a snifter for her grandfather. The rest she'd used to disinfect the pilot's nasty leg wound before they'd set out from the village on foot.

The seconds dragged by as they listened intently. A twig snapped. Ice-crusted leaves rustled. Then an owl flapped out of a tree, showering them with snow.

Anne-Marie breathed a sigh of relief and then whistled softly in a prearranged signal. When a gnomelike figure rose out of the ditch on the other side of the road, she stood on cramped legs and gave the pilot a hand up. "Follow me."

The road they needed to cross was coated with a thick, slick layer of ice, making it hard for the limping aviator to keep up with her. Normally the crews of shot-down Allied planes escaped back to their bases through northern France, near the Belgian border. The Gestapo had recently infiltrated the Resistance network that repatriated them, however, so he'd been passed farther south by a friendly railroad man and was being flown back tonight.

"You're late," Guy Compain scolded, raising his wrist to check his cheap steel watch as they approached. He was Anne-Marie's age but had taken to wearing little boys' shorts, even in winter, to appear too young for forced conscription. So far, the Germans had been too busy trying to capture the more illustrious Resistance leaders to bother with some village idiot who didn't have enough sense to wear long pants when it snowed.

"Sorry, old chap," the Englishman gasped, "but I'm a bit wobbly on the pins."

"The leg wound he received when his plane went down is infected." Anne-Marie had switched back to French for the explanation. She slid a supportive arm around the pilot's waist and motioned for Guy to do the same on the other side. "Since my grandfather won't have any sulfanilamide powder until the Lysander comes, I poured a little cognac on it and gave him some aspirin for his fever."

"Let's go," Guy snapped.

He hadn't wanted any part in helping the pilot escape, which was what they'd been arguing about when Henriette's father had seen them coming out of the woods. Too dangerous, he'd declared, reminding her that they would automatically be given the death penalty instead of a prison sentence if they were caught. It was too late to back out now, she'd countered. The pilot was here and he was hurt.

Guy had finally relented when Anne-Marie urged him to remember Miriam Blum, on whom she'd always suspected he'd had a crush.

Moonlight guided the slow-moving trio's path. A copse of trees lay straight ahead. On the south side was a lake where the villagers swam in summer; on the north, a large field that had been cleared of snow so the small British Lysander could land.

Silent as ghosts, several other figures came out from behind the trees. Like Anne-Marie and Guy, they were all dressed in dark clothes and knit caps. One carried a Sten gun, which had been delivered in a previous drop, while the others created a flare path with their obstacle lights.

Tonight's mission was the partisans' most daring to date. Their supplies were usually dropped with black parachutes on moonless nights. Since this was their first pick-up, though, they'd decided to risk exposure instead of a crash.

"I hear . . . the plane." Now that escape was so close at hand, the fevered pilot began to shake.

"You'll be home soon." Anne-Marie kept a tight hold on him, finding that his weakness somehow gave her strength.

On the ground, everyone watched anxiously as the Lysander approached the makeshift airfield they'd prepared. They'd been warned that timing was of the essence in an operation of this sort. Once the plane landed, they would have three minutes to unload the precious cargo it carried and to get the wounded pilot aboard before it took off. Any longer than that and the German patrol might spot it and sound the alarm.

"Vite, vite!" Guy reminded them to hurry in a harsh whisper.

The instant the tiny aircraft came to a stop on the four hundred-yard runway, the waiting réseau members got to work. Outgoing "mail" diagramming the location of railway depots and bridges so the Allied bombers could further disrupt the Germans' supply routes went on, while medical supplies, boxes of ammunition and orders for continuing the clandestine sabotage of Nazi travel came off. Last but not least, the injured aviator was made as comfortable as possible in the cramped interior.

Then, before the Lysander even lifted off, the partisans vanished into the night as quickly and quietly as they had earlier appeared.

Anne-Marie stuffed the package meant for her grandfather under her sweater and took off at a run. Snow whitened the ground under the trees, but otherwise it was hard with frost. The ski boots she'd bought on the black market made a ringing sound when their iron supports struck a frozen rut in the road.

Traveling alone, it hardly took any time to reach the village. Only once, when two bicycles came along with their blackout lights flickering unevenly, did she have to sink into the bushes alongside the road. Like her, the riders were breaking the midnight curfew, and she wondered on an increasingly rare romantic whim if they were secret lovers hurrying home to avoid the German patrol.

She clenched her chattering teeth, then shoved her bare hands in her pockets and tucked her chin into the curly lamb collar of the old coat she'd found in her grandmother's armoire and remade for herself, waiting until the bicycles faded around the next curve.

The rue de Bretagne, the main street in Ste. Genviève, was deserted now. Still, she looked carefully before crossing it because the Nazi nights had a thousand eyes. Even though the patrol car wasn't due to pass for another few minutes, there was no telling who might have gotten up to use the bathroom and then stopped to peer out the window on the way back to bed.

Her grandfather's house was as dark and tightly shuttered as a tomb. She slipped around to the back, took off her boots, and tiptoed in through the door that opened to their cramped kitchen. On stockinged feet then, she started across the living room.

Skirting the massive mahogany sideboard that stood against the same wall as the door to the vestibule, Anne-Marie permitted herself a small smile at how well things were going. First, she would set the sulfanilamide powder in her grandfather's medical cabinet. Then she would duck into the tiny downstairs bathroom to strip off her clothes and put on her night-gown before sneaking back up—

A light flared on just as she reached for the doorknob.

She spun, her heart in her throat, to find her grandfather sitting in the harsh glare of a gas lamp near the draped and shaded window that faced the street. Despite the fact that he was on call for emergencies all night, they suffered the same gas cuts as the rest of the village. Which meant that he'd been waiting for her under cover of darkness.

The lamp hissed steadily as she studied him in the gloomy silence. He looked as if he'd just awakened from a long nightmare. His white hair was mussed, his face flushed, and the fraying ties of his black silk robe lay limp and wrinkled in his lap. On the small table beside his favorite reading chair with the worn frieze upholstery sat the crystal snifter, empty now, into which she had poured the pilfered cognac.

"'Tiger Lily!'" He practically spat out the *nom de guerre* she'd taken when she'd joined the Resistance movement.

Anne-Marie sighed in resignation. She couldn't deny it. He'd caught her in flagrante. Nor could she look him in the eye and lie. He'd see right through her. The only option she had left was to try to contain the damage.

Toward that end, she spoke softly so as not to wake Henriette. "How long have you known?"

"I have eyes, I can see. I have ears, I can hear." His own voice quavered with quiet dignity. "Or do you think I'm too old, too blind and deaf and senile to know what you've been up to all these months?"

"Of course not." With more aplomb than she felt, Anne-Marie set her ski boots on the floor, unbuttoned her coat, and pulled off her black knit cap. Her hair, gleaming almost gold in the light from the gas lamp, fell past her shoulders. She reached up under her sweater and removed the precious parcel of sulfanilamide powder he needed to treat his patients, many of whom had been beaten by the Germans or badly wounded by Allied bombs.

"You—" As he took the package she proffered, his dark eyes widened in dismay. "Where did you get this?"

"That," she said gently, "you're better off not knowing."

His shrewd expression told her he wasn't as gullible as she thought. "Are you crazy?"

"War is crazy." Still too wound up to sit down, Anne-Marie paced the room. She moved as lithely as a dancer, her hair swirling as she turned the corner of the heavy old table where they took their meals. "And as pretentious as it sounds, I want to help bring an end to the insanity."

"By hiding pilots and derailing trains?" he demanded hoarsely.

Her jaw clenched. "If that's what it takes."

"The Germans have threatened reprisals—ten of us for one of them."

"As if they need another excuse to torture and kill the French!" she scoffed.

He gave her a penetrating look. "And if you're captured?"

"I carry a cyanide pill." When he flinched, she realized she'd gone too far and rushed to soften the blow. "But only as a last resort."

"This war . . ." With his beard spreading like cold ashes below his cheekbones, her grandfather looked older and more tired than ever. "It's not like other wars. Only men fought them—not women."

Giving in to her sudden fatigue, Anne-Marie sank down on the arm of his chair. Her heart constricted at the realization that she had added to the burden of grief and worry he already carried. But to do nothing, to simply surrender to the occupiers of her homeland because she was female, to blindfold herself in order not to see what was going on around her . . . it was unthinkable!

"We don't look at each other as men and women." She ran a smoothing hand over his hair and imagined her grandmother smiling down at her from on high. "We see one another as comrades in arms, fighting side by side for a common cause."

But her grandfather was beyond such simple appeasement. "Is Henriette a partisan?"

"No. But Maurice is threatening to take to the mountains."

"The Maquis?" He blanched at the news that his oldest grandson was thinking of joining the guerrilla fighters. "My God, what is this world coming to?"

"It's dying, *Grand-père*," she said sadly.

"And you think you can save it?" he concluded in a flat tone.

"Not by myself, of course." She lifted her chin to a proud angle. "But I need to do my part."

Some of her grandfather's old spirit reared its head as he peered up at her and put a new twist on the argument he'd been making for a good year now. "What you need, young woman, is a man to keep you home at night!"

Chapter Two

KANSAS CITY, MISSOURI

*S*econd Lieutenant Mike Scanlon was feeling the beer, but he'd yet to get really a good handle on the curvy blonde who'd made herself at home on his lap.

No sooner had he sat down with John and Charlie and their girls than the blonde had strolled boldly up to the table and asked him if he was saving that empty chair for someone. He'd taken one look at her abundant breasts and promptly pulled it out for her. Now if he could just recall the name she'd shouted at him over the swoony blare of "I've Got It Bad and That Ain't Good. . ."

Bully's on Broadway was the best juke joint and the worst kept secret in town. Soldiers, sailors and marines stood three deep at the bar, seeking a respite from the constant drumbeat of war news coming out of Asia and Europe. Between drags on their cigarettes and drinks from their bottles or glasses, they eyed the women dressed in their Friday night best who were coming in the door. Not to be outdone, the women eyed them right back.

The couples who'd already connected were dancing beneath dimmed lights and dangling strands of leftover Christmas tinsel. Raucous cheers from the craps table in the next room said that some lucky sonovagun had made his point. An interservice-shouting match near the jukebox had attracted the bouncer, who was trying to break it up before it escalated into a fistfight.

The loud music and even louder voices fell on deaf ears as Mike concentrated on his own battle plan. His objective was simple. First, he wanted to talk Blondie into leaving the bar with him; second, he wanted to take her to bed. The obstacles he faced, however, were a hell of a lot more complicated.

For one thing, he'd taken an oath to conduct himself as an officer and a gentleman. So far he'd managed to remember he was the former. But given the golden opportunity that had landed in his lap, he was increasingly hard-pressed to remain the latter.

And for another, he was running out of time. He'd been ordered to report to Camp Shanks, New York, with seven days leave home enroute. After eight months of training other men to become overseas replacements, he knew damned good and well what that meant. It was his turn to ship out.

Mike finally resolved his dilemma with a maneuver as smooth as any he'd ever directed on a field of fire. He picked up the brown glass bottle with his left hand and slid his right from the cradle of the blonde's slender waist to the side of her lush breast. Mission accomplished, he crowed silently when his wandering thumb encountered an erect nipple beneath her tight black sweater.

"And people say we don't know what we're fighting for," he toasted dryly, before taking a drink of beer.

Blondie jiggled when she giggled.

First Lieutenant John Brown and his fiancé, Kitty Martin, were too engrossed in each other to notice the shenanigans going on across the table from them. They exuded intimacy, sitting as close together as their chairs allowed. His right arm was draped across her shoulders and her cheek rested against his uniformed chest.

"I know what I'm fighting for," John said around the cigarette dangling from the corner of his mouth.

Obviously tipsy from that second gin rickey she'd just finished, Kitty looked up and batted her eyelashes flirtatiously at him. They'd met at Randolph Field, Texas, where she'd been a typist and he an Army Air Corps cadet. Even though they weren't yet formally engaged when he received his commission, she'd quit her job to follow him from training camp to training camp—and, ultimately, to Kansas City.

"What're you fighting for, Flyboy?" she demanded in a voice that was more slurred than sultry.

Still nursing his first beer, John was drunk on love and happiness. And why not? He'd completed his combat training with a "very high" rating and was scheduled to report to Chatham Field, Georgia, next week to begin final processing for assignment overseas. To top it off, he was going to marry the most beautiful girl in the world before he left.

His answering grin was almost sappy. "I'm fighting for the right to spend the rest of my life with you."

Kitty's reaction to his declaration shook him to the core. She sat bolt upright and stared at him, her eyes growing misty and her smile wobbly. For no apparent reason, she then buried her face in her hands and burst into tears.

John didn't know what to make of her sudden crying jag, but the sight of her, weeping and wretched, spurred him into action. He yanked the cigarette from his mouth and stubbed it out in the overflowing ashtray. Then he put his other arm around her, gathered her close again and held her. Just held her.

"Aw-w-w," Blondie crooned from her perch on Mike's lap. She leaned forward, propped her elbow on the tabletop and put her chin in her hand. "Ain't that sweet?"

Mike took advantage of both the situation and her position by cupping the weight of her full, firm breast in his palm and giving it a gentle squeeze.

"Sure is," he agreed, and took another swig of beer.

Buck Private Charlie Miller, sitting to Mike's right, was in no mood for this maudlin crap. He'd delayed joining up until he got his draft notice, then quit his soda jerk's job to enlist. Only to be rejected by the Navy because he had insufficient chest expansion and the Marines because he wore glasses. The Army, however, hadn't been the least bit bothered by either his shallow chest or his visual impairment. To the contrary, they'd welcomed him into their ranks with an embarrassing "short-arm" inspection.

So now, with basic infantry training behind him and orders to report to cook's school safely packed in his duffel bag, this dogface was home on furlough and ready to howl. He tossed back the remainder of his whiskey as the jukebox began wailing, "I'm Walking the Floor Over You." Then he wiped his mouth on his uniform sleeve and turned to the girl who was sitting quietly beside him.

"Wanna dance?" He didn't wait to hear her answer but simply scraped back his chair and stood.

Daisy English didn't have to be asked twice. She leaped to her feet, almost spilling what was left of her beer in her haste. After steadying the swaying bottle, she rushed to catch up with Charlie, who was elbowing his way toward the dance floor.

Mike drained the last of his beer and set the empty on the table. He scanned the low-ceilinged room, looking for their waitress so he could order another round. Seeing that she was busy, he turned back to the couple still wrapped in their darkly passionate embrace.

"Tell me again." He had to shout to be heard above the din of that god-awful song. "What time is the wedding tomorrow?"

John, his cheek still resting on the crown of Kitty's hair and her face still buried against his chest, raised his own voice to reply, "Ten-hundred."

"I know what that means," Blondie chirped. "It's military talk for ten o'clock in the morning."

Mike flashed her a grin, then rewarded them both by copping another feel. He was standing as best man because John and he were Catholic and Charlie wasn't. Except for that and for the few months' difference in their ages, however, they might have been triplets.

They'd grown up on the same block, gone through the same grade school and graduated from the same high school. Hell, they'd even dated some of the same girls. But now, at the ripe young age of twenty-one, they were going to be fighting this damned war in completely different outfits.

After making a mental note to hit the sack early tonight—with the blonde, he hoped—Mike finally caught their server's eye. When the empty bottles and glasses had been cleared and replaced with full ones, he paid for them from the rapidly diminishing roll of bills he'd received last payday.

Big fuggin' deal, he thought as he added a hefty tip for the waitress. With the future he was facing, what better way to spend his money than on wine, women and song? Any song, that is, except "I'm Walking the Floor Over You."

When Blondie made to stand, he tightened his arm around her. "Where're you going?"

"I've gotta get rid of that last beer before I start on another one." She grabbed her purse off the chair she'd abandoned earlier and got to her feet. Then, as if to guarantee he wouldn't disappear while she was gone, she also snatched his officer's hat off his head and put it on her own.

Mike watched her walk away, his hat tilted at a jaunty angle on her bottle-blonde hair and her hips working smoothly beneath her straight black skirt. Looking around, he noticed that he wasn't the only one who was watching. Every other man in the joint seemed to appreciate the fully orchestrated anatomical symphony playing out before his eyes.

Anticipation swam sweetly along with the beer in his bloodstream. If this was a preview of what he was in for later tonight . . .

Turning his head, Mike was amused to see that even the engaged John wasn't immune to some gentle voyeurism. Their eyes met over Kitty's bowed head and, together, they grinned. At the same time, someone punched in the "Pennsylvania Polka" on the jukebox.

"Why don't they play some Glenn Miller?" he griped.

"Or Sinatra," John suggested.

"Spit on me, Frankie, I'm in de toid row!" Mike's falsetto impersonation of one of the New Jersey crooner's fans, complete with an ecstatic facial expression, brought a chuckle from John. Even the melancholy Kitty managed a small laugh.

He should have quit while he was ahead, but he had just enough of a buzz on that he didn't stop to think before he blurted out, "So, has your mother changed her mind about coming to the wedding?"

Wrong question, Mike realized, sobering instantly. Because even in the dim light, the flush that climbed John's face was clearly visible.

Kitty had been raised a hard-shell Baptist, but had agreed to be married by a Catholic priest. When she'd called her parents in Houston to invite them to the wedding, they'd been horrified to hear that she was actually going to marry that "mackerel snapper" and had hung up on her. Naturally, she'd been devastated by their rejection.

Now the reminder that John's mother had also declined to attend the nuptials of her only son, saying she certainly hadn't raised him to see him married in a priest's parlor instead of at the altar where she took daily Communion, brought a fresh batch of tears from his bride-to-be.

"I *promised* to raise the baby a Catholic!" Kitty cried against his chest. "What more does she want?"

"She'll come around." John's comforting words aside, his bleak expression said he didn't believe for a moment that his dogmatic mother would budge an inch on this issue. Or that his browbeaten father would dare go against her.

Wishing he'd kept his big mouth shut, Mike reached for his beer. He wasn't surprised to hear that Kitty was pregnant. The passions of war were prompting shotgun weddings from coast to coast. He was just glad that *he'd* managed to avoid that particular trap.

Not that he didn't want to get married and have a family of his own someday. He did. But it was bad enough worrying about how his widowed mother and younger sister and brother would take the news if he were killed in combat. He couldn't even begin to fathom the thought of leaving a wife and child behind.

Frowning, he glanced toward the dance floor just as Charlie and Daisy waltzed by. And had to bite the inside of his cheek to keep from laughing out loud. Charlie was a pump-her and grind-her, raising and lowering Daisy's arm in time to the music and rotating his pelvis against hers with every other step.

An adoring Daisy didn't appear to care that her parents considered Charlie to be rude, crude and a drunk in the making. It was no secret that she was madly in love with him. She'd started chasing him when they were seniors in high school, then had continued her pursuit when he left for the Army by sending him letters liberally splashed with "Evening in Paris" perfume. Now that he was back, her gap-toothed grin seemed to promise, he was finally going to catch her.

Restlessly, Mike checked his watch and wondered what could be keeping the blonde. She'd been gone a good ten minutes and should have finished her business by now. He lifted his beer to his lips and let his gaze wander toward the back of the room, past the newly acquainted couples who were sitting around the cluttered tables and the small knot of soldiers still standing at the bar . . . and stopped cold.

Instead of coming out the bathroom door, Blondie was coming *in* the back door. Right behind her was a sailor wearing a sheepishly satisfied grin and crookedly buttoned bell-bottoms. They were careful not to speak to each other as they parted ways, but given the fact that she was now wearing his hat with the bill turned backwards, Mike had no doubts about what they'd been doing in the alley behind the bar.

As if to confirm his conclusion, she wiped a smear of lipstick from the corner of her mouth with her pinkie finger while making her way back to the table.

Cursing himself for a fool, he set the bottle down with a bang. This was his own damned fault. He'd thought about calling up one of his old girlfriends and asking her out, but he'd been gone so long that he didn't know anymore who was married and who wasn't. So he'd gotten exactly what he deserved—some khaki-whacky who wasn't shy about spreading it around.

He waited until she came to a stop in front of him before he stood and yanked his hat off her head.

Blondie blinked twice, obviously taken aback. "Hey, what's the matter with you?"

"I stand in line for inspection and I stand in line for chow. I even stand in line to shower and sometimes to shit." Mike pulled on his hat without bothering to smooth back his dark brown hair, then lowered his scowling face dangerously close to her surprised one. "But the one thing I *don't* stand in line for is a woman."

"You're home early."

Mike snapped his head around at the sound of his mother's hushed voice and just barely made out her shadowy figure seated in her favorite living room chair. He hadn't come straight home from Bully's. Instead, he'd drive by some of the landmarks on the compass of his childhood—Jeeter's Market, where he used to deliver groceries on his second-hand bike; Paseo High School, where John and he had played varsity football and Charlie had lugged water for the team; and the Bijou Theater, where he'd stolen his first kiss in the last row of the balcony.

Taking a right onto Garfield Street, he'd realized with a sharp pang that those days were long gone. And that the happily-ever-after he'd always dreamed of might never happen. He'd parked the old Buick in the gravel drive that he'd helped his father build the summer before he died and entered a darkened house that had led him to believe everyone was asleep.

Now, he slid the front door's chain lock into place and hung his hat on the hall tree. "I've been in the Army for three years, Mom," he reminded her quietly. "You don't need to wait up for me anymore."

Millie Scanlon switched on the floor lamp behind her mission oak rocker, then stood and crossed to the Christmas tree she'd stubbornly left up until he got home. There were no lights on it because of the blackout. Still, she rearranged a couple of shiny ornaments that weren't hanging straight enough on its drying branches to suit her.

Finally satisfied, she resumed her seat and fixed her oldest son with a reproving look. "You know how mothers are. We wait on and for our children from the day they're born."

"Well, you can rest easy, ma'am." Mike gave her a mock salute. "I'm home for the night."

Millie pursed her lips, obviously remembering the time she'd gotten up to use the bathroom and caught him sneaking out to keep a late date with Mary Frances Walker in the hollow behind their house. He'd been in the tenth grade then and was already taller than his newly widowed mother, but he would never forget the way she'd cut him down to size. Now here he stood, a grown man, with her blistering lecture about treating girls with respect still ringing in his ears.

"Something tells me I'm not the only one who performs bed check," she surmised.

He grimaced. "I had a battalion commander in California who believed that two weeks on KP was the cure for breaking curfew."

"And was it?"

"If I never peel another potato, it'll be too soon."

She laughed softly. "Three cheers for Uncle Sam."

Mike grinned, flashing the Scanlon dimple which, along with his height, he'd inherited from his father. He didn't just love his mother. He liked her. A lot. She knew when to push and when to pull back. When to punish and when to praise. More important yet, she'd managed to keep her family together after her milkman husband succumbed to pneumonia.

Following the funeral, he'd offered to quit school and go to work full time to help make ends meet, but his mother wouldn't hear of it. Neither one of his parents had graduated from high school and they had both been determined that their children would go to college. It was his father's dying wish that he complete his education, she'd argued—using guilt when all else failed—and it was his duty to fulfill that wish.

So Mike set a goal of a law degree and, after graduating from high school, got a job as a pipe fitter's apprentice to save money toward college. To augment his income, he also joined a field artillery regiment of the National Guard. Six months later, his unit was mobilized and he was inducted into the Army of the United States.

Like the majority of servicemen who'd grown up during the

Depression, he came from a family that was too poor to take vacations. Which meant that his exposure to America's mountains and oceans and monuments was limited to what he'd studied in school. But thanks to Uncle Sam, he'd seen more of the country in these last three years than most hoboes.

Mike started his tour of duty at Camp Robinson, Arkansas. There, he spent part of the time building sidewalks for the new recruits who would soon be arriving and the rest on maneuvers in Louisiana, slogging through the swamps with a broomstick for a gun. When he learned that his first leave was scheduled for Christmas, he wrote his mother to start looking— and cooking!—for him.

The attack on Pearl Harbor put the kibosh on his holiday plans. His battalion entrained for California, where he ate his Christmas dinner out of a mess kit. After sitting in several different gun emplacements above the coast to guard against the possibility of a Japanese invasion of the United States, he applied for and was accepted to Officer Candidate School at the Fort Sill, Oklahoma, Artillery School of Fire.

If war was hell, he quickly discovered that OCS was purgatory. For three months he worked day and night in both classroom and field. His diligence paid off in a commission, and Mike could honestly say that the proudest moment of his life—surpassing even the winning touchdown pass he'd thrown to John in the city high school championship game— was having those gold bars pinned on his epaulets.

His first assignment as an officer was to Fort Bragg, North Carolina. He'd spent half his time putting men through obstacle courses and the other half serving as defense counsel for the Court Martial Board. From there, he'd reported to Camp Butner for a refresher course and to do his duty in the field as a forward artillery observer.

Now his next stop, Mike guessed glumly, was Merry Olde England.

"I have something for you," Millie said.

That lifted his spirits. "What is it?"

Smiling, his mother reached into her robe pocket and pulled out a small wrapped package. "A belated Christmas present."

"I thought I opened everything last Sunday." Mike had come home to a hero's welcome and to his favorite meal of fried chicken, mashed potatoes, gravy and home-canned green beans from last summer's Victory garden. For dessert there'd been a chocolate cake with fudge icing that must have cost a month's sugar ration. After dinner, there'd been presents to open—a pen and pencil set from his mother, hand-knitted socks from his sister, and some stainless steel Kant Rust razor blades from his brother.

He hadn't returned exactly empty-handed himself. For his sister, a fashion-conscious high school senior, he'd brought two pairs of nylon hose at the PX; for his gangly fifteen-year-old brother, he'd picked up some paratrooper's boots that hadn't been off his feet all week. For Millie, he'd arranged an increase in her monthly allotment to be withheld from his overseas pay to supplement her stenographer's salary.

"This is special." His mother's eyes shone as brightly as the silver Service Star she proudly displayed in the living room window. "And since you'll be busy with the wedding tomorrow and you leave so early on Sunday, I wanted to give it to you tonight."

Mike sat down in the glider chair beside her rocker to open his present. He remembered to pass both the wrapping paper and the ribbon back to her so she could use them again next Christmas. Then he just stared at his gift with glistening eyes.

It was a soldier's Bible, with the word "Godspeed" written in his mother's fine hand inside the metal cover and, on the very first page, a mimeographed message from his Commander-in-Chief, President Franklin D. Roosevelt.

"Thanks, Mom." He cleared his throat, then leaned over and kissed her cheek. "I'll carry it in my shirt pocket until I come home."

Millie wiped her own damp eyes with a handkerchief. She'd done her best to put up a cheerful front this week, Mike knew. On more than one occasion, though, he'd caught her looking at him as if she were trying to impress her memory indelibly with the image of someone she might never see again.

"Oh, I almost forgot," she said on a sniffle. "You have a letter on the telephone table. It's got a California postmark."

He knew immediately that it was from the naval officer's daughter he'd dated while he was stationed in El Cajon. "I'll read it later."

"Is it from a girl?" His mother didn't ordinarily pry into his personal affairs, but this was an extraordinary occasion.

"Yes."

"Are you serious about her?"

"I can't get serious about anyone right now," he said gravely.

"I understand." She gave him a last, sad smile before she stood and kissed him goodnight. "I love you, Michael Vincent Scanlon."

"I love you too, Mom." After hugging her tightly, he watched her make her way into the front bedroom she now shared with her daughter. Then, still too restless to head into the back bedroom where he was bunking with his brother, he crossed to the telephone table to get the letter from the girl he'd left in California.

The blue envelope exuded the same floral scent she'd been wearing the night he'd met her at that USO dance. Her father had been at sea in the Pacific, her mother a Red Cross volunteer. She had worked in a war plant and had proudly called herself a "Bomber-Dear."

Mike thought of those late summer evenings when he'd lain in a backyard hammock, eating baby lemons peeled by the dark-haired girl kneeling in the grass beside him. She'd laughed when he'd puckered up after she first dropped the fruit into his mouth. And then one night, when the big orange sun had sunk into the sea and full darkness had enveloped them, she'd crawled into the hammock with him, licking the sweet-tart juice off his lips and whispering "Let's make love" into his ear.

She hadn't been a virgin, which was a relief. Nor had she been shy about expressing her needs. Still, he'd felt a twinge of guilt because he'd yet to tell her that he'd been accepted to OCS and would be leaving soon. But with her firm breasts pressed against his chest and her eager hands undoing his belt buckle, no power on earth could have kept him from taking her.

They'd kissed until her lips were swollen and his own felt raw. Her cotton dress had risen about her hips, and he'd caressed her through the thin rayon of her panties. Then he'd slipped his hand under the band and she'd opened her thighs so he could stroke the soft, damp velvet of her.

When he'd entered her, they'd lain in the swaying hammock, locked in the ecstasy of an embrace as old as time, until their yearning young bodies had begun to move and they'd come together like an electric shock.

Mike stared down at the envelope for a long, reflective moment. He knew he should probably write her back, but after "thanks for the memories," what more could he say? Without opening it, he tore it into tiny pieces and dropped them in the wastebasket beside the table.

"For richer or for poorer," Father Campbell intoned solemnly.

The priest's parlor smelled of oil soap instead of orchids or roses. A hissing radiator provided the music, and three straight-backed chairs served as pews for the guests. Though there were none of the tears that were normally shed at weddings, there was an aura of sadness about the couple who now faced each other and their impending separation.

Still, the groom cut a handsome figure in his "pinks and greens" uniform. And the bride looked as pretty and fragile as a hothouse flower in her floppy hat and a blue jersey dress that didn't quite hide the slight swell of her expanding tummy. But it was the maid of honor, a leggy redhead standing across the semi-circle that the wedding party had formed in front of the priest, who held the best man's attention.

Mike took a chance and smiled at her. If he thought she would blush or dip her head or demurely avert her eyes, he had another think coming. She looked straight at him and smiled back.

"In sickness and in health," Kitty repeated softly.

Mike knew he should be paying closer attention to the ceremony so that he'd know when to produce the ring that was nesting in the pocket of his dress uniform pants. But he was leaving tomorrow morning, he'd dumped that blonde last night, and the maid of honor might be the last

American female he had any contact with for a while. A very long while.

Pressing his luck, he winked at her.

She winked back.

"'Til death do us part," John vowed gravely.

Father Campbell cleared his throat then, and Mike realized that it was time for the blessing of the rings. He laid the bride's slender gold band on the paten the priest extended toward him. When the redhead placed the groom's wider one beside it, a ray of the chilly gray light washing the eastern window glinted off the matched set of diamonds on her left hand.

Matron of honor, Mike thought resignedly. He didn't have many rules where women were concerned, but he lived by one. Never with another man's wife.

"You may kiss the bride," the priest said in conclusion.

From the corner of his eye, Mike watched the matron of honor watch the newlyweds exchange a chaste peck. Then he did what he'd just sworn he wouldn't do. He looked directly at her.

As if she sensed him staring at her, she turned her head and met his gaze head-on. Her eyes were green, large and slightly upturned at the corners, her nose a little too short and pert to balance them against her full, scarlet mouth. Almost daring him to break their visual connection, she moistened her lips in a way that had him mentally placing them and that saucy pink tongue where they'd do him the most good.

"Time to cut the cake." Agnes Dill, the priest's spinster housekeeper, had slipped out of the room the instant the ceremony ended. Now she wheeled a serving cart into the parlor. On it was a pot of freshly perked coffee and a one-layer cake she had baked and decorated herself.

"Oh, how pretty!" Daisy leaped to her feet, almost overturning her chair, then managed to step on Mike's toes in her rush to take a picture of Agnes's culinary masterpiece.

Charlie, who was slower to rise and even slower to follow her across the room, had lost his sad-sack face and was wearing the look of a well-loved man.

The small party gathered around the serving cart, trying to make the occasion as festive as possible. Neither the bride nor the groom could muster much of a smile for their wedding picture, though. With both sets of parents conspicuous by their absence, it was hard to keep up the pretense.

After the reception, John and Kitty were taking the one o'clock train to St. Louis. They'd reserved a hotel room and were going to live out of their suitcases until it was time for him to leave for Chatham Field. She would return to Kansas City then to await the birth of their baby.

Mike had driven John to the church, so Charlie and Daisy, who were having lunch with her parents in hopes of discussing his going to work in her family's appliance store after the war, had offered to drop off the newlyweds at Union Station.

Out in the parking lot, John loaded Kitty's and his luggage in Charlie's trunk. Then, while the others were busy saying goodbye, he drew Mike aside and said, "I want you to do me a favor."

"You name it, you've got it."

"Promise me."

Mike felt John's fingers close on his wrist. "Say, what is this?" he laughed. "You need money?" He reached into his pocket with his free hand. "It's yours."

John waved away the small wad of bills he'd pulled out. "I want you to promise me that if I'm killed in combat—"

"Don't even think that, much less—"

"—you'll keep an eye on Kitty and the baby. She'll have my life insurance policy and a pension, so she'll be okay financially. But between her folks and mine, I'm afraid she won't have the kind of family support she'll need."

Mike sighed. "Has it ever occurred to you that I might be the one who doesn't make it?"

"You will. You're a survivor." John's earnest brown eyes bored into his. "Now just promise me, okay?"

Mike felt both honored and humbled by his friend's request. He looked away, wondering if he would really be able to keep the promise he was being asked to make. But if the tables were turned, he reminded himself, and he were leaving a family behind, the first person he would ask to watch over them would be John Brown.

"I promise," he said, and proffered his hand.

"Hey, you two, get over here!" Charlie hollered. "Daisy wants to take a picture of the three of us in uniform."

They posed in front of his parents' Chrysler. Charlie, being the shortest, stood between Mike and John. Their arms rested companionably on each other's shoulders.

"Smile!" Daisy instructed before she captured their image for posterity.

The party ended then with a few tears, a flurry of hugs and handshakes, and reminders to write. John and Kitty climbed into the backseat, Charlie and Daisy into the front. The old tin cans that Mike had dug up and tied to the bumper jangled out "Just Married" to everyone within earshot as the Chrysler pulled away.

"How about giving me a ride home?"

Mike had completely forgotten about the redhead, who was standing beside the passenger door of his Buick and smiling expectantly at him. She'd been introduced to him as Kitty's roommate during the reception but he'd let her name slide by for the simple reason that she was married. He'd figured there was no sense in rocking a boat—even a dreamboat—that he couldn't row.

Now he squared her in his sights. "Call your husband."

She tucked a stray wisp of flame-colored hair into the luxuriant pageboy roll that fell at the nape of her neck. "He's stationed at Paris Island, South Carolina."

"A Marine, huh?"

"The original lean, mean fighting machine." She lingered bitterly over the last word.

Mike cocked his head in curiosity. "How'd you get to the church?"

"I shared a cab with Kitty because I ran out of gas coupons for my car, and now I'm out of money."

"War's hell on the homefront," he said dryly.

"Isn't it, though." Reaching up, she ran a scarlet-tipped fingernail over the crossed brass branch insignia on his uniform lapels. "I like your guns."

"Cannons."

Her green eyes arrowed into his. "They look dangerous."

"They are." Mike had made enough passes, both on and off the football field, to know when he was on the receiving end of one.

"I live at Thirty-third and the Paseo." She hadn't buttoned her coat, and the January wind played peek-a-boo with the hem of her short, swingy dress.

His conscience raised a ruckus as his gaze moved down to her shapely legs. "That's a long way to walk."

"Alone," she added meaningfully, her expression softening when his eyes met hers again. "At least until Kitty gets back next week."

"I leave tomorrow morning." As if he needed another reminder that time was at a premium, the bell in the church tower chimed the noon Angelus.

"Have you ever pulled down your blackout shades in the middle of the day?" Her glossy lips parted in a wide, wicked grin. "I do it when I take a nap and it makes the room dark as night."

Damning the consequences, he unlocked the passenger door and opened it for her. "Ready?"

"Willing and able, too," the redhead parried silkily as she slid into the car.

The seductive way she crossed her legs, flashing him just a glimpse of smooth white thigh where the tops of her stockings met the tips of her garters, told Mike that he was probably in for the ride of his life. He should have been rarin' to go; instead, he found he was dragging his feet as he cut around to the driver's side. And when she reached over to unlock his door with her ring hand, he couldn't help but think that whoever said "All's fair in love and war" must've had heels like himself in mind.

Chapter Three

"My darling Kitty—
 I got your letter yesterday. My new birthday picture of you, too. To answer your question—again—no, you don't look fat and ugly. You look six *gorgeous* months pregnant. I only wish I were there to rub your back and your feet when they ache. Or to hold you on my lap, with your head on my shoulder and my hand on your belly, feeling our baby move inside you . . ."

John Brown took a drag on his cigarette and studied his wife's latest picture, which he'd propped up against the wall in front of him. Last month, while on "stand-down" due to bad flying weather, the officers in his squadron had contracted with a builder in the nearby town of Altamura to replace their pyramidal tents with small houses made of white tufa block and tile roofs. A reporter from *Stars and Stripes* had dubbed it "Bomber City."

His crew had moved into their new quarters on April Fool's Day. So for a couple of weeks now he'd had cement walls instead of canvas. Better yet, he was no longer tripping over five other men and their stuff all the time because he had a small single room with a door he could close when he wanted some privacy and a window he could open to let in fresh air.

There wasn't much space for anything besides a clothesline and the cot he was sitting on the edge of, but he'd scrounged up a couple of spare cement blocks and cut down a piece of raw lumber to make himself a crude writing desk. He kept Kitty's letters with the Air Medal he'd earned after five missions in a locked metal box but had left her pictures out, lined up against the wall. That made them the last thing he saw every night before he turned out the lights.

> "I really like your new hairdo. Makes you look like Gene
> Tierney in *Heaven Can Wait* only prettier. Now I know
> what I'll dream about tonight . . ."

He'd never told her or anyone else about the nightmares. About the planes that went up in brilliant but silent explosions in his sleep. Or the ones that were shot down and went spiraling at two hundred miles or more toward the earth. No, the nightmares were something he was going to have to deal with on his own. Either that, or ask to be grounded. Which seemed like the coward's way out of this damned war.

Exhaling smoke, John wondered what to say next. She already knew he was in Italy, but for security reasons he couldn't tell her where. Nor was he allowed to tell her that he'd exercised his pilot's prerogative and named his B-24 Liberator the "Kansas City Kitty" after her. And he damn sure wasn't going to waste his precious V-mail paper trying to settle the ongoing dispute between his wife and his mother!

As if he didn't have enough to worry about, Emmagrace Brown had finally broken her frozen silence and written him a long letter criticizing the amount of money Kitty was spending on things like maternity clothes and gin. And that redheaded roommate of hers! Married or not, his mother had declared, that girl was a tramp.

Kitty, on the other hand, complained that Emmagrace had started stopping by the apartment unannounced. She was always snooping around too, opening her closet door or checking the liquor cabinet under the sink. And would he *please* tell his mother to quit being so rude to her roommate, his wife had demanded.

Just thinking about it, John ground his teeth in frustration. How either one of them expected him to settle their ongoing dispute from almost half a world away, he couldn't imagine. So he simply ignored it, hoping for the best, and continued writing.

"Did I tell you I got birthday cards from Charlie and Mike? Charlie graduated from cook's school with sergeant's stripes, and says Daisy has set their wedding day for May 6. Buy them a nice present from us, will you? Maybe one of those tea sets or some matching picture frames. Mike's in England gearing up for the invasion of Europe, and seems to be getting along okay . . ."

The last part of that sentence wasn't exactly true. Mike had been assigned to a light armored artillery battalion that had already been through North Africa and Sicily. In the note he'd included in his birthday card, he'd said that the combat hardened "redlegs" weren't all that receptive toward their new green "shavetail." But he'd sworn that he was going to earn their respect, if not their friendship, in the practice firing missions he was observing for them later this month.

John decided not to repeat the bawdy Latin pun Mike had coined regarding his encounter with an English prostitute. Kitty had enough on her mind, what with the baby coming and his mother driving her crazy. There was no sense in making her worry about whether her husband was remaining faithful to her when he hadn't so much as *looked* at another woman in the two-plus months he'd been here.

"It was swell hearing from the guys. I just wish we were all back together at Bully's right now, having a beer. But we'll do it again someday, I'm sure. (And the sooner the better!) Mike told me to tell you hi. 'Junior', too . . ."

Rereading the word "Junior," he smiled. That was Kitty's nickname for the baby. She wanted a boy, but he honestly didn't care whether it was a boy or a girl, as long as it was healthy. But one thing for sure, he resolved as he resumed writing. Even if his son or daughter eventually married an atheist, *he* wouldn't miss their wedding!

"Better close now. I've got a busy day tomorrow . . ."

His squadron had been put on alert this evening. A bombing mission was on for the next day, and wake-up time had been set for 3:30 A.M. He hated those early calls because they almost always meant an especially long mission. Which made him think they were probably going back to Bucharest.

> "I miss you, sweetheart, more than words can say.
> Sometimes I lie awake at night, remembering our first
> date or how beautiful you looked on our wedding day,
> and I could fly back into your arms without a plane.
> God, I can't wait until I belong to you again instead of to
> Uncle Sam! Remember, I love you. Now and forever—"

John signed his name, then set the unsealed letter atop the pile of folded clothes he planned to put on in the morning so he wouldn't forget to drop it off at the censor's desk on his way to breakfast.

He sat back on his cot then and stretched, trying to get rid of the kinks in his neck and shoulders. Two months of intermittent rain and snow and overcast skies had finally broken, and tomorrow's mission would be his fourth in six days—which would make a total of fifteen since his arrival in late January. With a schedule like that, he should have been exhausted. For some reason, though, he was too keyed up to sleep just yet.

When he'd finished formation training and started flying combat, he'd been told that after fifty missions, with a credit of two for one over Germany, he would be rotated home for a rest. He'd figured it out on a mathematical basis—how many months it would take him to finish his stint—and realized that he might well be home when Kitty had the baby.

But Mother Nature had thrown a monkey wrench into the works. In addition to February's bad flying weather, Mount Vesuvius had erupted in March for the first time in almost forty years and volcanic ash had drifted down with the snow. The grit had covered everything and everyone, even getting into the food. It had also forced the cancellation of all missions for a whole week because it could damage engines.

So thirty-five, more or less, after tomorrow, John reminded himself as he butted out his cigarette, and he could go home.

Right now, though, he was going to bed.

"Let go of your cocks and put on your socks."

John sat up on his cot with a start when he heard the assistant operations officer in the hall. His chest was heaving and his mouth was dry from having silently screamed in his sleep. Another damned nightmare, he told himself, throwing off the covers and the vestiges of his bad dream in disgust.

No sooner had he swung his legs over the side of the bed than the door creaked open and the Ops officer shone a flashlight in his eyes.

John squinted against the flame and said, "I'm up."

"Breakfast at 4:30, sir, briefing at 5:30."

The grumblings and the stirrings of the other men in the "Officer's Quarters" filled the air as John reached for his own flashlight and headed for the latrine. No one spoke or joked. They just moved from the sinks, where they washed and shaved in the clammy water, to the urinals. Or vice versa.

Back in his room, John turned on the overhead light but left the black-out curtain drawn as he started getting dressed. He'd slept in his woolen long underwear to ward off the chill. Spinnazola was the anklebone in the boot of Italy, which should have made for warm weather. But the mountain ridge that ran parallel to the landing strip often meant long, cold days and even longer, colder nights.

Over his long underwear he wore a dark Army shirt and trousers. Regulations required a tie. Sitting on the edge of his cot, he pulled a pair of heavy socks over his silk ones, then double-knotted the laces on his high-top combat shoes to keep them from snapping off his feet if he had to bail out. Later, in the equipment hut, he would put on a pair of fleece-lined boots over his shoes and zip into a flying suit, which he could heat electrically by plugging it into an outlet on his plane's instrument panel.

As always, he wore his leather A-2 flying jacket. He never carried a gun, though, because the Germans could treat him as a spy if they caught him with one. But he did have a Swiss pocketknife, with a blade under six inches to conform to the Geneva Convention. And a silk scarf, on which a map of the Balkans was printed to help him avoid capture, went into his other pocket.

John couldn't help but smile as he tucked the scarf away. He'd first become fascinated by the idea of flying in grade school, after Charles Lindbergh had flown to France by the seat of his pants. And in high school he'd been an avid reader of "G-8 and His Battle Aces," a pulp magazine devoted to World War I aerial battles. In his dreams, he'd been Captain Eddie Rickenbacker, his white scarf streaming behind him in the wind as he flew over the trenches and maneuvered the enemy's plane into his gun sights.

Then the war had offered him a chance to make his dreams come true. His country needed flyers, thousands upon thousands of them. And now here he was, dressed to answer the call.

His letter to Kitty in hand, John turned out the light and left the room. There was no sense in opening the blackout curtain. By the time he returned, it would probably be dark outside again.

"Good morning." He met his copilot at the censor's desk by the door.

Bob Kiefer hunched his shoulders against the first shock of cold as they headed outside. "What's good about it?"

"Thirty-five to go after today."

"Yeah, well, I missed a pass to Bari because of this damn mission."

John laughed. "Don't worry, the wine will still be there when you get back."

Bob smiled crookedly. "It's hard to say which is aging faster—the *vino* or me."

They crossed through the olive grove to the officer's mess. The morning of his first mission, John had been struck by the irony of walking by olive branches—the symbol of peace—on his way to war. Now he just passed them without giving it a second thought.

At the door of the mess, they put down one military lire each and picked up one orange and one egg apiece. Then, seeing that the navigator and bombardier of the "Kansas City Kitty" were seated and already eating, they joined them at the table.

"Sunnyside up, Lieutenant?" the waiter asked as he took John's egg to give it to the mess sergeant.

He nodded, added Spam, pancakes, toast and coffee to his order, and then started peeling his orange.

Bob seconded his order, but asked for a bowl of fresh figs in canned milk to finish it off.

Their bombardier, Pat O'Toole, pulled a face at that last. "Figs give me the runs."

Norm Sandrich, the crew's navigator, made a scoffing sound. "This from a guy who can't wait to get home so he can have some of his mama's greens?"

"At least greens don't have seeds," the Arkansan drawled.

John cleaned his plate when it came, knowing he probably wouldn't eat again until tonight. Unlike some of his crew, who carried C-rations to warm on the heat vents and eat on the way back from a mission, he couldn't stomach food until he was safely on the ground again. Sitting back, he lit a cigarette and had a second cup of coffee while the others finished.

After breakfast, the four officers walked to the briefing room. They were early, but the two-by-sixes that had been laid across building blocks were almost full. A stage with a curtained wall behind it rose in front of the makeshift seats.

From the doorway, John spotted the six enlisted members of his crew. Bob said he'd go save four places in front of them, Pat and Norm went to get their pre-flight materials, and John picked up a mission briefing card. On the way to his seat, he stopped to confer with the Ops officer.

"You'll fly deputy lead, in the number two position," the officer told him.

"Roger." John accepted the assignment without question or complaint. If the mission lead dropped out of the formation for any reason, his crew's job would be to assume the lead and complete the mission.

Given the early hour, the six enlistees greeted him with more enthusiasm than he'd expected. He attributed it to the fact that all of them were younger than he. At age twenty-two, he was older than everyone in his crew.

"Have you checked out the ship yet?" As flight engineer and top turret gunner, Dirk Ellington was worried about their plane, which had sustained some flak damage on their trip to Bucharest the day before yesterday and had been sent to the hangar for repair.

"I walked over and talked to the ground crew after lunch yesterday," John told him. "They promised to work all night if necessary to finish patching it up."

Dirk nodded, then turned his attention to the papers he'd picked up at the door.

John grinned at his radio operator. "Got your Purple Heart on, Bill?"

Crewman Bill Burnside had been burned in the groin area by a short in his electrical suit during a raid over Nis, Yugoslavia, and John never failed to kid him about the decoration he'd received while recuperating from his injury.

"Right here." Bill opened his jacket and flashed his brag rag.

Pat came over, carrying a packet of evasion materials that the crew would use if they were shot down. In addition, Dirk had a box of hard candies and Bill a first-aid kit. After each mission Pat had to turn in his kit, but the crew usually ate up the candy on the way back to the base, and Bill always kept the medical supplies.

"Ten-HUT!"

Everyone stood at attention when the group commander and the briefing officers mounted the stage. After they resumed their seats, a junior officer opened the curtain to reveal a wall map on which the flight track from base to target and back to base was plotted. Two days ago there'd been groans and grimaces all around when the aircrews saw that the target was Bucharest. But today, when the map showed the same target, silence settled over them like a shroud.

"That's right," the group commander declared, "we're going back to Bucharest." He stuck the tip of the pointer he carried at the target. "As you all know, the master plan calls for stepped-up activity against the Germans' Romanian oil refineries as well as their oil transportation capabilities. We're an essential part of that plan. So we're going to hit these railyards again and, this time, we're going to wipe 'em out for good."

John noticed that he wasn't alone in rolling his eyes. The commander seemed to have conveniently forgotten that their previous mission to

Bucharest had been a toss-up as to which would be wiped out first—the bombardment group or the marshalling yards. Even worse, they'd lost two planes and their entire crews to antiaircraft fire.

The flak officer came next. The munitions, weather, maintenance and taxi-control officers followed him. Finally, to the commander's solemn countdown of "Five . . . four . . . three . . . two . . . one . . . HACK!" the pilots all synchronized their watches.

After the briefing, each crew huddled together to decide if there was anything special that needed to be done before they headed to the equipment hut.

"Have we got enough ammo?" Technical Sergeant Larry Shaffer asked.

"For all the good it'll do us against the flak." The expression on the face of the right waist gunner, Jerry Watson, was a grim reminder of the gauntlet of enemy gunfire they'd barely survived two days before.

The crew split up then, some of them going to finish last-minute chores and others making a beeline for the rooms behind the stage where chaplains of all faiths were waiting to tend to their spiritual needs.

After receiving Holy Communion and the Last Rites of the Roman Catholic Church, as he always did before going on a mission, John made the short walk over to operations to chat with the duty officer. He left encouraged by the news that his crew would probably be on an every-other-day schedule for the next couple of months. It was a killer rotation, no doubt about it. But the sooner he got this tour over with, he reminded himself, the sooner he'd be reunited with Kitty.

In the equipment hut, he put on his electrically heated flying suit and fleece-lined boots, then slipped a life preserver—jokingly called a Mae West—over his shoulders and checked both CO_2 cylinders to make sure they worked. Rumor had it that some of the guys had been using the cartridges to cool their beer and returning them empty. His were full. A parachute harness with tight leg straps and two chest straps went over the Mae West; white silk gloves would later go under his heavy leather mittens to ward off frostbite at high altitudes.

His sandwich-board-shaped flak suit, which he regarded as almost useless because it left his arms and legs unprotected, would rest behind his seat during the mission.

"Load 'er up!" Jerry had commandeered a truck and a driver to carry the crew, their equipment and the machine guns out to the plane.

Over his personalized leather helmet, John put on his flak helmet. It contained earphones and snaps for his oxygen mask, which had to be tightened constantly. He didn't like the helmets with built-in microphones because the water condensing from his breath froze the instruments at high altitudes. Instead, he used a throat mike—two hard rubber pill-shaped devices that fit against his larynx by a strap around his neck.

Wearing the umbilical cords that would connect him to his crew and his aircraft, much the way his unborn child was connected to his wife's body, he climbed into the truck with the other men.

The priest stood on the shoulder of the taxi strip. As each truck passed, he made the sign of the cross and said, "Take care of yourselves, boys. And God go with you."

John spotted three ground-crew members standing by his plane when the truck stopped at the circular hardstand. While the other men piled out to perform their own individual pre-flight chores, he went through a sequence of instrument and control checks with the crew chief. That done, he walked around the plane with the mechanic he'd talked to the day before. First, they examined the steel patches that had been soldered over the holes sustained during their last mission to Bucharest. Then they checked to be sure the main fuel tanks and the auxiliary tanks were full, and that ten 500-pound bombs hung in the bay.

"Looks good," John told him.

"Give Hans hell for me, sir."

The flight crew climbed into the plane, where they spent the final few minutes before engine starting time getting into their takeoff positions.

"Anybody need their sinuses unplugged?" Bill opened the first-aid kid and held up a bottle of nose drops. Hearing no takers, he treated himself to a snort before putting the bottle back.

"Everybody wearing their dog tags?" Bob asked as he slid into the copilot's seat next to John's.

"The rosary my mother gave me, too." Tommy Murphy reached down the front of his flight suit and pulled it out. He wore it around his neck on every mission, believing it brought him luck.

Ever the clown, Ed Harrigan grabbed the blue beads from behind and pretended to twist them around Tommy's neck, saying in a bad German accent, "Start praying, *Ami.*"

Tommy crossed his eyes and made a gagging sound. Everyone laughed, releasing some of the pre-flight tension. Then the assembly officer gave the signal to start the engines.

John checked his watch as Bob reached for the starter engines. The base exploded with sound as thirty-six olive drab B-24 Liberators roared into life and the noise echoed off the mountain ridge. From the tower, a white signal light arced upward, with two stars falling from it.

It was time to go.

The ground crew gave them thumbs-up, the brakes were released, and the "Kansas City Kitty" moved off its hardstand to join the other planes in a single-file counterclockwise path around the perimeter taxi strip.

Fifteen minutes after the squadrons engines started, the lead plane lifted off the single metal strip. John waited thirty seconds so he wouldn't get caught in its prop wash before following. The knot of tension in his stomach tightened as the plane surged forward and the crew checked off.

"Gear up."

"Wing flaps up."

"Climb configuration."

John tasted rubber, cold and bitter, through his oxygen mask as they lifted off. He'd seen so many aborted takeoffs, with at least two resulting in aircraft and bombs exploding at the end of the runway, that he couldn't relax until they'd passed the first danger point in the mission. When they were finally airborne, he sighed with relief.

"Bombs activated," Pat notified the pilots after they'd begun their hour-long assembly into box formation.

John's stomach tightened on hearing the statement. He couldn't count the number of hours he'd spent in the States practicing precision bombing until he could hit a "pickle barrel" from twenty-five thousand feet. But where he'd grown up believing that war involved only military men and military targets, he sometimes found himself bombing industrial towns that were largely populated with working people much like the members of his own family. So whenever the bombs dropped away and his aircraft leaped forward, free of its burden, he had ambivalent feelings. While he was glad to have a more maneuverable plane to fly, he felt guilty at the thought that he'd probably just killed a lot of innocent women and children.

On the lighter side, the sky was clear in all directions. People on the ground looked up. Some had their hands shading their eyes against the rising sun as they watched the growing air armada assemble. Others waved to them for luck.

John wished he could wave back. A war-weary Italy had surrendered last September, allowing the Allies to set up their air bases in the south, but the Germans were still fighting in the north. Bridges had been blown, villages destroyed and railroad ties demolished in an attempt to slow the Allied advance. It was that devastation, coupled with the abject poverty of the Italian people, which helped to remind him that he was on the right side of this cursed conflict.

"Oxygen check," Bob called fifteen minutes into the flight.

"Pilot OK," John replied as he relinquished the controls.

Disembodied voices crackled over the intercom—tail gunner OK, nose OK, right waist OK, left waist OK, radio OK, top turret OK, bombardier OK, navigator OK.

The squadron flew in tight formation over the Adriatic Sea and into Yugoslavian airspace. It was the best protection they had because it maximized their firepower against the emplaced German gunners on the ground. But with the good came the bad. When a plane in close formation was hit by flak, there was a chance of it taking another one down with it. To minimize the risk, they usually relaxed the formation over target and then reformed for the trip home.

"How are we doing?" Bob asked.

John checked his watch against the clock on the instrument panel. "Exactly on time."

The outside air temperature showed minus forty-eight degrees Centigrade, warmer than the minus sixty degrees that they'd recorded last week over Knin. The only clouds in the sky were the white contrails streaming from every wing tip.

"Oxygen check," John called when it was his turn to resume control of the plane.

"Copilot OK," Bob confirmed.

A few miles ahead, John spotted several cushiony puffs of flak below the formation. He didn't worry about the flak he could see, though. It was the flak he couldn't see that was the killer.

"*Too-ra-loo-ra-loo-ra,*" Pat warbled.

"Bing Crosby, you're not," Norm cracked.

"*Too-ra-loo-ra-li . . .*"

"Hush, *I'm* going to cry."

Because time passed so slowly over enemy territory, some of the guys sang or told jokes or talked about the wives and sweethearts they'd left back home.

John just tried to think about the mission. When that didn't work, he talked to the Man Upstairs. He prayed that he would do the right thing in an emergency. That he wouldn't let his crew down. And, if worse came to worse, that he would meet death like a man.

So far, with the exception of a few bad flak attacks, his prayers had been answered.

"Got any names picked out for the baby?" Bob asked him now.

"John, Jr., if it's a boy."

"And if it's a girl?"

"We can't decide between Mary and Margaret."

"How about Mary Margaret?"

"Mary Margaret." John mulled that over for a moment, then smiled. "I like it."

As they crossed the Romanian border, thick puffs of black smoke filled the sky, blotting out the sun. From dead reckoning, John placed the antiaircraft guns about a hundred miles from target. The shells exploded well to the right of the formation. But like ants at a picnic, he knew, there were plenty more where those had come from.

"Oxygen check," Bob clipped out.

"Pilot OK," John said tersely.

They were nearing Bucharest now and everyone was on full alert. Going in on a bombing run, they were bound to attract heavier flak than when they were coming out. After all, an empty bomber couldn't hurt anyone. The cloudless sky was no comfort, either, because it gave the German gunners a clear shot at them.

John had just taken over the controls again when he heard it . . . a faint sound, like gravel being thrown on a tin roof.

"Did you hear that?" Narrow-eyed, he scanned the instrument panel but saw nothing out of the ordinary.

Bob frowned. "Hear what?"

There was no mistaking the second hit. It tore through the ship with a thunderous roar, shattering the windows and buckling the floor. A hunk of hot metal caught Pat in the throat, killing him instantly.

"Oh, my God!" Bill screamed as he stared at the mittened hand with which he'd just wiped his face. "I'm bleeding!"

"Everybody into their flak suits," Bob ordered as the sky suddenly erupted into a sickening mass of smoke and flame and spheres of exploding steel.

B-24s began going down all around them. The lead plane went into a steep dive with both wings trailing bright orange flames. Another one barrel-rolled onto its back and plummeted toward the ground. Yet a third plane took a direct hit in the bomb bay and disappeared in a cloud of oily black smoke.

"Two o'clock low, sir," Norm directed.

John had already moved up to the lead position when he looked to his right and saw those ugly black spots climbing ever closer to their altitude. They missed completely. But seconds later the plane lurched again, as if swatted by some giant hand in the sky, and red-hot shrapnel ripped through the ship.

"Mary, Mother of God." Norm sounded surprised as he slumped forward in the rear of the nose—blown back there by the flak blast.

"I smell smoke!" the tail gunner cried.

"Right waist gunner to pilot, we're on fire."

Smoke from the battery of antiaircraft guns protecting the marshalling yard boiled up before John's eyes. He tried to blot it and everything else out of his mind and concentrate on flying. The controls had gone soft on him but the railroad tracks he was following told him he was right on target.

"Hit the bailout bell," he snapped as he started losing altitude.

Bob did as he was ordered.

"Get out, you guys." John feathered the prop to cut down on drag and air resistance, then pulled up so that his remaining crewmen could jump. "I'm going in."

Fumbling with his parachute straps, Bob looked at him like he had oatmeal for brains. "You're coming, too."

"I can't." An icy calm descended on him as he glanced down and noted that his right leg had been severed and was hanging by just a few shreds of skin. His life's blood gushed from the torn tissue but, oddly, there was no pain—only a merciful numbness. "I'm hit. Bad."

"I'll help you hook up your pack," his copilot insisted.

"Get the hell out of here," John shot back.

"You gutsy sonuvabitch, you." Bob's voice shook with emotion as he squeezed John's shoulder hard in farewell. Then he dropped to his knees and began crawling behind the other crewmen through the choking smoke toward the escape door.

John thought of his beautiful wife, Kitty. And of the baby he would never see. It was enough to make a grown man cry. But just before his bomber hit the railyards and exploded in a ball of fire, he smiled.

Chapter Four

 lessent mon coeur d'une langueur monotone," the announcer intoned.

Kneeling beside her radio set in the attic, Anne-Marie Gérard was stunned by the impact of the words she'd just heard. "Wound my heart with a monotonous languor" was the second line of one of her favorite poems—"Song of Autumn" by Paul Verlaine. The first line had been broadcast two nights ago, putting French partisan groups on alert. Now this was the last half of the message telling them that the Allied invasion of Europe would begin within the next forty-eight hours.

Which meant she had work to do.

Before she got started, though, she had two other coded messages to listen for. Sitting back on her heels and clenching her hands together in her lap, she strained to hear the BBC broadcaster's voice over the static created by the early June storm that was sweeping through the village. The messages she was waiting for would confirm that the underground's prearranged sabotage plans against the Germans were to go into effect tonight.

"It is hot in Suez . . . It is hot in Suez." The announcer's solemn voice triggered off the "Green Plan"—the sabotaging of railroad tracks and equipment.

Time seemed to drag out interminably in the crackling silence following that first message. Anne-Marie bit her lip to keep herself from screaming at the broadcaster to hurry up. Then she heard it, the second message.

"The dice are on the table . . . The dice are on the table," he said, calling for the "Red Plan"—the cutting of telephone lines and cables—to begin.

Overcome by emotion, Anne-Marie bowed her head and allowed herself a moment to collect her thoughts. It wasn't quite seven o'clock in the evening, and the attacks couldn't begin before dark. But the freedom for which so many of her countrymen had been fighting and dying these last four years was finally close at hand.

Fear prickled across the nape of her neck as she prayed for courage for everyone involved. It was going to be a long and dangerous night for French resisters. An even longer and more dangerous day lay ahead for the Allied soldiers who would soon be confronting the Germans.

The announcer droned on, delivering messages to various other resistance units. Having already heard the ones that concerned her, Anne-Marie concentrated on her next move. She needed to contact Guy Compain, who'd been receiving airdrops of explosives and stockpiling them in a cave near the village, and tell him that the signal had been given. In turn, he would inform the demolition experts within their group that it was time to blow the main trunk line leading out of the village and into lower Normandy. Yet other subagents would go to work smashing the steam injectors on the railway cars sitting unguarded behind the depot.

Then the Maquis, perhaps the noblest saboteurs of all, would step in to engage as many German patrols as possible before the Allies began disembarking on the beaches.

Anne-Marie smiled—a small, bittersweet smile. While she still didn't know exactly where or when the invasion would take place, she was elated to hear that it was imminent. At the same time, she was heartsick that it was coming too late to save Henriette's brother, Maurice.

Last month, a German company had attacked the forest camp where he and his comrades were training new recruits to the Maquis. By all accounts, the fighting had been bitter and brutal. Maurice had escaped with minor wounds, only to be discovered the next day hiding out in a farmer's barn.

Now, remembering how his lifeless body—tortured and beaten almost beyond recognition—had been dumped on her aunt and uncle's doorstep, she was more determined than ever to see the Germans defeated.

Thunder boomed, loud as a cannon shot, as she switched off the radio and got to her feet.

Downstairs, her grandfather was dozing in his chair. His neck was bent at an odd angle and the medical journal he'd sat down to read after dinner had fallen to the floor. Something inside of him seemed to have died with Maurice. He could barely drag himself out of bed in the morning and he just picked at his food. When he wasn't working, he slept.

Anne-Marie hated to disturb him, but she didn't want him to wake up later and be alarmed by the fact that she was gone. Besides, he wouldn't be able to turn his head tomorrow if he didn't change positions pretty soon. She finished buttoning her raincoat, then leaned down and gently kissed his brow. He opened his eyes and looked up, staring at her in confusion.

"I have to go out," she told him.

"Is it still raining?"

Her face softened. "Yes."

"You should wear a scarf."

"I will."

Once he might have grilled her. Demanded to know where she was going and why, and when she would return. Now he simply nodded and began drifting back to sleep.

The rain was coming down straight as a measuring stick when she went out the back door of the house and into the garage. She would have to ride her bicycle because there was no gasoline in her grandfather's car, and she only hoped that the new patch on her front tire would hold. If it didn't, she could always hide it in a ditch and complete her errand on foot. That would add almost an hour to her journey, though, and time was of the essence.

Anne-Marie was fairly certain that no patrol cars would be out on such a foul night. Still, she kept a weather eye out for them as she pedaled along the street. Rain soaked her scarf and cold droplets ran down the back of her neck, but she took comfort from the thought that, even if the Germans caught and killed the messenger, they couldn't kill her message.

The Allies were coming!

OMAHA BEACH, FRANCE; JUNE 6, 1944

One minute Mike Scanlon was stationed behind the Landing Craft, Tanks' lowering ramp with his rifle in his hand, ready to hit the beach; the next, he was hurtling through the air sans rifle.

They'd hit an underwater mine; it had blown the ramp off and sent him flying.

He felt weightless—like an eagle soaring. Which seemed impossible given the gas-impregnated coveralls, heavy boots and steel helmet with the white officer's stripe up the back that he was wearing. Only when he came splashing down in front of the crippled craft did it occur to him that he could easily become hamburger if the current pulled him under and the propellers caught him up.

To his relief, his lifebelt inflated, keeping him afloat. But his heart sank like a stone when he opened his eyes and saw the carnage before him.

The body of the first lieutenant who'd been standing to his right was now bobbing facedown in the water. The scarlet stains on his back told Mike that machine-gun fire from the German pillboxes on the bluffs had gotten him. Another body, that of the staff sergeant who'd been standing behind him, drifted faceup—dead from a bullet to the throat.

A spray of water exploded in front of him, and he realized with a start that he was the target now.

"Need a hand?" a loud voice called above the spanging of shells on steel.

Mike glanced up and saw a Navy crewman, hunchbacked in a bulky life vest, looking down at him over the side of the beached craft he'd just been blown off of. Without waiting for an answer, the sailor threw him a line. Geysers of water from machine-gun fire erupted around him as Mike grabbed hold of it and let himself be pulled aboard.

Except for the two of them, the LCT was deserted. The water was knee deep. None of the self-propelled guns or jeeps from Mike's battery had debarked.

"Want a drink?" The sailor proffered a half-pint-sized bottle that was about three-quarters empty.

Still too shocked to speak, Mike nodded and grabbed it gratefully. He took a pull, careful to leave some for the other man, and felt bourbon whiskey blazing a trail down his throat and into his stomach.

As he lowered the bottle, salvos straddled the small craft, shaking it and dousing them with yet more water. On the beach, a mortar scored a direct hit on a tank. Within seconds, it was a roaring inferno.

"Holy shit!" Mike's throat was raw from the saltwater and bourbon he'd swallowed, tight with emotion he couldn't afford to let loose as he watched two men, their clothes afire, leap out of the tank's turret and fall like a couple of spent matches onto the sand.

The explosion served its purpose, though. It snapped him back to concentrating on the job at hand. And that job was to survive this fiasco and find his battery so he could start fighting back.

He thrust the bottle at the sailor, who waved it away. "I've had plenty," he said. "You finish it."

Mike emptied the bottle in a head-back, walloping gulp. Then, full of Dutch courage, he jumped off the front of the landing craft and started wading to shore.

And stepped into the jaws of hell.

He'd never been exposed to small-arms fire before, much less mortar fire, so his heart, if not his feet, was doing double-time. Despite the fact that he'd just wet his whistle, his mouth felt as dry as cotton. Slogging through the waist-deep breakers and the blood-red water, he couldn't help wondering whether the rest of his life could be counted in minutes or hours. Days and years didn't even enter the equation.

Without his rifle, he felt totally defenseless. He took refuge behind a beach obstacle shaped like a giant jack. Then, soaking wet and shivering with fear, he tried to figure out where he was in relation to his battery. With their guns still aboard the landing craft, they were obviously going to have to regroup.

"I'm hit!"

Mike looked to his right, into the white face and frightened eyes of a young soldier. A boy, really. Not much older than his own brother. Instinctively, he made a grab for the kid and yelled at the top of his lungs, "Medic!"

"Maa-maa . . ."

"Hang in there." However frantic his thoughts, Mike's voice was calm as he dragged the badly wounded boy behind the obstacle with him. "Help's on the way."

But the medic got there too late. He took one look at the motionless soldier, his eyes glazed and his mouth frozen on that agonizing call for his mother, and shook his head. Then, ignoring the bullets kicking up spurts of sand at his heels, the corpsman moved on to do what he could for some other casualty.

Mike felt rage burn like a hot iron inside his head. It was time to do some killing of his own. For that poor dead kid lying beside him. And for John Brown, shot down in the prime of life.

He took his .45 service automatic out of the plastic he'd wrapped it in before the landing and found that it was sticky with salt and gritty with sand. When he pulled the slide back to load a round into the chamber, it stuck halfway. Cursing a blue streak, he tossed the useless pistol aside and reached for the dead soldier's Browning automatic rifle, only to discover that it was similarly fouled.

"A gun, goddammit." He needed a gun.

The beach was strewn with them, and with bangalore torpedoes, ammo belts and bandoliers of grenades—all discarded in either death or disgust. He thought about trying to grab the closest carbine, then thought again when a burst of machine-gun fire flung sand in his face. That was when the enormity of the situation hit him. Instead of a well-trained, well-equipped fighting man, he was half-drowned and helplessly disarmed before the enemy.

On paper, the invasion plan had looked foolproof. At first light the Air Corps would bomb the beaches for a half-hour to soften them up for the troops. Then the Navy would weigh in with its own bombardment to knock out the Germans' concrete pillboxes on the bluffs so that the combat engineers could go to work blowing mines and clearing lanes for the landing craft.

But nothing was working according to plan. The beach was a shooting gallery, the Americans sitting ducks. And with their pillboxes virtually untouched by either the air or naval bombings, the Germans were having a field day.

Mike hunkered down behind the beach obstacle, alone with the dead soldier and trying to buy some time for himself. But time was as much his enemy as those mortars and machine guns. The longer he stayed there, the greater his chances of getting hit.

The question was, where should he go next?

Behind him, even lightly wounded men were drowning in the tide. Around him, other men were falling and crawling and crying and dying. Straight ahead of him, along the seawall, hundreds of men—many of them wounded—were lying out in the open, exposed to the mortar fire pouring down from the bluffs.

His best bet was an exit. The closer the better. And the closest one, a sunken dirt road bordered by a high earthen bank on one side and a few twisted trees that had somehow survived all the shelling on the other, was only a couple of hundred yards to his left.

Mike's legs were trembling like he was palsied, but he decided to make a run for it. If he was going to die, he'd rather die doing something than to bite the dust doing nothing. Just as he got to his feet, making sure to keep his head down, he heard a tremendous roar that damned near broke his eardrums.

Glancing back, he saw two destroyers pulled broadside to the beach, blasting away at the bluffs.

The heavy smoke from their guns provided the cover he needed. He made the sign of the cross, and then he made his break. He ran like hell, zigzagging through a withering hail of bullets and hoping to high heaven that he didn't zig when he was supposed to zag.

He dove behind a dirt embankment near the base of the exit and hugged the ground. How long he lay there, panting from exertion and praising the Lord that he'd made it in one piece, he couldn't begin to guess. But when he finally raised his head, trying to get his bearings, he saw a GI bent down on one knee a few feet away from him.

He wriggled up beside him, tapped him on the shoulder and yelled, "Hey, do you know where Headquarters Batt—"

The soldier keeled over, dead from a bullet hole right in the middle of his forehead.

Cursing viciously now, Mike picked up the other man's M-1, blew the sand off its sights and threw back the bolt. Satisfied there was a live round in the chamber, he stood and, with his finger on the trigger, started working his way up the draw. His only goal, besides survival, was to find his outfit. But if it happened to be his turn to die, he wasn't doing it alone. He was taking as many Germans with him as he could.

He advanced like an outlaw, keeping his eyes to the front and his back against the bank. Partway up, he realized he'd acquired a following. He turned his head and found himself practically nose to nose with a soot-faced private who was mimicking his every move.

"Where are you going?" he barked.

"With you, sir!" the private shouted back.

Apparently that sounded like as good an idea as any to the dozen or so other leaderless men staggering up the road. Not only did they nod their helmeted heads in agreement with the private but they also looked to the second lieutenant in front of him for direction.

Just what he needed, Mike thought. A bunch of stragglers to bring the wrath of the Germans raining down on him. But being an officer, he couldn't very well leave them milling about like a herd of lost cattle. And the guns they carried would come in handy at the top of the hill.

"Spread out! Half of you on one side of the road and half on the other!" No sooner had he bellowed the order than a volley of machine-gun fire from a nest on the crest stitched a dividing line down the center of the road.

The soldiers scrambled to obey.

On the high ground, Mike crouched down behind a hedgerow in order to catch his breath and signaled the others to do the same. The steady *b-r-r-rip* of machine guns on the other side of the tall, thick shrub pulsated in his ears. He thought for a minute, trying to come up with a plan for disabling them. When he did, he turned to the private who'd become his shadow.

"Got a hand grenade?"

"Right here, sir."

A sergeant squatting beside a tree directly across the road from them produced one too.

Mike doffed his helmet, broke a long, sturdy stick off the shrub and put his helmet on the end of it. "Pull the pin," he whispered to the private, "count to five, and then throw your grenade over the hedgerow."

The private semaphored the order to the sergeant.

The instant Mike eased his helmet up, machine gun bullets started spinning it like a top. Two grenades went sailing over the hedgerow. In the wake of their explosion, the guns went silent.

"Let's go!" Mike plopped his bullet-riddled helmet back on his head and waved the men to follow him. Still keeping to his defensive crouch, he cut around the hedgerow and found three dead Germans and one disabled machine gun in a concrete trench.

A fourth German, wearing a field cap, a greatcoat and a stunned expression, sat crumpled in the corner beside a second gun that had somehow survived the grenades.

"*Kamerad,*" he muttered hoarsely as he clasped his hands over his head in surrender.

"What should we do with him, sir?" one of the men asked.

"They told us not to waste time taking prisoners," the sergeant said.

Mike had come to France with vengeance in mind. Still mourning John Brown, he'd vowed to kill every German he could. But what kind of example would he be setting for the other soldiers if he shot an unarmed man, he wondered now. He was an officer, sworn to follow the rules of engagement, not to commit atrocities. And deep down inside, he knew it wouldn't bring his friend back.

"Frisk him and send him down to the beach," he snapped.

While the other men were doing that, he reached inside his coveralls and pulled out the waterproof pouch in which he'd carried his situation maps ashore.

"Can you use this, sir?" A corporal held out a brown leather map case that he'd taken off the German.

Nodding his thanks, Mike slung the straps around his own neck and stooped to spread the map on the ground so he could see where he was and where he had to go to catch up with his battery.

A rifle slug split the air where his head had been just seconds before and ricocheted off the concrete wall.

"Sniper!"

"Hit the floor!"

Mike rolled over until he was behind the German machine gun that the hand grenades hadn't destroyed. Then he hosed the hedgerow across the road, sending leaves and limbs flying every which way. Shrieks of pain, followed by dead silence, told him he'd partially evened the score for John.

Two thunderous explosions coming from the beach suddenly bracketed the trench.

"Damn!" The same naval fire that Mike had blessed earlier he now cursed.

The floor trembled and shook beneath an answering barrage of German artillery fire.

"We're getting' it from both sides!" the sergeant shouted.

The private, sporting a bubble of blood on his cheek from where a chip of concrete had nicked him, stammered, "W—where do we go now, s-sir?"

"First, let's see where we are." Still flat on his stomach, Mike reached for his map and finished spreading it out in front of him.

Where they were, he discovered, was in no-man's land—between the Germans' prepared positions on the bluffs and the Americans' renewed shelling from the beach. The only "safe" place he could find was a field of some sort across the road.

"We could probably dig in over there," the private pointed out.

"I've got an entrenching tool," the sergeant said.

"And I've got a shelter half," another soldier added.

"So do I," someone else chimed in.

Mike gave up on the idea of finding his battery. At least for now, anyway. Because if he abandoned these men and later found out they'd been killed, he couldn't live with himself. Resigned to his fate, he folded the map and stuck it in the leather case.

"Cover me," he ordered.

The makeshift squad fired a steady fusillade as he cut around the hedgerow and charged across the road. Then they took turns, one running and the rest shooting, until they all wound up in a flat field encircled by some more of those high damned hedgerows that made such good defensive cover for the Germans.

"We're safe, sir," the private panted.

"What makes you say that?"

"See that cow over there?"

Mike looked at the grazing brown-and-white bovine, with her big eyes and swollen udder. "So?"

"So, cows are curious animals, sir. If there was anyone else in this field, ol' Elsie wouldn't be chewing her cud. She'd be facing 'em, waiting to be milked."

Mike looked at him askance. "How'd you know that?"

"I grew up on a farm in Clay Center, Kansas, sir."

Cows spotting Germans made about as much sense as anything else Mike had seen or heard today. He started to shrug it off. Then it hit him that, as a forward observer, he might find this particular tip real handy in combat.

"I'll have to remember that, Private," he said appreciatively.

"Anybody know what time it is?" someone asked.

Mike dug his watch out of his pocket. He'd wrapped it in a condom before the invasion to keep it dry and was glad to see the ploy had worked. What surprised him, though, was seeing how late it was.

"Almost five o'clock," he said in amazement.

"No wonder I'm hungry!" The sergeant, a burly guy with a brush haircut, started digging around in his pack for something to eat. "I missed breakfast and lunch."

The other men followed suit, sharing everything from the apples they'd brought from England to the K-rations they'd been issued before the invasion with those who'd either lost their packs or, like Mike, had left them on the landing craft. With the fighting still raging around them, they didn't dare light a fire to heat water for their packets of Nescafé coffee. So except for a sip of water each from the one canteen that had survived intact, they didn't have anything else to wash down their food.

Until the private came up with an idea of how to remedy that. "Ever tasted fresh milk, Lieutenant?"

After wolfing down a cold ration of chopped ham and eggs, Mike found that his stomach was still sending out distress signals. Except for some seasick pills and those two slugs of bourbon, he hadn't had anything by mouth in over twenty-four hours for fear of being gut-shot. Now he set the empty ration can aside and reached for an apple, trying to make up for lost time.

"My dad used to bring it home sometimes," he said with a wistful smile.

The private grinned, a missing front tooth and that smeared face giving him an engagingly boyish appearance. "Well, you're about to taste it again."

Everyone watched in amazement as he squatted beside the cow's ballooning udder and held a borrowed canteen cup beneath the chosen teat. An expert milkman, he filled the cup to the brim and carried it back to Mike without spilling a drop.

"Here you go, sir."

"Thanks." Mike drained the cup, finding that the warm milk was as rich and creamy as he remembered.

Artillery shells and mortar fire whistled and whizzed over the field, but the cow stood patiently as the private returned for another cupful.

Milking a cow in the middle of a war suddenly struck Mike as ridiculous. He started laughing, letting it roll out of him in waves. Pretty soon the other men were howling along with him, releasing some of the tension built up over the longest, most miserable day of their lives.

As darkness came on, so did the cold. The sodden group decided to spend the night together and then try to find their own outfits in the morning. Besides, they all agreed, another cup of that fresh milk would taste mighty good for breakfast.

I made it, Mike thought as he flopped down in a ditch beside the hedgerow. Dog-tired yet still too wound up to sleep, he stacked his hands under his head and just laid there for a while, watching a path of tracer fire arcing in the distance and listening to that cow lowing contentedly in a corner of the field. But as his eyes finally drifted closed, he couldn't shake the feeling that he was living on borrowed time.

STE. GENVIÈVE, FRANCE

"Hold his head still."

Anne-Marie willed her hands to stop shaking and smiled down at the four-year-old boy who was lying on her grandfather's operating table. Unfortunately, little André Tardieu couldn't see her smiling at him because of the bandage covering his eyes. A larger bandage started just below his shoulder and nearly reached his elbow, and his hands were wrapped in gauze.

She noticed the smell of smoke lingering in his hair as she bent down and whispered in his ear, "We're almost finished."

"Maman!" André cried as Henri Gérard began probing for scattered splinters in the boy's cheeks and quivering chin.

But his mother was dead. As were his older sisters and baby brother. The only other member of his family who was still alive was his father, who had dragged the boy out of their blazing farmhouse after a German shell had hit it. An anxious Monsieur Tardieu, his own hands badly blistered, was now waiting in the anteroom for news of his son's condition.

Just a little over a month old, the war had already extracted a terrible price from the people of France. The Germans, furious at being caught off-guard by the Allied invasion at Normandy, had begun striking back at acts of sabotage with mass executions. The most egregious to date was when an elite Das Reich division on its way to the front rounded up all the inhabitants of Oradour-sur-Glane in the village's church and barns and set fire to them.

"Don't move!" Dr. Gérard sharply admonished the squirming André.

Still bent over the boy, Anne-Marie hummed a few bars of "*Frère Jacques*" to try and keep him immobile while her grandfather sprinkled some of their dwindling supply of sulfanilamide powder on his facial wounds.

When she straightened, she glanced out the operating room window and saw artillery flashing like heat lightning in the July dusk. The Germans, in a furious fight to hold their ground, were laying waste to the countryside. Wheatfields were pocked with shell craters and cows lay dead in the pastures. All that remained of her uncle's apple orchard were a few green leaves and twisted branches where his proudly tended trees had once stood.

The Allies would save France. Of that, Anne-Marie was certain. But sadly, she thought as she watched her grandfather peel off his surgical gloves and square his shoulders before going out to talk to Monsieur Tardieu, no one could save little André's sight.

SOMEWHERE IN NORMANDY

The village looked deserted. But looks could be deceiving, as Mike Scanlon had learned the hard way these past seven weeks. And small actions could easily turn into big conflagrations.

"Stop here," he ordered his driver on the edge of town.

Mike had already reported to the commander of the infantry division that he was going to shoot for and received an update on the mission. They'd gone in to mop up a friendly village, only to find that the Germans wanted it back. Now, using their artillery regiment, his job was to make sure that they didn't get it back.

"I'm going to scout around a little bit." Wearing his map case and carrying both his rifle and 536 radio, he jumped out of the jeep. He'd left his musette bag with his tank crew. It contained his first mail from home—birthday cards from his family, a birth announcement from Kitty Brown containing a picture of his new godson-by-proxy, John, Jr., and a thank you note from Charlie and Daisy Miller for the cash wedding present he'd sent them. Later, if there was a later, he would answer them all.

"I'll go with you, Lieutenant," his driver offered.

But the redheaded corporal, who looked barely old enough to shave, was Mike's third driver since the landing. His first had been killed by stray shrapnel from the rolling barrage the battalion had laid down for the crossing of the Vire-Taute Canal, while the second had asked to be reassigned after that close quarter defensive action at St. Jean-de-Daye—an action that had earned Mike a Bronze Star with a V for valor.

"No." Something was going to happen very soon, Mike could feel it in his bones, and he didn't like it one damn bit. Plus, he didn't want to lose another driver. "Keep the motor running and I'll relay the coordinates back to you."

The dominant building, as it was in all of the Norman villages he'd been in, was a church of square-cut stone with a tall, slender steeple stretching into the sky.

Seeing that steeple, he wondered why no one had bothered to shoot it off. It was the only logical point of observation for miles around. When the American infantry came through, thinking the town had been cleaned out, the German observer would be able to adjust fire right down on top of them.

He made a note of the coordinates on his map and then he wondered which way to turn—right or left?

Following his instincts, he turned right, went around to the back of a house in a long row of houses, and edged his way in a cautious crabwalk to the end. The main street looked empty—too empty to suit him—and the shutters were drawn on those storefronts whose windows hadn't already been shattered. Which told him that the villagers had either fled in panic or were huddled inside in fear of the battle to come.

His nerves blade-thin, he dashed across the street, then crept along behind another row of houses. Just beyond the last one, a small bridge spanned a creek. He slowed to an invalid's walk and peered at it and around it and past it . . . and stopped dead.

There, not a hundred yards beyond the bridge, in a field by the side of the road, sat a German panzer division.

As he looked through his binoculars, Mike could smell the heavy diesel odor from their engines hanging in the air. He made radio contact with his driver and gave him the map coordinates. Less than a minute later the artillery regiment fired, the shells screaming over his head on their way to the enemy. Seeing they weren't exactly on target, he relayed a correction.

"One-Fox to Fire Direction Center," he called then. "Fire for effect."

The ground trembled under his feet as exploding shells saturated the area. Thick black smoke from the stricken hulk of the closest German tank stung his eyes. The sweet-rancid smell of burning fuel, torn flesh and ruptured earth seared his nostrils.

Mission accomplished, Mike was just hopping back into the jeep when a bullet hit the hood and bounced harmlessly against the windshield. He glanced up and, sure enough, saw sunlight glinting off the scope of the German artillery observer's rifle in the church steeple he'd foolishly forgotten to target.

"Stay here," he told his terrified driver as he leaped out again. "I'll be right back."

There wasn't time to call in the coordinates, so he ran inside the church and headed straight for the stairs to the steeple. As the German opened fire on him from his new position in the choir loft, a bullet cut through Mike's carbine and shattered the stock.

He felt a burning sting in the side of his neck—from a fragment, he supposed—as he ducked behind the baptismal font. Ignoring the pain, he drew his pistol from the holster of his Sam Browne belt. Then he just crouched there, keeping his eyes focused on the stairway that led to the loft and waiting to see what happened next.

The silence below proved too tempting for the German to resist. His bootheels made soft scuffing sounds as he crept down the stairs. When he started a pew-by-pew search, Mike held his breath and told himself to be patient. The closer the German got, the easier he'd be to take out.

Suddenly the church was filled with noise as the jeep driver came bursting through the door and sent it crashing against the back wall.

The German whirled and shot the corporal.

At the same time, Mike vaulted to his feet and shot the German. The stone walls echoed the *chink* of the bullets that hit him, while the *crump* of artillery drowned out his dying screams.

"Am I going to live, Lieutenant?" His face white beneath his freckles and his fingers red with blood, the corporal was clutching his shoulder when Mike knelt beside him.

"To the ripe old age of a hundred, if you're lucky." Mike ripped open the uniform shirt that covered the torn flesh and protruding bone and saw that it was probably more than the battalion surgeon could handle. Which meant the corporal would be evacuated back to England and he'd be getting a new driver.

"I heard shooting, sir, and I got worried about you."

Mike felt a crack forming in the protective shell of numbness he'd developed to help him go on day after day. He understood now why the combat veterans in his battalion had kept him at arm's length when he'd joined them in England. And why he hadn't allowed himself to get too close to anyone, not even his tank crew, since the landing. With death just a fact of life in front-line combat, he didn't want to wind up losing any more friends.

"And now you've got the 'million-dollar wound'." He didn't have any sulfa powder with him, so he took out one of the morphine syrettes he carried on his belt and inserted the needle.

The corporal winced. "You're bleeding too, Lieutenant."

"It's just a scratch." After removing the needle, though, Mike unzipped the collar of his tank suit so that the knitted material wouldn't stick to his own seeping wound.

Two blue eyes blinked up at him. "I'm sorry, sir."

As angry as he was with the corporal for disobeying orders, Mike was even angrier with himself for letting his emotions get the best of him. He looked away, vowing he wouldn't make that mistake again, and asked in a gruff voice, "Is the morphine helping yet?"

"Yes, sir."

"Then let's get the hell out of here." He slid an arm under the corporal's good shoulder and half-carried, half-dragged him back to the jeep. After he'd settled him on the passenger side but before he slid behind the wheel, he radioed the coordinates he'd forgotten to relay earlier to the infantry's artillery regiment.

Mike felt no satisfaction as he watched the shells hit the church steeple, leaving behind a jagged spire spiking the sky—only a terrible weariness at the waste of it all.

Chapter Five

STE. GENVIÈVE, FRANCE

*T*he feeling of cleanliness was like a rebirth.

Mike had shaved and taken "whore's baths" out of his helmet on a regular basis, but he hadn't been wet all over since that quick shower back at Headquarters Battery about ten days ago.

Now, standing in the shallows of the lake, he soaped himself from head to toe, scrubbing off the vestiges of mud and blood he'd accumulated in the ensuing battles. He rinsed by wading farther out and diving beneath the cool, clear water, drowning out the sleep-haunting sounds of exploding shells and excruciating screams. Surfacing, he swam back to the bank and brushed his teeth, scouring away the pungent taste of cordite and the clouds of dust he'd been eating with his cold rations.

The murmurs of the men in their pup tents pitched among the trees and the clang of machinery being worked on rode a warm August breeze as he headed back to his own tent wearing only his dogtags and clean skivvies. His battalion had been pulled out of action for ordinance maintenance and had infiltrated in the middle of the night to make camp in this field. Except for an occasional day in reserve, it was his first real break since his baptism of fire on the beach, and he needed it with every fiber of his being.

Especially after Mortain, where the German counter-battery had been as heavy and damned near as deadly as anything he'd experienced on D-Day.

"Monsieur?"

The softly accented summons caught Mike off guard. He reached for his pistol, then realized that he wasn't wearing it. Or much of anything else for that matter, he reminded himself, as he pivoted on his bare heel to see who'd called to him.

If he'd been wearing socks, though, the willowy young woman pushing a bicycle with a patched front tire and a live chicken in the handlebar basket would have knocked them off.

Observation was second nature to him now, and for the first time since the landing he liked everything he saw. She was wearing a pair of cork-soled sandals with wedged heels, and a sleeveless blue dress that bisected her bare knees and was demurely buttoned to her throat. Tendrils of honey-blonde hair had escaped the heavy knot atop her head and clung damply to her long, slender neck.

His heart jitterbugged in his chest when she stopped a few feet away from him and lifted her chin. Even without makeup, she was a knockout. Dark brows arched over light brown eyes that were wide and a little wary. Her pale skin wore the natural blush of exertion, and perspiration glistened like dew on an upper lip that was bowed like a Kewpie doll's.

She extended a hand that was as clean and delicate-looking as the rest of her. "I'm Anne-Marie Gérard."

"You speak English," he said inanely.

"But of course!" Her proud smile staggered him like a bare-fisted punch. "And—"

"Wait here, I'll be right back."

Mike ducked into his tent and dropped the flap behind him. He knew it was rude of him to cut her off in mid-sentence like that. Ruder still to leave her with her hand hanging in midair, wondering if he'd lost his everlovin' mind. Which he probably had, but that was beside the point.

Because if he'd stayed, he might have done something even worse—like throwing her down on her back and taking her on the ground.

But what could he expect? He hadn't had a woman since England,

and that had been nothing but a fast financial transaction. A "quid pro quickie," as he'd jokingly called it in his birthday card to John Brown all those months ago. He'd been sealed in a marshaling camp after that, cut off from the rest of the world while he prepared for the invasion and wrote both his will and what might well be his last letter home.

Then war had become his all-consuming passion, blurring the lines between moral duty and murder as he'd shelled and maimed and sometimes shot his fellow man to death.

None of which excused what he'd wanted to do to her.

Mike really couldn't explain his reaction, except to say that she was his first contact with something normal since—Christ, he almost couldn't remember when! That shield of numbness had served him *too* well, it seemed. At some point he'd quit thinking about yesterday. Quit worrying about tomorrow. He'd quit feeling, too . . . until he'd found himself standing in a summer green field with a girl whose smile had unleashed in him a spasm of half-forgotten sensations and memories of another life.

Was she still waiting for him? God, he hoped so. He cocked an ear toward the tent flap, listening closely but hearing nothing, then decided there was only one way to find out.

It took him all of about three minutes to get dressed, because Supply Battery had yet to catch up with the rest of the battalion. He tossed his wet towel and toothbrush in the corner, then put on his cleanest dirty shirt and matching olive drab pants. His field jacket had seen better days, as had his combat boots, but they would have to do for now. Finally, he finger-combed his hair, reminding himself to get it cut when the barber arrived, and then stepped outside.

"Sorry about that." He was relieved to see that she was still there. Even more relieved when she smiled her forgiveness of his rude behavior. He jammed his hands in his pockets, where they would be safe, and introduced himself. "I'm Mike Scanlon."

Anne-Marie had heard the rumors about the American GIs' preoccupation with sex. And about the French women, many of them younger than she, who sold their bodies for a bar of soap or a pack of cigarettes.

She didn't purport to judge any of them because she didn't know their circumstances. Just so there was no mistaking *her* intentions, however, she had deliberately kept some distance between herself and the soldier she had spotted from the road.

She'd spent last night at the farm comforting Henriette, who was still in mourning for her oldest brother, Maurice. Then this morning, after putting the chicken that her grieving aunt had given her to cook for her grandfather's dinner this evening in the wire basket, she'd started back to the village. It was a clear, calm day, but it was hot enough to make her wonder if anyone she knew was swimming in the lake. Riding past the field, she'd almost driven her bicycle into the ditch when she saw the vehicles with white stars instead of swastikas parked there and the small tents sitting among the trees.

But the task she had impetuously set for herself at that moment would have been easier if this tall American weren't so . . . so dangerously attractive.

Damp brown hair as dark as his eyes had been raked back from a strong face made lean by war. Except for the pale line of demarcation across his forehead, where she presumed his helmet had perched, his skin was bronzed from exposure to the summer sun. His nose was straight, his cheekbones seemingly molded from steel, his chin a monument to both decency and daring. And that smiling mouth, with the dimple beside it, definitely drew her eye.

As did the breadth of his shoulders beneath the drab, olive-green jacket. There were muscles there; she'd seen them. And that memory, coupled with the remembrance of long, bare legs liberally dusted with dark hair, almost made her forget the reason she had approached him in the first place.

Searching for something less distracting to focus on, she looked at the silver bars, one each, pinned to his epaulets. "You are an officer?"

"A first lieutenant, yes." Mike had received a battlefield promotion last month, after the all-night pyrotechnics he'd sent crashing down on Cerisy-la-Salle.

"Then I should call you 'sir'!"

"Only if you want me to call you 'ma'am'."

The chicken in her handlebar basket cackled at his comeback and they laughed together, their eyes clinging even after their smiles had faded.

"Mike," she agreed shyly.

His dimple reappeared. "Anne-Marie."

"Is Mike your . . ." She faltered, trying to think of the right word. "Knickknack?"

He took a wild guess. "Nickname?"

"Oui!"

"Yes."

She bristled at his teasing smile but stood her ground. "You're making fun with me."

"No," he said, genuinely contrite. But he wished . . . God, how he wished!

A burst of raucous laughter erupted from the far side of the bivouac area, where the enlisted men had pitched their tents. Somebody bellowed, *"Vin!"* Someone else bawled, *"Cherchez la femme!"* A chorus of lusty voices, closer by, began singing, *"Roll me o-ver . . . Roll me o-ver! Roll me over, lay me down and do it again!"*

She stole a glance in that direction, and he felt his gut tightening when the wariness returned like a shadow to her expressive amber eyes.

"Michael." He stepped sideways, blocking her view of the bivouac area, and succeeded in drawing her worried gaze back to him. "My full name is Michael."

"In French we say *Michel.*" Her smoky voice breathed such exotic new meaning into his name that his mouth watered for more.

He swallowed before he started drooling all over her. "What can I do for you?"

Anne-Marie hesitated only because she didn't want Mike to see her as a beggar. Then she reminded herself that pride was a small price to pay when peoples' lives were at stake. So she resolved to do what she had come to do, even if it made her look bad in his eyes, and then go home.

"My grandfather is a doctor," she began, "and so many of our villagers have been wounded by bombs or bullets—"

"Collateral damage," he muttered under his breath.

"Comment?" she asked in confusion.

"That's the military term for civilian casualties." But Mike would have been the first to admit that it took a tougher nut than he not to be moved by the sight of a small child who'd lost a leg and now used a crutch. Or a mother cradling a crying baby swathed in bandages from head to toes.

Anne-Marie was moved for a different reason. She saw the regret in the depths of his dark eyes and wanted, somehow, to reach out to him. She wheeled her bicycle a little closer and laid her hand on his forearm. "To make an omelet, you have to break eggs."

"You're not bitter about the damage then?" He balled his own hands into fists in his pockets, wondering if she knew that everything about her, from the way she rolled her *r's* to the reassurance of her touch, was tying him in knots.

"We've waited a long time for you." Feeling his muscles tense beneath her fingers, she withdrew them and grabbed hold of the handle-bar again, surprised to discover she needed the support because her knees were unsteady.

Her simple words warmed him as the sun could not, and he suddenly felt like he was awakening from the long, violent nightmare of war.

For this moment, he was a man at peace with himself and with his surroundings. He could hear the birds caroling in the trees. Smell the purple and the yellow wildflowers growing at his feet. For this moment, he could see blue sky overhead and the beautiful young woman standing in front of him.

And for this moment, this brief, shining moment, he wanted that woman as he'd never wanted a woman before.

"You said your grandfather is a doctor," he reminded her gruffly.

"He needs sulfanilamide powder to treat our wounded, and I . . ." Still a little squeamish about what she was asking, she squared her shoulders and forged ahead. "I thought that if your group had some to spare, I could take it to him."

He willed himself not to look at the soft swell of her breasts beneath her blue cotton bodice. "I could write you a note to give to the battalion surgeon."

"A surgeon—*oui!*" She hoped her voice didn't betray her nervousness as she thought about walking through the noisy bivouac area. "And where would I find him?"

Mike knew what he had to do. He'd wanted some privacy after spending the better part of two months cooped up in a tank with four other men, so he'd pitched his tent near the lake and away from the crowd. But sending Anne-Marie into a field full of sex-starved soldiers, he acknowledged now, would be like sending a lamb to the slaughter.

"Why don't I go get it for you?" he offered.

Relief swelled through her. "You wouldn't mind?"

"I need to talk to my tank crew." Most of whom, he suspected, were busy "liberating" the tall bottles of wine and the squat bottles of cognac they'd been given by the grateful French who'd lined the roads as they'd rolled through their newly freed villages. He took three steps away from her before he stopped and did an about-face. "Wait here, I'll—"

"Be right back," she finished for him.

"Count on it." When she smiled at him again, Mike suddenly had the sensation of all the world slipping away so that only he and she were alone in it together in this place and at this time.

As she watched him walk away, Anne-Marie pressed a hand to her jittery stomach. For some reason, it felt as if she had just swallowed one of the butterflies fluttering about the bird-foot violets and the genet blooming in the field. Her heart was behaving erratically, as well. It seemed to be thundering at a thousand pulses a minute.

She attributed her strange reaction to the heat. Either that, or to the excitement of knowing that she would soon have the life-saving medicine her grandfather needed. She refused to even consider that it might be the man now carrying the wooden box back from the bivouac area who excited her so.

How could she repay his kindness? *That* was what she should be concentrating on, she chided herself. Yet her unruly mind kept recapturing the memory of the taut, well-muscled torso beneath the uniform.

Determined not to be caught staring at him, she studied the small chicken still roosting in her bicycle basket. Ordinarily, it would feed only two people. Now she decided that extra vegetables and wine would stretch it enough for three.

"Tell me the name of that dish again."

"Coq au vin."

Mike didn't even attempt to repeat it for fear of making a fool of himself. He just hopped into the jeep he'd parked at the curb and nodded his appreciation. "It was delicious."

"Even the turnips?" Standing on the step in front of her house, Anne-Marie wore a floral-patterned skirt, a simple white blouse and a mischievous smile.

He grinned, remembering the surprise he'd received when he'd forked what he'd thought were mashed potatoes into his mouth and discovered they were puréed turnips. He must have made a grotesque face, because she'd flashed him a concerned glance. But then, as the turnips' sweet, buttery taste had melted over his tongue, both his facial and his throat muscles had relaxed, and they'd gone down with surprising smoothness.

"Even the turnips," he admitted on a laugh.

"And the coffee—"she splayed her slender fingers at the open collar of her blouse—"it wasn't too bitter for you?"

It had tasted like something out of a test tube, but he couldn't tell her that. "No, it was fine."

She saw through his lie. "We can't get good coffee yet, but soon."

"It was fine," he repeated. "Really, everything was just great."

Dinner had been a convivial, bilingual affair, but now the sun had disappeared below the horizon and GIs in combat boots either sat in groups at the sidewalk café in the square or walked arm in arm with local girls along the dusky streets of the village.

"I'm sorry the room was so dim," Anne-Marie apologized for at least the third time since Mike had arrived. "But our electrical wires are still being repaired."

"The candles gave us enough light." And he'd enjoyed watching their soft flames flicker across her face as she'd sat between him at one end of the table and her grandfather at the other, serving as their interpreter through the meal.

She stepped down, onto the narrow sidewalk that ran past the house. "The *girandole* belonged to my grandmother."

"The what?"

At his puzzled expression, she searched for the appropriate English word to describe the silvered bronze and crystal table accessory. "Candelabra."

He cocked her a grin. "Gotcha."

"It was a wedding present from her parents."

"Very pretty." But not nearly as pretty as she was right now, Mike thought. She'd brushed out her hair, and the evening breeze was sending the honeycomb strands dancing around her face and along her neck and throat. He gripped the steering wheel with both hands to keep himself from doing something he was sure he'd later regret. Like reaching over to grab her and kiss her senseless.

Anne-Marie clasped her own hands together in front of her and twisted her fingers together nervously, wondering if she had said or done something to offend him. What else could make his eyes go so dark and his expression so grim? Or him so obviously anxious to leave?

"My grandfather asked me to thank you again for the medicine," she said on a rush of breath.

"I'm glad I could help." But recalling the way the candlelight had thrown the bones of Dr. Gérard's face into sharp, almost skeletal relief, he wondered if she knew the old guy was dying.

"And for the cigarettes, too."

He'd gotten his hair cut and picked up his clean uniform. Then, remembering his manners, he'd stopped by the Red Cross Clubmobile to see if there was something he could take as a sort of hostess gift. At a loss, he'd bought a carton of Lucky Strikes.

"I didn't know if either one of you smoked—"

"No, we don't. But American cigarettes are more valuable than francs. Especially for bartering."

"Maybe you can trade them for more turnips," he said, deadpan.

She raised one of those dark brows that provided such a striking contrast to her pale skin. "I'll call you when they're ready to eat."

The two wits smiled at each other in the lavender twilight.

"Well," he said with a philosophic shrug, "it's getting late."

Disappointment swamped her as the silver bars on his broad shoulders winked goodbye to her. "When does your battalion have to leave?"

"I don't know." He shrugged again. "Our equipment is in better shape than anyone expected, so March Order could come any day."

"Do you think you'll still be here tomorrow?"

"If I had to guess, I'd say yes." But in the skewed reality that was war, he'd learned, yesterday was always long ago and tomorrow was always far away.

"Then we have time," she said when he reached to start the jeep's motor.

He retracted his hand and tilted his head at her. "Time for what?"

Anne-Marie felt her face flame as she gazed into his eyes. She'd never been one to flirt, not even before the Occupation, and she had always spurned the advances of the male Resistance members who became enamored of her. Now here she was, all but throwing herself at an American soldier who would probably forget her as soon as he was gone. And praying he wouldn't say no.

Or notice how shaky her smile was. "Time to go on a picnic."

Because she'd pronounced it "*peek-neek*," it took him a few seconds to translate. Even then, he stared at her blankly for another heartbeat or two. "A picnic?"

"Yes." She took a deep breath. "Tomorrow."

Actually, Mike had been thinking about swinging by that little French inn tomorrow, the one his tank crew had discovered today, and seeing for himself if the barmaid really was as easy as they claimed. They'd come back to camp reeking of cheap wine and even cheaper perfume just as he was getting ready to leave to have dinner with the Gérards. Only the memory of honey-blonde hair and amber-brown eyes had kept him from taking a detour.

Talk about a rock and a hard place, he thought now. Here he sat, torn between a broad who was rumored to have round heels and a beautiful woman who'd stood up to the Nazis at every turn. And surprising the hell out of himself when he nodded and said, "Yeah, a picnic sounds like fun."

"*Le nez.*"

"You don't pronounce the *z*?"

"No."

"*Luh nay.*" Feeling clumsy and foolish, Mike repeated phonetically the French words for *nose*.

Anne-Marie rewarded his latest effort with an enthusiastic, "*Bravo!*"

These past two days had been short, but sweeter than anything either of them had ever known before.

Over yesterday's picnic of pungent Camembert cheese, accompanied by slices of soft bread and crisp apple and topped off with a bottle of vintage *vin rouge* that she'd found in her grandfather's cellar, they'd told each other their whole lives.

Mike had felt her sorrow, as keen as a knife's edge, and his own slow-burning rage as she'd described the Stuka attack on Rouen that she'd survived and her parents and younger brother had not. And the story of how her cousin Maurice had died at the hands of the Nazis had poured kerosene on the fires of his fury.

Anne-Marie, in turn, had murmured regrets over the death of his father, expressed her deepest admiration for his mother's determination to keep her family together and sighed with envy when he showed her the small black-and-white picture of his sister and brother that he carried in his soldier's Bible. She would give anything, she'd said, to see even one of her deceased relatives again.

"My grandfather is dying," she'd whispered then.

"I wasn't sure you knew." He'd thought she might cry, providing him with the perfect excuse to take her in his arms, but she had remained in control of her emotions.

She'd raised her chin, her eyes shining like liquid amber, and said, "He misses my grandmother."

A skylark's song, as melancholy as it was melodious, had accompanied their accounts of John Brown and Miriam Blum. Had he reached for her hand first, or she his? Neither remembered but both became increasingly aware that they were sharing more than just a sense of loss.

Their war stories had fallen on the lighter side. And deliberately so. Each of them had seen enough of its horror in their young lives without having to revisit it.

So she'd laughed until her stomach ached when he recounted bedding down in a barn in the dark of night on what he thought was a haystack and waking up the next morning to discover he'd been sleeping atop a pile of manure. And he'd shaken his head in utter astonishment when she told him about the German patrolman, unaware that she carried sabotage plans in her bicycle spokes, who'd helped her patch the front tire.

Finally, he'd revealed his artillery call sign and she her Resistance code name.

"'Ello, One-Fox," she'd said saucily.

He'd gazed at her in a steady, serious way that made her uncomfortably warm. "Hello, Tiger Lily."

Embarrassed, she'd glanced away. "I have to go home now."

Mike hadn't kissed her goodbye. Though Lord knew he'd wanted to.

Instead, he'd filled her bicycle basket with packets of Nescafé and made her promise to come back first thing tomorrow.

So this morning, wearing her summer-white Sunday dress and a straw boater hat that had belonged to her grandmother, Anne-Marie had ridden out to the field to attend Mass with him. Accustomed to the pomp and ceremony of her village priest, she'd been amazed when his battalion's chaplain simply spread a snowy white altar cloth across the hood of a jeep and called his flock to worship. She'd never felt closer to God or more afraid for a man than when she'd knelt in the lush green grass beside the American soldier who would be leaving her soon.

The gathering storm clouds had scuttled their plans to go swimming after Mass, so she'd hung her hat from her bicycle handlebars, he'd bought them each a bottle of Coca-Cola from the Clubmobile, and they'd taken a long, leisurely walk around the lake. When the wind picked up, raising gooseflesh on her bare arms, he'd loaned her his field jacket to wear over her light cotton dress and helped her roll back the too-long sleeves. In return, she'd offered to give him a French lesson.

Mike had spread his sleeping bag on the same secluded patch of the small beach where they'd picnicked the day before, then dropped down on it, Indian-style. Anne-Marie had tucked her skirt beneath her and folded her legs in ladylike fashion to sit beside him on its cushiony surface. He'd proved to be an apt pupil as she'd taught him the words for *head* and *eyes* and *nose*.

But now, ready to move lower, he looked at her soldier's dream of a mouth that had kept him awake for two nights running and asked, "Lips?"

"*Les lèvres*," she answered, moistening her own with her tongue in a way that made the skin on the back of his neck prickle.

Thunder grumbled in the distance. Or was it gunfire? They both looked in the direction it had come from; they both felt time rushing away like grains of sand in an hourglass; they both looked back with the terrible knowledge that this might well be their last day together.

Mike got to his knees and brushed a finger down her cheek. Then he coiled a windblown strand of her soft, silky hair around that same finger and gently drew her up until they were kneeling face to face. He wanted to see, just once before he left, if she tasted as good as she looked.

"How do you say, 'I want to kiss you'?"

Anne-Marie stared into his intent brown eyes for a breathless moment. She'd been raised to believe that the sin of the flesh started with a kiss, and had always been careful to stop any boy who tried to go beyond a chaste peck. Yet even knowing that this was a man who would take everything she had to give, she couldn't refuse him.

"Je veux t'embrasser."

He didn't try to repeat the strangely pretty words. He just slid one hand into her hair, tilting her head back, then slipped an arm beneath the field jacket she was wearing and clamped it around her waist. Slowly then, he lowered his mouth to hers.

Anne-Marie had been kissed before, but never like this. He touched the corner of her lips with his tongue. Took soft, plucking bites with his teeth and applied a gentle suction that generated a moan, low and deep, in her throat. On and on he went, teasing her and tempting her until her head buzzed, her blood raced and her breathing rasped as if she'd been bicycling uphill.

A jagged streak of lightning divided the sky as she wrapped her arms around him and parted her lips for more.

Mike was no longer thinking "just once." No longer thinking, period. She was soft and supple and as sweet as a feast after a long fast. Craving more, he sampled and savored her mouth. Used his tongue to trace the provocative curves that had been driving him stark, staring crazy. And then he plunged deeper, knowing he could never get enough of her.

Thunder clapped as the kiss turned ravenous, slanting this way, then that.

He wouldn't give her promises he couldn't keep. Couldn't give her permanence when he didn't even know where he would be this time tomorrow. So with hands that were as strong as they were sensitive to a woman's needs, he gave her pleasure.

And what pleasure it was . . .

She shivered with it when he cupped her breast. Quivered with it when he shaped the soft flesh to fit his palm. Then thought she would die from it when he flicked his thumb over her nipple and brought it to full, aching bloom.

Desire zipped up her spine when his other hand moved down to her derrière and pressed her closer. She felt the steely evidence of his arousal through the thin material of her dress. And was amazed that she found no shame in letting him fondle her so intimately.

Two days ago they'd been complete strangers. Yesterday they'd become friends. Today, if nature took its course, they would be lovers.

Mike knew the French phrase for asking a woman to go to bed with him. Hell, the whole damned battalion had been practicing it since well before the landing. But Anne-Marie was so classy and *"Voulez-vous coucher avec moi?"* suddenly sounded so crass.

He nuzzled his way to her ear. Nosed her silky hair out of the way and sketched the sensitive shell with the tip of his tongue. Then he left his lips there to whisper, "How do you say 'I want to make love with you'?"

Anne-Marie felt a skitter of panic as she turned her head and looked into his face. His dark hair fell onto his brow and his dimple had deepened beside his smiling mouth. But it was his eyes, filled with breath-stealing tenderness, which had her shrinking away from him.

This was all her fault, she knew. It was she who had thought he would be satisfied with a few kisses. She who had melted like warm candle wax in his arms. Now it was she who had to put a stop to this.

"I'm sorry," she murmured.

He shook his head to clear it. "What?"

She scrambled to her feet. "I said—"

"I heard you." He stood and propped his hands on his hips, his breathing as harsh as the wind that now rose between them.

"I can't," she said on a note of regret.

Mike knew he couldn't blame her for pulling back without also blaming himself for trying to push her too far, too fast. But that didn't slake his pent-up lust. Nor did it keep him from behaving like a class A bastard.

He took a menacing step closer to her and snarled, "Can't or won't?"

Anne-Marie couldn't believe the change that had come over him. His mouth had tensed, his dimple had disappeared, and his eyes had developed an edge. A dark and dangerous edge that told her what a fierce warrior he must be.

Still, she met his challenging stare levelly. "One thing you must know about me is that I always say what I think."

He nodded curtly, trying his damnedest not to admire her show of spunk as he waited for her to finish.

"I've never known a man." She saw his surprise, something deep and shadowed in his eyes, and went on in a jagged whisper, "But I think you've known many women."

He couldn't deny it. Didn't even try. He just continued to stare at her, steeling himself against emotions he couldn't afford to feel.

"What do you want from me?" he finally demanded.

"Nothing." That wasn't true, but it didn't matter now.

"Then why are you—"

"But for myself," she said, lifting her chin to that proud angle, "I want to be more than one of many."

There was a time when Mike would have lied to her. He would have taken her in his arms and told her that she was the girl of his dreams, his one and only, the woman he'd been waiting for his whole life. Hell, he'd have told her the moon was made of green cheese if it meant she'd go to bed with him.

But that was two months and a thousand lifetimes ago. Now he could no more look into those golden-brown eyes and lie than he could sprout wings and fly. And besides, he reminded himself in a throbbing fit of frustration, there was always that barmaid.

"Goodbye, Anne-Marie."

She swallowed the sting in her throat and met his eyes directly. They were remote, as if he'd already put hundreds of miles between them, and his face was so wooden that it might have been carved from one of the stately oak trees that surrounded them. But it was his tone of voice, so flat and so final, that broke her heart.

"Adieu, Michel."

The wind whipped her hair across her eyes, almost blinding her as she turned and, still wearing his field jacket, ran toward her bicycle. She felt as if she'd barely avoided a tumble from a cliff. And realized she already regretted not taking the plunge.

"March Order!"

Enraged at the sudden awakening, for it was the middle of the night and he'd just barely gotten to sleep, Mike sat bolt upright in his sleeping bag.

"Hubba, hubba!"

Mike recognized his battalion commander's voice. He heard men grumbling, jeeps backfiring and tank engines growling to life. Sounds that told him the peaceful interlude was over and the war was starting again.

Rain pelted the sides of his tent as he rolled out of his sleeping bag and, telling himself that it was time to move on, began getting dressed in the dark.

After Anne-Marie left, he'd gone to see the barmaid. With her flashing eyes and full lips, her swaying breasts and supple hips, Gi-Gi was just the ticket he needed. Or so he'd thought as he'd sat at a corner table, letting her fill his glass with wine and his head with fantasies.

Problem was, the woman he kept picturing had honey-blonde hair instead of black. A slender body, not a blowzy one. The woman who haunted him was the one he couldn't have.

He'd done everything he could to forget Anne-Marie. He'd ordered more wine, trying to drown his frustrations. Bummed a cigarette from another soldier, then crushed it out after one acrid puff. He'd taken that other woman's hand in his, let her lead him up to the loft and down to the disheveled bed where she did her "entertaining." Tasted other men when he kissed her and told himself it didn't matter.

But he was wrong, dammit. It did matter. A hell of a lot more than it should have. Because when Gi-Gi's avid mouth was on him, coaxing his body to climax, his mind wasn't on her. When he closed his eyes and found his release, it wasn't her face he saw behind his lids or her name that rang through his head. And when he left her with a large tip for her time and trouble, he still wasn't satisfied.

He still wanted Anne-Marie.

"Moving out!"

Thunder boomed, as loud as an artillery barrage. As violent as the beating of his heart. Now he was fighting two wars. The one with the Germans and the one within himself.

Anne-Marie's heart was pumping as fast as her legs were pedaling.

It had quit raining at dawn.

She knew because she'd watched the sun come up. While working with the Resistance, she had become accustomed to living on a lot of nerve and a little sleep. The fear of discovery, even more than the idea of death, had burned in her like a low-grade fever day and night. She would go to bed exhausted and get up exhausted. And tell herself, *"C'est la guerre"* when she didn't think she could stand it another moment.

But last night she hadn't slept at all.

She'd done her best to forget Mike, knowing there was no future for them. She'd tried a long hot bath and a little warm brandy. She'd told herself they were of the war and nothing more as she'd climbed the stairs to her bedroom. Then she'd put out the light, plunging the room into darkness. Only to see his face when she closed her eyes.

This morning, wearing his borrowed field jacket over her dress, she had left the house before breakfast.

Her front tire hit a rut in the road, splashing dirty water on her bare legs. She didn't even notice. Her eyes were focused on the field she was fast approaching and her thoughts were centered on the man who had touched her where no other man ever had—her mind and her heart.

Now she wanted him to touch her body. Touch it and teach her how to touch his in return. She wanted him to love her, if only for a little while, as she knew she would love him for the rest of her life.

Unlike yesterday, today was beautiful. The sky was a cloudless blue, the surface of the lake sparkled in the sun and the tree branches swayed in the breeze. Birds sang. And the air, after the storm, smelled fresh and full of—

Anne-Marie stopped her bicycle with a jerk of brakes. Her hands clutched the handlebars so hard that her knuckles went white. A soundless cry tore at her throat.

Mike was gone!

Her heart sank with despair as she stared at the deserted field. All that remained of the tanks and jeeps and self-propelled guns that had been parked there the day before were the herringboned ruts their tires had made in the mud when they'd departed. The grass was matted and yellowed where tents had stood and soldiers had strolled.

Numbly, Anne-Marie pushed her bicycle toward the spot where Mike had pitched his tent. Her eyes were burning dry but, inside, she was weeping. The tears would come later, she knew, when she'd fully absorbed this terrible loss.

Then she saw it—an empty green Coke bottle turned upside down on a stake driven into the ground, with a folded piece of paper inside.

Anne-Marie reached for it with a trembling hand. Mike was gone, yes. But he hadn't forgotten her. For as she discovered when she shook the paper out of the bottle and unfolded it, he'd left his address and asked her to write to him.

Chapter Six

Aachen, Germany

The colonel commanding the engineer combat group was clearly disgusted. And with good reason. "We've taken that hill twice, Lieutenant Scanlon," he grumbled to his newly assigned forward artillery observer, "and we've lost it twice."

"So I've heard, sir." Mike was careful to keep his voice neutral, not wanting to sound like he was criticizing a superior officer's performance.

They both knew that Aachen wasn't an important military objective. Strategically speaking, though, it was a different story. Not only was Aachen the birthplace of Charlemagne, it was a sacred symbol of the Holy Roman Empire—the First Reich. Hitler, who'd frequently prophesied that his own Third Reich would also last a thousand years, had exhorted the city's residents to hold out at all cost. To engage in house-to-house fighting, if necessary, in order to protect their precious heritage. None of which had deterred the Allies, who'd decided that a strike at Aachen could be the fatal blow to the heart of Nazi faith.

So the colonel had a right to be frustrated. The hills and ridges surrounding the city were the keys to reducing it. And in his first experience leading an infantry mission, he'd let those keys slip through his fingers . . . not once, but twice.

He raised his binoculars and peered out the second-story window of the farmhouse-cum-observation post, through the steady October rain and the thick yellow smoke from the Allied dive-bombers. Then he lowered the glasses and looked directly at Mike. Beneath the brim of his steel helmet, with its dangling chin straps bracketing his gaunt face, his eyes were narrowed and his jaw was set in a determined line.

"I want that hill back, Lieutenant."

"Yes, sir." Mike spoke without any hint of nervous apprehension, but his palms were sweaty, his stomach felt hollow and his pulse was keeping time with the heavy concentration of artillery and mortar fire that was pouring down on the dug-in city.

Twenty-four hours with no sleep and nothing to eat could do that to a man . . . as could the knowledge that he'd already outlived the odds against forward observers.

After leaving Ste. Geneviève in the dead of night, his battalion had been reattached to their old armored division for the final battle at Argentan-Falaise. With the Gap closed and those Germans who'd escaped capture on the run, they'd spearheaded east. Tomatoes were just coming into season as they thundered through Corbeil, south of Paris, and the French civilians who'd lined the roads had generously shared the ripe, red produce with their Yankee liberators.

They'd met some opposition when they crossed the muddy Seine River on pontoon bridges, but it was quickly overcome. Leapfrogging across northern France, they'd passed through territory that was painfully familiar in American history. In the space of twenty-four hours, they'd rumbled by Château-Thierry and Belleau wood—places where, in World War I, many of their own fathers had crawled forward foot by bloody foot.

Now history had put them in the driver's seat, and nothing could stop their momentum. Victory was in the air, as sure as the season's turning. The Germans were in full retreat, the Allies in hot pursuit, and "Win the War in 44" was their battle cry.

They were riding high when they entered the Low Countries, with hysterically happy crowds lining the roads and cries of "*Allemande-Kaput*" ringing in their ears.

Going through Charleroi, Belgium, they'd looked more like the Tournament of Roses parade than a fighting unit on its way to battle. Flowers pelted their vehicles, beer flowed like water, and the people dancing in the streets slowed the armored march to a crawl. To top it all off, a group of Belgian Resistance fighters, drunk as skunks and armed to the teeth, commandeered the battalion CO's jeep and led the military police a merry chase up and down every side road in town.

But the joy ride had ended in September. Not with a bang, either, but with a sputter. The Allies had run low on gasoline and ammunition, giving the Germans time to regroup along their own border, and every mother's son on the offensive front had started praying that he'd get "Home Alive in '45."

And twice since the Allies had reached a stalemate at the Siegfried Line, those jagged roadblocks of concrete and steel that the Germans boasted no enemy army could penetrate, Mike had thought he was a goner.

The first time he'd been on reconnaissance, scouting out a new observation post, when an SS combat patrol had come out of nowhere. His radioman had been killed and one of his wiremen severely wounded in the firefight that followed. The second time his tank had been knocked out while breaching the "dragon's teeth." He'd been thrown clear with only the sharp piece of shrapnel that was still in his leg, but the rest of his crew had burned to death in the subsequent explosion.

Now here he was, he thought grimly, sitting on Germany's doormat like one of the milk bottles his father used to deliver, wondering when his own number was finally going to come up.

"Do you have a plan of attack, Lieutenant?" Given his two previous failures to hold the hill, the colonel had no choice but to ask. He did so with both a lack of the hubris that normally accompanied rank and a note of hope in his voice.

"Yes, sir, I do."

His throat sore and scratchy from all the smoke he'd swallowed and his nerves screaming from lack of food and sleep, Mike removed his map from the leather case he'd worn in action since D-Day. He crossed the room, his boots crunching on the rubble of fallen ceiling plaster, and lit the Coleman gas lamp that was sitting on a field table he'd shoved against the wall and away from the window. The lamp hissed and sputtered as he dusted off the tabletop with his sleeve, then spread out the map and motioned his commanding officer over so he could explain the plan.

"There's a little valley on the other side of the hill where the Germans have dug in," he pointed out.

"The perfect defensive position."

Mike nodded in agreement but remained focused on the problem at hand. "And here, overlooking the valley, are three abandoned houses—"

"They're still standing after the shelling?"

"They were when I left at daybreak."

"You went up there?" his CO asked, aghast.

"Just long enough to get a look-see. Anyway, there's a three-story house right here" —Mike put his finger on the spot— "with a half-moon window in the attic—"

"The perfect observation post."

"The best I've seen."

The colonel stroked his beard-stubbled chin. "How will you get into the house?"

"Through the back door."

"It's unguarded?"

"And unlocked," Mike confirmed.

"It'll take you half the night to get up there."

"I'll start as soon as we're finished here, sir."

The table rocked and the floor shook as one of their own artillery shells fell short of its target. A high-explosive shell, judging by the hot white and orange flickers that shadow-danced on the walls. Neither one of the men bent over the map even noticed the new plaster filtering down from the ceiling or the dust flying up around them.

"When do we jump off?" the colonel asked.

"At dawn." Which meant another sleepless night for Mike.

"Catch 'em with their pants down, hey?"

Mike's mouth hooked in a mirthless smile. "In a manner of speaking."

"How many men will you need?"

"Three, besides myself."

Silently, the commander strained his red-rimmed eyes over the map. "And while you're figuring your coordinates," he said at last, "we can finish consolidating our positions."

"By this time tomorrow, sir, you'll be king of the hill."

"Unless the Germans counterattack."

Mike had already thought of that. "I'll smother 'em under another blanket of hot steel."

"And if they figure out where you're shooting from?"

"I'll head for the basement and box us in with artillery."

His CO gaped at him speechlessly, as if he couldn't quite decide whether his FO was a fool or a genius.

"Defensive fire?" he demanded when he found his voice.

"Yes, sir."

"Dangerous as hell."

"But effective." Mike straightened and shrugged his weary shoulders. "What do you think, Colonel?"

"I like it." The frown he'd been sporting eased into a smile. "Like it, hell. I wish I'd thought of it myself."

Mike's answering grin could have been construed as a grimace. "Wait until you've been at this as long as I have."

"No, thanks!"

The two men laughed at his quick, heartfelt rejoinder, then spent the next few minutes reviewing the details of the plan. Mike had left nothing to chance. Besides the necessary element of surprise, it called for dovetailed timing. If it worked the way it was supposed to, the hill was theirs for the taking.

"How's your leg, Lieutenant?" the colonel asked before he left to get his men in position.

"I won't be entering any dance contests for a while, but I can still kick German butt."

"Yes, well . . ." The commander clicked his tongue. "I was sorry to hear about your tank crew."

Mike had thought he was too numb to feel. Too detached to care. But the night his tank crew died, he'd burrowed into his sleeping bag and bawled like a damned baby.

Now he just nodded and said, "They were good men."

"Aren't they all?"

The sharp thunder of outgoing artillery was the only answer the colonel's rhetorical question required.

"By the way," he said then, "our mess sergeant rustled up some hot steak sandwiches if you'd like to eat before you leave."

Mike still made it a rule not to eat before going into battle, but now his long-empty stomach growled noisily at the mention of food. He looked down at his mid-section, then up at his CO, and grinned in embarrassment. "Sounds good to me, sir."

"Well . . ." The colonel paused, clearly awkward when it came to good-byes, then snapped his helmet strap under his chin and said brusquely, "I'll see you at the top of the hill, Lieutenant."

"Yes, sir," Mike replied as he snapped off a crisp salute.

At the door, the colonel stopped and turned back, his grave expression softening with concern. "Godspeed, son."

"Same to you, sir."

Mike could hear the colonel clumping down the wooden stairs, shouting orders all the way, as he folded his map and put it away. The thought of a hot steak sandwich instead of a cold K ration had his mouth watering. And him hurrying to grab one before he started up the hill.

He got sidetracked, though, when he was replacing the straps of his leather map case around his neck and his hand bumped against the small Bible he always carried in his shirt pocket. In addition to the pictures of his brother and sister and his godson, he now had a snapshot of Anne-Marie Gérard. Her cousin Henriette had taken it, she'd explained, and she had enclosed it in one of her weekly letters—most of which had burned along with his men and the Bronze Star he'd yet to send home for safekeeping when his tank was hit.

Her letters had become his lifeline in the midst of all the death and destruction. When he received one, he ripped it open and read it immediately. Then he reread it every chance he got. He rarely retained what she said because the noise and the confusion made it difficult to concentrate. But whenever he heard his name at mail call, it was like music to his ears.

He hadn't had a chance to write back to her, what with his being constantly on the move or in the thick of battle. Besides, he wasn't sure he could find the right words to tell her how often he thought of her—when he had the time to think, that is. If he'd had the time or the words, though, the first thing he would've told her was how much he appreciated her picture.

"*I'm standing in front of my house,*" she'd written in her fine hand on the back. *"Do you recognize?"*

Mike wasn't sure if Anne-Marie was asking whether he recognized the house or her, but he hardly needed a reminder of what she looked like. Hell, she haunted his dreams. When the battalion coiled for the night, he had only to crawl under his tank and close his eyes to conjure up the honey-gold bounty of her hair and the pale oval of her face in the empty blackness.

But whenever he opened the Bible to look at the small black-and-white picture, as he did now, and remembered the way her topaz eyes had glimmered with tears and her rose-kissed lips had trembled with regret when he'd told her goodbye, the guilt that raged in him was so strong that he almost didn't care who won the goddamned war.

Just as long as he lived to apologize to her in person.

Anne-Marie had been running on sheer willpower for two days now, ever since her grandfather died, and she was drained to the point of exhaustion.

The fierce November wind howled around the corners of the house as she closed the front door on the last of the funeral party. She rubbed her arms, wondering if she would ever feel warm again, then reached to the coat-track for her sweater. As she slipped it on, she thought of Mike's field jacket. It was hanging in her armoire, and she frequently took it out at the end of the day and wore it to bed over her nightgown.

She was tempted to run up and put it on right now. To bury her nose in the collar, breathe in the scent of him that still clung to it and pretend that he was close to her. But she knew if she did, she would probably crawl under her comforter, curl up into a ball and cry herself to sleep.

Her knees nearly buckling under the weight of her fatigue, not to mention all the major decisions she still had to make about her future, she crossed the painfully empty living room to tend the fire. The clock on the mantle confirmed she'd made the right decision in settling for the sweater. It was only a few minutes after four—too early for bed and too late for a nap.

Yesterday morning, when her grandfather had failed to come down for breakfast, she'd felt a foreboding so strong that it had sent her racing up the stairs. Trying to control the panic in her voice, she'd called out to him in the ominous silence as she'd moved toward his room. Hearing no answer, she'd opened the door and slipped in.

And discovered his body in bed.

"Mon Dieu!" she'd whispered, too stunned to cry as she'd taken his lifeless hand in hers and held those cold, knobby fingers to her cheek.

Her grandfather had died in his sleep, simply slipped away from her in the middle of the night as she had so often slipped out of his house when she was working with the Resistance movement, and she'd known immediately that there was nothing she could do to revive him.

The next few hours had been a greater test of her love and her resolve than all of her missions against the Germans combined.

Gently, though her hands shook, Anne-Marie had closed her grandfather's sightless eyes and kissed his stubbled cheeks before calling the farm to deliver the terrible news. Then, determined to restore her grandmother's standard, she'd rolled up her sleeves and gone to work preparing his body for burial. By the time her aunt and uncle and cousins arrived, she had already shaved him and trimmed his snowy hair and was busy pressing his best suit.

And today, as the wind swept down from the Arctic and a thin gray veil of sleet fell from the clouds, a nattily groomed Henri Gérard had been laid to rest beside his beloved Yvonne.

The funeral had been almost unendurable. Her aunt had sobbed convulsively throughout the requiem Mass, almost drowning out the village priest's ancient Latin words. Even her surprisingly sober uncle had choked back tears as the procession moved from the church to the cemetery. Her surviving male cousins had stood, somber as three old men, while the coffin was lowered into the earth. And poor Henriette, who had earlier confided that she was pregnant by Guy Compain and praying desperately that he would marry her before she started to show, had wept hysterically when it was her turn to toss a handful of cold, muddy dirt onto the lid.

Only Anne-Marie had remained stoic and dry-eyed. In spite of her grandfather's sometimes-gruff demeanor, she had loved him dearly. And she knew he had loved her —perhaps more than any of the others. As such, she felt it would dishonor his memory to set aside her dignity and surrender to the wrenching grief that tore at her heart.

Mourners had come from the village and the outlying farms to make their *adieux*. They'd brought food and wine, as friends and neighbors do for such occasions. More important, they'd brought stories of the doctor who had delivered their babies, diagnosed their ailments and driven untold miles in weather fair and foul without regard as to whether they could pay his bill. Stories of a well-loved, well-respected man who had always put people before money.

It was those stories, as well as her own fond recollections, which now had Anne-Marie perilously close to tears. They filled her eyes, blurring her vision as she all but stumbled across the room to sit in her grandfather's chair. While the upholstery was worn and the seat lumpy, its welcoming arms enveloped her like a warm hug.

Not bothering to switch on the lamp, she sat in the sepia-toned light, vignettes of those carefree August holidays that her parents and her brother and she had always spent in Ste. Genviève flashing through her mind.

Some mornings the entire family would climb into her grandfather's coupe and drive to the coast. After a day spent exploring the historic abbey at Mont St. Michel or building sand castles on the beaches of St. Malo, they would arrive home tired but happy. Over that evening's apéritifs, they admired the souvenirs they'd bought in the shops leading up to the abbey or the seashells they'd found on the beach before sitting down together to one of her grandmother's delicious dinners of lamb or freshly caught fish.

Even if there'd been no excursion planned, they'd had fun. Her brother often bicycled out to the farm, where he would pester their rural cousins by jumping off the haystacks they'd baled or accidentally dropping the eggs their hens had just laid. If it was sunny, Miriam Blum and she would go swimming in the lake or sip *citron pressé* in the shade of a tree; if it was raining, they would shut themselves in Miriam's room and confide their secret dreams to each other. And at least once during their two-week stay, the whole lot of them would pitch tents in the woods and pass the long, dark night scaring each other silly with ghost stories.

But it was those simple evenings spent *en famille*, with the scents and the sounds of summer drifting in through the open windows and doors, which would forever live in her heart.

A log hissed in the fire, shooting out a tongue of blue flame, as Anne-Marie rolled her head sideways and looked across the room. Even now, she could see her mother and grandmother sitting at the lace-covered dining table, shoulders hunched and nimble fingers flying as they patched the knees of her brother's pants or lengthened the hems of her school dresses. While they sewed, they discussed everything from what the latest fashion designs were to when French women would finally be granted the right to vote.

Forcing herself to look away, she focused on the chair opposite the one she occupied. If she listened carefully, she could hear one of Josephine Baker's jazzy solos on the gramophone, providing the background music for a spirited political or philosophical debate between her father and grandfather.

And there, on the threadbare carpet, her brother refighting Trafalgar with his tin soldiers while she sprawled on her stomach, chin in hand, reading one of her beloved romances.

They were gone now, all of them, and she was alone.

Alone.

The devastating realization that she'd lost almost everyone she'd ever loved struck her like an assault. Four years of holding back, of bottling up her tears and her fears, built like floodwaters against a damn. Sorrow clawed inside her, demanding release, as she covered her face with her hands and began to cry.

She cried for her parents—for a mother who had always smelled of jasmine and a father whose mustache had always made his kisses tickle. She cried for her sunny-faced brother, her brave cousin Maurice and her sweet friend Miriam Blum. She cried for her grandparents—for a grandmother who'd endured such horrible agony and a grandfather who'd remained true to her and to himself to the bitter end. She cried for her country, now lying in ruins, and for her people, so many of whom had paid the ultimate price to be free.

And when that storm subsided, when her eyes were puffy, her nose stuffy and her entire body aching with sadness for all she had lost, Anne-Marie wept for Mike.

Rocking back and forth to give herself some small comfort, she wept for the ugly way they had parted. For her refusal to make love with him. And for the yearning regret which stalked her yet.

Then she wept for the dangers he faced. As the uncontrollable tears seeped through her fingers, the news from the radio broadcasts that she listened to nightly replayed in her mind. The battle for France had been won but the fighting along the German front was fierce and bloody, and the Allied losses were staggering.

She didn't know where Mike was, of course. Didn't even know if he was dead or alive. And while she prayed every day that he was warm and safe and had enough to eat, it was the not knowing that sparked her nightmares. She was constantly fighting off the terrible specter of his fiery death, the flames racing over her own flesh and boiling her own blood, the thick, black smoke choking off her own breath, so that she would come awake in the dark, flailing against the demons that haunted her and crying out his name.

How long she wept she couldn't say. Gradually, though, her sobs quieted and the hot tears slowed. And her pain, finally purged, eased.

Anne-Marie dropped her hands and raised her head, astonished to find that what little natural light there had been earlier was gone, swept away by the onset of evening, and that the room had grown dim. She fumbled in her sweater pocket for a handkerchief with which to dry her eyes. Then she sagged back in the chair and faced the very bleak but very real prospect of a future without Mike.

He hadn't told her he loved her. Nor had he made any rash promises to come back for her. He'd simply asked her to write to him. Which she had, faithfully. Except for the photograph he'd sent to her almost a month ago, however, she'd received no replies to her letters.

She turned her gaze to his photo, which she had framed for display on the chairside table, and studied it in the flickering firelight. It had come as a complete surprise because she'd given up hope of ever hearing from him. But she'd gotten an even bigger surprise when, in the privacy of her room, she'd slit open the thin blue envelope and found that it contained only a black-and-white print.

At first she'd been disappointed that he hadn't taken the time to write her a letter telling her where he was and how he was doing. Then she'd turned it over and read what he had written on the back. And had burst out laughing.

"*I'm standing in front of my jeep,*" he'd scrawled in his large, firm hand. "*Do you recognize?*"

Now, as she recalled what she'd penned on the back of the picture she'd sent to him, a small, wobbly smile curved Anne-Marie's lips. She loved Mike's quick wit. His rich, ready laughter. Loved them almost as much as she loved the man himself.

And yes, she recognized. His dark hair, cropped *en brosse*, and his handsome face. The breadth of his shoulders and the bronze of his flesh. Oh, she remembered everything about him so clearly! That intriguing dimple in his cheek and the timbre of his voice, as tantalizing as the caress of his hand.

Her smile faded into a frown, though, when she touched his glossy likeness through the glass. Feet braced apart and hands fisted on hips, he appeared to be standing atop a hill. But despite the triumphant pose, there were deep grooves of exhaustion on either side of his mouth. Grooves that told her that he was as sick and tired of this war as she was.

He'd lost weight, too. She could see it in the slightly baggy fit of his new field jacket. The lean and hungry planes of his features. More worrisome yet were his eyes. They stared out at her like spent bullet shells, with no life behind them, as if a part of him had died during his grueling climb to the top.

Anne-Marie felt her heart swell painfully at the thought. She'd heard nothing from him since he'd sent the photograph. *Rien.* Still, she would write to him this evening, as she had every week for the last three months, and tell him the sad news about her grandfather. Then she would give some serious thought to where she went from here.

But first, she decided, as she raised the picture to her lips and tenderly kissed his image, she would rest for a few minutes.

She fell asleep in the chair, holding his picture.

Chapter Seven

THE EIFEL-ARDENNES

*T*he snow was ass-deep to a tall Indian, the December wind had a razor's edge, and the fog that had rolled in with the night was so thick that a man could barely see his hand in front of his freakin' face.

Sergeant Charlie Miller still couldn't figure out how he'd gone from running a combined mess hall at Camp Fanning, Texas, to standing guard on the Ghost Front in just two months' time. One day he'd been serving shit-on-a-shingle to corporals and steaks to captains, nipping a little vanilla when nobody was watching to tide him over till payday, and writing dutifully to his pregnant wife, who was staying with her parents back in Kansas City for the duration. The next, he'd been reassigned to an infantry division, retrained in combat technique, and ordered to ship out immediately.

He'd put off calling Daisy until the evening before he'd left.

It wasn't a call he'd looked forward to making. At five months along, she was over the morning sickness that had been plaguing her but was prone to some pretty wild mood swings. Her doctor had attributed it to hormone changes and said it was perfectly natural for a woman in her condition. But seeing as how she'd gotten pregnant on their wedding night, when his GI condom broke, Charlie had a sneaking suspicion that she was just using that as an excuse to get back at him.

Then there was the little matter of money. Marriage had proven to be a more expensive proposition than he'd anticipated. No sooner had he finished paying off Daisy's wedding ring than he'd had to start in on her doctor bills. And then there was her allotment, which was automatically deducted from his check every month. So add it all up, and he was walking around flat broke most of the time.

"But you're a cook, not a killer!" she'd cried when he'd called her—collect—to give her the bad news.

Charlie knew himself well enough to know he was no hero. He'd never fired a shot in anger, and he had no idea how he would react if someone shot at him. To hear Daisy tell it, though, he was just some weak sister who'd fall apart at the first sign of trouble.

"For your information, I hit the target three times with my carbine today." On the defensive, he didn't bother to explain that that was out of a clip of fifteen rounds. He felt certain, however, that her old man—who'd never liked him—would be more than happy to supply his only daughter with that minor detail.

"And you're going to be a father next February!" Daisy's voice rose, cracking on a shrill note before falling to a pleading whisper. "Can't you just ask them to keep you stateside until the baby's born?"

"In case you've forgotten," he reminded her testily, "we're at war."

"How can I forget?" She sounded more in control of herself, but also a little condescending. "It's all I read in the newspapers. All I hear on the radio."

"Then quit reading and listening."

"What else is there for me to do?"

He fought a sudden urge to slam down the receiver in her selfish ear. "Try rolling bandages for the Red Cross. Or volunteering to write letters for wounded vets."

She must have realized she'd upset him because she adopted a placating tone. "What I'm saying is, I don't think it's good for a pregnant woman to be exposed to all that bad news."

Charlie tried to picture Daisy sitting in her parents' cozy pink-and-white kitchen. But all he could see was her mother, always looking down her nose at him as if the son of a trashman wasn't good enough for her daughter. The bitterness he felt surprised him, though it shouldn't have. He'd already learned that his wife wasn't above belittling those she considered beneath her, either.

"I also think it's wrong to put an expectant father in harm's way," she added belatedly.

"The Red Cross will notify me when the baby's born," he reassured her.

"I know, but it's not the same as your being here."

"Even if I was stateside, the Army wouldn't let me come home."

She sighed fretfully. "Well, what I don't understand is why they won't give you a furlough before you leave."

"Because they need replacements, and they need 'em now."

"Replacements?"

All sorts of dismal thoughts chased each other across Charlie's mind as he tried to come up with a gentle way to phrase it. He finally gave up and just said it flat out. "For the men who've already been wounded or killed."

"Don't say things like that, Charlie."

"I'm sorry, Daisy, but it's the truth."

"Oh, God." Her voice trembled, as if she were on the verge of tears. "I can't stand the thought of getting one of those Western Union telegrams like Kitty Brown did."

Charlie couldn't even think about John Brown, much less talk about him, without getting all choked up. He felt that familiar sting in the back of his throat as the face of his lifelong friend swam before his eyes. *Jesus!* He still couldn't believe it. John Brown . . . dead.

He swallowed hard, trying to drown a sorrow that refused to die, then changed the subject. "Did you see the doctor today?"

"Yes."

"What did he say?"

She snorted. "According to him, I'm healthy as a horse."

Sensing an unspoken "but," he waited for her to continue.

And continue she did. In addition to the same old complaints about her expanding waistline and falling arches, Daisy had a new one. No matter that her obstetrician kept saying that everything was fine, *she* claimed that she was carrying too high. That the baby's head was growing right in the middle of her ribcage and giving her heartburn so bad she was forced to sleep sitting up in a chair every night.

Charlie had listened to her, biting his tongue until he could get a word in edgewise. Then, before she could say anything else, he'd told her he loved her, promised to write and hung up the phone.

"My Buddy" was playing on someone's radio when he got back to the barracks, reviving memories of all the good times that John and Mike Scanlon and he used to have. His assistant cook, seeing how low he was, had offered to buy him a drink. They'd closed down the noncoms' club that night, and he'd had a bad case of the whiskey jitters the next morning when he'd boarded—

Now, a sound like a twig snapping jarred him out of the past, reminding him of the Germans' well-entrenched presence not more than eight hundred yards away.

Charlie spun in the direction the sound had come from and aimed his M-1 rifle toward the snow-covered trees that marked the perimeter of his company's defensive position. Visibility was poor enough because of the pitch-blackness and the fog, but the thin layer of ice that glazed his glasses made it even harder for him to see. He wiped the lenses with the heel of one gloved hand, which did more to smear them than to clear them, and started to challenge with the standard "Halt!"

Then he barely made out a familiar red glow some twenty yards away.

His shoulders wilted and his breath rushed out on a cloud of relief at the realization that the sound he'd heard was just one of the other GIs standing guard down the line flicking his Zippo to light his cigarette.

The cold cut at Charlie's face like a rusty saw-blade as he relaxed his grip on the rifle and reshouldered it. God, what he wouldn't give for a drink right now! Something to warm his insides and take the edge off his nerves. Something to help him forget that this was the miserable end to a long, miserable journey that had begun in late October, when his division had sailed from the States for England.

Twelve days crossing the North Atlantic had caused his stomach to revolt. Not that the sea had been unusually rough, but there'd been something about the ordinary pitch and toss of the swells that had left him clinging desperately to the rail. Every time the ship heaved, it seemed, so had he. Adding insult to injury, the briny wind had spit it all back in his face.

England, with its cloudy skies and constant drizzle, was an equally wretched experience. After another three weeks of combat training, with no time off to see the sights of London, his division embarked for France. The weather in the English Channel was so bad that they couldn't land, so he'd spent four more sea-sick days aboard the Landing Craft, Infantry, wondering if this was how Mike had felt before the invasion and wishing God would just go ahead and strike him dead.

When they finally landed, his division was broken up and the separate companies sat around in the muddy staging camp for twenty-four hours, waiting for the next snafu. It came in the form of open trucks—normally used for transporting supplies, not men. Which meant another two days spent in soaked, numbed misery as the convoy crawled across the bombarded countryside of northern France and up and down the roller-coaster terrain of Belgium.

The trucks carrying Charlie's company finally halted at the foot of an ice-slicked hill, giving the green troops that clambered out their first glimpse of their "new home."

Home sweet home, it wasn't. Their sector of the front was an isolated ridge shrouded by low-hanging clouds and covered with snow-laden pine trees. A shell-pocked farmhouse, its front door hanging ajar on its hinges and its windows shattered, had apparently been abandoned by its owners. No chickens clucked in the side yard, no cows mooed in the surrounding fields. Even the birds were silent in the trees.

Charlie had been inundated with war news for three years, ever since the Japanese bombed Pearl Harbor. And he'd read the stories in both *Stars and Stripes* and *Yank* about the American tankers who'd charged across the Siegfried Line in mid-September, only to be driven back into Belgium a week later by a remobilized German army. But nothing he'd heard or seen could have prepared him for the carcass of a charred Sherman tank on the side of the road or those makeshift crosses sticking out of the snow, marking the graves of its crew.

Or for the big signboard with the large block letters that greeted him with the warning, YOU ARE ENTERING GERMANY. BE ON YOUR GUARD.

He'd gotten an even bigger shock when, at the end of a two-mile hike to their forward combat positions, he'd seen the condition of the men they were replacing. Their faces were unshaven and black with smoke from their cooking fires and their uniforms were stiff with mud from their foxholes. Those who hadn't been supplied with winter overshoes had wrapped their feet in rags and newspapers to ward off frostbite.

The accommodations were rougher yet—freezing cold trenches in the forest floor, a pit crosshatched with logs for a latrine, and a timber-roofed dugout that served as the command post.

What had spooked him the worst, though, had been the transfer reports indicating that they were little more than a snowball's throw from the Germans, who'd established their positions on the very next ridge.

"Sergeant Miller?" A nasally voice from behind punctured the graveyard silence now, snapping Charlie out of his morbid memories.

He whirled, almost tripping over his own feet, and saw a fog-blurred figure plowing toward him through the snow. At the same time, it occurred to him that he'd stupidly forgotten the night's password. A bubble of panic rose in his throat as he leveled the rifle and demanded hoarsely, "Who goes there?"

"Private George Aylmer." The soldier who'd come to relieve him stopped and saluted crisply. "Reporting for guard duty, sir."

"Jeez," Charlie said peevishly, shivering partly because of the cold and partly in delayed reaction. "Scare the hell out of me, why don't you"

The young GI's grin flashed whitely in the night shadows. "Gettin' nervous in the service, Sarge?"

"Try freezing and starving," he fired back.

"Well, there's hot coffee back at the CP. And rumor has it that the kitchen trucks will be here in time for breakfast."

"Christ, I hope so." All Charlie had had to eat in the last forty-eight hours were a couple of D bars—" Hitler's Secret Weapon," as someone on the way to the latrine had called the sickly chocolate concentrate.

"And Captain Quinn says we're going to have turkey and dumplings for Christmas dinner."

"I'll believe it when I taste it." Charlie made a scoffing sound, but at the mention of the upcoming holiday he felt a wave of homesickness so powerful that it brought tears to his eyes. Regret followed in its wake as he remembered how curt he'd been with Daisy the night before he sailed. He promised himself he would write to her later today. Tell her how much he missed her and how sorry he was that they were spending their first—

"My mama always cooks a big, fat goose on Christmas Day," the private continued in a faraway voice. "And sausage stuffing that's brown and crispy on top and all—"

"No offense, kid," Charlie interrupted, salivating at the memory of the roast chicken and cornbread dressing that were his own mother's specialties. "But I've been standing here for so long that my feet feel like blocks of ice."

The private blinked as if he'd been slapped and slung his rifle over his shoulder. "Any changes to report, Sergeant?"

Charlie shook his head, then took off at as fast a clip as his winter boots and wool overcoat would allow. Numb from exposure and frozen to the marrow, he concentrated on that hot coffee the private had mentioned. It would probably be as thick as sludge and taste like sh—

It hit him about halfway across the compound that he was wrong. That there *had* been a change. A minor change, true, but one he'd failed to report.

The Germans hadn't sung "Lilli Marlene" even once on his watch!

Charlie stopped, his breath coming so hard it hurt his chest as he recalled the comments that the guide from the company they'd replaced had made when he'd met them at the foot of the hill almost three days ago.

"You guys sure struck it lucky," he'd said.

"How so?" one of the new men had asked.

"Well, for one thing, the only casualties we've had lately have been head colds and trench foot."

"And for another?"

The guide had rolled his eyes. "Except for the Germans singing 'Lilli Marlene' at the top of their lungs when they go to the latrine, it's been so quiet up here that we've taken to calling it the 'Ghost Front'."

"Here's hopin' they don't get diarrhea in the middle of the night!" one of the other replacements had exclaimed to a round of nervous laughter.

Now, Charlie didn't know which way to turn. Should he retrace his steps and warn the private to stay on his toes? Just in case the Germans' silence meant something besides a major case of constipation. Or should he keep going? Let the kid figure it out on his own.

To hell with it, he finally decided, hotfooting it toward the warmth and temporary shelter of the command post. He was off duty, dammit. And besides, he reasoned as he entered the reinforced dugout, the private would have to be stone-deaf not to notice that they'd quit singing that damned beer-hall ditty.

But when he finished his coffee and stepped out into the silent night to head for his foxhole, Charlie could only hope that this wasn't the quiet before the storm.

Rolling thunder jolted him out of a restless sleep.

Charlie jackknifed into a sitting position, shearing off his helmet when he bumped his head against the heavy pine boughs he'd used to cover his foxhole.

Still wearing his coat and his gloves, with his wool blanket wrapped around him and his M-1 cradled like a baby in his arms, he'd been dreaming about the Christmas that John and Mike and he had all gotten BB guns. And the trouble they'd been in when Mary Frances Walker's father had caught them using their outhouse down in the hollow for target practice. He'd taken his punishment as manfully as the other two, but to his ever-lasting embarrassment, he was the only one who'd missed the mark.

In a nightmare of bewilderment now, Charlie checked the luminous hands of his watch, saw that it was only 5:30 A.M. and wondered if all that noise meant the kitchen trucks were finally here.

"The Germans have broken through!" someone shouted.

"Counterattack!"

Enemy artillery started falling like rain then, one explosive drop after another descending in a savage barrage upon the slumbering compound.

His skull rattling from the concussion of the salvos and his hands shaking with fear, Charlie groped around in the darkness for his helmet. He finally found it, lying behind him, then somehow managed to knock his glasses askew when he plunked it back on his head.

"Get up!" someone hollered.

"Everybody up!"

Charlie was trying to get up, dammit, but he was all tangled up in his blanket. He suddenly realized that he was sitting on the edge of it and, in a fit of frustration, yanked it out from under him. Free at last, he pulled on the boots he'd taken off to let dry, but didn't bother tying the laces. Then he grabbed his rifle with his right hand and shoved the sheltering tree branches away with his left.

Just as he stood to leap out of his foxhole, a lightning-bright flash of shellfire flowered in front of him and threw him backwards.

He lay in the trench, dazed and confused and winded, until there was a slight break in the barrage. Then he raised his head ever so cautiously to peer out over the top. A red drapery of blood ran down over his glasses, blocking out his sight, and he realized he'd been hit.

Oh Jesus, oh God, oh no, was he *blind*?!?

His heart hammering frantically in his ears, Charlie ripped off his glasses, breaking an earpiece in the process. As he bent his head to wipe the lenses on the front of his coat, more blood dribbled onto the bridge of his nose. Tentatively, he touched his forehead and felt a sting over his eyebrow but below his helmet brim. A sting that told him that a stray fragment had probably nicked him.

But that was the least of his worries.

Praying like he'd never prayed before, he stuffed the broken earpiece in his coat pocket and carefully slid his glasses back on . . . and went limp with relief when he found he could see again.

What he saw was the sky falling in.

Searchlights played off the low-hanging clouds, creating a kind of artificial moonlight that reflected onto the forest floor and bathed the Germans' targets with an eerie glow.

Those targets were the American soldiers, still befuddled from sleep, now pouring out of the trenches and the command post to man the company's emplaced machine guns and mortars.

A chill raced up Charlie's spine when a tree burst scythed the top off a pine, showering fragments of red-hot metal downward and dropping three GIs in their tracks.

"Medic!" a fourth screamed in agony.

A corpsman wearing the big Red Cross on a white background that was supposed to give him immunity rushed out to pull the wounded soldier to safety, only to disappear himself amidst the flame and smoke and fire of an exploding shell.

"You dirty bastards!" Another dough stood and shook a furious fist in the direction that the enemy artillery was coming from.

As if to answer his epithet, a piece of shrapnel severed the arm attached to that fist as neatly as if it had been a surgeon's scalpel.

His face hollow with shock and surprise, the maimed man fell to the ground.

Sickened by the sight of that shoulder bone gleaming whitely through the bloody gore, Charlie retched, the remains of the coffee he'd had a couple of hours ago boiling up into the back of his throat.

"Move up and man those guns!" Captain Quinn roared.

Charlie forced himself to swallow the bitter, burning bile, then staggered to his feet to follow the company commander's order.

"Hit the dirt!" someone else bellowed over the stomach-churning howl of incoming "screaming meemies."

Diving back down into his frozen hole, Charlie hugged the ground, nearly paralyzed with terror under the lethal barrage. He could feel the earth heaving from the force of the mortar bursts and hear stricken men crying out for a medic who was no longer there. The stench of fresh blood filled his nostrils. His eyes burned from the cordite, and the smoke was so thick he could hardly breathe.

"Help!" a vaguely familiar voice shrieked in the chaos of explosions.

Charlie looked up, past a grisly array of corpses, rifle clips and combat boots, and saw the private who'd relieved him as sentry come charging out of the trees and into a hail of splinters and metal that sent him sprawling, face down, into the snow.

"Fuck this shit!" A terror-stricken GI burst from his ditch and ran a broken field pattern toward the captain's jeep, which was parked in front of the CP. "I'm bugging out!"

"Hey, wait for me!"

Charlie watched, horrified, as a mortar scored a direct hit on the jeep's hood and the two men who'd just jumped into it went flying through the air when its engine exploded.

The German shelling continued unabated for what seemed like hours, knocking out most of the company's guns and keeping the American defenders who might have used them to repel the attack bogged down in their trenches.

And then, almost as abruptly as it had started, the terrible bombardment stopped.

That wasn't the end of the horror, though, as Charlie discovered when he gathered enough courage to lever up and look out into the gloomy half-light of dawn.

Hundreds of German grenadiers stepped out from behind the fog-bound pine trees that encircled the American camp. Draped in white sheets, they were beautifully camouflaged by the snow. They had even covered their machine pistols with white cloths.

We're surrounded, Charlie thought, his heart sinking as his gaze swept over the ghostly figures that had obviously stolen into their positions during the blitz.

"Surrender!" the German commander demanded in English.

But his American counterpart had not yet begun to fight. Captain Quinn scanned the anxious faces of his men, now down to less than half their original strength of two hundred, then cupped his hands around his mouth like a megaphone and yelled back, "Go to hell!"

The Germans advanced on the Americans from all sides then, shooting on the run and shouting something that sounded like, *"Sturm!"*

Standing behind the machine gun he'd stepped up to, Quinn waited until the grenadiers were about twenty yards away before ordering, *"Fire!"*

Charlie adjusted his broken glasses and sighted his rifle, planning to do exactly that. This was his first chance to prove himself, and he wanted to do it right. But when he squeezed the trigger, nothing happened.

"My gun's frozen!" the man in the foxhole next to his cried.

"Work the bolt!" Quinn directed.

"No time!"

Charlie's jaw dropped in utter disbelief when the dough urinated into the chamber of his M-1, trying to provide enough heat to thaw it out.

"That one's for the medic!" he declared not two minutes later, after he'd mowed down a German with his now-working rifle.

Realizing that his gun was probably frozen too, Charlie reached inside his coat for his fly . . . and found that he'd already pissed in his pants.

"The hell with it!" A disgusted GI threw down his disabled weapon and sat back to await his fate.

That fate, Charlie was stunned to see, was a German bullet between the eyes.

"Stay down!" a scared rifleman warned as slugs flew over the trenches from north and south, east and west.

"Stand up to the sonsuvbitches!" Quinn countermanded above a steady volley of machine-gun fire.

Desperate for a weapon to use, Charlie threw his ice-bound M-1 aside and started to climb out of his foxhole to retrieve one of the rifles littering the snow. But a bullet whizzed past his head like some berserk bee and he had to slide back down.

"Fight back, goddamn you!" an enraged Quinn ordered when he saw how easily his men were being overrun.

But dazed by the devastating barrage and demoralized by both that withering crossfire and their own inability to return it, many of the Americans were breaking down their rifles and raising their hands.

The German commander called a halt to the attack and, as the firing died away, repeated firmly, "Surrender!"

Bleeding profusely from a gaping hole in his thigh, Captain Quinn reeled at the sharp directive but somehow managed to remain on his feet.

His ruddy face seemed to crumple in on itself with grief as he looked at the wounded and the dead piled up around him. With a visible effort, he pulled himself together and turned to the men who'd survived the onslaught but had failed to follow his orders. He glared at each of them in turn, telling them without words that they had been weighed in the balance and found wanting.

Then Quinn drew his service revolver out of his shoulder holster and brandished it in their wincing faces. "Stand and fight, you yellow-bellied—"

A crescendo of cracks ruptured the air. Bullets hit him from all directions. His head snapped back and his body thrust forward from the impact, and he was dead before he reached the ground.

Several Germans stepped forward in the ensuing silence. One kicked Quinn's pistol away. Another picked it up for a souvenir. Yet a third expertly looted the deceased's pockets, taking his cigarettes and his money, while a fourth slid his watch off his wrist.

"At least he kept his honor," one of the besieged GIs muttered under his breath.

"Quiet!" the German commander barked.

"Blow it out your ass, you motherfu—"

A single deafening explosion cut off the GI in mid-curse. He slumped back in his hole, his head falling forward as if he were peacefully taking a nap. Only the small scarlet circle staining the front of his graycoat indicated that he'd died violently.

No one moved for several shocked seconds. Finally, the remaining GIs let go of their weapons and got to their feet. In a final token of defeat, they removed their helmets before they raised their hands in surrender.

Figuring that this was the end, that he was going to die without ever having fired a shot in his own defense, Charlie said a silent goodbye to both his wife and his unborn child and followed suit.

The victorious Germans swarmed in, machine pistols at the ready, and started rounding up the vanquished Americans.

Charlie was still standing in his foxhole when he was shoved from behind. A sudden, murderous rage shivered through him, supplanting the stark terror that had rendered him totally impotent during the shelling and the subsequent firefight. He swung around, hands fisted, and found himself facing the barrel of a burp gun.

He looked up, into Teutonic blue eyes that blazed like acetylene torches in the bleak morning light. At the same time that his pride goaded him to fight, every muscle in his body tensed for flight. But there was nowhere to run, he realized as his gaze widened to encompass the furious orange fire staining the horizon behind the trees. And even if by some miracle he did manage to escape into the woods, something told him there was no safe place to hide for miles around.

Overwhelmed by a rush of shame so profound that it damn near drove him to his knees, Charlie dropped his eyes, relaxed his fists and surrendered without a fight.

The cold steel barrel of that burp gun burned into his temple as his German captor said in guttural English, "For you, the War is over!"

Chapter Eight

STE. GENVIÈVE, FRANCE

Except for the late February chill having driven the patrons of the sidewalk café inside, the village looked pretty much the same as he remembered it.

Mike stood in the square, where the driver of the Army truck had left him, feeling as if he'd stepped into another world. A peaceful world, away from the blood and the mud and the misery of war. He looked around him, at the store windows with their meager display of goods for sale, and couldn't help but smile when two children ran out of the bakery, laughing. It had been ages since he'd heard the laughter of children. And something told him that it would be a long time before he heard it again.

"*Bonjour, m'sieur,*" said a woman carrying a long loaf of bread under her arm as she followed the children out of the shop.

He nodded in a friendly manner but his smile disappeared as soon as she ducked into the butcher's. There was no use getting accustomed to the sights and the sounds of normal life. No sense in relaxing his guard too much. Because in four hours there would be another truck—a truck full of replacements rolling east, toward Germany. And by this time tomorrow, he would be back at the front, directing fire on the enemy and sweating bullets himself.

But today—or for these next few hours, anyway—he was a man on an entirely different kind of mission.

Mike shouldered the strap of his musette bag, then picked up his bedroll and struck out in the direction of Anne-Marie's house. It felt good to stretch his legs after the long, bumpy truck ride. To breathe in fresh, clean air instead of the foul odors of death and decay. Best of all, though, was being able to walk down a street without having to worry about what lay around the next corner.

He turned his face to the noon sun, its pale rays doing as much to bolster his spirits as those two weeks in a hospital bed had done to heal his body.

Just that morning he'd been released from the 168th General Hospital back at Omaha Beach. The beach was a place he'd sincerely hoped to never visit again, but he'd had no choice in the matter. After being wounded twice in action and surviving the German breakthrough in the Battle of the Bulge, he'd damned near died from a botched tonsillectomy.

He'd been plagued by colds and a low-grade fever since Christmas, so he hadn't been overly concerned when he went to the battalion aid station for yet another sore throat. Expecting the standard swabbing with gentian violet, he got a surprise instead. The surgeon said that his tonsils were badly infected but that he didn't have the time or the proper equipment to remove them, so had sent him by jeep to a field hospital some fifty miles away.

The scene in that unheated field hospital, with row after row of stretchers full of wounded men and medics walking up and down between them weeding out the most urgent surgery cases, had reminded Mike of one from *Gone with the Wind.* He took a seat in the back of the gymnasium-sized room to wait his turn. Five, maybe six hours later, a nurse came by and gave him a whiff of something she euphemistically called an "anesthetic." The next thing he knew a tall, tired-looking surgeon stopped in front of him and told him to "Open wide."

He'd done as he was ordered, and the doctor had reached down his throat with an instrument that looked like a pair of ordinary mechanic's pliers and yanked out a couple of pieces of bloody tissue.

The next morning, hemorrhaging from his nose and throat and burning up with fever, Mike had been flown by liaison plane to the hospital on the beach. He'd lain there for almost a week, drifting in and out of consciousness and dreaming about Anne-Marie. When he finally awoke, the recollection of her pretty face and pixie smile was still in his head. That was when he decided to stop and see her on the way back to his battalion.

Now he was standing on her doorstep, showered and shaved and dressed to kill . . . or be killed.

The orderly had stripped him of his old tank suit when he was admitted to the hospital, and a new one had been issued to him upon his release. Supply had even replaced the cumbersome combination of combat boots and buckled overshoes he'd been wearing with snowpak boots, which had tall leather tops sewn to a rubber shoe. While they weren't insulated, they were light and warm over the socks his sister had knitted for him.

He'd left his helmet at the aid station, so he was wearing a campaign cap with the silver bar of his first lieutenant's rank pinned at the front. A wool Eisenhower jacket for extra warmth was folded at the bottom of his musette bag. Figuring the Gérards could use them to barter for food or medical supplies, he was also packing two cartons of Lucky Strikes that he'd picked up at the hospital PX.

Mike had mentally rehearsed what he was going to say during the long ride from the beach. First, he wanted to pay his respects to Dr. Gérard. Then he wanted to talk to Anne-Marie alone for a few minutes and apologize for his crude manhandling of her six months earlier. Despite the erotic nature of some of his dreams, he'd kept his needs under lock and key since leaving Ste. Genviève. Yet he harbored no illusions that he would come away today with anything more than a clear conscience.

His drills were for naught; no one answered his knock.

Puzzled, he checked the name on the mailbox and saw that it still read *Gérard*. Then he double-checked the address, number 23, even though he'd easily recognized the white stucco house with the neat blue trim from his previous visit. He leaned first to one side, then the other, trying to look through the windows that faced the street. But the shades had been pulled and he couldn't see inside.

Finally he tried the door. It was unlocked and swung open to his push. He stepped out of the dank cold of the street and into the dreary warmth of the vestibule.

The doctor's waiting room, to his right, had been emptied of furniture. As had the combination living and dining room to his left. The smell of woodsmoke lingered in the air, but the dark rectangle on the wood floor where the rug had once laid told him that someone had rolled it up and carted it off.

But who? And why?

Things had been a blur since the Bulge, and his mail had been delivered sporadically at best. Right before he got sick, though, he'd had a letter from his mother containing the bad news about Charlie Miller being reported as missing in action and presumed dead. And now that he stopped to think about it, Mike remembered another letter—one from Anne-Marie in late November or early December telling him that her grandfather had died and that she was moving to Paris to attend the university there.

She was probably long gone, he realized, but he called out her name anyway. "Anne-Marie?"

There was no answer, save the echo of his voice.

He tried again—louder this time. "Anne-Marie!"

And still, the silence drummed in his ears.

He considered dropping a note in her mailbox for the postman to forward to her in Paris. Or asking one of her old neighbors if they knew her new address. Wondering if he had anything to write on, he turned toward the front door.

Then he turned back, something beyond his ken prodding him to set his musette bag and bedroll on the floor and take a quick look around.

Dr. Gérard's office door was closed.

Mike resisted the urge to kick it open, a method he'd perfected during the hellish months of house-to-house fighting, and knocked once, politely. Then twice, sharply. Getting no response, he reached for the knob and shouldered the door open.

Both it and the small bathroom next to it were vacant.

He left those doors standing ajar and crossed to the living area. The kitchen was at the back of the house, as he recalled. But the cupboards that had once been crammed with dishes and cooking utensils were now bare and the stove was cold to his touch.

A scuffling sound overhead set his skin to prickling.

Mike pulled his pistol from his shoulder holster and, using the door that led upstairs as a shield in case someone decided to shoot first and ask questions later, eased it open.

Anne-Marie was in her bedroom, where she had just finished buttoning up her black wool dress and was starting to fix her hair, when she realized that someone had opened the door downstairs.

She wasn't expecting company, though she'd certainly had more than her share of it lately. A steady stream of friends and neighbors had stopped by to bid her farewell. And her family had come three days in a row to remove the furniture and pictures and rugs.

Nor had she heard anyone enter the house. But that was no surprise. She'd been walking around in a daze all morning, her head reeling and her stomach clutching as she'd wandered from room to empty room, taking a last look around to make sure she hadn't forgotten anything before she caught the evening train to Paris.

She'd sold the house to a young doctor who was moving in with his family and his own equipment tomorrow. After dividing the proceeds from the sale with her aunt and handing the keys to her grandfather's coupe to her uncle, she had given all the furnishings to Henriette and Guy as a belated wedding present and donated the medical supplies to the village hospital. Besides her clothing, all she was taking with her were her grandmother's candelabra and Mike's picture. Those she had carefully wrapped in his field jacket so they wouldn't get broken when her trunk was heaved into the train's baggage car.

Now, thinking it might be someone else who'd stopped in to say goodbye, she crossed the hall to the top of the stairs and called down to ask who it was. *"Qui est-ce?"*

The man who stepped out from behind the door and looked up at her in the dim light of the stairwell was the answer to all of her prayers.

She stood there dumbly for a moment, drinking in the sight of him. Emotions raced through her body so powerfully, she felt as if she glowed with their electric force. She sensed an equally puissant tension about him as he holstered the pistol, doffed his cap and met her disbelieving eyes with his dark ones.

"Mike!"

"Hello, Anne-Marie."

Almost breathless with joy, she started down the stairs. "You came back!"

"Only for a few hours."

She stopped halfway down, her heart stumbling in disappointment. "A few hours?"

"I'm on my way back to Germany."

"No."

He nodded. "Yes. I report tonight."

Tonight! Anne-Marie gripped the banister rail, her knees growing wobbly at the thought. She needed, wanted time. But there was no time, she realized. No past or future, only the present. And the present was a tyrant, demanding satisfaction now, today, with no promise of tomorrow.

The present was this man.

She took a deep breath and let go of the rail. *"Je veux de faire l'amour avec vous."*

Mike felt the space between them dissipate in that instant. He searched her burnt-honey eyes in the shadowy light, and his blood sizzled with the hope that she'd said what he'd waited six long months to hear. Just to be on the safe side, though, he decided he'd better ask for clarification.

He cupped a hand to his ear. "Come again?"

"That's how you say, 'I want to make love with you'." Her posture was broomstick straight and her hands were tightly fisted at her sides, but her voice rang as true as fine crystal.

He cleared his throat, and it sounded unnaturally loud in the narrow confines of the stairwell. "Are you sure?"

In response, she practically flew the rest of the way down the stairs. He dropped his cap at his feet, then caught her around the waist and crushed her to him, burying his face in the golden mass of hair she'd yet to pin up for traveling. She wreathed her own arms around him and rested her cheek against his solid chest, reveling in his strength and his clean masculine scent.

Precious minutes ticked by as they stood at the bottom of the stairs, clinging to each other as if they had all the time in the world.

Mike finally moved one hand, bringing it up from her waist and increasing the pressure on her back until her breasts were flattened against his chest. His other hand glided down to conform to the curve of her bottom, drawing her so close to the burning length of his body that she could feel his heat and his hardness through their clothes. Then, holding her still, he rubbed himself against her with desperation born of long denial.

Arching against him with rivaling urgency, Anne-Marie tipped her head back. Through the haze that blurred her vision, she could see his hungry mouth descending to take possession of hers. And then she could taste him, his tongue as hot and sweet as the fire it ignited deep inside her.

Passion exploded between them, fueled by the terrible knowledge that these few hours might be all they would ever have. One kiss melded into another . . . wet, open-mouthed kisses that dissolved the weary days of death and danger that lay behind them . . . tender, tongue-twining kisses that would have to sustain them through the lonely nights of deprivation still to come.

After the last time, Anne-Marie had thought she was ready for the intensity of the feelings that Mike aroused in her. But the shivers that chased each other down her spine as his hands skimmed up her sides stole her breath. And the sparks that showered inside her when his thumbs brushed the sides of her breasts all but melted her bones.

Her own hands went where they'd dared not go before. She caressed his taut buttocks. Clutched at his narrow hips. Then, summoning up every ounce of courage she possessed, she reached down and laid her palm over his erection.

"Oh, God, that feels so good." His lips trailed fiery paths across her cheeks, her eyelids, her chin, burning away the chill that permeated the stairwell. "But if you don't stop, I'll be finished before we even get started."

Anne-Marie snatched her hand away, her stomach suddenly tied in knots. She knew he wouldn't deliberately hurt her, but she was nervous about what was going to happen next. The only thing to do, she decided, was to tell him the truth.

"I'm frightened," she admitted softly.

Mike raised his head and looked down at her, resigning himself to the fact that she had probably changed her mind. And resolving not to bully her into doing something she might regret. His own regrets would come later.

"If you don't want—"

She laid a silencing finger on his lips. "I want. But I don't know what to do."

He smiled in relief and kissed the sensitive pad of her finger. "I'll show you."

A frown pleated her forehead. "We still have a problem, though."

"Oh?"

"I don't have a bed."

He could take her now, fast and hot and furiously, right where they stood. The speed would release this terrible pressure that burned like a proximity fuse inside him. But he wanted more. And God knew, after all he'd already put her through, she deserved more. Much more.

"I have a bedroll."

In her fantasies, Anne-Marie had always envisioned a feather bed. A big, soft bed with a hand-carved headboard. And Mike, laying her down as gently as a bridegroom upon the white satin comforter, then stretching his lean length beside her and taking her in his arms to teach her the secrets of the dark.

That reality would be an Army bedroll cast upon the cold, hard floor of a vacant room didn't disillusion her in the least. She loved him. And for now, that love was enough to warm her. For now, that love was enough to fill those empty spaces that would return with a vengeance when he left her.

"Where is it?"

"In the vestibule."

She lifted a hand to his cheek. "You get the bedroll and I'll make a fire."

"*We'll* make a fire." He turned his lips into her palm, then released her.

There were enough live embers beneath the ashes of last night's fire to catch quickly when Anne-Marie touched a match to the kindling under the logs that Mike had laid on the grate.

As the blaze grew, its orange-and-crimson flames brushing heat across their faces and lighting the dark corners of the unfurnished room, he retrieved his bedroll from the vestibule and, together, they spread it in front of the hearth.

He unlaced his snowpak boots and toed them off. Following his lead, she stepped out of her sensible traveling shoes and met him in the middle of the wool blanket that covered his canvas shelter half. Seeing that he'd already removed his shoulder holster and partially unzipped the top of his tank suit, she reached to undo the buttons down the front of her dress.

"Let me," he said huskily, laying a staving hand over hers.

No fantasy, no matter how richly woven, could have prepared her for the way he lingered over undressing her.

One by one, he slowly undid her buttons and slid her dress off her shoulders. She shivered, but not from the cold, as he lowered his head and savored the satiny curve of her neck. First one side. Then the other.

Her slip came next. Hooking his thumbs under the straps, he drew the undergarment down until it landed in a cottony pool at her feet. Both of his arms went around her, and she felt her brassiere go tight, then loose, then fall away.

The sound that rumbled in his throat when his gaze shifted downward made her stomach tremble. "Beautiful."

Her lashes swept down shyly, then lifted. "I'm small."

"You're perfect." To prove it, he cupped her breasts in his hands, holding them as if they were fragile glass that could be shattered by a careless touch. "Just perfect."

Her breath quickened when his thumbs feathered over her nipples. Her heartbeat accelerated as he teased them to aching fullness. Her pulses pounded and her hands gripped his wrists, urging him to soothe that which he'd so skillfully inflamed.

And still, he didn't hurry. He slipped his hands inside the waistband of her rayon panties and peeled them and her ribbed stockings past her hips and over her slender legs. On his knees now, he slid his warm palms up and down the backs of her thighs while he nuzzled the soft, tawny curls at their juncture.

If she had been thinking straight, she would have been shocked. As much by what he was doing to her as what more she wanted him to do. She swayed, dizzy from the onslaught, and dug her fingers into his shoulders.

Mike was dying to taste her. To ravish and plunder and devour. But because this was her first time, he put the brakes on desire, got to his feet and skimmed a finger along the delicate ridge of her collarbone.

"I've dreamed of seeing you like this."

Anne-Marie wondered how he could touch her so gently yet look at her with such simmering violence. Her hand trembled as she finished unzipping his tank suit top. Fumbled a bit when she spread it open.

"And I, you."

Firelight licked the planes and hollows of his face as he shucked off his tank suit, skivvies and socks. In the nude, he was every erotic statue that she had seen or imagined. Her gaze held a connoisseur's gleam as it swept from his broad shoulders to his flat stomach, from his bold erection within the dark nest of his loins to—

She gasped at the sight of the inch-long scar high on his muscular thigh. Before she could stop herself, she reached out to touch it. "*Mon Dieu*, what happened?"

He savored the slow up and down rub of her finger for a few seconds before he took her shaking hand in his. "A piece of shrapnel."

Tears welled up in her eyes as the war, which they'd managed to hold at bay thus far, came crashing back into their midst. "You . . . you could have been killed!"

"But I wasn't." He brushed a tear from her cheek and pulled her into his arms.

"Was it painful?" she persisted, unable to bear the thought of him suffering.

"I'm all right, Anne-Marie." His voice was as gentle as the hand he stroked down her back.

She wrapped her arms tightly around his waist and pressed her cheek to his hair-matted chest. "Make love with me, Mike."

"I will," he promised.

"Now." She threw her head back, the embers of an age-old need flaring in her eyes. "Please, now."

His gaze caught her fire and returned its golden radiance. She felt her head spinning and clutched at him for dear love, afraid she was falling. But he was just lowering her to the thin cushion of the bedroll before following her down and easing himself over her on his hands and knees.

"I wish it was a feather bed." His gruff voicing of her girlish fantasy brought a new stinging to her eyes.

She blinked back her tears and wound her arms around his neck. "We'll pretend it is."

The heavy drone of planes in the sky rattled the windows of the house and shook the floor as he bent his head and kissed her. He drew her tongue into an erotic duel in which there were no losers. But on the battlefield to which he was returning, she knew, there could only be one winner.

"*Je t'aime*," she murmured as he continued to kiss her and caress her until her body arched instinctively against him, seeking more. "*Je t'aime, Michel.*"

Mike knew in his heart that Anne-Marie was saying she loved him. He could hear it in the soft intensity of her voice. Could see it in her eyes, her face. But with his two best friends already gone and himself just a fugitive from the law of averages, he couldn't say it back. Couldn't bring himself to tell her how very much she meant to him.

So he did the next best thing. He moved her hands from his neck to his hips, then slowly entered her. And as the firelight cast a glow over their entwining limbs, he stroked her and he stoked her and he showed her that love has a language all its own.

"Again."

Mike didn't say in case it was the last time, but he didn't have to. Lying cradled in the curve of his arm in front of the fire, Anne-Marie heard the urgency, raw and rough-edged, in his voice. Understood that time, not the Germans, was their worst enemy now.

Swallowing her tears and her fears, she looked down. At the luminous dial on the watch he still wore. At the dark hairs swooping down from his forearm to curl about that serviceable wristband. At his long, strong fingers strumming restlessly from her waist to her hip to her thigh and back again.

Then she looked up, into the molten force of his eyes, and felt a heat that had nothing to do with the flames at her back rising inside her.

"Yes," she agreed, her own voice shaky but certain. "Again."

Her arm tucked securely in his, Anne-Marie walked with Mike to the square.

They'd remained in the house, hidden away from the world, until the last possible moment. She had promised herself she wouldn't cry when it was time for them to leave, and she hadn't. But as they approached the corner where the Army truck would pick him up, she could feel her eyes beginning to sting and her chin to quaver.

Determined as much for his sake as for her own to maintain her composure, Anne-Marie took a deep breath and said calmly, "I've heard that in Paris I can get a kilo of sugar for a pack of American cigarettes."

"That's only—what?—a little over two pounds."

"Enough for one person for a month or more."

Mike's throat ached as he glanced down at her and saw her staring straight ahead. The sun had ducked behind a bank of late-afternoon clouds, but her hair shone like gold in the cheerless light. She wasn't wearing gloves, and her hand looked pale and pretty against his olive drab sleeve. Her taut fingers, however, reflected her inner turmoil.

"Well," he drawled, giving her arm an affectionate squeeze as they approached the square, "as long as you don't trade 'em for turnips."

She smiled up at him, but her eyes bespoke a sorrow that resonated in his soul.

Before she could reply, though, the canvas-topped Army truck rumbled into the village and came to a stop with a squealing of brakes and a grinding of gears.

It was better this way, Mike thought as he looked to the east, toward the German front and away from Anne-Marie's haunting amber eyes. Already he could hear the sounds of shells exploding one right after the other. He could see the smoke rising and smell the acrid odor of gunpowder. Already he could feel that familiar tightness forming in his gut as he once again faced the prospect of his own death.

The truck driver leaned across the seat and opened the passenger door. "Wanna ride up front, Lieutenant?"

Ignoring the envious looks of the young replacements crammed onto the rail seats in the rear, Mike tossed his bag and his bedroll into the cab. Then he turned back to the woman standing quietly behind him and kissed her, quick and hard. And, perhaps, for the last time.

Anne-Marie felt her lips tremble and prayed that she would get through this without falling apart. She tried to smile at him but couldn't quite manage it. "I'll send you my address when I find a place to live in Paris."

He wanted to tell her that, address or no, he would find her. To this point, though, he hadn't made any promises he wasn't positive he could keep. And he damned sure wasn't going to start now. So he just nodded and said, "I'll look for your letter."

Then he climbed into the cab and closed the door.

Mike sat woodenly on the front seat, with his eyes on the road ahead, as the driver shifted gears. He'd sworn he wouldn't look back, and he didn't. But if he had, he would have seen Anne-Marie weeping openly as she waved goodbye to him.

STALAG 58, GERMANY

The prisoner of war camp sat in a peaceful green valley beneath a warm April sun. Apple trees wore blossoms as white and frilly as a bridal veil. Wildflowers grew in wild profusion at their feet and birds flitted through the spring-blue sky overhead.

Everything and everyone was quiet.

Until a vast panoply of American tanks and open-topped M-7s, their engines growling like panthers and their guns rattling a warning, crested the grassy hill.

And the hundreds of hollow-eyed internees crowded behind the rusting barbed-wire fence raised a cheer that echoed throughout the valley.

Mike ordered his tank driver to stop on the high ground. Then he focused his field glasses on the compound for a moment before calling down to the emaciated man who was riding point, "I don't see any guards in the towers."

A new hope seemed to light the escapee's eyes as he looked back from the front end, where he was standing with one arm hugging the gun. "They must've heard us coming and made a run for it!"

"You think it's a trap, sir?" the artilleryman to Mike's right shouted over the noisily idling engines.

"There's only one way to find out."

"Go in with triggers fingered."

Leaving Anne-Marie was the hardest thing Mike had ever done. She'd become a part of him, like the shrapnel in his leg: hot and painful and impossible to ignore. And as he'd strapped on his gun in the waning light of a day that might have been their last, he couldn't help feeling bitter about having to return to the war.

But as bad as he had it, the mission was still his priority. It had to be. Especially if he wanted to live long enough to see her again. So when he rejoined his battalion, he rolled up his sleeves and got down to the sordid business of destroying everything in his roundabout path to Paris.

His first day back, he'd helped clear the high ground on the enemy side of the Prüm River for an infantry division that was attacking across it. A couple of weeks later, he'd laid a highway of hot steel for an armored drive toward Frankfurt. And just last week, he'd fired one smoke mission after another to cover his own battalion as they crossed the Rhine River on pontoon bridges for the final thrust into the evil heart of the Fatherland.

How he'd gone from directing fire missions to leading a rescue mission was another story altogether.

At the crack of dawn, while the battalion was warming up its engines for today's push, an escapee from the prison camp had staggered into their command tent after walking all night. His eyes fever-bright, his remnant of a uniform hanging on his skeletal frame and his boots coming apart at the seams, the young corporal had looked certifiably crazy. Yet he'd sounded perfectly coherent as he'd explained to the CO that there were almost a thousand American soldiers, most of whom had been captured during the Battle of Bulge, being held in a German prison camp some five miles away.

"We have to hurry, sir," he'd said. "Some of the men were wounded during the Bulge and never received proper medical care. Others suffered frostbite when they were force marched out of the Ardennes." He'd squared his coathanger shoulders then. "All of them are starving."

"*We?*" the colonel had queried as he'd eyed the scarecrow of a man swaying unsteadily across the stack of C-ration cartons that served as his desk.

The former POW's face had twisted with pain as he'd leaned forward and said, quietly but firmly, "I promised the men I'd bring help or die trying, sir."

Mike had gone into headquarters to pick up his observation maps just a few minutes ahead of the escapee. As he'd listened to him talk, he couldn't help but think of the terrible fate that had befallen John Brown and Charlie Miller, whose wife Daisy had given birth to an eight-pound boy in early February. Something in his eyes or his facial expression must have reflected his growing determination to help those other men, as he had not been able to help his two best friends, because he'd come out with orders to liberate the camp.

Now he gave the go-ahead sign and the column, guns pointed outward in case the Germans were playing a deadly game of cat and mouse, moved slowly but steadily down the hill. Ambulances and jeeps full of medics followed closely behind. Yet more armor brought up the rear.

They came to a stop facing the entrance gate. For a moment, no one on either side of the fence moved. Then half of the tankers dismounted and spread out, carbines at the ready, while the other half remained aboard to man the big guns.

Inside, the internees stood as still as statues. The maimed clung to the able-bodied, the blind to the sighted. Bruised and beaten, but not broken, they had obviously formed a brotherhood that transcended the ties of blood.

"Why aren't they coming out?" someone asked.

"The gate's wired shut," the escapee answered.

"How'd you get out?"

"Let's just say there's no gold under that ground."

"You *tunneled* out?"

Mike swiveled his head and hollered, "Anybody got a pair of wire cutters?"

"Right here, sir."

"Thank you, sergeant."

Wire cutters in hand, Mike dismounted and headed for the gate. He had to breathe through his mouth to block out the heavy stench of illness and infection that hung over the compound. Hearing about the condition of his fellow soldiers was one thing. Seeing it firsthand was enough to bathe his world a furious red.

"Sir?" someone behind him said.

Mike was so focused on freeing the prisoners that he hadn't realized he was being followed. He stopped just a few steps short of the gate and spun. Then he blinked to clear his vision and found himself facing a bona fide hero.

The escapee extended his claw of a hand, palm upward. "May I?"

Mike couldn't have explained it if he'd tried. Not even to himself. But the sight of that hand pierced his heart like a bayonet.

"What's your name, soldier?" he demanded in a voice gone coarse with emotion.

The former prisoner snapped to attention and clicked his heels. "Walker, sir. Corporal Tim Walker."

Mike gave him the wire cutters and a battlefield promotion he would write up later. "Get those men out of that hellhole, *Sergeant* Walker."

"Yes, *sir!*"

Bedlam reigned as the gate creaked open and the prisoners, free at last, came limping and hobbling out on legs like sticks. The medics rushed forward to carry those who couldn't walk. More than one rough, tough redleg—Mike among them—had to wipe the wetness from his eyes as the gaunt and grateful survivors said thanks before being loaded into the ambulances.

Only one man remained behind the barbed wire.

A spiraling of concern swept down Mike's spine when he saw him sitting on the grassless ground with his back against the wooden barracks wall and his head hanging in utter defeat.

His hair was so dirty and matted it was hard to tell whether it was light or dark, blonde or brown. An earpiece was missing from his glasses, a scraggly beard hid the lower half of his face, and his khaki shirt had been stripped of all identifying insignia. He wore a regulation combat boot on his right foot, but the bare and blackened toes of his left stuck out from a swaddling of rags.

Mike waited until some of the confusion died down, then drew the newly minted sergeant aside and asked, "Who is he?"

"I don't know, sir." Walker shook his head. "We came in about the same time, but I never got his name. Most days, he just sat like he is now. Then he ate, if they bothered to feed us, and went to bed."

"What's wrong with his foot?"

"Frostbite. He was missing a boot when he got here, so I assume he lost it in the Ardennes."

The medics were too busy tending to the soldiers who'd already left the camp to notice the one who'd remained behind.

Mike slipped in through the gate, intent on bringing the man out even if he had to carry him. As he crossed the dusty compound, he caught a whiff of something stale and sour and downright sickening. Once he got where he was going, it didn't take him long to figure out what the smell was.

The poor guy had pissed in his pants—numerous times, in fact, judging by the stains on the front of his trousers.

"Hey, buddy," he said with as much joviality as he could muster, "the Krauts are kaput and you're free to go."

But imprisoned in some hell of his own, the man neither moved nor spoke.

Mike had seen many a brave warrior lose his nerve or his will to fight back during the hell of an enemy artillery barrage. And he wasn't ashamed to admit that there'd been plenty of times when he'd thought he couldn't take it anymore himself. Yet he'd never seen anyone with such a bad case of shell shock before.

He crouched down beside the stiff and silent figure, then reached over and gently clasped his shoulder, feeling more bone than flesh beneath that tattered shirt. "Can I give you a hand up, soldier?"

It might have been his comforting touch. Or maybe it was his consoling tone of voice. Whatever, the man slowly lifted his head and looked sideways.

Mike felt a kick of recognition that almost knocked him backwards as he stared into the familiar brown eyes of the lifetime friend he'd given up for dead.

"Charlie?" he breathed.

The man blinked, as if awakening from a trance, and a lone tear leaked out from under the frame of his broken glasses and rolled down his dirty cheek.

A knot coiled in Mike's chest and it was all he could do not to cry himself. The filth and the foul odors aside, he grabbed hold of his old friend and wrapped him tightly in his arms. "My God, it's Charlie Miller!"

Chapter Nine

*H*e said h-he loved me!" the girl sobbed.

Anne-Marie had been in no mood for company when she got home from work. Not even her own. She'd been cranky from the June heat, exhausted after being on her feet all day, and frustrated at having had to rebuff the amorous advances of the dozens of fresh-faced American GIs who'd lined up at her sales counter in the Galéries Lafayette to buy a souvenir of "Gay Paree." Worse, she'd been crushed to discover that yet another week had gone by with no letter from Mike.

None of which had kept Brigitte Duprée, her neighbor across the hall, from rushing into her room without knocking and promptly bursting into tears.

"H-he even asked m-me to marry him!" Brigitte cried now, devastated by the tragic turn her *affaire de coeur* had taken. In her first serious relationship, she had fallen hard for the wrong man—a GI whom she'd met three months ago, while he was recuperating from his battle wounds at the American Hospital in Paris. She'd been writing him long, passionate letters since his return to the front. But with the war over, her erstwhile lover had callously written back to tell her that he was going home without her.

Sitting on her narrow bed with her arms wrapped around her heartbroken neighbor, Anne-Marie wanted desperately to say something that would ease her pain. And perhaps to dispel some of her own fears where Mike was concerned. Words failed her, however, so she simply tightened her embrace and let the poor girl cry it out.

"Oh, why did he tell me he loved me if it wasn't true?" Weeping wretchedly, Brigitte answered her own question. "To get me to go to bed with him, that's why!"

At least Mike had been honorable enough not to lie to her, Anne-Marie thought with a small, poignant smile. He hadn't said he loved her, not even after she'd said it to him. Nor had he asked her to marry him. He'd taken what she'd gladly given. And had given her beautiful memories in return.

Still, moisture beaded on her own lashes as she looked around the tiny, third-floor room she had rented almost four months ago on the *rive gauche*.

It measured five steps exactly from wall to wall. Besides the single bed, a small table with two chairs and an unpainted cabinet in the corner completed the furnishings. Her grandmother's candelabra sat on the table. Inside the cabinet was the last of the coffee and sugar she had bought on the black market with her American cigarettes. Atop it was the framed picture of Mike—taken, he'd told her in a flat tone, as they'd lain entwined in front of the fire, after the battle for Aachen.

The room's saving grace was the window; it overlooked a bend of the Seine River, which shimmered like a silver ribbon beneath the lowering sun.

Was it only last month, Anne-Marie wondered in amazement, when Brigitte and she had stood at that window to watch powerful floodlights spread a "V" for Victory across the night sky and to listen to the joyful ringing of the church bells all over Paris? Instead of joining the jubilant crowds in the streets, they had celebrated the end of the war by sharing a bottle of wine and singing the "*Marseillaise*." A little light-headed then, they had clasped hands and prayed together for the safe return of the servicemen they loved.

But today, with Brigitte's sergeant having summarily ended their wartime interlude and Anne-Marie's lieutenant yet to be heard from since their stolen afternoon in Ste. Geneviève, the future looked much gloomier than either of them could have imagined that glorious night.

"I'm sorry." Brigitte hiccuped and raised her head.

"Sorry?" Smiling quizzically, Anne-Marie released her. "For what?"

"For burdening you with my problems when you have worries of your own."

Anne-Marie realized that Brigitte was referring to Mike, but she wasn't ready to talk about him just yet. Instead, she turned the topic back to her neighbor's predicament. "What are you going to do now?"

"I don't know." Brigitte blinked sorrowful blue eyes at her and shook her head. "What Frenchman would have me after what I've done?"

"And what exactly have you done?" Anne-Marie exploded as the heat and her own disappointment finally got the best of her. "Loved a man who said he loved you!"

"Yes, but—"

"A man who lied to get you into bed!"

"True, but—"

"Well then, *he's* the one who should be ashamed, not you!"

"I know, but—"

"But what?" Anne-Marie demanded in a near shout.

"But will you please let go of my hand before you break it?"

Anne-Marie didn't remember taking hold of her neighbor's hand. Now she looked down and realized that she had it in a bone-crushing grip. Laughing softly, she let go.

A sniffling Brigitte failed to see any humor in the situation. "What *am* I going to do?"

Unable to resist, Anne-Marie reached over to ruffle Brigitte's wispy black cap of hair. They were the same age, and they had moved to Paris from their respective villages at approximately the same time. For reasons she couldn't fathom, though, she thought of her neighbor as the younger sister she'd never had.

"You could always become a *zig-zig* girl." She was only teasing, of course, but Brigitte took her seriously.

"It would serve him right if I wound up walking the streets!"

"Or you could say 'yes' if Pierre Dumas ever works up enough nerve to ask you to have coffee with him."

Brigitte's eyes clouded with confusion. "Pierre Du—the baker around the corner?"

"He's a fine man."

"You're just saying that because he always saves you bread."

"Not a bad friend to have in a city full of shortages." Anne-Marie took it as a good sign that Brigitte hadn't rejected her suggestion out of hand. "Besides, Pierre has asked about you every morning since he saw us together on the street."

"He does have kind eyes," Brigitte conceded.

"More important, he has a kind heart."

Brigitte mulled that over for a moment. "I wonder what he would think of my having . . . been with an American soldier?"

Anne-Marie waited a beat. "Did I tell you that the girl he was engaged to ran off with another man?"

"A GI?"

"Worse, an English officer."

"So he's suffering, too."

"Maybe you can ease each other's pain."

Brigitte nodded contemplatively. "What time does he open the bakery?"

"The line begins to form about five in the morning."

"Five?" Normally a late sleeper, Brigitte looked appalled. "But I'll be all night getting ready to go see him!"

"Best to get your beauty rest instead," Anne-Marie counseled.

"You're right." Brigitte spurted to her feet and started toward the door. "I'll go to bed now and get up at four."

"Bring me a croissant," Anne-Marie called after her.

"It may be day-old bread by the time I get back!"

As Brigitte left her laughing, Anne-Marie opened her window to let out some of the heat entrapped in her room. Then she changed out of her work clothes and into a sleeveless blue chemise. Habit had her inspecting her cotton skirt and blouse for wear before she hung them in the shallow alcove that served as her closet. In the small bathroom hidden behind a flowered curtain, she washed her face and pinned her hair up off her neck.

The terrine she'd eaten at noon still sat like a lump in her stomach and it was too hot for coffee, so she stepped to the window to watch the church spires vanish into the twilight and couples stroll out of the mist to walk arm-in-arm along the banks of the Seine.

L'heure bleue, the hour of long shadows and lovelorn hearts, was when the heavy hand of aloneness smote Anne-Marie the hardest. She'd been alone before. When her parents and her brother were killed. And after her grandfather died. But never had she felt as lonely as she did when she thought of living without Mike.

The nights were the worst. During the day she stayed busy enough with the temporary job she had taken until she started school in the fall. And there was her volunteer work at the reception center, helping to repatriate the French civilians who had survived the German prison camps while trying—fruitlessly so far—to learn the fate of her friend, Miriam Blum. Come the dark, though, she would don her nightgown, brush out her hair and turn off the light. And then, like some old woman whom life has passed by, she would climb into her narrow bed and remember—

A sharp rap at the door cut into her reveries.

"*Entrez*," she invited over her shoulder, assuming that it was Brigitte again.

"I hope that means 'come in'," a familiar masculine voice said into the dimness of her room.

Anne-Marie felt a dizzying sense of *déjà vu* as she wheeled away from the window to see Mike closing her door behind him.

For a small eternity, she stood where she was, sating herself on the sight of him. Tall and tan and tautly muscled, he looked every inch the conquering hero. His square-cut hair was neatly combed, his face freshly shaved. On the shoulders of his dress uniform gleamed his single silver lieutenant's bars while a colorful tier of campaign stars and battle decorations lay over his heart.

He looked so strong. So handsome, standing in her ugly little room. So alive.

"Mike," she marveled softly.

"You were expecting maybe *The Hunchback of Nôtre Dame*?" he said with a wry smile.

Her saucy little chin shot up a notch. "Do I look like Esmerelda?"

That devilish dimple pocked his cheek. "You look like a dream come true."

Before she could stop herself, Anne-Marie did something she'd never done in front of him before. She burst into tears. Hot tears that made her eyes feel as if they were on fire.

"You're here!" she sobbed. "You're really here!"

Alarmed by her loss of control, Mike crossed the room in half the number of steps it normally took her and enfolded her in his arms. His own emotions were dangerously close to the surface. On the one hand, it felt so right to hold her again. To bury his face in her sunlit hair and to fill his senses with her moonflower scent. On the other hand, it terrified him to think that this wouldn't end the way he wanted it to.

"Hey," he said, trying to cheer her up, "I've got a bicycle taxi waiting down—"

"A bicycle taxi!" She lifted her shocked face to his smiling one. "But that must be costing you a small fortune!"

He shrugged indifferently. "I've also got three months' worth of combat pay in my pocket and a seventy-two hour pass—"

"Seventy-two hours?" she repeated, both her voice and her heart breaking at the realization that this, then, was how it would end between them.

His dark eyes speared into her distraught ones. "Do you know I've been here for a good ten minutes and you haven't even kissed me hello?"

Anne-Marie made a painful but practical decision in that instant. She could cry as much as she wanted after Mike left her to go back to America. Until then, he wasn't going to see another single tear.

She rose up on tiptoe and drew his head down. No coyness sparked in her eyes when they met his. She was his woman for the next three days and nights, and he was her man. And in the years to come—the lonely years, far ahead and long away—she knew she would look back on their time together with no regret.

"'Ello, Mike," she whispered against his mouth.

He crushed her against him as their lips melted in an ardent kiss. Their tongues swirled together in an erotic *pas de deux*. His hands moved possessively over her body, leaving fire wherever they touched, and she could feel his living heart pounding in tempo with hers.

She clung to him and to the wonder of the moment. He was her first lover, her *bien-aimé*, and she couldn't bear the thought of losing him. But lose him she must. The war that had brought them together had been won. He had a home and a family waiting for him back in Kansas City, and she had goals of her own to pursue here in Paris. So instead of worrying about the future, she would simply appreciate the precious present.

"I thought of you every day," he murmured.

"I prayed for you every night," she admitted.

Mike smiled, but his brown eyes were shadowed with memories of war that Anne-Marie knew would haunt him forever. "Sometimes in the middle of a fire mission, I'd swear I could see your face in the smoke. Then I'd blink and, poof, you'd be gone."

She nodded. "Every so often I'd see an American soldier on the sidewalk who reminded me of you. I'd start walking faster, trying to catch up with him" —now she shook her head ruefully— "only to realize he was a complete stranger."

They kissed again, tenderly. And again, deeply. Finally, fighting for breath, they broke apart.

"Do you want to send the bicycle taxi away and stay here tonight?" she asked him.

"No."

"Why not?"

He grinned down at her. "Because I have a surprise for you."

"A surprise?" She smiled up radiantly at him. "Oh, but I love surprises!"

Actually, Mike had several surprises in store for Anne-Marie, but after a cursory glance around her tiny but tidy room, he decided that this was neither the time nor the place to spring them on her.

"What is this surprise?" she demanded, scarcely able to contain her curiosity.

"Put on your prettiest dress," he said silkily, "and I'll show you."

The door opened into her fantasy boudoir. Subtly striped moiré papered the walls, cut velvet draped the windows, and a simply patterned Savonnerie carpeted the floor. A carved bed, its white satin comforter already turned down, dominated the suite.

"It is to your liking, *m'sieur?*" asked the anxious concierge who'd ridden up in the hotel lift with them.

Mike tilted his head consideringly at Anne-Marie. "What do you think, *mademoiselle?*"

"C'est magnifique!" Peeking into the luxurious, marble-mosaicked bathroom, she caught a glimpse of her reflection in the gilded mirror above the sink, seeing a woman who had been liberated by love . . . and, standing behind her, the man who had set her free.

Coming here with Mike might have been a mistake, Anne-Marie knew, because she would surely end up weeping when it was time for him to go. But as she'd changed out of the chemise and into her white crepe suit—a prewar Chanel she'd found in a secondhand shop—she'd felt ridiculously happy. And in the taxi on the way to the hotel, where he'd already arranged for them to stay, she'd renewed her vow to enjoy what time they had together.

We deserve this, she told herself now. After all we've suffered, everything we've survived, we deserve this.

She squared her shoulders and started to turn back to him. Then stopped, her eyebrows shooting up in surprise when she saw the bottle of Mumm Cordon Rouge chilling in a silver cooler beside the small brocade sofa.

"Champagne!" she said with a laugh.

The concierge lifted the bottle from the bucket, expertly removed the foil, then popped the cork and poured.

As she accepted the flute, Anne-Marie noticed a tray of hors d'oeu-vres—crackly disks of thin crust daubed with briny black drifts of caviar or cool crème frâche—sitting on the sofa table.

She smiled coyly at Mike. "Now I see why you didn't want to stop for dinner."

"No turnips, *m'sieur.*" The concierge's tone said he didn't quite understand the reasoning behind that particular request but that he'd ful-filled it precisely.

Seeing the puzzled expression on the man's face, Anne-Marie choked back her laughter and sipped champagne. It was delicious. But the fizz in her throat was nothing compared to the bubbling of her blood when she looked at Mike and saw the naked want on his face.

His eyes never left hers as he reached into his pants pocket and pro-duced an American ten-dollar bill. "That'll be all, thank you."

Clutching the precious paper money that would probably buy him more than he earned in a month, the concierge backed out of the open door, then executed a courtly bow before he closed it.

"We need to talk, Anne-Marie," Mike said in a grave tone that sent a shiver of premonition down her spine. "I have a lot of things to tell you, and something I want to ask—"

"No." Not yet ready to hear him say that he was going back to America, she set down her flute and started toward the bed. "No talking tonight."

Determined to have his say, he followed close on her heels. "But I want—"

She spun and silenced him the only way she knew how, with a desperate kiss that left them both shivering with desire. Then, before he could utter another word, she kicked off her shoes, unbuttoned her suit jacket and stepped out of her skirt. Clad only in her lacy brassiere, garter belt and the silken stockings she'd been saving for a special occasion, she took hold of his tie and towed him down to the mattress with her.

"A feather bed!" she squealed in delight.

"How does it feel?"

"It's so soft."

And he was so hard and ready lying between her thighs that Anne-Marie simply couldn't resist. All seductress now, she reached down between them and undid his fly. Her eager fingers circled him and stroked him until he made a noise in his throat, part moan but mostly growl. Then she let him go and lifted her hand to caress his cheek with melting tenderness.

Mike's blood pounded a drumbeat in his ears as he looked down at the wanton picture she made with her tawny hair fanning across the potpourri-scented sheet, her amber eyes so soft and shiny, and her skin gleaming like satin in the golden light from the bedside lamp. Talking be damned, he decided. Right now, he had more pressing needs to tend to.

His mouth captured hers and moved over it greedily. She twined her arms around his neck, parting her lips to receive the thrilling thrust of his tongue as she opened her thighs to accept his hot, pulsing hardness. He gripped her hips and drove his body into hers. In response, she locked her legs around him and arched her back like a bow. His hoarse gasps mingled with her glad cries as they found release where they'd left it . . . with each other.

The pale light of dawn outlined the velvet drapes when Anne-Marie awakened. She lay unmoving for a moment, staring at the elaborately worked plaster ceiling. Then she turned her gaze to Mike, sleeping soundly beside her.

He'd had a bad dream in the middle of the night. She hadn't known what to think when his shouts first pierced her ears. But when he'd sat bolt upright in bed with his eyes closed and his fists clenched and sweat beading on his skin, she'd realized that he was reliving some unspeakable horror of war. Remembering her own harrowing nightmares when she didn't know where he was or whether he was even alive, she'd wrapped her arms around him and held him, simply held him, until his muscles relaxed and he drifted off peacefully again.

Now, being careful not to disturb him, Anne-Marie slid out of bed and began putting on her clothes. Mike's seventy-two hours were up today, and it was time for her to go. She hated the thought of leaving him like this, with no note of explanation and no kiss goodbye, but she was taking with her a lifetime's worth of wonderful memories.

The days had passed in a blur as she'd given him the grand tour of the "City of Light." She'd taken him from the top of the Eiffel Tower, where they'd clung dizzily to each other as they'd looked straight down, to the underground tunnels of the métro, where they'd necked like teenagers in a darkened car. From the Louvre to the Arc de Triomphe, from a religious service at Nôtre Dame to a risqué show at the Casino de Paris, he'd seen them all.

But at night, he took the lead. Time and again, he celebrated her body with a tender skill that had left her limp and sated and more in love than ever. Later, she would lie cradled in the curve of his shoulder, listening to the receding thunder of his heart and the relentless ticking of his watch.

Finished dressing, Anne-Marie found her purse on the sofa table, where she'd dropped it the night before while being carried to bed. Tucked inside her bag were the franc notes she would use to buy a round-trip train ticket to Ste. Genviève. She was sure her aunt would be happy to see her. And she hoped she could be of some help to Henriette, who was due to give birth any day and whose husband Guy was working to reconstruct the very railroad tracks that he and the other Resistance members had destroyed. Mostly, though, she needed to get away from Paris for a little while so she could begin learning to live with the pain of Mike's absence.

She stooped to pick up her shoes, then straightened to study his beloved face one last time. It was then that her tears came—silent sobs that began somewhere in her soul and shook her chest. She had to get out of here. Now. Before her heart shattered and the sound of it breaking into a million irreparable shards awakened him.

Carrying her things, she tiptoed to the door and reached for the knob. Two hands suddenly snaked around from behind her and kept her from opening it. She sagged against the wood, knowing she was caught.

"Where are you going?" Mike demanded, his voice rough with sleep and his breath warm against her neck.

Anne-Marie spun and faced him squarely. "I'm leaving you before you can leave me."

He fisted his hands on his naked hips and frowned down at her. "What makes you think I'm leaving you?"

"You said you only had seventy-two—"

"I also said I had a surprise for you."

Still holding her purse and her shoes, Anne-Marie waved her arms to encompass the suite. "I thought you meant this."

Mike grinned and shook his head. "That's only part of the surprise."

"And the rest?" Her voice reflected her anxiety.

"I've been given a choice." His expression turned somber. "I can use the points I've earned in combat to go back to Kansas City next week. Or I can accept a promotion to Captain and stay in Paris another six months with the Army of Occupation."

She was almost afraid to ask. "Which are you going to do?"

"That depends."

"On what?"

"Not what, but who."

"Who?" she parroted.

"Or is it *whom*? I can never remember—"

"*Whom?*"

He bent his head and brushed his lips over hers. "You."

"Me?" she all but squeaked.

"I love you, Anne-Marie."

On finally hearing the words, she bumped her forehead against his chin to hide her tears. "I love you too, Mike."

He looped his arms around her waist and pulled her closer. "You're brave and you're beautiful and you gave me a reason to go on living when it seemed like everyone I knew was dying."

"That's why you didn't write to me," she said with sudden insight.

"I was afraid of putting my feelings on paper," he admitted. "Afraid that I'd tell you I loved you one day and then jinx it by getting myself killed the next." His self-deprecating laugh rumbled deep in his chest. "I was even afraid that, after the way I'd built you up in my mind, you'd find someone else you loved more and wind up jilting me."

She snorted indelicately at that last. "So you waited to tell me in person."

"I had to come to you whole."

Anne-Marie thought of all the soldiers she'd seen who were missing an arm or a leg or an eye. Or burned so badly that their own families would have trouble recognizing them. And then there were the men who looked physically fine but whose minds had been permanently scarred. In a way, their wounds were the deepest and most devastating of all.

She said a small, silent prayer of thanksgiving that Mike had been spared before tipping her head back and smiling up at him tremulously. "And now that you're here?"

He tightened his hold. "Now I'm asking you to marry me. And to go home with me when I'm—"

"But—" Reeling at how fast this was all happening, she said the first thing that popped into her head. "America has such bad laws about the strangers!"

"Strangers?" Now it was his turn to play the parrot.

"People from other countries." Before he could correct her erroneous impression by telling her that America was the greatest melting pot on earth, she bombarded him with her other concerns. "What would I be? French or American? Would I be able to go to school? I want to become a history teacher, like my mother. And what about *your* mother?"

"My mother?"

She dropped her gaze. "How would she feel about her son marrying a French girl?"

"If I love you, so will she." That settled, he tried to answer her other questions in the order she'd asked them. "You'll always be French by birth, but as my wife you'll have the opportunity to become an American citizen. And yes, you can go to school. I'm planning to go too, on the GI Bill that our Congress has passed, because I want to be a lawyer."

He felt his heart swell as she lifted her eyes, her beautiful amber-brown eyes, and said haltingly, "My father was a lawyer."

"If I could bring even one of them back for you, I would."

She coughed rustily to clear her throat. "I know."

"But all I can do is offer you a new family. The family we'll make together." He gently cupped the sides of her face. "So, what do you say? Will you marry me?"

"*Oui,*" she whispered. And then, just so there would be no mistaking what her answer was, she practically shouted, *"Oui, oui, oui!"*

Mike didn't need an interpreter to tell him that Anne-Marie had just said "yes." He understood her perfectly. And when she dropped her shoes and her purse and flung her arms around his neck, he knew that the war was truly over and that their life together was about to begin.

PART
TWO

Passion Flower

Chapter Ten

KANSAS CITY, MISSOURI; 1968

G ood evening, my fellow Americans." President Lyndon Baines Johnson looked earnestly into the camera as he began his televised address to the nation.

Catherine Brown hated coming home to an empty house. Especially on Sunday—the loneliest day of the week if one was leading the "single married life" of a soldier's wife. So she'd turned on her portable TV when she got back from that student teacher's weekend seminar, more to keep her company while she went through her mail and scrounged up something to eat than because she was interested in the news. After all, the news never changed. If the networks weren't showing "peaceniks" like her younger brother burning their draft cards in public or marching on the White House chanting "Hey, hey, L.B.J., how many kids did you kill today?" they were broadcasting footage of soldiers fighting and dying in Vietnam.

But now, still in shock, she was sitting on the sofa with Johnny's letter in her hand, staring vacantly at the black-and-white screen.

"Tonight," the President said in his slow Texas drawl, "I want to speak to you of peace in Vietnam and Southeast Asia . . ."

Peace? Cat frowned as the word penetrated the fog of despair that surrounded her. She blinked her eyes and looked around her, noting almost absently that the late March sun had set and the living room of her two-bedroom rental house had grown dark. The only light came from the television that sat on the four-wheeled stand in the corner.

"We are prepared to move immediately toward peace through negotiations . . ."

She needed to move too, Cat realized numbly, but she was so tired, so confused, so sad, that she couldn't make herself do it. Her legs felt like lead and her arm was so heavy that she couldn't raise it to turn on the lamp. Even her tears seemed to be dammed up in her eyes.

"With America's sons in the fields far away . . ."

Johnny! Cat sucked in a sharp breath and curled her hands into fists, crumpling his one-page letter. Because he wasn't much of a writer, they usually exchanged cassettes to play on their matching recorders. It felt awkward at times, speaking of her love for him and her dreams for their future into a machine, and she absolutely hated the way her voice sounded on tape. But it was always comforting to listen to her husband's deep voice expressing his own feelings and emotions in return. She hadn't heard from him in a couple of weeks, though, so finding a letter from him when she got home had come as a pleasant surprise.

Certainly more pleasant than the shock that had followed it.

As the memory lanced through her, Cat finally moved, folding her arms across her stomach and doubling over until her head almost touched her knees. She had just finished reading Johnny's letter and was wondering what to make of it when the knock came. Thinking it was probably one of the neighborhood kids selling tickets for the school carnival or candy bars for their baseball team, she had instead opened the door to a man in uniform who had solemnly introduced himself before saying those awful words, "It is my duty to inform you . . ."

" . . . with America's future under challenge right here at home . . ." the President continued.

Cat shut her eyes against the wave of guilt that swept over her. She was supposed to see Johnny in Hawaii next month for his R & R, and it was a trip she had really been looking forward to. Partly because they'd never had a honeymoon to speak of—only an overnight stay at the Phillips Hotel, courtesy of her parents, before he'd helped her move into the house and then left her to arrange their furniture on her own. And partly because final exams had kept her from meeting him in Hong Kong during his first tour of duty. But mostly because she'd hoped they could start all over again after their bitter arguments during his thirty-day leave home about his volunteering for a second tour in Vietnam.

" . . . with our hopes and the world's hopes for peace in the balance every day . . ."

Three days ago, the Air Force chaplain had said. Now she wondered what she'd been doing at the time. It almost killed her to realize that, three days ago, while she was either giving a spelling test to her second-graders at Hale Cook School or working part time as a sales clerk at Harzfeld's to help defray her college expenses, Johnny may well have been dying in some faraway jungle.

Sitting up, Cat opened her tear-blurred eyes and looked at their wedding picture, which she proudly displayed on the wicker end table for all the world to see.

Images of the past filled her mind as she studied the smiling bride in white satin and lace and the square-jawed groom resplendent in his dress blues. Johnny and she had married a year-and-a-half ago, after he'd graduated from pilot training and before he'd shipped out to Vietnam the first time. He'd wanted them to wait until he finished his stint—just in case something happened, she was sure—but she simply wouldn't hear of it. She had known him all her life, had loved him since she was a little girl in pigtails, and she believed with fairy-tale certainty that he was her Prince Charming.

As she reached out to touch his likeness behind the cool, unyielding glass, it suddenly seemed impossible that his heart could have stopped beating without her own breaking in half. But in retrospect, she realized that she had felt nothing. Neither a falter nor a fissure. Which told her that one of two things had happened. Either the ties that bound them had been sundered by their physical distance and differences that seemed almost petty at the moment. Or, he was still alive.

She retracted her hand and drew a shuddering breath, clinging like a drowning woman to that hope.

" . . . I do not believe that I should devote an hour or a day of my time to any personal partisan causes."

How long had she been sitting there? Cat wondered now. She squinted down at her slim gold watch—a wedding present from Johnny—and was astonished to see that nearly three hours had passed since her world had been turned on its head. Then she reached up woodenly to switch on the table lamp and smoothed out his letter so she could read it again.

The black ink that he'd used seemed to dance before her confused eyes as she scanned the words that he'd scrawled on the thin airmail sheet. It was a short letter, only three paragraphs long. He'd spent the first thanking her for sending those cotton socks to help keep his feet dry and the packages of grape Kool-Aid that made the drinking water more palatable, and the second telling her how his plane's computer had fouled up and thrown a bomb into the boonies.

"Accordingly, I shall not seek, and I will not accept, the nomination of my party for another term as your President," Lyndon Johnson said in a startling conclusion to his speech.

But it was the third paragraph, especially the last sentence, which completely baffled Cat. She read it over and over, struggling to make sense of it. Then she stopped, trying to fathom what kind of terrible premonition had prompted such an urgent plea on Johnny's part.

If *anything*—underlined twice—happened to him, he'd written, if he was reported as missing in action or presumed dead, she was to contact a man in Saigon by the name of Cain. Whether Cain was the man's first or last name, he hadn't said. He'd just scribbled an address on Truong Minh Gian Street, then closed by saying, "And remember, no matter what, you're the only woman I ever really loved."

Cat was still staring at the letter, dumbfounded, when she made her decision. If it meant that much to Johnny, she would contact this Cain. But first, she would call her parents.

Mike Scanlon elbowed that messy stack of papers aside before setting the plates he'd carried in from the dining room on the kitchen counter. "I don't know what's gotten into that boy, but I'm sick and tired of these stupid leaflets littering up every room of the house."

Anne-Marie Scanlon shrugged and began scraping garbage into the disposal. "Think of him as a modern-day Thomas Paine."

But her husband refused to be placated. "Thomas Paine, my ass." Picking up the top sheet, he read the smudgy mimeographed words aloud. "'Make Love, Not War.' What kind of crap *is* this, anyway?"

"Free speech." Still infused with an immigrant's straightforward patriotism, she ranked the Constitution right up there with the Bible and Dr. Benjamin Spock on her list of required readings.

"Free, hell." He balled up the leaflet and sent it sailing across the kitchen. Two points, he congratulated himself when it landed in the wastebasket. "Who paid for the paper and printing?"

"Drew did."

"With what?"

The plates rinsed, she reached for the silverware. "With the money he collected at the peace rally in Volker Park."

"And where did all those political Katzenjammer Kids get their money?" he retorted as he began filling the dishwasher that had been installed when they'd remodeled the kitchen. They'd spent a small fortune having walls knocked out to turn three rooms into one and innumerable layers of linoleum pried up to expose the original pine floor. Still, his wife insisted that the family sit down together every Sunday evening at the dining room table that was graced by her grandmother's candelabra. "From the hardworking parents they take such delight in denigrating as 'Tools of Capitalism', that's where."

Sensing another futile argument about their son's anti-war activism in the offing, Anne-Marie turned off the water and dried her hands on a towel. Then she reached up to run her fingers through the sideburns he'd let grow a little at her urging. Despite the silver that was beginning to fleck his hair and the fine lines that already flanked his eyes, he was as handsome as ever.

Mike responded to her caress by pulling her into an embrace. He rested his chin on the crown of her head, while his arms slid around her waist and linked at the small of her back. It never ceased to amaze him, how much strength and comfort he drew from her slender body. Or how easily she could distract him with a gentle touch or her trademark sass.

"It's a nice suggestion, no?" Her French accent had faded somewhat, but her voice was as soft and smoky as it had been that long-ago August day when he'd first heard it.

"What?"

"'Make Love, Not War.'"

"Don't humor me, Anne-Marie." But knowing she'd outmaneuvered him yet again, Mike tipped her chin up and bent his head to cover her mouth with his own.

Nearly twenty-three years of marriage hadn't cooled their passions. *Au contraire.* As their family and friends liked to tease, they still had the "hots" for each other. They also had three healthy children, a comfortable old Craftsman-style home just south of Loose Park, and careers that both challenged and fulfilled them.

Now if their son would only quit threatening to flee to Canada after he graduated from high school in June in order to avoid the draft . . .

Despite his success as a lawyer, Mike was beginning to think that he was a complete failure as a father. At least where Drew was concerned, anyway. There were times, like this evening, when he wished the boy would go ahead and make good on his threat. Lord knew, he wouldn't miss those dinnertable diatribes that invariably left him reaching for the Alka-Seltzer! Then there were other times, like late last night when he'd peered into Drew's room and watched him sleeping the innocent sleep of a child, when the thought of losing his son damn near reduced him to tears.

For her part, Anne-Marie was more worried about the conflict at home than the one half a world away. She understood why her husband was upset. He'd answered his country's call without question, and was justifiably proud of the part he'd played in defeating the Nazis. She also knew where her son was coming from. He was a good student and he wasn't into drugs like so many of his peers, thank God, but one of the very first words out of his baby's mouth had been "Why?" Caught in the middle, she did what all mothers do. She hoped for the best and prayed that she would never have to choose between them.

When the phone rang, Mike broke off their kiss and raised his head with a groan. He waited to see if one of the kids would answer. As usual, he waited in vain.

"I'll get it." He released Anne-Marie on the second ring.

"If it's David, tell him I'll call him right back." Sixteen-year-old Mary—named for Anne-Marie's long-lost friend Miriam Blum—stuffed the tablecloth down the laundry chute and then hit for the stairs. David was her boyfriend, a junior to her sophomore, and a member of the Young Republicans. Every night she spent at least an hour closed in the bedroom she now had to herself talking to him about everything from the presidential election this coming fall to their own plans for attending the same law school someday.

"If it's Sammye, tell her I'm on my way over with the leaflets." Eighteen-year-old Drew—named for Mike's father, Andrew Scanlon— passed his sister on her way out of the kitchen. Sammye, who was lank of hair, long of body and big on Bobby Kennedy, was a true flower child. "Can I borrow your car, Mom?" Before she could ask "Have you finished your homework yet?" or remind him to tune the radio back to the classical music station she liked to listen to, he dug the keys to her '61 Corvair out of her purse. While he was at it, he grabbed a dollar for gas and stuffed it in the pocket of his bell-bottom jeans.

"Why doesn't anyone think that it might be a client calling *me*?" Mike grumbled as he stalked toward the wall phone.

"Because prisoners are locked down at night." Drew's gibe about his father's criminal law practice earned him a glare. As did the shoulder-length hair he'd tied with a shoelace at the neck of his fringed vest.

"I could work *pro bono*," Mike shot back as he picked up the receiver on the third ring. "But I'd hate like hell to see you starve."

Anne-Marie expelled a sigh and turned back to the sink.

"Hi, honey." Mike's mood brightened considerably when he heard his oldest daughter's voice on the other end. Here, at least, was a child he could talk to without getting a lot of grief in return. Cupping his hand over the mouthpiece, he informed his wife, "It's Cat. She's back from her seminar."

"Tell her that some of my ROTC students are going to write letters to Johnny tomorrow." Anne-Marie taught World History at Southwest High School. She'd started college when her youngest child had started first grade, and she didn't regret a single one of the nights she'd burned the midnight oil while the rest of her family slept. Having witnessed the atrocities of war firsthand, she believed that people who lost memories of their ancestors' holocausts were people doomed to seeing the horrors repeated.

Mary came dashing back into the kitchen. "Ask her if she'll go shopping with me next week for a new dress for the Spring Fling."

"Better ask the old man if he can afford to pay for it first," Drew muttered under his breath. Leaflets and keys in one hand, he flashed his family the peace sign with the other as he started toward the back door.

"What?" Speaking into the phone again, Mike felt his knees go weak and his mouth go dry. His shoulders slumped as he fell back against the wall. "Oh, Cat, no!"

Reading his shattered expression, Anne-Marie put down the casserole dish she'd just picked up and rushed to his side. "What happened?" she demanded fearfully. "Is she hurt? Where is she?"

Drew stopped at the door and turned back. There was no counting the number of times that Cat and he had gone at it about the war. She supported sending troops to help South Vietnam remain independent as strongly as he opposed paying the price for their freedom in American blood. They never attacked each other personally or mocked the other's motives, but their arguments invariably ended with him feeling frustrated by her faith in the military-industrial complex and her seeming both saddened and bemused by his efforts to turn duty into dishonor.

But now his love and concern for his older sister's safety was plainly etched on his young face. "Was she in a car accident?"

Mary simply stood in the middle of the kitchen, her eyes growing watery and her hands clasped prayerfully under her chin.

"We're on the way, honey." Mike's face looked haggard as he hung up the phone and told his anxiously waiting family, "It's Johnny."

"Mon Dieu!" Anne-Marie whispered in horror.

"Is he . . . dead?" Mary asked hesitantly.

Drew jingled his mother's car keys in a nervous motion.

"His plane disappeared and he's been reported as missing—" Emotion clogged Mike's voice; he couldn't continue.

Tears streamed down Anne-Marie's cheeks as she put her arms around his waist. She shared his pain because Johnny was more than just his godchild or their daughter's husband. In their hearts, he was their second son.

His mother, Kitty Brown, never remarried after her husband John was killed in combat in World War II. She couldn't forget her first and lasting love, and had tried to drown her sorrow in alcohol. Eventually she developed stomach cancer, which the people closest to her believed was partly the result of too many years of pain at the core of her being. When she'd passed away at the age of thirty-five to spend eternity with her "Flyboy," Mike and Anne-Marie had brought her fifteen-year-old son home from the funeral to live with them.

Drew, who'd learned how to play "Capture the Flag" and to build model airplanes from Johnny, said in a choked voice, "I'll drive."

"The telegram says they're making every effort to locate him." But Anne-Marie's soothing words fell on deaf ears.

"I-it . . . also says . . . he could be held by h-hostile . . . forces." And it was that possibility, more horrific than certain death, that had Cat sobbing against her mother's shoulder.

The telegram from the Defense Department, which had arrived shortly after her family, was a more detailed confirmation of what the Air Force chaplain had told her in person several hours earlier.

Perched on the end of the sofa where his wife and daughter were huddled, Mike reread the dryly worded particulars of Johnny's disappearance. He'd been on a combat mission and it was believed that he'd been maneuvering his plane to avoid hostile fire when radio contact was lost. Another pilot had observed an explosion, but it had yet to be officially determined whether that was hostile fire or Johnny's plane.

"It's kind of ironic, huh?" Drew asked.

Mike folded the telegram carefully and replaced it in its envelope before looking down at his son. Except for mumbling "I'm sorry" and patting his sister awkwardly on the back, Drew had been unusually quiet. Now he was sitting cross-legged on the avocado-green shag carpet beside a large cardboard box that he'd dragged out of Cat's spare bedroom. Inside the box were some old pictures and medals and citations—all that Johnny had ever had of his father—along with a smaller metal box containing the letters that his parents had exchanged during their short-lived marriage.

There was another telegram, too . . . one that had been read so many times over the years that its edges were frayed and its creases were worn thin.

"Ironic?" Mike repeated.

"First Johnny's father, and now—"

"Tragic is more like it," Mary said, her voice quavering as she knelt down next to Drew, reached into the box and lifted out the framed citation that had accompanied John Brown, Sr.'s Medal of Honor, awarded posthumously.

Mike nodded and tried to stay focused on the situation at hand, but he couldn't shake the image of a toddler sitting on a blanket playing toy soldiers. Or of a scared little boy on his first bicycle. Then there was the seven-year-old in Indian headdress holding the bow and arrow that "Santa" had brought him.

The pictures kept coming, running through his mind like those reels of family movies the kids used to watch by the hour. He saw a teenager in his too-big black suit turning tearfully away from his mother's grave. A high-school graduate kneeling somberly beside the simple white cross in the American Cemetery at Anzio, Italy, that had been erected in memory of the father he'd never known. The most recent and most poignant, perhaps, was a newly commissioned lieutenant waiting at the altar for his beautiful bride-to-be.

Swallowing against the tightness that was building in his throat, Mike rubbed his leg where that old shrapnel scar still nagged him sometimes. When he'd come home from Europe, he'd done everything he could to keep an eye on John's widow and son. That Anne-Marie, a war bride with a newborn daughter named for the mother she'd lost in the German *blitzkrieg*, had always encouraged him to make good on his promise had only deepened his love for her.

"Dad?"

He shook off the images and saw Cat looking back at him over her mother's shoulder. Her long red hair framed her pale face like parentheses and her changeable hazel eyes were luminous with tears. But it was the way she was biting her lower lip, just like she used to do when she was a little girl and something had hurt or upset her, that really got to him.

His little girl, he thought, and his own eyes stung at his inability to spare her this terrible heartache. "What is it, honey?"

"Is there anyone you can call? Someone in your old reserve unit, maybe, who can find out more about . . .?" Her voice broke apart.

Mike all but leapt to his feet, grateful for something to do. Like many returning servicemen, he'd remained in the Organized Reserve Corps. It had been as much of a financial decision as a patriotic one. The weekly meetings and yearly training camps had been a hassle, and sweating out Korea until he'd learned that his unit wouldn't be mobilized had been pure hell. But the checks, added to his monthly living allowance under the GI Bill and a part-time job clerking for the police department, had helped to feed his growing family while he'd finished college and law school.

"I'll use the kitchen phone." He wondered if he should call Charlie or Daisy Miller while he was at it, then decided against it. Their son, born while Charlie was a prisoner of war, had been busted for selling hard drugs to an undercover agent and had died of a heroin overdose while he was out on bail awaiting trial. Mike hadn't seen either one of them since the funeral, but he'd heard that Charlie, who'd lost one foot to frostbite after his terrible ordeal, now had the other one in an alcoholic's early grave. And that an embittered Daisy, who'd since divorced him, was working herself to the bone trying to keep her family's appliance store going in order to support herself and their surviving daughter. No, he thought as he left the living room, the Millers had enough on their plate without his adding yet another helping of tragedy.

Cat tossed her sodden tissue atop the growing pile on the coffee table. As she reached for another one, she caught a movement out of the corner of her eye. She turned her head, then yanked her body straight and glared at her brother.

"Don't open that," she hissed at him.

Drew glanced up guiltily from the small metal box he'd taken out of the larger one. "I was just going to look—"

"Those letters belong to Johnny."

"We used to read 'em together."

She surged to her feet. "Well, you don't share a room with him any-more. Or anything else, for that matter."

"That's enough," Anne-Marie warned. "Drew loves Johnny, too."

"Oh, that's right, I forgot." Cat realized that she was blowing this all out of proportion but she couldn't stop herself. It was as though her control, stretched to the breaking point by grief over Johnny's uncertain status and her own guilt about the way they'd parted, had suddenly snapped. She skirted the coffee table, then grabbed the small box out of her brother's hand and put it back in the larger one. "It's the war he hates, not the warrior."

"Johnny hates the war, too." Drew blinked back tears, obviously hurt by her unprovoked attack.

"Give me a break," she scoffed.

"Cat, please," Anne-Marie begged, rising to position herself between them.

"What could he possibly know about what Johnny loves or hates?"

"I know a lot more than you think."

"Like what?"

Drew pushed to his feet and pressed on. "Like why he was so nervous when he was home. And why he couldn't sit still or couldn't concentrate on anything."

He couldn't sleep, either. Cat recalled waking up in the middle of the night on more than one occasion to find Johnny's side of the bed empty and him pacing like a caged animal in the kitchen. Then, she'd attributed it to what he'd seen in the war. But now . . .

"Of course he was nervous." Her voice wobbled. "He was going back to Vietnam."

Drew frowned. "That wasn't all that was bothering him."

Mary tilted her head inquiringly at her brother. "What else was there?"

As Mike paused in the kitchen doorway, Anne-Marie turned questioning amber eyes to him. He shook his head, silently telling her that he hadn't been able to reach anyone who could help them learn anything more tonight about Johnny's situation than they already knew.

"Answer Mary's question," Cat prodded Drew in a caustic tone.

He lifted his shoulder in a single shrug. "All I know is what Johnny said after you two had that last big fight about him going back to 'Nam."

"He *told* you about that?" She hadn't breathed a word to anyone, not even her parents. That Johnny had gone behind her back—and to her younger brother, no less!—seemed like the ultimate betrayal on his part.

"You weren't speaking to him," Drew reminded her, "and he needed somebody to talk to."

Cat held her breath against the memory of all the angry things she *had* said to Johnny. That if he really loved her, he wouldn't leave her again. Or that he'd already done his duty, dammit, and now it was time for him to stay home and for them to start a family. And worst of all that she might not be waiting for him when he returned.

"I tried to talk to him," she whispered shakily. "But all he would say was that he was going back."

"Well, while you were student teaching one day, Johnny signed me out of school for lunch"—Drew shot an apologetic look at his parents—"and we wound up spending the rest of the day together."

Mike, seeing that Cat was on the verge of tears again, moved to her side. "What did you talk about, son?"

"He didn't want to go back, Dad, he really didn't. And believe it or not, he said I was right to keep protesting the war."

"What?" Mike looked skeptical.

"It's true." Drew appealed to Cat now. "He said the morale of our troops is so low, it's pitiful, and that Americans are being fed a pack of lies—"

"Lies?" Anne-Marie gasped.

"About how heavy our casualties really are and how bad the drug problem—"

"That's why we need Richard Nixon for our next president," Mary piped up.

Drew rolled his eyes. "So he can bomb Southeast Asia back to the Stone Age?"

"So he can end the war and bring our boys—"

"That's enough, you two." Mike shot a quelling look at Mary, then nodded at Drew. "Go on."

"Johnny said it was a sad day when the most powerful country on earth can't find officers who can read a map or a compass." Drew's frown deepened as he stared at his father. "And he said that even though you're retired from the reserves now, you could still probably call in a better air strike or artillery barrage than all of those 'Saigon Generals' who are sitting on their butts behind desks combined."

Cat swallowed hard. "Then why did he want to go back?"

"He didn't say . . ." Drew hesitated for a few seconds before adding, "Exactly."

"Exactly?" Being a trial lawyer, Mike picked up on equivocations like that.

"He told me that he had some unfinished business to take care of, and that he needed to talk to some guy named Cain—"

A car backfired out in the street, the sharp burst of sound reverberating through the small living room and cutting Drew off in mid-explanation.

"Cain?" Cat echoed, thinking she'd heard him wrong.

"Do you know him?" Mary asked in a tiny voice.

Cat shook her head at her sister, then turned bewildered eyes to her father. "But Johnny mentioned him in the letter I opened today."

"Let me see it," Mike said.

Anne-Marie handed him the letter, then stood at his elbow to read it with him.

"He was worried about something, all right." Mike stated the obvious.

But a bemused Anne-Marie wondered just what Johnny had meant by that last sentence.

"You've got to help me, Dad," Cat pleaded, knowing now what she needed to do.

"But of course he will," her mother hastened to assure her.

"It's too late to call anyone else tonight," Mike said. "First thing tomorrow, though, I'll get on the phone to the Defense Department and see if I can open some channels there." He folded the letter and passed it back to Cat. "You stay home from school in the morning in case—"

"No, that's not what I mean."

He gave her a blank look. "Well then, what do you mean?"

Cat took a breath that was remarkably steady, given the momentousness of the announcement she was about to make. "I want you to help me get to Saigon."

Chapter Eleven

SAIGON, VIETNAM

"To put it bluntly, Mrs. Brown, this Cain is a disgrace to all red-blooded, right-thinking Americans."

Flabbergasted, Cat rested her elbow on the arm of her chair and pressed her fingers to her temple. "Colonel Howard, are you sure we're talking about the same man?"

"Sure as God made little green apples." The colonel's thin mouth twisted sourly as he handed back the sealed envelope across the inlaid wood of his desk. "He fancies himself some kind of soldier of fortune when he's nothing but a dirty, low-down mercenary. Smuggling drugs, running guns—you name the crime, he'll name his price."

More confused than ever, Cat tucked the envelope in the zippered section of her shoulder bag, next to Johnny's letter. She'd written to Cain and told him that she was coming to Saigon. And had received her unopened letter back stamped "Return to Sender." Now, on top of everything else, she had to worry about how her husband had gotten mixed up with some shady man for hire.

"Why haven't you arrested him?" It seemed like the logical question to ask, but the colonel's back stiffened.

"Because we haven't caught him with the goods." He looked like he couldn't wait to put the elusive Cain on the gallows and personally watch him hang as he added in an ominous voice, "Yet."

"Have you thought about setting him up?" She remembered the police doing that to one of her father's clients. And her father tearing the prosecutor's case apart in court.

His face went blank. "What?"

"You know, one of those sting op—"

"In case you haven't heard, Mrs. Brown," Howard replied in a tone that told her that his patience was fast running out, "there's a war going on."

Cat's own patience was none too plentiful at this point. She was so hot and tired and discouraged that she wanted to scream. Or throw something. Preferably something heavy, like that halved shell casing full of cigarette butts that was sitting on his desk.

"I'm painfully aware of the war, Colonel Howard," she said, struggling to keep her temper under control. "But even if I weren't personally involved, even if I weren't—to stretch the term some—a casualty of war myself, how could I *not* know what's going on over here when it's on the news at home every night in living color?"

"Damn television reporters have no respect for the military." He pulled a cigarette out of the pack in his shirt pocket, flipped open his Zippo and bent his head to the flame.

"Colonel—"

"Non-clotting, bleeding-heart liberals, every one of 'em," he sneered, snapping his lighter shut. "I've heard they've even taken to calling their daily briefings the 'Five O'Clock Follies'."

"Please—"

"It's not like our last two wars, that's for damn sure." Leaning back in his swivel chair, Howard blew a stream of smoke toward the lazily rotating ceiling fan. On the wall behind him hung a huge plastic-overlay map of Indochina on which battles were tracked in grease pencil. "I was still in high school when World War Two ended. And by the time I got to Korea, I was just another cop on the beat at the 38th Parallel. But back then the press was our ally, not our enemy."

"About Cain," Cat persisted through clenched teeth.

"Last I heard, the sonuvabitch had left Saigon," he snapped, and sat up straight.

His statement caught her like a cuff to the chin. "Left? When?"

"Right before the Tet Offensive."

"But that was in—what? Late January or early February?" She didn't recall the exact date when the North Vietnamese forces had launched their surprise attack against the South. She did, however, remember being glued to the TV with tears streaming down her face as she'd watched the flag-draped coffins of those brave Marines who had died defending the American Embassy being loaded onto a transport plane for the long trip home.

"It began on 31 January, the Lunar New Year." Howard's eyes turned flinty and smoke curled out of his flaring nostrils. "Seems to confirm what I've been saying about where that turncoat Cain's loyalties lie, doesn't it? His leaving two steps ahead of the Viet Cong?"

"And Johnny's letter is dated March 23." She had shown it to him first to help him understand why she was so determined to get in touch with Cain.

"Your husband was under a lot of stress when he wrote that letter, Mrs. Brown." Pulling rank, or perhaps simply dismissing her, he set his burning cigarette in the metal ashtray and reached for a briefing book on a corner of his desk.

"How would you know what kind of stress my husband was under, Colonel Howard?" Cat's voice dripped a scorn born of sheer frustration as she looked around his small but well-appointed office in the old French colonial bungalow that was now being used by the American military for administrative purposes. Taking in the comfortable furniture, sisal rugs and glass-fronted bookcases, she couldn't help but hear Drew repeating Johnny's scathing description of the commanders who were running the war.

Eyes bright with indignation, she returned her gaze to the one whose hand was frozen in mid-air just an arm's reach away from her. "'Saigon

Generals' like you sit behind a desk all day while men like my husband fight your wars."

"That's enough, young lady," he snapped, and stood.

"Yes, it is." She stood too, graciously unfolding her long legs, then shouldered her purse and spun on her heel. After opening the door to the reception area, though, she stopped and took a last look over her shoulder at Colonel Howard. With his crew-cut hair, neatly pressed khakis and shiny brass, he reminded her of one of those recruiting posters back home.

A trap, she realized with a sudden, bitter clarity. That's all those posters were. Just cleverly posed, professionally photographed traps meant to lure patriotic young men like Johnny into the deadly maws of war.

"I'll find Cain myself," she vowed. "And when I do—"

"Tell him for me that he's a goddamned traitor."

"Tell him yourself, Colonel Howard." She lifted her chin and let him have it with both barrels. "Or do you expect others to fight your verbal battles as well?"

A muscle rippled in his clean-shaven jaw but his voice remained calm. "Go back to Kansas City, Mrs. Brown, and get on with your life."

"What life?" she retorted.

"You're what"—he looked her up and down—"twenty?"

"Twenty-one." Her birthday, on February 11, had been the second one in a row she had spent without her husband. She didn't dare think about her first wedding anniversary or she might start crying—something she was determined not to do.

He glanced down at Johnny's file, which still lay open on his desk. "No children, right?"

She tightened her grip on the doorknob as a pang of regret struck deep into her soul. That Johnny had rebuffed her pleas to have a baby and insisted that she continue taking her birth-control pills was none of the colonel's business. "What's that got to do with anything?"

"You're young, you're unencumbered." He reached for the cigarette he'd left burning and took a drag. Exhaling smoke, he delivered the coup de grace. "You'll be remarried before you're twenty-five."

Cat reeled at his callous prediction. "Johnny's been reported as missing in action, Colonel Howard, not dead."

"Not yet."

"How can you say—"

"Go home, Mrs. Brown," he warned her again, "before you get hurt."

Only when Cat had spent her anger by slamming his door shut behind her, causing the young Vietnamese secretary sitting at the reception desk to look up at her in alarm, and then storming out of the air-conditioned building into the blistering early May heat did she realize what she had done.

Cain.

She had exhausted her last, best hope of finding him. And perhaps ruined all chance of ever learning why Johnny had wanted her to contact him in the first place. Tears stung her eyes at the realization, and a niggling little voice in the back of her head told her that she was probably a fool for not following Colonel Howard's advice about going home.

But she'd come too far to turn back now. She hadn't spent a fortune on long-distance calls or the better part of a month getting her visa to be so easily deterred. Nor had she resigned her student-teaching position to fly almost ten thousand long miles, hitting practically every island in the Pacific on her way, only to be stopped short of her goal by yet another rear-echelon desk jockey.

Cat slid on her sunglasses, her mind made up. She'd gone the official route—not once, but twice—and had found it barricaded both times. Now she was going native.

And she knew just the place to start.

She squared her shoulders and marched down the narrow walk, past a sadly neglected garden and dried-up goldfish pond, to the jumble of sandbags and concertina wire that had turned the small courtyard into a compound.

"Good afternoon, ma'am," said the MP who had checked her visa and had her sign the visitor's log on her way in. At first glance, he didn't look much older than her younger brother. But his ancient eyes, combined with that bandage on his neck and the M-16 slung over his shoulder, proclaimed him a veteran of war.

Cat was tempted to stop and ask him if *he* knew where Cain was, but she just acknowledged his farewell with a nod and kept moving. At the curb, she raised her hand to hail one of the cyclo cabs, a cross between a taxi and a motorbike, streaming along the street amidst the trucks and busses and jeeps. Then she changed her mind, dropped her arm and joined the swarm of pedestrians parading along the sidewalk. Her feet felt like melons in her square-toed pumps, but she was only a couple of blocks from her hotel. And she could use the time to plan her next move.

Despite the fact that the ravages of war were everywhere in Saigon, that its people were still reeling under the impact of Tet, the city continued to throb with its normal peacetime pursuits.

Take the Central Market, for example.

She'd gone there yesterday to walk off her anger after a dead-end meeting with that pompous, patronizing attaché at the American Embassy who'd kept calling her "honey" while he'd cleverly avoided answering her questions about Cain.

As she'd wandered from stall to stall, rubbing elbows with women in loose black peasant pajamas picking their way among fish and fruit, inhaling the pungent garlic and pepper aromas that permeated the air, and listening to the singsong exchanges between businessmen in immaculate white suits and merchants in soiled aprons, it had occurred to her that a person could buy everything from thousand-year eggs to turtledoves in elaborate bamboo cages.

Now she took heart from the idea that, for the right price, that same person could probably buy the most precious commodity of all—information.

Before she went shopping, though, she was going to cool off. She hadn't been outside even five minutes yet and already her hair was wilting, her makeup was melting, and sweat was pouring down her back and pooling between her breasts. Even the sleeveless mint-green skimmer that she'd put on only a couple of hours ago was wrinkled now from neck to hem.

Hang convention, she decided as she limped up Tu Do Street, a half-mile long avenue of carnal pleasures ranging from gaudy bars featuring blaring rock music to head shops to doorways full of Vietnamese prostitutes in miniskirts and white go-go boots hustling young American GIs in their filthy jungle fatigues or ill-fitting "civvies." It was too damned hot for pantyhose. And she had a pair of Capezio sandals in one of her suitcases that—

"Mrs. Brown?"

Cat was standing at the intersection, waiting for the traffic to clear so she could cross Le Loi Boulevard, when she thought she heard someone call her name. It was impossible to tell over the chain-saw buzz of the cyclo cabs and the gritty strains of "I Can't Get No Satisfaction" blasting out of one of the open-doored bars. Not to mention the clatter of those Huey helicopters overhead and the roar of that jet taking off from Tan Son Nhut Airport just a few miles away.

Her ears were probably playing tricks on her, she mused as she glanced first to her right, and then to her left. Either that or the ruthless rays of the sun had finally fried her brain.

"Mrs. Brown!"

There was no mistaking it this time. Someone really was calling her. Turning, she saw a petite Vietnamese woman running to catch up with her. While she looked vaguely familiar, Cat couldn't place her to save her soul.

"I'm sorry, Mrs. Brown." The pretty young woman spoke in both staccato gasps and perfect English tinged with a slight French accent. "But I wanted to talk to you, and I couldn't do it in the office."

"Who are you?" Cat asked when she paused to catch her breath.

"My name is Nguyen Kim Chi." She pronounced her first name *newyen.* "And I am—"

"Colonel Howard's secretary," Cat said in a burst of recognition.

The smile that curved the girl's lips revealed teeth as tiny and shiny white as the pearls at her ears. Her long, loose hair was black and silky-looking and her pale complexion was flawless. But it was her almond-shaped eyes, so dark and yet so sincere, that made Cat believe she could be trusted.

"As I was saying, Mrs. Brown—"

"My friends call me Cat."

"And my American friends call me Kim." She glanced around them warily, as if afraid someone might be eavesdropping, then grabbed Cat's arm in a surprisingly strong grip for someone of her size and pulled her back from the sun-drenched curb and into the shade of a building.

She rose up on tiptoe then and whispered, "I know where Cain is."

Cat gaped at her. "Where?"

"He was in Hanoi over Tet—"

"But that's the capital of North Vietnam!"

"Please believe me when I say that Cain is an honorable man. He helped me get my job, although Colonel Howard doesn't know that. More important, he asked nothing of me in return." The way Kim leaped to Cain's defense, combined with the look in her eyes, made Cat wonder if there wasn't more than just gratitude in the girl's heart.

Which was none of her business, she reminded herself firmly. "Where is he now?"

"He was wounded while he was in Hanoi—"

Cat's stomach clenched. "Is he all right?"

Kim nodded. "He's recuperating in Cholon."

"Cholon?"

"The Chinese quarter of Saigon."

Pulling the returned envelope out of her purse, Cat showed it to Kim. "So is this his address or not?"

"His old one."

Cat's fingers closed around a ballpoint pen. "And his new one?"

Now Kim shook her head, causing her long hair to swirl about her narrow shoulders. "I promised him I wouldn't give it to anyone."

"I won't tell—"

"But my oldest brother, Loc, drives a staff car for the American Embassy. Cain helped him find employment too, after his jewelry store was bombed during Tet."

A question flowered, full-bloom, in Cat's head. If Cain was as bad as

Colonel Howard claimed, how was he able to get these people such good jobs? She was still trying to come up with a plausible answer when she realized that Kim was looking at her expectantly.

She blinked and blew her drooping hair out of her eyes. Her tongue, when she ran it across her lips, told her that they'd long since lost the "Peach Petal" frost she'd applied that morning. And judging by how damp and sticky her underarms were, her Secret deodorant was turning tattle-tale on her.

"I'm sorry," she apologized. "The heat must be getting to me. Did you say something?"

"I asked you where you're staying."

"Oh, the Continental." Her father had made her reservation on his old reserve commander's recommendation. It was the hotel of choice for many of the American correspondents who were covering the war. It was also supposed to be one of the more secure buildings in Saigon.

"Loc finishes work at six o'clock, so he'll meet you in the lobby at six-fifteen."

Before Cat could ask Kim how she would recognize her brother or thank her for helping, the girl turned on her spiky high heel and ran back the way she had come.

Her "cool" shower had consisted of little more than a tepid dribble of water, her ceiling fan barely stirred the muggy air, and she didn't have any ice for the grape Kool-Aid in her glass.

And yet, being half-French, Cat was wholly intrigued by the almost seamless blend of East and West in the city that had once been touted as the "Paris of the Orient."

From the balcony off her hotel room, she could see the red-bricked twin spires of Nôtre Dame Cathedral. Johnny had mentioned attending Mass there in one of his tapes, and she planned to do the same if she was still here on Sunday. In the opposite direction, the phoenix-shaped roof of a Buddhist temple rose out of the surrounding rubble of the Tet Offensive.

Her room was high enough that she could, if she chose, watch the fire-and-light show of war in the distant hills. She chose instead to watch a huge freighter sailing upriver from the sea, toward the Port of Saigon. In its wake, junks and house barges bobbed and a fisherman angled for shrimp from a small sampan with a red eye painted on its bow to protect him from demons.

Closer to home, the lowering sun dimly penetrated the polluting haze of diesel smoke that hung thickly in the air and the heat that radiated off the shell-pocked pavement. But come the dark, Cat knew diners would crowd around tables at the outdoor cafés or into the tiny noodle shops that lined the boulevards and crammed the alleyways. The rooftop restaurants that specialized in venison steaks and French fries and front row seats on the ever-present violence in the streets would attract their share of patrons as well. And the neon lights would wink on along Tu Do Street as those Vietnamese bargirls smiled their enticing smiles at American GIs whose own smiles didn't quite reach their eyes.

A cacophony of screeching brakes and honking horns drew her attention to the street below.

Motor scooters whizzed in and out of the traffic to shouted curses and shaking fists. Jeeps and Army trucks claimed the right of way, drawing resentful looks from the automobile drivers who ceded it. At the corner, a Mercedes bus with screens bolted over its windows to keep out hand grenades wheezed to a stop, disgorging a blue-gray haze of exhaust smoke along with a knot of passengers.

The sidewalks were as busy as the streets. A woman carrying leafy produce in a net bag scolded a man toting a live pig under his arm. Shopkeepers stood in front of their stores, alternately smiling at passersby and scowling at the Vietnamese war casualties who sat on their haunches, hands outstretched, like a living version of the Stations of the Cross. Children wearing blue-and-white school uniforms wove their bicycles in and around the foot traffic as children the world over are wont to do.

"*Song voi,*" Johnny had called it, just shortly after he'd dropped the bombshell that he'd volunteered for a second tour of duty in Vietnam. "It means 'fast tempo'."

Then, Cat had been too dazed by his news to fully absorb his description of the city's frenetic pace. She'd sunk down on the wicker sofa she'd slip-covered in an avocado, rust and gold print for his homecoming and listened to him rattle on and on about the exotic place and the foreign people she'd only read about in magazines and newspapers or seen on a television screen. To hear him tell it, war-buffeted Saigon was a veritable Shangri-La.

"You sound like a man in love," she'd said when she finally found her voice.

Johnny had hesitated just long enough to make her wonder if he was hiding something, then had brushed off her remark by taking her in his arms and murmuring, "I *am* in love. With you."

Unfortunately, the memory of his tender lovemaking that night didn't alleviate her lingering guilt over their ugly fight the next morning. Or the fights that followed it. All it did was strengthen her resolve to meet Cain. And to ask him when, where, why and how he'd met Johnny.

The question was, would he have the answers she was seeking?

Cat had wrapped herself in a seersucker robe after her shower. Now she glanced down at her watch and saw that it was six o'clock straight up. Time to get dressed. She turned back into her room, making sure to close the louvered doors behind her before draining the last of her lukewarm Kool-Aid and setting the empty glass on the bureau.

In deference to the heat, she'd tied her hair back into a ponytail with a scarf and decided against wearing any makeup. Getting ready to go then was simply a matter of pulling on a gauzy yellow sundress that was hemmed just above her knees and slipping her bare feet into her sandals. And of checking to be certain that her suitcases were locked.

After dinner at the hotel's rooftop restaurant her first night here she had returned to her room to find the balcony doors ajar. Convinced that she had interrupted a burglary in process, she'd slammed the door and, eschewing the elevator, had run the four flights down to the lobby, screaming for the police all the way. A hotel security officer who had reminded her of a young Peter Lorre had accompanied her back upstairs and helped her search the room.

To her relief, nothing was missing. Nor was there anyone hiding in the closet, the bathroom or under the bed. But as he'd closed the louvered doors, the officer had cautioned her not to leave anything of value behind when she went out because the maids would probably come back while she was gone and steal it.

"The maids?" She'd found it difficult to envision the tiny, work-worn woman who'd furnished her with an extra towel to dry her hair as a thief.

"Like everyone else in Saigon," he'd said with a shrug, "they get by any way they can."

Now, shuddering at the thought of strangers pawing through her personal things, Cat put the keys to her suitcase in her purse along with her visa, her money and those two letters before she left the room to meet Loc.

"Mrs. Brown?"

While the Vietnamese man who greeted her when she stepped out of the elevator and into the lobby spoke with the same French accent as his younger sister Kim, he looked nothing like her. His hair was gray and cropped close to the skull, his skin had been baked to a leathery brown by the sun, and his smile showed betel-nut-stained teeth. Instead of the uniform of an Embassy driver, he was wearing a bright orange T-shirt with **DOW SHALL NOT KILL** printed on the front, baggy black pants and flip-flops on his feet.

"You must be Loc," she said.

He bowed his head, closing his eyes in a gesture of Oriental respect. "At your service, Mrs. Brown."

"Call me Cat, please."

Nodding, he moved his arm as if drawing aside a curtain. "Shall we go?"

"How far is it to Cholon?" she asked as she fell into step with him.

Loc's head swiveled as if it were mounted on a turret. The reporters had already left for their briefing, but the lobby was crowded with guests. Four silk-clad Oriental women were playing mahjong at a rattan table. A middle-aged man, dapper in white linen, was sitting on a plump sofa sipping red wine from a crystal stem-glass. GIs in clean jungle fatigues were standing around in small groups, swapping stories of battles lost and beauties won.

"It's best not to discuss our destination until we're in the car," he cautioned her under his breath.

"But why would anyone here care where we're going?" She lowered her own voice to a whisper, though, when she noticed a man sitting in a fan chair near the door. His face was hidden behind a newspaper, yet his cold weather attire—gray flannel suit and black wing-tipped shoes—made him stand out like a sore thumb in this tropical climate.

"People are not always who they seem in Saigon," Loc replied in that same undertone.

It was the second such warning that Cat had received since her arrival two days ago. No, she thought, remembering how Kim had contradicted Colonel Howard's vitriolic assessment of Cain, it was the third. All at once, she felt totally alone. And more than a little frightened. If what everyone was saying was true, she had no way to judge who were friends and who were enemies.

Loc led her out of the air-conditioned lobby and into the late-day heat. His '67 black Pontiac Tempest was illegally parked in front of the hotel, but his diplomatic license plate apparently gave him immunity. Or else the policeman at the intersection had been paid to turn a blind eye.

Cat had just stepped down from the curb to follow him around to the passenger side when she felt a tug on the hem of her skirt. Startled, she turned and saw a little boy standing right behind her. Except for the conical straw hat that shaded his shiny black eyes and the rubber sandals that shod his tiny feet, he might have been one of her former students.

"You buy?" The child peddler plucked a bright red balloon from the bouquet of balloons in his hand and held it out to her.

Before she could ask him how much the balloon cost, Loc stepped between them, angrily waving his arms and shouting at him in a rapid-fire barrage of Vietnamese.

His lower lip trembling, the boy turned and ran.

Cat scowled at Loc. "Why did you chase him off?"

His expression hardened as he opened the passenger door for her. "The Viet Cong use their women and children to kill Americans in Saigon."

"But it was only a balloon," she argued, still standing in the street. "And he was just a little boy."

"Last month another balloon seller—a girl, this time—asked an American soldier to hold her wares while she made change for him. The balloons, which had *plastique* explosives in them, blew up."

"Wha . . ." Her voice cracked and she cleared her throat. "What happened to them?"

The sadness in Loc's black eyes made her sorry she'd asked. "Both she and the soldier died."

Her stomach churning at the thought of Americans being so hated and innocent children being used for such evil purposes, Cat got into the car. "I'm sorry," she whispered when he swung in behind the wheel. "I had no idea that kind of thing was going on."

"There are atrocities on both sides in this war."

She wondered if that explained his T-shirt, which protested against the chemicals being used to defoliate the jungles where the Viet Cong usually hid, but didn't pursue it.

He turned on the ignition. Then he turned into a maniac. He threw the Pontiac into gear, floored the accelerator and rocketed away from the curb with a force that plastered her back against the front seat.

The drive from downtown Saigon to Cholon took less than ten minutes, but it was the longest ten minutes of Cat's life, with Loc flying through busy intersections, rounding corners on two wheels and careening across lanes like some berserk bumper-car driver at an amusement park.

"What's the hurry?" She gripped the armrest with one hand and the dashboard with the other, trying to brace herself as he hit another one of the potholes that cratered all the streets. In her peripheral vision, she could see huts fabricated of sheet metal, wood scraps and cardboard whizzing by. Through the open car windows she could smell the malodorous Ben Nghe Canal mingling with the aroma of a cabbage dinner cooking on a charcoal stove for some luckless family that lived along its banks.

"I need to be sure we're not being followed." He glanced into his rearview mirror, then did a one-eighty in the middle of the road, barely missing a truck carrying a load of chickens. Apparently satisfied that he'd done enough zigging and zagging and backtracking to lose anyone who was trying to tail them, he slowed to a crawl and turned onto a dim back street.

Cat's head was spinning crazily as Loc braked to a stop. Still glued to her seat, she breathed a sigh of relief and smiled over at him. Only to find herself facing the back of his head.

"Foreigners are not welcome in Cholon after dark." He continued staring out his window as he spoke.

Hearing herself called a foreigner, even though it was true in this instance, made her feel strange. She sat up with the intention of asking him if there was an alley they could use so no one would notice their coming and going. But peering across him and seeing the dump Cain lived in struck her dumb.

Chapter Twelve

t's six-thirty now," Loc said. "I'll pick you up at seven."

Cat blinked in dismay. "You're not coming in with me?"

"I have business of my own here in Cholon." He turned his dark eyes back to her. "And the less I know about your dealings with Cain, the better for me."

"Oh, of course . . ." Embarrassed to realize that she hadn't even considered the potential consequences of the risk he'd already taken on her behalf, she grabbed hold of the door handle and said as she alighted, "I'll see you at seven."

As the Tempest pulled away, Cat set her jaw firmly and started toward Cain's house. It was even more dilapidated than it had appeared from the curb—like something out of "The Munsters." Which made her wonder what he did with all the money he was earning from his criminal activities.

The white stucco exterior was stained with black mildew caused by the moisture from the nearby rice paddies, while the red barrel-tiled roof was broken and jagged in places. Some of the shutters were closed, others partially open, giving the house the air of an old unshaven drunk staring at her through half-closed eyes. A mangy yellow cat digging through the pile of smelly garbage that littered the courtyard hissed at her as she passed through a wrought-iron gate hanging rusty and broken on its hinges. And a beady-eyed rat crossed her path when she approached the front door.

No one answered her knock, but the door creaked open of its own accord.

"Cain?" She called his name into the dim interior, but got no response. Clearing her throat nervously, she tried again. "Mr. Cain?"

The chippering of a sapphire swift as it swooped across the sky was her only reply.

Maybe Loc had gotten the address wrong, Cat stewed. Or maybe Cain had left Saigon again. There was one way to find out, of course, but the idea of entering someone else's house without their permission—especially when she'd already been warned that she wasn't welcome in this part of town—scared her silly.

She dashed a trickle of sweat from her cheek with the back of her hand. Reached up and tucked in a tendril of damp hair that had escaped from her ponytail. Waved away an annoying fly. Then another one. Finally, she checked her watch and saw that she'd already wasted five of her allotted thirty minutes waiting for someone to answer her.

Forcing down her trepidation, she entered the house and stopped just inside the door. The sudden shift from daylight to gloom nearly blinded her. Long shadows cut a swath through the small front room and the shuttered windows admitted only enough light to limn the cracks in the bare walls and gild the dust motes drifting through the stale air. When her eyes finally acclimatized, she looked around.

And was horrified to see a man lying face-up on a cot in the middle of the otherwise empty room.

Cat's first thought was that he was dead. Despite the drugging heat, which the snaggle-bladed ceiling fan did nothing to dispel, she felt a sudden chill. She covered her mouth to keep herself from screaming and wondered if she should call the police. But there was no telephone in the room. And even if there had been, she couldn't have relayed her concerns to anyone because she didn't speak Vietnamese.

The man drew a deep breath and let it out on a loud snore.

Her shoulders wilted with relief at the realization that he was asleep, not dead. She laid her palm over her still racing heart. Then she took a tentative step forward. And froze when he fisted his right hand. Irritated at this new delay, she wasted yet another precious minute or two waiting for him to relax his hand before taking her last cautious steps toward the cot.

Up close, he looked more like a charity case than he did a soldier of fortune.

His muddy jungle boots hung over the end of the small bed, his fatigue pants were ripped up one long leg and a black patch covered his left eye. She wondered how he'd lost his eye, then remembered Kim telling her that he'd been wounded in Hanoi and was in the process of recuperating. Which probably explained that blood-soaked piece of white cloth tied around his right bicep. As well as the seeping cuts that criss-crossed his bare chest and flat abdomen.

There were other scars—a thin silver one that circled the corded column of his neck, a puckered pink starburst in his lean side—that read like a map of too many rivers run, too many jungle trails followed and too many brushes with the law.

But it was another, more deadly reminder that she had entered the netherworld that drew her eyes.

Her knees nearly gave way when she saw the pistol that had been shoved into the waistband of his fatigue pants. Given the nature of his profession, she assumed that he probably needed to keep it handy. Then again, he might just be trigger-happy.

How long she stared at the gun, Cat didn't know. But it suddenly occurred to her that if he woke up and found a complete stranger standing over him, he might shoot first and ask questions later. Her body jerked as if from the recoil and her heart pounded with fear. Still, determined to talk to him, she held her ground.

"Cain?" She whispered his name so as not to startle him into doing something rash—like pulling that gun. "Mr. Cain?"

He snorted and he snuffled, but he didn't wake up.

Refusing to think about the gun, she concentrated on his dirt- and

FRAN BAKER

sweat-streaked face. And felt a strange shiver pass over her from head to
toes. His shaggy black hair fell across his forehead, his nose was bold yet
finely chiseled, and his strong jaw was shaded with several days' growth
of beard. But it was his bowstring mouth that made her tingle. In a face
that was all lean planes, hard angles and five o'clock shadow, that tautly
drawn upper lip and sulky lower one were almost blatantly sexual.

He startled her into taking a step backwards when he began moaning
and mumbling and twitching restlessly as if he was either in the throes of
a nightmare or terribly ill. Reminding herself that he'd recently been
injured, she stepped forward again to see if he needed help. She bent
down, causing her ponytail to fall over her shoulder, and reached out a
hand to check his forehead for fever. Then she got a whiff of his breath.

And realized that he was drunk.

Oh, Christ, he'd died and gone to Donut Dolly Hell.

That was all he could think when his eye grated open and he saw the
shadowy face of the woman who smelled like Dove soap and sweet
dreams but who was staring down at him with the sort of repugnant
expression he'd had his fill of in an earlier life.

"Cain?"

He winced as her voice went through his head like a spear. Then he
winced again because it had hurt so damn much the first time. At great
expense to his pain threshold, he shifted a little on the cot and let his eye
droop to half-mast, trying to get a bead on her through the screening veil
of his lashes.

Not bad, he admitted. But not his type, either. With that bonfire of
hair and velvety-looking vanilla skin, she was too All-American girl for a
jaded half-breed like him. Still, she was quite a picture. Her eyes were
brown with a little green mixed in for good measure, her cheekbones
were sharp enough to cut glass, and her perfect nose belonged on a prom
queen. Her mouth . . . despite the disdain that puckered them now, he

would've bet his last piaster that her lips were full and—

"Mr. Cain!"

But her voice! God, it rapped his muddled consciousness like a judge advocate's gavel. He touched guarded fingers to the goose egg on his temple and groaned, "Go away."

She straightened, giving him his first good look at her slender figure and just a hint of her long legs, and snapped, "Not until you sit up and talk to me."

Cain thought about whipping out his .45, just to see her jump, but the knife-wound that those two bully boys had put in his arm last night was throbbing as badly as his head. It was small comfort to remember that he'd managed to do a little slicing and dicing of his own before it was over. Because right now he had another problem on his hands.

He fixed that problem with a ferocious glare. "If I weren't so sick—"

"Sick, my foot," she fired back. "You're drunk!"

No, he was hungover. Wrung out and strung out to beat the band. He'd spent the better part of last night swilling beer with his contact in Madam Wu's before ol' mama-san had sicced her boys on him. Now his mouth tasted like the cat had crept in, crapped and crept out, his teeth felt like they'd grown fur and his stomach was in imminent danger of emptying itself.

Hair of the dog, Cain decided groggily. That was what he needed. His taste buds perked up as he reached down under the cot and closed his fingers around the half-empty bottle of Ba Muoi Ba beer that he'd stuck there the night before, after he'd torn up what was left of his T-shirt to bandage his arm.

But no sooner had he raised the bottle to his lips with a shaky hand than Dolly snatched it away from him, held it out to her side and poured the rest of the warm bom-de-bom on the filthy tile floor.

"Hey!" he croaked, making a feeble but ultimately futile attempt to grab the bottle back. "What the hell are you doing?"

She dropped the empty bottle on the cot and smiled down at him as though he were a dolt. "I'm trying to get your attention, Mr. Cain."

Oh, she had his attention, all right! And if he hadn't been in such bad shape, she'd have had his hands around her throat, too. He scowled up at her, wishing he had the wherewithal to wipe that supercilious smile off her face.

Cat was no more enamored of Cain at this point than he was of her. From his undisciplined mane of hair to his mud-caked jungle boots, he looked every bit as dangerous and disreputable as Colonel Howard had declared him to be. She was sorely tempted to go find a pay phone and call the MPs. Tell them where this debauched specimen of humanity was hiding out so they could haul him off to the hoosegow.

But that would be tantamount to betraying her two new friends' trust. The police would want to know who had led her to him, and would likely detain her until she told them. Which could put Kim and Loc's jobs, if not their lives, in severe jeopardy.

And as galling as it was to admit, Cat needed Cain. He could glower and growl at her all he wanted. She really didn't care if he liked her or not. He was her only link to Johnny, and she'd gone to too much trouble and too much personal expense to retreat now.

She looked down at her watch and was disheartened to see that she had a little less than fifteen minutes left to get some answers out of him.

At the same time, he levered up on his good elbow and asked in a raspy voice, "In a hurry, Miss . . .?"

"Don't get your hopes up, Mr. Cain." She held out her left hand so he could see the simple gold band that adorned her tapered ring finger. "And it's Mrs.," she corrected. "Mrs. Johnny Brown."

In the past two years, Cain had perfected a near mastery over his reflexes. He'd learned to control his reactions in situations he'd never experienced before, and in others he hoped he'd never experience again. Which was a damn good thing. Because when his still-sluggish mind finally put a face to the name, red flags went up and alarm bells went off.

"Air Force, right?" With some half-million American soldiers in Vietnam, he wanted to be sure they were talking about the same Steve Canyon look-alike who had rubbed him the wrong way on more than one occasion.

"Right." Cat started to add that Johnny had graduated first in his pilot's class, then decided that was beside the point and let the single word stand.

Cain swallowed thickly against a wave of nausea, trying not to disgrace himself by puking all over her strappy little sandals. "Second tour, as I recall."

Now she gave him a bob of the head that he took for a nod.

He swung his legs over the side of the cot and sat up woozily. His head was hurting like a son of a bitch, which didn't improve his mood. But since neither his memory nor his vision was impaired, he didn't think he'd suffered a concussion.

"So," he said, smiling thinly, "how is ol' Johnny, anyway?"

Bridling at his sardonic tone, she replied more sharply than she'd intended, "He's been classified as Missing in Action."

"I'm sorry, Mrs. Brown." He was surprised to realize that it was the truth. Even though he'd never liked the guy, he always hated to hear that another American had gone down.

She tilted her head. "You didn't know?"

"I've been on the move." The dim light cast her face in shadows, but he could see the sadness in her eyes. With everything else that was coming down right now, though, he couldn't afford to feel for her. "When did it happen?"

"March 28."

"Have they found the plane?" He thought that was kinder than asking if they'd found the body. And he was sure that somewhere out there in that green hell of a jungle there was a body. Otherwise, he'd have been notified by now.

"Not yet." But she needed to call her parents when she got back to the hotel to see if they'd had news to the contrary.

"Did they say where he went down?" He'd heard through the grapevine that, despite their denials, the Americans had stepped up their bombing of the Viet Cong's infiltration routes from Laos.

She shook her head. "Over North Vietnam, I suppose."

"That covers a lot of territory."

"They also said he could be a prisoner of war."

Cain realized that she was asking him for a measure of hope, no matter how scant, that her husband was still alive. He couldn't bring himself to deny it to her. "There is that possibility."

"It's the not knowing . . ." Cat looked up at the water-stained ceiling, fighting to keep her emotions in check, then down at him. And uttered a small gasp. "You're bleeding."

He touched his arm, and his fingers came away smeared with red. "The bandage is coming loose."

She resisted a ridiculous urge to reach out and help him as he made an awkward, left-handed grab for one end of the makeshift binding. Weaving the way he was, it took him two tries to catch it. But then, when he bent his head and seized the other end in his mouth, it was more than she could stand.

"Oh, for heaven's sake." As she plopped down beside him on the cot, he peered up at her with that piece of cloth trapped between his straight white teeth. "Let go." She chucked him under the chin, ignoring the sandpapery rasp of his beard against her skin. "I'll do it."

"Be careful." He squirmed in apprehension when she set her shoulder bag aside and reached for the bandage.

"Sit still." Gingerly, she slid her index finger into the top loop of the knot and gave it a tug.

To his relief, he felt only a mild discomfort when it came undone. "So far, so good."

Cat finished unwrapping it, then felt herself blanch at the sight of the nasty gash in his arm. "You need stitches."

"Just tie the bandage back on, okay?"

"Have you seen a doctor?"

"I disinfected it myself." Cain tensed as she began dabbing at the blood that trickled from the wound with the cleanest end of the dirty cloth. But he needn't have worried. Her touch was as gentle as before.

"Disinfected it with what?"

"The beer you poured on the floor."

Cat gave him a retiring look. "Beer hardly qualifies as a disinfectant, Mr. Cain."

"Make do with what suffices, Mrs. Brown," he said dryly.

She frowned at the caked blood that had come away with the cloth. "Have you got a clean bandage?"

He let his gaze drift around the empty room, then twisted his upper body toward her, narrowing her field of vision to his broad shoulders. "Sorry, but I'm fresh out of clean bandages."

Quickly averting her eyes, Cat set about the business of rewrapping his wound. And felt her pulse leap when the backs of her fingers grazed the hard, bronzed bulge of his bicep. Telling herself it was the heat that was causing all these untoward reactions, she tied a square knot that would have made her old Girl Scout leader proud.

"Did this happen while you were in Hanoi?" she asked conversationally.

"No, it happened last night." He did a double take then that made his poor, sore head spin like a propeller. "And just how did you know I was in Hanoi?"

"I have my sources." Smiling smugly, she admired her handiwork.

He made a mental note to check them out. "So it seems."

"Then it happened here in Cholon?" she persisted, bringing him back to the subject.

"No."

"Oh?"

"It happened in downtown Saigon."

Startled, Cat looked up at Cain. And noticed for the first time that his eye was a pale gray, with a charcoal ring around the outer rim of his iris. Given the darkness of his hair and brows, his tawny, almost amber complexion, she had assumed that his eye would be dark as well.

"Where in downtown Saigon?" she demanded nervously.

"No place you're likely to frequent." His pirate's grin was anything but reassuring, however.

"Where?"

"In an alley behind a bar."

That figured, she thought, but only said, "I'd hate to see the other guy."

His grin curled into a snarl that was nothing short of feral. "Now that I've marked them, you'll recognize them easily enough."

"Them?"

"One is missing his nose—"

"You cut off someone's *nose*?"

"And the other one's ear."

Cat couldn't say which appalled her the most—the horrible injuries he'd inflicted on two other human beings, or his obvious relish in recounting them. Shouldering her bag again, she stood and looked everywhere but at him. "That should hold you until you can see a doctor."

Too late Cain realized that he should have kept his big mouth shut. He'd witnessed so much senseless violence and needless death since his arrival in Vietnam that he'd become inured to it. But all she knew of this goddamn war and the grisly counting of its toll was what she read in newspapers or watched on television, where the bodies with their faces blown away or their innards spilling out or their legs gone were always bagged before the cameras were turned on. And seeing her standing there, all stiff and guarded, he suddenly felt as if that knife had been plunged into his gut instead of his arm.

He stared up at her until she looked him in the eye again. "It was them or me."

"I'm sure it was," she responded tersely.

He felt like saying to hell with it and telling her that there were really two wars going on over here. There was the media spectacle where all the Walter Cronkite wannabe's in their khaki bush jackets spent their time heckling the generals who proclaimed it fitting and proper to die for one's country instead of talking to the grunts in the jungles and the mountains and the rice paddies who were doing the actual dying. And then there was the behind-the-scenes battle that was being fought against the growing force of North Vietnamese regulars who'd been seeping into Saigon since Tet to mingle with the Viet Cong and to kill those South Vietnamese who were working with and for the American "enemy."

Because that would prompt questions he wasn't at liberty to answer, though, he just cupped his arm and cocked her a smile. "Thank you."

"You're welcome." The words sounded stilted, even to her, but she relaxed her stance somewhat.

Silence fell, as sharp and crystalline as his eye.

"Tell me something," he encouraged her after a moment. "Why are you here in Saigon instead of back home in—"

"Because Johnny said I should contact you if anything . . ." To her humiliation, her voice began to quaver.

"And it never occurred to you to just write to me?" he asked quietly.

"I did." Cat unzipped her shoulder bag and fished out the letter from Johnny and the one to Cain. "But as you can see," she said as she handed them over, "you'd already moved."

Cain's expression hardened subtly as he scanned Johnny's letter. Given all he knew, that last sentence was almost laughable. Almost, but not quite. He didn't bother opening the envelope addressed to him on Truong Minh Gian, but just passed both it and the letter back to her.

"Let me get this straight," he said as she returned them to her purse for safekeeping. "When you got my letter back, you decided to hop on a plane and fly halfway around the world, into the middle of a war zone, to look for me."

She hadn't realized how imprudent it all sounded until he'd said it aloud. "Not exactly."

"Then what, exactly?"

"At first I was just going to write to you and leave it at that. But then my brother told me that one of the reasons Johnny volunteered for a second tour in Vietnam was because he needed to talk to you." She briefly recapped the sequence of events that had brought her to Saigon.

Cain's jaw locked tight as he listened. Damn that Brown for being such a blabbermouth. And double damn him for dragging his wife into this seething hellhole of plots and cabals and schemes. She was out of her element. Totally. Worse, she had no idea that what she was poking and prying into could blow up in her face.

"What do you want from me, Mrs. Brown?" he asked when she finally wound down.

She twisted the wedding band on her finger. "I want you to answer some questions for me, Mr. Cain."

The planes of his face shifted slightly, until his mouth hovered on the edge of a smile. "Why don't you drop the 'Mister'? Call me Cain."

She gave him another nod, and then she gave voice to her worst fear. "Is Johnny in some kind of trouble that I should know about?"

Cain pushed to his feet, towering over her own five-feet-seven, and pulled his Zippo and a hard pack of Swisher Sweets out of his pants pocket. He took his own time, lipping a cigarillo and lighting it with a spin of the wheel. Then he took a deep drag and blew the smoke out slowly before proffering the pack to her.

Cat shook her head and eyed him askance, waiting for him to quit stalling and start talking.

Truth was, he wasn't so much stalling as he was trying to come up with a way to deflect her questions without arousing her suspicions. Too many lies had already been told. Too many lives had already been ruined. There was no way he was going to add another name to the casualty list if he could possibly avoid it.

Squinting at her through the cigarillo's smoke, he answered her question with one of his own. "What makes you think he's in trouble?"

"I don't know," she admitted, frustration sharpening her voice. "I just have this feeling—well, you read his letter." The third paragraph, especially that last sentence, was burned into her brain. "It was almost like he had a premonition that something bad was going to happen to him and he was trying to prepare me for—what? Another woman, a divorce . . ."

Her gaze met his in a direct challenge. "You saw him last. You tell me."

Cain looked at her with grudging respect. He'd never been married. Had never even come close. But gut instinct told him that not many wives would have confronted the possibility of their husbands cheating on them with even half of her composure.

Too bad he had to ruffle her pretty little feathers.

"Sounds to me like you're more concerned about being dumped than you are about Johnny going down," he said derisively.

To her credit, she didn't flinch. Nor did she back off. She raised her chin defiantly and took a shot of her own. "Go to hell."

"I probably will, Mrs. Brown." He shouldn't taunt her like this, Cain thought. Shouldn't be so deliberately cruel. But dammit, he had to get her out of here before she got drawn into the danger that swirled about him like a deadly gas. "In the meantime, why don't you go home and wait to hear from the Defense—"

"Excuse me."

As one they turned and saw Loc standing in the open doorway, his anxious eyes darting between them.

"It's seven o'clock," he announced.

"Well, well, well." Cain pivoted on his bootheels to face Cat. "You do get around, Mrs. Brown."

She arched an eyebrow at him. "Colonel Howard sends his regards."

His laser-beam gaze homed in on her with what could only be called malicious intent. "If Kim loses her job because of you—"

"She sought me out and offered to help." Cat had the eerie sensation that Cain saw more with that one eye than most people did with two.

"That's true." Loc vouched for her from the doorway.

She smiled at him, then frowned at Cain. "You still haven't answered my question."

"Go home, Mrs. Brown," he said in a weary voice.

"It'll be dark soon," Loc reminded her.

"Oh, all right." Exasperated with the both of them, she stamped across the room.

Cain followed her out of his house and into that sorry excuse for a courtyard. The rat she'd seen on the way in appeared to have moved on to greener pastures, thank God. But that mangy cat, which had hissed at her, purred for him.

"I'm leaving now, but I'll be back tomorrow," she warned the barbarian at the gate. "And every day after that until I get some answers."

At the curb, Cain flipped his cigarillo into the street with a fillip before he rudely turned his back on her and began speaking to Loc—not in English or Vietnamese, but in French.

He had no way of knowing, of course, that French was practically Cat's mother tongue.

Clenching her teeth against a frisson of rage, she listened to him tell Loc to take her back to the hotel tonight and then see to it that she was on the first plane out of Saigon in the morning.

When the conversation ended, her compliant driver cut around the Tempest and, obviously assuming that she was right behind him, opened the passenger door for her.

"Mister . . . Cain." Still standing on the curb, she addressed him like a drill sergeant, with a *thousand-one, thousand-two* pause between the first and second words.

He turned. And saw her in a whole new light. The last rays of the sun struck her red hair and set it afire. Long auburn lashes curled over hazel eyes that sparkled with secret amusement, and a faint blush rode the high ridges of her cheekbones. Her parted lips were as full and soft as he had earlier bet they would be.

The need to cover those tantalizing lips with his own slammed through Cain. Everything in him prodded him to close the distance between them. To break his long self-imposed period of denial and satisfy the hunger that suddenly twisted his gut.

Savagely reminding himself that she was another man's wife—at least until she was formally notified to the contrary—he tipped his head and drawled in a deceptively civil voice, "Yes, Mrs. Brown?"

Cat waited a beat, savoring the anticipation, before reiterating in French that, like it or not, he would be seeing her again. "*Au revoir.*"

Chapter Thirteen

She awoke with a start at the hand that covered her mouth. "Don't scream, Mrs. Brown," Cain warned her, his voice low and urgent in the night shadows.

Still dazed from awakening to find him in her room, Cat nodded to let him know she understood.

"Get dressed." He tossed a pair of black peasant pajamas at her, then crossed to the closet. "You're leaving."

She swept her sleep-tousled hair off her forehead and pushed herself up on her elbows. From this distance, her uninvited guest was a formidable silhouette of dark shadows, dimly illuminated by the moonlight streaming in from the open louvered doors that she distinctly remembered closing before she went to bed. When he moved closer, carrying her sandals, the scent of soap that accompanied him told her that he'd showered since she'd left his house. She could also see that he was wearing a long-sleeved black T-shirt and a pair of button-front blue jeans with a knife sheathed at his belt and that familiar gun tucked into the waistband.

Which reminded her that she was wearing nothing but a thin white nightgown. She dropped her head back down on the pillow and pulled the sheet up to her chin. "I already told you, I'm not going anywhere until I—"

"Think again, Mrs. Brown." Cain contradicted her with a steely resolve that set her teeth on edge. "You're leaving in five minutes, clothes or no clothes."

Despite her bravado, Cat was beginning to feel that she was staring defeat in the face. "What's going on?"

"This place is about to blow."

Her jaw dropped in disbelief. "The hotel?"

"Saigon."

"Oh, my God!" Panicked now, she threw off the sheet and bounded out of bed. Then clutching the pajamas he'd thrown at her in front of her revealing nightgown, she backed into the bathroom.

"Leave the light off," he said when she reached to switch it on.

Cat got dressed in the dark. She hadn't thought to grab a dry bra and panties out of the bureau drawer, and the ones she'd hand-laundered earlier in the sink and hung over the shower rod were still damp. With time at a premium, she gritted her teeth and put them on. The thin cotton pajamas that Cain had brought for her were too short in the arms and legs, but they would simply have to do.

When she came out, he was standing at the balcony doors, watching flares dropping like many moons of pale gold around Saigon.

"I talked to my parents this evening," she said to his back.

He turned to face her, his brows pulled together in a scowl.

Cat cleared her throat, which ached from having cried herself to sleep after she'd hung up the telephone, and clasped her hands together in front of her. "The Air Force has officially changed Johnny's status to a Presumed Finding of Death."

Cain wasn't surprised by her news, but he was staggered by his own visceral urge to go to her and comfort her. There was nothing prurient in his sudden desire. She just looked so fragile, standing there with tears glittering in her eyes and her milk-white wrists and ankles sticking out of those black pajamas, that he simply wanted to take her in his arms. Smooth back her hair and press his lips to her brow. Hold her and offer her his shoulder to cry on.

But the don't-touch-me vibes she was giving off warned him that that would be a big mistake on his part, so he scotched the idea and asked her gruffly, "They found the plane then?"

"No, but they talked to another pilot in Johnny's squadron, and his report led them to assume—"

"Sometimes that's all they have to go on."

"'Presumed' . . . 'assumed' . . ." Her voice was breath and blood and heartache as she quoted the wishy-washy words her father had read to her over the phone. "How can they just leave people in limbo like that?"

He could have told her how. First they dropped the bomb, and then they dropped the ball. Instead, he regarded her with piercing intensity. "I take it you're not going home."

She lifted her chin determinedly. "Not until I get some answers."

A flare in the night sky lit up the room, revealing the adamant line of her full lips and the angry jut of his clean-shaven jaw.

"Let's go," he said harshly.

She dug in her heels. "What about my clothes and—"

"Kim will collect your things in the morning and keep them for you."

Cat glanced over her shoulder, out the open doors, when gunfire erupted in the street below. "How long are we going to be gone?"

"Ever heard of Lot's wife?" Cain taunted as he took a step toward her.

She turned her head back and looked up at him. He tilted his head and looked down at her. They stood so close she could feel his body heat, could smell his spicy after-shave mingled with a tantalizing hint of male musk, and she suddenly sensed that she was facing a far more devastating danger than any that could be found on the streets of Saigon. Only sheer determination kept her from backing down.

"Where are you taking me?"

"Someplace where you'll be safe."

"I'll go on one condition." She held his gaze until he looked away. Taking that as a concession, she stated her terms. "That you'll promise to tell me why Johnny wanted me to get in touch with you."

Knowing that she was going to regret it, knowing somehow that he would too, he reluctantly agreed. "You win, Mrs. Brown."

"Cat."

"What?"

"My name is Catherine, but everyone calls me—"

An orange fireball outside illuminated the room's interior with a hellish glow.

He grabbed her hand and yanked her toward the door. "Let's go, goddammit."

"Wait!" She pulled free of his grasp and backstepped to the bureau.

"Now what?"

"I need my purse."

Cain ground his teeth in frustration, wondering if he was going to have to resort to dragging her out of the friggin' hotel by her waterfall of red hair. "Peasant women don't carry purses."

"This one does." Cat snatched up her bag and hooked the strap over her shoulder and across her breasts so that she was wearing it like a bandolier. Properly armed, she caught his hand again. "Lead the way."

Brandishing the .45 and hugging the wall, he led her down the back stairs of the hotel. When they reached a side door, he jerked to a halt. Cautiously he poked his head out and surveyed the immediate area.

"Keep your head down," he warned her. "There could be snipers on the roofs." All but crushing the bones in her hand, he made a dash for the curb.

She put on the brakes and gaped at the vicious-looking motorcycle that was parked there. "Surely you don't expect me to ride—"

An explosion ripped through the night, changing her mind about their mode of transportation.

Numb with shock, Cat swung her leg over the padded seat. When she was situated, Cain climbed on in front of her. He reached behind him and took her hands in his, then folded them together just above his waist and pressed them against him.

"Hold on tight!" he shouted at her above the revving of the engine and the riot of gunfire.

She glued her front to his back and splayed her hands wide over his stomach, feeling oddly comforted when her fingers brushed the hard barrel of the gun he'd tucked back into his waistband.

The cycle bucked and shot forward.

Rockets and mortar fire shook the city as they rounded a corner and sped up the street. Buildings went by in a blur and people spilled out of houses, bars and hotels, crying and screaming at the top of their lungs. A three-wheeled Lambretta taxi, abandoned by its driver and filled with TNT, went up in a million lethal pieces. The eggbeater rhythm of American helicopters added to the noise and confusion as they swept down, guns blazing, like giant metal dragonflies.

Cat's head was buzzing and her mouth had gone dry. She'd never been on a motorcycle before, and there was something utterly terrifying about having only those two wheels between her and the macadam that sped past beneath her. Convinced that she was going to die before the night was over, she closed her eyes and said a silent but sincere "Act of Contrition."

When she opened her eyes, she saw an American armored personnel carrier rolling relentlessly toward them.

Cain saw it, too. He veered to the right and cut through a cemetery. But it seemed that even the dead weren't allowed to rest in peace in Saigon. As the cycle corkscrewed past tombstones inscribed "*Mort Pour La France*," it ran a gauntlet of machine-gun fire being exchanged between Vietnamese marines positioned on one side of the graveyard and Communist guerrillas dug in on the other.

A stray bullet shattered the glass that had previously been one of the bike's rearview mirrors.

They zipped out of the cemetery through an open side gate and onto a street where a small squad of Viet Cong was hoisting their blue and red and gold starred flag on a light pole, sniping at passing vehicles and holding a group of panic-stricken refugees at gunpoint.

"Hang on!" Cain yelled back at her.

Cat held her breath and hung on for dear life as he opened the cycle's motor to full throttle and flew by them all like an angry hornet. The hot wind whipped her hair about her face, making her wish she had a scarf, and the steady vibration of the motor thrummed up through her thighs and belly and breasts. Behind her, she could hear blood-curdling yells and gunshots popping as the surprised Viet Cong opened fire on them. Her ears rang and her heart pounded in her throat at the realization that her back was exposed to their bullets.

But they were either terribly poor shots or their bullets were no match for a target that was moving at warp speed.

"You all right?" Cain turned left, toward the river and away from the incoming fighter-bombers swooping low to deliver their deadly cargoes of high explosive on insurgents and innocents alike.

Too wilted to even ask where they were going, Cat laid her cheek against his back and nodded her head.

For all the chaos in the city, it was business as usual at the Port of Saigon. Ammunition dumps and fuel depots ranged far and wide. Jeeps and tractors raised a lot of dust. Stevedores, many of them female, carried bags of grain on their shoulders off a freighter. The trucks at the bottom of the gangplank would then cart them to the American bases in the field.

Cain slowed down as they approached the port. When he finally braked in front of a huge metal warehouse, Cat raised her head. And blinked twice when she saw a big sign tacked over its open double doors that said THINK RICE.

"There's no white potatoes over here," he explained after he cut the engine. "So they're trying a mind over matter strategy with our troops."

Her knees almost buckled beneath her when she climbed off the padded seat, and she needed a moment to get back both her breath and her bearings.

Cain didn't give it to her. Before she had time to regain her equilibrium, he clamped onto her wrist and towed her into the cavernous, floodlighted warehouse. Cat felt dwarfed by mountains of bags of cement and fertilizer and pyramids of boxes containing everything from roto blades for helicopters to cases of Seven Up. Beyond a pile of jukeboxes, a forklift truck stacked crates full of ammunition for pistols and submachine guns.

As if there wasn't already enough noise to wake the dead, someone had cranked a radio up to full volume and Ruth Brown was complaining in her black-and-blues voice, "*Mama, he treats your daughter mean.*"

Halfway through the warehouse, Cain reached into an open box with **WASHINGTON STATE** stamped on the side and picked up a couple of delicious-looking red apples. When they finally came to a stop in the back, he let go of her wrist. Then he took a bite out of one apple and held the other out to Cat.

She refused with a shake of her head. "You stole them."

"Sure did," he admitted, and took another bite.

"But they're supposed to go to our front-line troops."

"Not if rear-echelon bastards like Howard can divert 'em."

She gazed at him in mute astonishment for several seconds. "Are you telling me that our officers are stealing food from—"

"And they call *me* a thief." He tossed the core of he apple he'd scarfed down into an overflowing trashcan, then passed the one he'd taken for her under her nose, tempting her with its sweet-tart scent. "Think of it as the one that Howard won't get."

In a complete reversal of the transaction in the Garden of Eden, Cat took the apple from Cain. Then she bit into it. And found that it was as delicious as it looked.

"Hey, you one-eyed river rat!" a voice boomed from behind her.

She wheeled, wondering who could be so cruel as to mention Cain's affliction, and saw a mahogany version of Mr. Clean leaving a messy desk with a transistor radio sitting on it to lumber toward them. The man wore khaki swim trunks and thongs and the sweat of hard physical labor. A gold front tooth glittered in his wide, friendly smile but those massive shoulders and that sawed-off pump shotgun he carried gave fair warning that he wasn't a man to be messed with.

Instead of taking offense at the epithet, as Cat had expected, Cain stepped past her and stuck out his hand. "How ya doin', Tiny?"

Tiny's ham-sized hand engulfed his. "Everyone I can, man."

"Is the boat loaded?"

"To the gills."

Cat stifled a scream as a distant explosion shook the warehouse from the floor to the rafters. If she'd had a choice at that moment, she might have given up her objective and gone home. But it was too late and she was in too deep. She just prayed she wasn't in over her head.

Tiny scowled toward the open doors. "What's Charlie up to now?"

Cain raked a hand through his windblown hair. "Looks like Tet all over again."

"Oh, man, why don't they just give it up?"

"Maybe it's us who ought to give it up."

"Then I wouldn't have a job," Tiny countered. "And you'd be up sh—"—he glanced at Cat, then cleaned up his language—"the river without—"

Cain snapped his fingers. "Extra ammo?"

"You got it."

Another earth-shaking roar, this one closer than the last, caused the floodlights to flicker.

"Yeah," Cain murmured, "but have I got enough?"

Cat, tired of being treated as if she weren't even there and scared out of her wits by the encroaching explosions, tossed her half-eaten apple in the trash can, stepped between the two men and glared up at Cain.

"Is this the 'safe' place you were taking me to?" she snapped. "Because if it is, I have to tell you that I don't feel very safe."

The skin across his cheeks tightened as he met her seething gaze. He hadn't forgotten her, if that was what she was worried about. Quite the opposite, in fact. He remembered only too well how right it had felt to have her sitting behind him on the motorcycle. To have her breasts pressed against his back, her arms wrapped around his waist and her thighs cradling his hips. For the duration of their wild ride through the rebellious streets of Saigon, they'd been as close as a man and a woman could be without—

He pulled a frown. And his mind out of the big soft bed he'd like to get her in. "No, Mrs. Brown—"

"Cat," she reminded him shortly.

"No, Cat," he conceded, thinking that she looked like she was ready to sink her claws into him. "We've still got a ways to go—"

"Well then, what are we waiting for?"

"Good question." He flashed the peace sign, minus his index finger, at a grinning Tiny, who gave him the black power salute in return, then took her arm and steered her out the back door of the warehouse.

His doughty but aging French gunboat sat broadside to the wood-planked dock.

She was a beauty—and he always thought of boats, with their fluid lines, as females—if he did say so himself. He'd found her at an abandoned French junk base down near Vinh Binh. After giving her a whirl to make sure she was still seaworthy, he'd picked her up for a song. Then he'd spent a small fortune and cashed in every favor he'd ever extended fixing her up.

He'd filled her hull with foam, plexiglassed the wheelhouse, plated her engine area with ceramic and customized the muffler so it exhausted silently underwater. In addition to the turret-mounted .50-caliber machine gun she already carried, he'd added some extra firepower. He'd also devised a way to man his defenses from the helm. James Bond never had it so good. Because if necessary, Cain could control the speed of the boat with his right hand, steer with his left, and fire the bore-sighted .30-calibers or .106 recoilless rifles with a foot lever.

When he'd finished, he'd thought about painting her a pristine white. She would have stood out too starkly, though, on those dark nights that he needed to slip up or down the river after curfew, so he'd left her a weathered gray color, draped her guns with fishing nets for camouflage purposes and concentrated on fixing up the main cabin. He'd torn out the tiers of bunks the French colonials had used and replaced them with a small but efficient living area. And below that, in the hold—

"Permission to come aboard," Cat said in a saucy voice as they crossed the dock.

"Granted," Cain replied in that same teasing vein, and offered her a helping hand.

She caught the lines he tossed her as he jumped aboard. Then she just stood there, not knowing what to do with them. He coiled and stowed them before heading into the wheelhouse. The engines came on with a grumble she felt through the soles of her sandals as she stepped in behind him.

The moon was almost full and the stars were out in spades. He left off all the lights except the muted red ones on the instrument panel, not wanting to attract the attention of the Navy river patrols that were sure to come racing in to try and restore order. Frantic voices crackled over the radio net. He squelched them, wanting to maintain silence for safety's sake.

Using the built-in starlight scope, which sucked in all available moon- and starlight and painted the world the eerie green of penicillin mold, he scanned the waterway. Soon, he knew there'd be an entire flotilla of sampans and junks and house barges clogging it as they fled the chaos of Saigon. For now, though, it was clear sailing ahead.

A charge blew in a terrible, ear-splitting roar.

Cat stared at the orange fireball rising above the warehouse through the bulletproof glass that enclosed the wheelhouse, then turned back to him anxiously. "Will Tiny be all right?"

His gaze intent on the water, his profile backlit by fire glow, Cain nodded. "Pity poor Charlie if—"

"Who exactly is Charlie?"

"It's slang for Viet Cong."

"Johnny called them gooks. Or slants."

"I know." His voice was dry, and more than a little bitter.

Thinking of Kim and Loc now, she sighed. "I kept telling him that they're people, just like us, but—"

Automatic weapons fire burst out to the right, along the bank of the river, and she could see several men, small in the distance, shooting at their boat.

Cain steered left and sent her stumbling against him.

Cat suffered a slight vertigo when her breast bumped his arm. Attributing it to frayed nerves and lack of sleep, she righted herself and started backpedaling. "What should I do now?"

"Stay low. Go below." He glanced at her over his shoulder, carefully schooling his expression so it wouldn't reflect his own churning reaction to their brief encounter. "Brush your hair."

"Oh, Lord." She raised a self-conscious hand to the wind-snarled hair tangled around her face. "I must look like a witch."

Cain turned his attention back to the water before he could tell her how beautiful she looked against the backglow of fire. Or how much he admired her fortitude. He studied her reflection in the glass. Saw her bite her lip when a string of floating claymore mines blew along the bank. The coup must've scared the hell out of her—it had him—but she hadn't screamed or cried or fainted. Brass act that she was, she'd just hopped on, hung on and gone along for the ride.

Still standing behind him, she cleared her throat. "How do I go below?"

"The hatch is on deck."

"Hatch?"

"Two doors. A right and a left. Built into the deck." He met her hazel eyes in her reflection. "There's a head and a bed in the cabin."

"A head?"

"Bathroom."

Her eyes gleamed with relief. "Is there a kitchen?"

He nodded. "The galley, such as it is, is part of the main cabin."

"Would you like a cup of coffee?"

"How about a beer instead?"

Remembering how he'd wolfed down that apple, Cat smiled. "Is there stuff for sandwiches?"

Cain reached into a crevice of the instrument panel for the soapbox he stashed his cigarillos in to keep them dry and got one out. He wasn't going to light it, not now, but just having it parked in the corner of his mouth would help take the edge off. "Knowing Tiny, there're enough bologna and cheese slices in the refrigerator to feed the Big Red One."

"A beer and a bologna and cheese sandwich, coming up." She threw him a saucy salute, turned and dropped down on all fours.

He spun when she disappeared from his sight. "What the hell are you doing?"

"Staying low," she called over her shoulder as she crawled across the deck.

Good thing, too, because the concussion from the B-40 rocket that went throoming over their heads could have blown her overboard. Which reminded him . . .

"Hey," he hollered, "put these on while you're down there!"

Cat looked back. And got a face full of pantyhose. "What?"

"I said put 'em on."

"Why?"

Facing forward again, he noticed a little blip on the radar screen and bent his head to scope it out. "They'll keep the leeches off if you fall in the water."

"*Leeches?*"

"And there's mosquito repellent in the medicine cabinet."

Fruitlessly, she checked the pantyhose for size and some clue of their origin. "Where'd you get these?"

"Out of your drawer." Spotting a ferryboat cutting toward the east coast of Saigon about a hundred meters ahead, he eased his foot toward the firing lever just in case that sucker was loaded with Cong. And if the recoilless didn't sink 'em, he had a mini-gun he'd literally stolen out from under a navy commander's nose that would.

"My drawer?"

"While you were getting dressed." After getting a closer look at the passengers crammed onto the ferryboat, he retracted his foot, idled the motor and let it pass unassailed. Even if everyone on board had suckled at the breast of Ho Chi Minh himself, he didn't get off on killing women and children. "I stuck them in my pocket and forgot I had them until just now."

Scalding color rushed to Cat's cheeks at the thought of Cain's hands on her lingerie. Which was ridiculous. Her room had been dark, so he couldn't have actually seen anything. Still, just knowing he'd touched the lacy bras and silky panties that had lain atop the pantyhose made her go hot all over.

Another flash of bright light, followed by a thunderous *BOOM*, had her groping frantically around on deck for the hatch doors. She found them, flung them open, then took a quick, backward look at the fireball in the sky over Saigon before slamming them closed. A lantern and matches on a beveled ledge lit her way down the metal stairs and into the cabin.

To her surprise, it was all spit and polish and shine.

The small galley sink and two-burner stove were spotless, the brass on the wall lamps at the head and foot of a bunk that appeared to double as a sofa shone in the lantern's light, and there wasn't a speck of mold in the shower.

Cat used the cramped bathroom to brush her hair, put on the pantyhose she hadn't planned to wear again until she got home and spray herself liberally with mosquito repellent, then headed back to the galley to make Cain a sandwich.

Halfway across the cabin, she stumbled over a woven bamboo throw rug that lay in the middle of the floor, kicking it askew. Bending to straighten it, she found another hatch—one that appeared to lead down to a lower level—beneath it. Curious, she tried to open it. And discovered that it was locked.

Colonel Howard's words—*Smuggling drugs, running guns*—came back to her with such a sudden haunting clarity that she glanced up to be sure he wasn't standing over her wearing an I-told-you-so smirk.

A chill raced up Cat's spine as she hastily straightened the rug and stood, wondering what she should do next. She had literally placed her life in Cain's hands. Without him, she had no chance of surviving the coup. No hope of ever finding out what his connection to Johnny was, either. So like it or not, they were essentially comrades in arms. What she hadn't planned on, though, was becoming his partner in crime.

She crossed to the sink and peered out the galley porthole. Fire still rained down on Saigon from American planes and gunships. The Viet Cong continued to reply with machine guns, mortars and rockets. She saw a great flash, and then she saw a helicopter spinning, spinning, spinning toward the ground.

And where was she while it was all going down? Trapped on a river of terror with some rogue warrior who was wanted for treason! Worse, she had nobody to blame for her current predicament but herself.

"When will she ever learn? When will she e-ver learn?" As she paraphrased the refrain of the popular folk song that Johnny had considered little more than antiwar propaganda, Cat hung the lantern from a hook over the sink and set about the business of making Cain a sandwich.

True to his prediction, the compact refrigerator held two packages each of bologna and cheese slices. An unopened carton of milk lay on its side, next to a container of eggs that she trusted weren't of the thousand-year variety. The tiny pantry boasted bread and mustard along with a whole host of cellophane-wrapped chocolate cupcakes with white squiggles of icing on top. Plastic silverware and paper plates sat on the bottom shelf. Under the sink was a wooden ice chest with an opener hanging from one handle by a string and, inside, at least a dozen bottles of beer.

Leaving the lantern on the ledge at the top of the stairs, she carried the beer and the meal she'd slapped together into the wheelhouse. The worst of the flames from demolished buildings and the smoke from white phosphorous shells appeared to be behind them now. But God only knew what lay ahead.

"Here you go." She set the plate on the instrument panel.

He took the beer. "Got your sea legs already, huh?"

"Growing up, I used to water ski at the Lake of the Ozarks every weekend."

"Your parents have a sport boat?"

"And a lake house." She smiled with remembrances of golden times. Before they were tarnished by war. "That's where we were when Johnny . . ." A pang that was becoming all too familiar tightened her throat. She looked down, wishing she'd never brought the subject up.

"When Johnny what?" he prompted softly.

She raised her head and met his gaze. "Proposed to me."

A strand of hair had blown across her lips. Cain gripped the wheel hard with both hands to keep from reaching over and brushing it aside. "Sounds like a real nice memory."

"Yes." Cat hadn't thought of it in quite that way before. She smiled a secret little smile that told him she'd temporarily left him and this whole hellacious scene behind. "Yes, it is." Then she tucked that tempting strand of hair behind her ear and widened her smile to include him. "Thanks for reminding me."

What the hell was going on? he asked himself. He should be focused on the mission, and the mission alone. Instead, he felt himself being pulled, tugged at, by the woman standing beside him. A woman who no more belonged in his world than he did in hers.

"You're welcome." Disgusted at himself for letting her get to him, he scoped the water again, almost wishing Charlie would pull out of one of the myriad canals that fed into the river and pick a fight with him.

"And for rescuing me." She was still amazed at how instinctively she trusted him. With that raven hair and black eye patch, he looked like a pirate, a man who not only attracted danger but also actively courted it. Yet she felt completely safe with him.

He gave her that half-smile again, the one that just barely curled his lips. "It was either take you with me or leave you there to talk the Viet Cong to death."

Ignoring his gibe, she squinted at the riverbank and saw nothing but unrelieved blackness. "Where are we, anyway?"

"We just passed Shanty Town."

"Wherever that is."

"The last and largest slum on the outskirts of Cholon."

"We're going south." It wasn't a guess; she'd glanced at the compass.

"Very good." His plan was to tool a few miles down river, then find a safe berth in some little canal off the beaten path. Since Charlie favored the night, he figured they were better off traveling by day.

"I got an A in geography," she said smugly.

He bit back a smile at the sudden image of her in a parochial school pinafore, starched white blouse and saddle shoes. "Then you can navigate."

Cat yawned and looked over at Cain sheepishly. "Sorry. It's been a long night."

"And it's not over yet," he said, watching white tracers arc across the sky.

She glanced at her wrist and realized she'd left her watch on her bed-side table. "What time is it, anyway?"

He checked the clock on the instrument panel. "Almost three."

"And we left the hotel—"

"A little after midnight."

She yawned again. "It seems like days ago."

He took a drink of beer. "Why don't you go below and get some shuteye?"

"You believe Johnny is dead, don't you?"

Her question caught him off-guard, like a Surface-to-Air missile at ten thousand feet. For a moment he was dumbstruck. He studied her in pro-file. She was the picture of calm, staring out the glass. But like the river, he knew, she was roiling beneath.

"Lots of guys have come walking out of the jungle after a crash that should have killed them." He couldn't tell her that he was living proof of that. Not without blowing his cover. If he closed his eye, though, he could still see the doctor looking down at him sympathetically and saying how sorry he was that they couldn't save the other one.

"But?"

"They're the exception, not the rule."

Feeling her control starting to frazzle, she lowered her head and looked at her hands. Later she could grieve. But now, not knowing what waited around the next bend, she needed to keep it together.

"I guess I'll go lie down for awhile."

"I could be wrong, you know."

She raised her head and smiled, but her heart wasn't in it. "Good night, Cain."

He stared down at her for a long reflective moment before he turned his attention back to the river. "Good night, Cat."

Chapter Fourteen

ood morning."

"What time is it?"

"Why?" Cain grinned at her over the mug of coffee he'd poured from the pot on the stove, his eye gleaming like polished silver. That was the only thing about him that could even remotely be called "polished," though. His hair was rumpled, his clothes wrinkled, and a night's growth of dark stubble shadowed his jaw, carving intriguing hollows in the planes of his face. "Are you playing 'Beat the Clock'?"

"Very funny," Cat sniffed as she swung her legs over the side of the bunk and sat up. Then she shoved her own disheveled hair out of her eyes and squinted at him. She'd only meant to lie down for a few minutes, to cry for a little while, and had never dreamed that she would actually go to sleep. But the rocking of the boat and the rumbling of the engines had been so soothing that she'd just drifted off. And had slept like the proverbial log.

Now the sun was peeking through the porthole, almost blinding her with its brightness, and the smell of freshly perked coffee filled the cabin.

She breathed in its delightful aroma. "Is there enough of that to go around?"

"Sure is." When she made to get to her feet, he waved her to remain where she was and set his own mug aside. "I'll get it."

"Oh, thanks." She planted both palms in the small of her back and arched it, stretching her cramped muscles.

"Milk or sugar?" he asked her over his shoulder.

"You have sugar?"

What he had was a small pink-and-white box of cubes in the pantry, which she'd apparently overlooked the night before. "One or two?"

"Two, please." It felt strangely intimate, watching him pour and stir sugar into her morning coffee. She squirmed, discomfited by the thought, and wished that she'd just gotten up and done for herself.

Waiting on her didn't seem to bother him in the least, however. To the contrary, he appeared happy to do it. He was neat too, sponging off the counter after setting the pot back on the burner and replacing the box in the pantry. Much neater, she mused, than—

Mentally Cat sprang erect. There was no comparison between Johnny and Cain. None whatsoever. Johnny was her Blue Angel, while Cain was . . . She skimmed her gaze over the unruly hair, the broad shoulders that stretched the seams of his T-shirt, that tough, street fighter's body. Cain was the devil's own.

"One coffee, two sugars." He caught her studying him from behind when he turned to face her. For an instant their gazes locked, reinforcing the feeling of intimacy that had so flustered her only seconds ago. Then that buccaneer's grin curled his mouth, and he handed her the mug.

Flushing slightly, she smiled her thanks and took a sip. The sweet, steaming liquid scalded her tongue, but she wouldn't have spit it out if her life had depended on it. Feeling as if she'd swallowed a flaming sword, she racked her brain for something—anything—to say.

"I didn't hear you come down this morning," she finally managed.

"I washed up, but I figured showering and shaving would be pushing it." The sunlight caught his wide, white smile in his beard-darkened face.

She looked away from that disturbingly attractive smile. "Did you get some sleep?"

"Couple of hours." He'd backed into a narrow canal, out of the line of fire, and had gone below to see if she was all right. She'd been curled up in a ball on his bunk, the silvery paths of her tears streaking her pale cheeks. Before he could do something stupid, like bury his face in her copper-penny tangle of hair that provided such a striking contrast to those black pajamas, he'd gone back up on deck and stretched out on the portside bench. And had awakened with an erection like a telephone pole.

"Where are we now?"

"About thirty miles south of Saigon."

"How much farther do we have to go?"

"You're a regular Baby Snooks this morning, aren't you?"

Back on familiar ground, Cat tossed him a cheeky smile. "Keep that up and I won't offer to make you breakfast."

"You can cook, huh?"

"I make a mean cheese omelette."

"A cheese omelette I can handle." Leaning back against the sink, Cain took another sip of his cooling coffee and eyed her across the cabin. "But mean"—he shook his head and smiled slowly—"it's way too early for mean."

He was coming on to her, she realized, and felt herself go cold all over. And she, a married woman, was coming right back at him. Blocking out an unbidden image of Johnny's serious face, she pushed to her feet

"I'll wash up, and then I'll fix us something—" Her voice broke, and though she turned away quickly, he saw the tears spring to her hazel eyes.

He saw the ghosts, too. The husband who had disappeared without a trace and the life she had planned with him shredded by the winds of this stinking war. Vexed, he topped off his coffee and headed for the hatchway.

"I'll be topside if you need me for anything." And she would need him, he told himself. Before this ended, she would need him as much as he was beginning to need her.

Cat felt so hot and sticky and smelly that she decided to take a shower. In lieu of shampoo, she washed her hair with soap. After she'd toweled off, though, she was in a dilemma as to what to put on. She couldn't force herself to wear her underclothes again until she'd rinsed them out in the sink, so she settled on the pantyhose and black pajamas.

She combed her hair and left it loose, figuring the sun would bake it dry. Found toothpaste in the medicine cabinet, next to the mosquito repellent, and spread some on her index finger to brush her teeth. Then, praying that the bra and panties she'd left hanging on the only towel rack got dry before Cain needed to use the bathroom again, she went back out into the cabin and whipped up their breakfast.

The heat and the humidity that greeted her on deck staggered her almost as much as the tricolors he was flying.

"What's with the French flag?" She'd almost dropped the paper plates and plastic forks she was carrying when she saw it hanging limply from the mast that speared up into the bleached blue sky.

Cain smelled his soap on her skin when she entered the wheelhouse and decided that the second—okay, the third—best route to a man's heart was through his nose. Nodding his thanks, he took the first and dug in. "I found it when I was tearing this baby apart and figured it might come in handy someday."

Since Johnny had left, Cat had eaten most of her meals alone. Now, even though it meant she had to stand, she opted for company. "But given the hundred years of bad blood between the French and the Vietnamese, isn't that a little like waving a red flag in front of a bull?"

He swallowed and shook his head. "Not this week."

She paused with her fork halfway to her mouth. "Why not this week?"

"Great omelette, by the way."

"Thanks."

"Nice and fluff—"

"The French flag," she reminded him.

He savored the last bite. Swallowed it reluctantly. "Charles de Gaulle said something the other day that really pissed off the Americans. Now he's back in Charlie's good graces."

"Charles de Gaulle?"

"The president of—"

"And the leader of the Free French during World War Two."

"You certainly know your French history." The language too, he recalled with a rueful smile.

"I ought to."

"Why's that?"

"My mother is French. She met my father during World War Two, and they were married in Paris."

Finished eating, he set his empty plate on the instrument panel. "Ah, that explains the cheekbones."

She tilted her head back just as he turned to look at her. "Whose cheekbones?"

His smile deepened as he took her plate from her limp fingers. "Yours."

"Mine?"

"Accents *grave*"—his forefinger grazed first her right cheekbone, then her left—"and *aiguè*."

Shivers chased over her skin. At the same time, the air in the wheelhouse grew heavy and thick, making it hard for her to breathe. Thrilled yet terrified by the tenderness of his touch, she stepped back on legs that had jellied and looked past him.

Cain read the fear on her face and blamed himself for putting it there. "I'm sorry, Cat, I shouldn't have done—"

"There's someone out there." She said it so softly that it took a few seconds for her words to sink in.

When they did, his pulse hit a lick and his nerves sang to life. He heard it now, the sucking sound of footsteps in the murky rice paddy that lay just a couple of klicks beyond the canal. Viet Cong returning from their hard day's night in Saigon, he wondered, or Americans tracking them down?

Panic beat like bat wings in Cat's throat when six Vietnamese guerrillas wearing pith helmets stepped up onto the bank, which was covered with knee-high saw grass, and pointed their guns at the occupants of the boat. Their faces were young, but sinister. All had the menacing expressions of men who weren't afraid to either kill or be killed.

"I can see— Oh, God—they've got—"

"Don't go off the deep end on me now, for Christ's sake." Cain's voice was low but harsh and brooked no argument. "Just do exactly as I tell you—no questions, no complaints—and we'll be fine. Understand?"

She made herself breathe in, breathe out, slow and normal. "Yes."

It was too late to curse himself for not getting an earlier start, Cain thought, as he pivoted on his heel and saw the guerrillas' hostile faces. Or for not locking and loading instead of fooling around with Cat. He only hoped it wasn't too late to talk them out of plugging him full of holes. God knew what they would do to her if they killed him.

Because he was smart enough not to do anything stupid in the name of heroism, he yanked the .45 out of his waistband and twirled it, presenting her with the butt of it. "Do you know how to shoot this?"

She took it, surprised at how heavy it was, and gripped it with both hands as she looked at him fearfully. "No. I—I've never even held a gun before."

"Lai day!" The tallest of the VC, who seemed to be in charge of the small squad, waved his Soviet AK-47 in an impatient come-here gesture.

Realizing he didn't have time to give her more than a quick lesson, Cain said, "Just point it at their balls and shoot." He grinned crookedly then. "If it'll help improve your aim, pretend it's me."

She answered with a sickly smile of her own. Then she watched, her stomach churning, as he stepped out of the wheelhouse and approached the rail with his hands raised. He'd dropped anchor in the middle of the canal. That was smart, she realized, because the guerrillas would have to swim if they wanted to confront them physically. Distance, however, was no barrier against their bullets.

Cat had no idea what Cain said when he spoke to them in Vietnamese, but was relieved to see the guerrilla leader's sneer turn into a smile. Then he pointed to the French flag he was flying and said something else in a vicious tone that caused all three of them to burst out laughing. Obviously relaxed by the "hail fellow, well met" atmosphere, he pulled a cigarillo and his Zippo out of his jeans pocket and fired up.

That prompted their leader to make a new demand.

Cain spoke to them in Vietnamese again, then addressed Cat in English over his shoulder. "Lay the gun on the floor and go below. In the drawer under the bunk, there're some cartons of cigarettes. Lucky Strikes and Chesterfields and Salems. Bring me a couple of each."

Knowing that he was fraternizing with the enemy, had probably even cursed America's presence in their country, didn't keep her from racing across the deck and down the hatchway to do as he'd ordered. She'd been so tired and depressed last night that she hadn't even noticed the drawer. Now, as she pulled it open with shaking hands, she discovered that it contained several dozen neatly stacked cartons of cigarettes.

Tell him for me that he's a goddamned traitor.

Colonel Howard's words rang in her ears as Cat slammed the drawer shut and carried the cigarette cartons back up on deck. Her arms loaded, she moved toward the rail. Cain threw his burning cigarillo into the stagnant brown water, where it drowned with a sizzle, then took the cartons from her and tossed them, one by one, to the guerrillas on the canal bank.

Their leader still wasn't satisfied, however.

He glanced at Cat speculatively, gestured at first himself and then her, and said something to Cain.

Despite the sweat that was beading on her face and pouring down her back, Cat froze. She might not understand the language, but she understood perfectly well what that leer on the leader's acne-scarred face meant. He wanted her.

His followers smiled their hearty approval of the suggestion.

To her relief, Cain replied with a negative shake of his head and an unequivocal, "No."

Cat relaxed her guard too soon. Whether Cain was simply taking advantage of the situation or trying to emphasize his point with the VC, she couldn't even begin to guess. But when he pulled her into his arms, tipped up her chin with a callused thumb and dipped his head, she knew exactly what he was going to do.

"Sorry," he said softly just before his hard mouth captured hers in a kiss.

Shudders coursed through her, liquid and hot, as his lips moved over hers. A whimper of protest issued from her throat and her hands made a futile attempt to push him away. She pressed her lips together tightly, trying to deny him access to that which he sought so avidly.

But his mouth was as skillful a thief as he was. It slanted against hers, taking her breath. It gentled on hers, winning her trust. Then it opened over hers, robbing her of the will to resist.

Her fingers clutched the front of his T-shirt and her head fell back. An aching deep inside her yawned wide. Her lips parted and his tongue arrowed home with a force that licked at her thighs, her stomach, her breasts. A tremulous sigh shook her whole body as feelings she'd thought she'd buried came flooding back. His heat seared her through their clothes. She welcomed it, wanted it, nurtured the flames it ignited in her.

Cain pulled back once to look at her face, saw himself in the cloudy depths of her eyes, and then his mouth crushed down on hers again. He hadn't meant for things to go this far. Had merely intended to show those stupid bastards that they couldn't have her. But now that he'd touched her, now that he'd tasted her, he couldn't let her go.

The sun beat down on them with fiery fists as he angled his head to deepen the kiss. She tilted hers, the better to accommodate him. Her world careened when he used his tongue to make slow, sweet love to her mouth. Her senses reeled when he cupped her derriere and pulled her higher and harder against the front of his body. She clung to him dizzily, her fingers sinking into the long, straight strands of his hair and surrendered to the power of his lingual persuasion.

Cat had never received such a blatantly erotic kiss. Not even from Johnny. Had always held something of herself back. Even from Johnny. Now guilt pierced her to the core at the realization that she'd given her all to Cain, and she shrank away from him. There was fire in him like nothing she'd ever experienced before, and she wanted to put it out before it was too late.

"Stop," she pleaded, batting at his hands and backpedaling to put some distance between them. "Please, stop."

His breathing was so harsh that it was several seconds before he could speak coherently. "What's the matter?"

"What's the matter?" she repeated stridently. "I'm married to another man, that's what's the matter!"

Ignoring the boiling cauldron churning in his stomach, he lashed back with, "A man who's officially presumed—"

"Don't say it!" She knew in her heart that it was true, and yet she wasn't ready for such a truth. "Presumed is a hell of a long way from confirmed."

Cain stood silently for a moment, watching her struggle with her emotions. He wanted to turn away, but forced himself to face the pain in her eyes. The pain he'd put there, he reminded himself in disgust.

"This is all my fault." He dragged a repentant hand through his hair. "I instigated it. You have nothing to feel guilty about."

Her face burned, as much from shame as from the scrape of his beard. "You still don't get it, do you?"

"I guess I don't," he admitted, his own ire rising now. "Why don't you tell me?"

"I'm as much of a traitor to my husband as you are to your country!"

The instant the words left her mouth, Cat wanted to snatch them back. She'd always had something of a temper. A sharp tongue on occasion, as well. Her father blamed it on her red hair, while her mother claimed it was because he'd spoiled her rotten. But she'd never intentionally hurt anyone before the way she had Cain just now.

And she *had* hurt him. She'd seen it in his bleak expression right before he'd turned his back on her. Saw it yet as he stood motionless at the rail, staring out at the bank. His feet were braced a shoulders' width apart. His hands, balled into fists, were held rigidly at his sides.

He'd risked his life to save hers—not once, but twice in less than twenty-four hours—and she had repaid him by calling him one of the vilest names in the English language.

True, she had incriminated herself as well. And deservedly so. She was still married. Still didn't know for sure if her husband was dead or alive. Still wondering if he might be lying wounded in a prisoner of war camp somewhere, so delirious with malnutrition or disease that he was unable to contact her.

Yet she had kissed another man. Gloried in his heat and passion and hunger. Tasted the violent urgency of his need. And then she had pointed the finger at him because he'd aroused that same need in her.

Now her conscience prodded her to go to that man and apologize, to beg his forgiveness, but her throat was so thick with guilt and with grief that she wasn't sure she could get the words out.

Cain was cursing himself up one side and down the other. He'd been called a lot of names in his twenty-seven years. Some he'd cultivated because they'd suited his purpose at the time. Still others he'd shrugged off, chalking them up to peoples' ignorance. But there was one name that he couldn't tolerate. One slur that could set him off like a SAM. The hell of it was, it was the same name that suited him to a T right now.

He was a bastard.

Not in the literal sense of the word, of course. His parents had met in the eye of another storm in another country, had married over both their families' and their societies' objections, and had welcomed him, their only child, into the world on a day that lived in infamy yet. The years that had been allotted to them had been painfully short but poignantly sweet. His father had died first, a fallen hero in a forgotten war. Then his mother, who'd suffered so many slings and arrows and indignities that it was a miracle she could function, had succumbed less than a year later to a broken heart.

But the fact that his parents still lived in his memory didn't make him any less of a bastard. He'd violated the sanctity of another soldier's marriage. It didn't matter that the soldier had been a philandering SOB. That was water under the bridge. Or that his wife's loyalty to the vows she had taken was about to be put to the ultimate test. That was her problem, not his.

His problem was with what James Lee Cain had done. And what he'd done had been inexcusable. He could only hope that what he was going to do next might right that grievous wrong.

Because from this moment on, he was keeping his mitts off Mrs. Johnny Brown.

He'd been standing at the rail, staring vacantly at the grassy bank. Now he blinked and scrubbed his hands over his face. And saw that the Viet Cong guerrillas who'd been there only moments ago had retreated back into the rice paddy from whence they'd first appeared.

"Guess we fooled them, huh?" he asked Cat over his shoulder.

When she didn't answer, he turned away from the rail and saw that she too was gone.

"You'd better put on a hat," he said when she came topside a couple of hours later, "or you'll be fried to a crisp."

Cat paused just outside the wheelhouse, surprised by his cordial tone. She'd never felt so humiliated or so furious in all her life as she had after their argument. She'd gone below, intending to throw herself on the bunk and sob her heart out. Instead, too agitated to lie still, she'd wound up pacing the cabin, cursing herself for a colossal fool. Cursing Cain, too, for making her feel like one. When she'd finally gotten her act together, she'd come back up to apologize and to take her lumps. Only to hear that he was concerned about her getting sunburned.

"I don't have a hat." She didn't even have dry underwear yet, though she wasn't about to mention *that.*

"Pop the lid on the portside bench." He lit a cigarillo. "There ought to be some in the storage area underneath it."

There were at least a half dozen conical straw hats stacked on top of each other.

Cat plopped one on her head and carried another into the wheelhouse for Cain. "You've gotten a little sun yourself."

"I was roasting in here, so I took off my T-shirt," he said as he pulled the hat low over his brow.

She'd noticed. In fact, her mouth had gone dry at the sight of the sweat-slicked, sun-baked muscles rippling in his lean back. To avoid staring temptation in the face, she focused on the river, which flowed by them like a giant spill of chocolate milk.

"Would you like something cold to drink? A beer? Some water? We've still got ice cubes in the—"

"You know what I really want right now?"

Baffled, she looked back at him and cocked her head. "What?"

He flicked her a glance. "I want you to quit beating up on yourself."

"I'm not—"

"Yes, you are."

She frowned at him, hating the fact that he could read her so clearly. "Yes. I am."

He blew out a stream of smoke, pleased that he was finally one up on her. "Now, how about that cold drink?"

Nodding, she turned to leave the wheelhouse. Then turned back in confusion. "What just happened here?"

His eye glinted like pewter under the brim of his hat. "You don't know?"

"I know that I came up here to apologize for calling you a—"

"I've been called a whole lot worse."

"By who?" Or was it *whom*, Cat wondered. Like her father, she could never remember—

"By myself."

Her mouth opened in a small o.

Cain was tempted to chuck it closed, but kept his hands firmly on the wheel. "I think I'll have a glass of milk."

"Milk?" she echoed blankly.

"And one of those chocolate cupcakes," he decided.

"Cupcakes?"

"You eat the other one so it doesn't go moldy."

Amazed, she went below to get milk and cupcakes for two and brought them back up.

"Your arm looks better." But she still winced when she looked at the red gash from which he'd removed the binding.

He grinned. "Nothing like a little beer to chase the germs."

"Drink your milk," she said primly.

"Yes, mother."

She gave him a look that told him he was pushing his luck.

"*Chin, chin.*" Cain raised his glass and, seeing her blink in confusion, explained, "That's the Vietnamese version of 'bottoms up.'"

Cat went him one better, lifting her glass to touch his and toasting his health in French. *"À votre santé."*

"I'll drink to that," he agreed, and did.

"So," she said, sensibly averting her gaze from the frothy milk mustache on his upper lip to peer out the plexiglass window from under the brim of her straw hat, "where are we?"

Chapter
Fifteen

They were in the Mekong Delta, which was as rich in people as in rice. It was also rife with Viet Cong. They generally played their lethal game of hide-and-seek by night, and they always played by their own rules. Mines could lurk under innocuous-looking water weeds. Vertical bamboo triggers could be concealed in swatches of tall grass. The soft ground of the jungle could hide punjy spikes—booby traps made of a rusty nail dipped in excrement, which could penetrate rubber boot soles, go right up through the foot and cause a nasty case of gangrene.

There was death in the delta. Swift and vicious and tragic, it bided its time on a maze of rivers and streams and canals. But now, late in the golden afternoon, there was a simple joy in survival.

Small villages, where people lived in shacks-on-stilts to protect themselves from the flooding that accompanied the monsoon rains, dotted the river's banks. A smell of charcoal drifted from a nearby bamboo fishing boat. Those food-bearing trees that hadn't been defoliated by napalm bombs were heavy with coconuts and mangoes and bananas.

"It's funny."

"What's funny?"

Cat was watching a group of laughing children who were taking turns sliding down the back of a big gray water buffalo soaking itself in the shallows of the river. There were three boys and two girls, none of whom appeared to be older than nine or ten, and they were having a ball. Sitting in wooden lawn chairs on the bank, out of reach of the sun's last glaring rays, their recently bathed mothers kept a careful eye on their offspring as they gossiped and giggled amongst themselves.

She turned back to Cain and saw by the smile that curved his lips that he'd been observing the pastoral scene as well. "To look at those children playing, you'd never know they were living in a war zone."

He frowned as it suddenly struck him that there were no male villagers in sight. This was, after all, the time of day when entire families—fathers included—came down to the river from the rice paddies to wash off the sweat and the grime of their day's labors before taking their evening meal. But seeing not a single man among the bathers told him they were either sleeping off their killing spree from the night before or getting rested up to launch a new one tonight.

"By this time next year," he cautioned her, "those kids will probably be killing Americans."

"Maybe the war will be over by then," she said optimistically, and went back to watching them at play.

"Yeah, right. And maybe General George Armstrong Custer will come back to share a peace pipe with Ho Chi Minh."

Ignoring his sarcastic comeback, Cat smiled yet again when a young Vietnamese woman lifted her baby out of a basket to carry him into the river. Then she wanted to cry when she saw that the baby had no legs. She turned her head away, wondering if her heart could stand any more of these terrible blows.

"My parents rarely talked about their war." She looked down at her feet, which were bare. They'd swollen in the heat and humidity, so she'd kicked off her sandals. Her pantyhose were riddled with runs—which would have made them fodder for the trash had she been at home—but she didn't even consider removing them now. "They both told me at separate times, though, that what bothered them most was seeing children hurt."

Cain heard the sadness in her voice and wanted to reach over and put his arm around her shoulders. But he kept his mind on the mission, his eye on the river and his hands to himself. "Children always suffer the worst in a war—whether it's from food shortages or disease or the loss of a parent."

"My mother's grandfather was a doctor, and she told me about helping him treat a little boy whose house had been bombed by the Germans." As she spoke, Cat watched a stork with about a six-foot wingspan swooping along the riverbank looking for a place to land.

"He was burned?" Cain knew that, as painful as it was for her, she needed to talk about the baby she'd just seen. Otherwise, it would fester inside her like an infected wound. The hell of it was, he thought, she was going to be seeing a lot worse before this was over.

"Yes, terribly."

"Did he live?"

"He lived, but . . ." She sighed and shook her head.

"But what?"

"Poor baby, he'd lost his sight."

Cat didn't even stop to think about what she was saying. She just blurted it out. Embarrassment, hot as the sun, climbed her cheeks as she looked over at Cain, trying to gauge his reaction. She wished the deck would open up and swallow her when she saw the defensive set of his jaw.

"I'm sorry if I hurt your feelings," she murmured, with a catch of undiluted emotion in the words.

"You didn't." But his voice sliced through hers like a razor.

She reached over and laid her hand on his forearm, ignoring the way his muscles knotted beneath her touch. "Were you in an accident?"

He couldn't tell her how high he'd been flying when he'd lost his eye, so he nodded curtly and said, "Yes."

Cat got the message. Subject closed. Over and out. Move on to something else. Before she could make another stupid blunder, she retracted her hand and searched for a more suitable topic of conversation. She finally latched onto food, which seemed like neutral territory.

"What shall we have for dinner?" she asked. "Bologna and cheese or . . . bologna and cheese?"

Cain relaxed his tense posture when she pulled back. Her gentle touch had gotten to him as nothing else could. She was the cleanest, most decent thing that had come into his life in longer than he could remember. And for just a minute there, he'd been tempted to let her see the man behind the mask.

"How about grilled shrimp?" he suggested.

She gaped at him. "Grilled—"

"With fried rice, of course."

"Fried—"

"And for dessert"—he kissed his fingers like a gourmand—"grapefruit sorbet."

"It sounds wonderful." Her stomach growled in agreement. "But just where, pray tell, are we going to find a feast like that?"

He cut the boat's engine and pointed. "A couple of klicks that way."

Cat looked around them then and saw that Cain had put into a small, peaceful cove. Behind her was a lush peninsula that appeared oddly untouched by war. Grapefruit trees reached for the sunset-red sky and velvety green plants that she couldn't even begin to name grew in their shade. Orange firecracker flowers flourished in rich soil cooled by the river.

"Where are we?" she asked him.

He doffed his hat and wiped the sweat off his brow. "Put your shoes back on and I'll show you."

Fear feathered down her spine as she stared into the dense growth behind the lovely plants. The longer she looked, the darker and more dangerous it appeared. It was a jungle out there. A jungle full of the kinds of creepy, crawly things that gave people nightmares.

"What's a klick?"

"A kilometer."

"Two klicks . . ." She did the math in her head. "That's a little over a mile."

"Maybe it's only one," he temporized as she began backing away from him.

"You go eat shrimp," she encouraged him in a high, strained voice.

"I'll stay here and have a sandwich."

He started to tease her about chickening out on him, until he saw the distress signals flickering in her eyes. Then he hastened to assure her, "There's nothing in there that will hurt you."

"No leeches?"

"You're wearing pantyhose."

"Bugs?"

"A few mosquitoes, maybe, but you've got on repellent."

"Snakes?"

"I have a gun and a knife."

She paled drastically as her imagination began running wild. "I can't go into that jungle, Cain."

"Listen to me, Cat," he began, his gaze softening.

"No!" She all but sobbed the word. "I hate bugs! I hate snakes! I hate—"

He caught her shoulders and shook her gently. "Stop that."

But terror had her in its clutches now. "I hate you!"

"I can handle that."

"I mean it!"

His face was grim as he looked at her. She'd stood up to so much without turning a hair that he hadn't expected her to fall apart like this. But she was becoming more frantic by the minute, and they were running out of daylight. "Cat, please—"

"I despise you!" Tears dripped down her cheeks as she jerked free of him. Panic rose in her at the thought of what could be waiting out there in the wilderness. She tore off her hat and sent it sailing across the deck. "And I hate this horrible place!"

Since reason wasn't working, Cain weighed his other options. He could slap her. Not real hard, but hard enough to bring her back to her senses. Or he could break his vow and take her in his arms.

He decided on the latter, pulling her close and hugging her tight. "We've come this far together," he whispered into the fiery curtain of her hair. "Now let's get off this goddamn boat and go the rest of the way."

"I hate the dark," she said hoarsely. "I don't know why, but I always have."

"It's sunny on the other side."

She let out a shaky breath. "And I hate being alone."

He gave in for an instant and pressed his lips into her hair. "I'm here."

Cat buried her face against his broad chest and burrowed in. He smelled of sweat and man and strength, and she wanted him to hold her forever. She wanted him to keep her safe. To protect her from the dangers that lurked in the jungle and the awful surprise that she suddenly sensed lay just beyond the—

She stiffened in his arms and asked achingly, "This has something to do with Johnny, doesn't it?"

Cain would have given his good eye at that moment to be able to reply with an unqualified "No." But that would be a lie. And after all the hell she'd gone through to get here, she deserved the truth.

"Yes." His throat felt like raw meat when he answered her. "This has everything to do with Johnny."

"Is his"—she couldn't bring herself to say the word *body*—"Is he there?"

He tightened his embrace, knowing what it had cost her to ask. "No."

"Then why should I—"

"Because"—it came to Cain like a bolt out of the blue, the answer that had been eluding him ever since she'd showed him that letter—"Johnny wanted you to."

She swallowed hard. "You think so?"

"I know so." He didn't have time to explain it to her, not yet, but it made perfect sense to him now.

She stepped back on legs that felt as brittle as sticks and clenched her hands together to keep them from shaking. As hard as she willed it, though, she couldn't stop her chin from trembling. "Okay, I'm"—when her voice threatened to break, she drew in a fortifying breath—"ready."

He didn't smile, but there was a faint softening of his hard features. "Let's do it."

While she went down to get her purse and the can of mosquito repellent, he pulled his T-shirt back on and tucked a couple of cigarillos behind his ear. He locked the hatch doors when she came back up and pocketed the keys. Then he flipped a rope ladder over the rail.

Cat forced her mind to go blank as she followed Cain down the rungs and into the thigh-high water. Refused to think about what it was that brushed against her leg when she began wading toward shore. Ignored the mud that oozed up over the soles of her sandals and squished between her toes.

At the edge of the jungle, he stopped and looked back at her. "I can't cut us a path because I don't want to leave a trail."

"I understand," she said woodenly.

"Grab hold of my belt and hang on tight."

Like a robot, Cat did as he ordered.

Cain wished there were a better way to do this. "And keep your eyes on my back at all times."

She shivered and looked away from him, telling him that she wasn't quite as immune as she appeared. He reached back, cupped her chin in his hand and brought her head around. Then he kissed her hard and quick for luck before leading her into the jungle.

A triple canopy of trees closed out the light, enveloping Cat in the heart of a darkness that utterly terrified her. But she had Cain to hold onto, and that's exactly what she did. She kept a death grip on his belt loop and her eyes trained on the solid shadow of his back.

Vines snatched at her hair like living fingers. She shook them off. Creatures stirred and birds squawked, causing her pulse to race and her breath to heave. Something cold slithered past her feet. Gnarled tree roots tried to trip her up. She stumbled, but she didn't fall. The sharp-bladed undergrowth slashed at her legs. She stayed the course.

"I made it!" was all she could manage when she saw the light change. She gulped out a sob as it brightened and dropped to her knees in the grass. *Real* grass, she marveled, soft and shimmering velvety green in the late-day rays of the sun.

Cain sat down beside her and began unlacing his boots. He yanked them and his socks off. Then he rolled up the legs of his jeans, took the can of mosquito repellent out of her purse and started hosing himself down.

"Don't look," he warned her just a tad too late.

"Oh, my God!" Cat placed a hand over her mouth to keep from retching when she saw the leeches, big and blue, that were falling off of him in droves.

"I should have grabbed a pair of your pantyhose for me, I guess." He got to his feet and unbuckled his belt, then undid the top button of his jeans.

"You, uh . . ." She stammered a bit when he reached for the second button. "You have leeches in . . . there, too?"

His silver-and-steel eye twinkled mischievously in the gathering twilight. "And I'm not wearing any underwear."

Neither was she. Her bra and panties were still hanging damply in the bathroom on the boat. Cat ducked her head and saw that the front of her black pajama top was clinging to her breasts, outlining their small but firm shape. Her eyes swung back up in time to catch Cain looking at her, and her cheeks turned a warm pink at the realization that his gaze had followed hers down.

She surged to her feet and turned her back. "Tell me when you're done."

While she waited for him to finish spraying the leeches, Cat studied the two-story white-stucco villa that crowned the small hill they still had to climb. It was, in a word, breathtaking. Pink coralvine splashed its arches and violet bougainvillaea climbed its walls. Tamarind trees, their limbs as graceful as those of a ballerina, shaded the terrace and the gardens.

"All done," Cain announced.

She nodded at the house. "Who lives there?"

"Come on." He extended his hand. "I'll introduce you."

"An old French planter?" she guessed as she tagged after him.

"Nope."

"A government official?"

His long legs ate up the ground, forcing her to walk faster than usual. "Wrong again."

"Well, it has to belong to somebody important."

"It does."

"Otherwise," she concluded breathlessly at the top of the hill, "it would have been bombed by now."

Cain crossed the flagstone terrace and rang the bell. A large crucifix fashioned of ivory and wood hung over the door. Nailed to the frame opposite the bell was a small font of holy water.

A church, Cat decided as she dipped her fingers and made the sign of the cross.

The diminutive woman in the starched white habit who answered the door told her that she was close. It was a convent. And the way the nun's little raisin of a face lit up when she saw the man who was standing there also told her that he was no stranger in the night.

"James Lee." She spoke his first and middle names with a lilting French accent.

Cat, who'd never heard him called anything but Cain, swiveled her head in surprise.

"*Soeur* Simone," he said respectfully.

"We've been waiting all day for you, young man." Even as the petite nun shook an admonishing finger in his face, her expression said she was more relieved than angry.

He bent to kiss her on both cheeks. "I was delayed by the coup in Saigon, but I'm here now."

"We prayed for safe passage for you when we heard about it on the radio."

He straightened and smiled. "Somebody up there must have been listening."

Sister Simone reached up and laid a soothing palm on his cheek. "He always listens, my son."

Cain opened his mouth as if to argue the point, then closed it with a click of his teeth.

The nun turned friendly brown eyes to Cat. "And who have you brought with you?"

She stepped forward and introduced herself in French. "*Je m'appelle* Catherine Brown."

"Mrs. Johnny Brown," Cain clarified for the nun's benefit.

Sister Simone's eyes went wide with surprise for a second, making Cat wonder if she'd known Johnny. Before she could ask, the nun recovered her equanimity and ushered both Cain and she inside. The tiled entry provided a cool respite from the tropical heat.

"Welcome to *Sacré Coeur*," the nun said formally.

"Thank you," Cat said, her gaze drawn to the lovely painting of the Sacred Heart of Jesus that hung on the wall and for which the convent was named.

"Where is everyone?" Cain asked.

"*Soeur* Francoise and *Soeur* Marie took the older children fishing, and—"

"Children?" Cat interrupted.

The nun looked at her quizzically. "James didn't tell you?"

"Tell me what?"

"This is an orphanage."

Wondering why he'd kept her in the dark, and what other surprises he might have up his sleeve, Cat pivoted on her heel and arched a quizzical brow at Cain. "No, he didn't tell me this was an orphanage."

Caught between the devil and her demanding hazel eyes, he took the easy way out. "Why don't we discuss this after we eat?"

"You would like to wash first, no?" the nun asked.

"Yes, please." Cat smiled tiredly and lifted her heavy hair off her neck.

"You use the bathroom down here," Cain said. "I'll use the one upstairs."

"Come, *mon enfant.*" The brown rosary beads cinched at her waist clacking every step of the way, Sister Simone drew Cat along the hall, around a corner and into a thoroughly modern bathroom.

Cat couldn't help but smile when she saw the child-sized sink for washing grubby hands and faces that stood beside the adult-sized one. A bathtub with built-in shower fixtures sat along the back wall. Two doors, one with a low knob and the other a high one, guaranteed privacy for the people big and small who were using the commodes. An open window covered with a voile curtain overlooked the back yard.

"Do I have time to take a quick shower?" Even if she had to put her dirty clothes back on, she was dying to feel clean again.

"But of course." Sister Simone opened the linen closet and took out two fluffy white towels. Before she closed the door behind her, she added, "And while you're doing that, I'll see if I can find you something else to wear."

The water was cool, the soap ninety-nine and forty-four one-hundredths percent pure, and the baby shampoo promised no more tears.

Cat wasn't sure about that last, but she knew that she would never take the convenience of a real, honest-to-God bathroom for granted again. She used one towel to dry her body and wrapped the other one turban-style around her head. Then she rinsed out the pantyhose that had kept the leeches off of her, resigned to putting them back on wet if she had to.

Sister Simone knocked politely on the door.

"Come in," Cat invited.

But respectful of her modesty, the nun only cracked the door open and reached in, then remained standing outside. "I found this *ao dai* and a pair of trousers that one of our girls left behind. She was tall and thin, like you. I brought you some thongs, too, since your sandals are still wet."

"Oh, thank you." Cat accepted the pale green gown, black trousers and thongs as gratefully as if they were *haute couture*.

"I pray they fit."

"I don't care if they're high-waters. Anything's better than those dirty pajamas."

"'High-waters'?" Sister Simone repeated in a low voice.

"Oh, it's an American expression." Cat stepped into the trousers and was delighted that they were long enough to cover her ankles. The *ao dai* was a perfect fit, as were the thongs. "It means too short."

"You studied French in school?"

"My mother is French." Cat found a plain black comb in the medicine cabinet and ran it through her hair. "She met my father during

World War Two."

"I met an American boy during the First World War." The partially closed door lent almost a confessional quality to the nun's quiet admission.

"You loved him?"

"Very much."

"Why didn't you marry him?"

"He died at the battle of Verdun, and I became a Bride of Christ."

"My husband died here, in Vietnam." It was the first time Cat had uttered the agonizing word that she'd turned her mind from these past five weeks.

"He was a pilot, no?"

"Yes." Almost dizzy with relief now that she'd gotten out the anguishing acknowledgment, Cat grabbed the edge of the sink with both hands. The grief, she knew, would come later. And after that, she prayed, there would be peace.

"I heard one of your officers say once that a good soldier is just a klick away from God."

Because the nun had pronounced it "*kleek*," it took Cat a second to get it. When she did, she smiled wanly. "Johnny loved to fly."

"And you loved him?"

"All my life, and with all my heart."

"But you never conceived a child."

"Johnny wanted to wait."

Sister Simone sighed wistfully. "I wanted children."

Cat's smile was equally wistful. "You have the orphans."

"And James."

"James?" Cat echoed, frowning. "Oh, you mean Cain."

"Every month he brings food and clothing for the children from Saigon on his boat," the nun explained.

Food and clothing he'd probably stolen, Cat thought uncharitably. "That's kind of him."

"He bought us this house, too, after our orphanage in Saigon was bombed during Tet."

What was he trying to do—buy his way into heaven? Cat wondered scornfully. "Who owned it previously?"

"A distant cousin of the former President."

"He was fleeing the country?"

"Actually, James traded airplane tickets to Thailand for him and his family in exchange for the house."

"So he really wasn't out any money?"

"Which is more valuable—money or life?"

"Cain's done well by you," Cat conceded as her vile sentiments gave way to a wave of guilt.

"He remembers how it feels to be an orphan."

Cat hadn't thought anything could surprise her anymore. She was wrong. "Cain was an orphan?"

"His father died in the Korean War, and his mother shortly thereafter."

"Another war, another tragedy."

"When men lose the ability to converse with one another," the nun returned gravely, "they start killing each other."

Bitterness clogged Cat's throat. "And women are left to wonder what happened to the lives they had planned."

"God has a plan for you, as he does for us all."

A teary-eyed Cat touched the trembling lips reflected in the mirror. "I feel so lost."

"He'll show you the way, if you'll only let him."

"He'd better hurry," the woman in the mirror muttered. "Because I'm drowning here."

Beads clicked in the silence following her statement. Glad shouts drifted in through the open window from the back yard. The nun sighed again then.

"It's sad, *n'est-ce pas?*"

Her ears ringing with the high-pitched giggles that were coming closer every second, Cat shook her head in confusion. "Sad?"

"How many children those young warriors leave behind to be raised by strangers."

It hit Cat then like a fist, almost doubling her over. Her temples were pounding and her palms were sweating. She rubbed at her eyes, scrubbing away at a truth she didn't want to face, fighting to hold back a sob.

"Soup's on!" Cain hollered down the hall.

"But you're having shrimp, not soup."

"He . . ." Cat sucked in a deep breath, as if oxygen could wash out the hurt. But it still hurt. Hurt so badly, she wanted to cry. "He means dinner is ready."

"You Americans have such strange expressions," Sister Simone tsked.

"Don't we, though?" Cat turned away from her stunned reflection in the mirror and crossed to the door.

Cain, who had showered and shaved himself, was blown away when she entered the dining room. Her red hair flowed to her shoulders, the gossamer *ao dai* was split to her slender waist, and the plain black trousers made the most of her from-here-to-eternity legs. The thongs showed off the high arch of her foot and her peach-frosted toenails.

But on closer inspection, conducted by the light of the chandelier, he saw that she appeared to be upset about something. Her color was too high and her eyes were shiny with unshed tears. She was biting her lip, which he'd already learned was a sign that there was a storm brewing inside her.

He pulled out a chair. "Sit down before you fall down."

She remained standing. "I'm not hungry."

"You need to eat."

"I said I'm not—"

"Then sit here while I—"

"Why didn't you tell me this was an orphanage?" Her legs began to tremble, and she groped with frantic fingers for the back of the chair he still held out for her.

"Cat, honey . . ." Unaware of the endearment that had sprung so naturally to his lips, Cain reached over with a stabilizing hand.

"Don't touch me!" She lurched away from him angrily.

He immediately lowered both his hand and his voice. "All right."

"And don't call me 'honey'."

"I hear you."

He heard the children now, too. The older ones were coming in the back door, laughing and shouting and bragging about the frogs and small fish they'd caught in the pond behind the house. And the freshly bathed babies upstairs were starting to fuss for their bedtime bottles.

Seized suddenly by a rage so fierce that she was afraid she might hit him, she backed up another step. "What does this damned orphanage have to do with Johnny, anyway?"

Cain ignored the shocked look that crossed Sister Simone's face as she set a bowl of fried rice next to the platter of grilled shrimp already on the table and concentrated solely on Cat.

"I can't tell you." Cautiously, he moved closer.

"Why not?"

"Because you have to see it to believe it."

"See it?" Cat was vibrating—with fury, with foreboding—yet her voice was remarkably tranquil. "See what?"

Cain took the last step to close the distance between them and drew her into his arms. She didn't fight him, as he'd feared she would. Neither did she lean on him, as he'd hoped she would.

She just stood there rigidly as Sister Simone slipped out of the dining room. Refused to soften when the older children—many of them the same age as the students she hoped to teach someday—ran in crying his name and clamoring to show him what they'd caught in their small fishing baskets. She didn't even acknowledge the greetings of the two nuns in muddy habits who rushed in after them to try and calm things down.

"Look, Cat," Cain said when Sister Simone stepped back into the room carrying a fussing, fidgeting bundle wrapped in a lightweight white blanket. He relieved the nun of her burden, which was barely big enough to fill the crook of his arm from elbow to wrist, and turned so it could be easily seen. Then, because he couldn't think of a way to break the news to her gently, he did it bluntly. "It's Johnny's son."

Chapter Sixteen

Cat pressed her fingertips to her lips as a tiny fist flailed up out of the blanket and cuffed Cain on the chin. She couldn't believe that this was really happening. But it was. She prayed it was just some bizarre dream from which she would soon awaken. But it wasn't. It was a wife's worst nightmare come true.

"No!" She shouted the denial.

"Yes." He extended the baby to her.

She dropped her arms to her sides and said fiercely, "I don't want it."

Sister Simone clapped her hands. "It's time for your baths, *mes enfants*."

But the children were much more interested in what was going on between the two adults at the moment than they were in getting clean.

"It's not mine!" Cat's voice teetered on the brink of hysteria.

"Calm down," Cain ordered as the baby began wailing at the top of his lungs.

"*Vite, vite!*" Sister Simone said briskly, shooing the children into two reluctant lines. "*Soeur* Francoise will supervise the boys, *Soeur* Marie the girls."

"You'd better take the baby, *Soeur* Simone." Cain passed the now-squirming, squalling bundle back to the nun, then grabbed Cat's hand and pulled. "We're going outside."

"Get your goddamn hands off me, you—"

"Little pitchers have big ears," he cautioned her.

"Rotten, no-good"—heedless of the fact that some of the children were still in the room, she hauled off and slapped him as hard as she could with her free hand—"son of a bitch!"

"And you, Mrs. Brown, have a filthy mouth." Face stinging and features contorted, Cain dragged her into the hall.

"Liar!" Cat screamed at him. "Cheater!"

"I'm going to pretend you've been talking about Johnny all this time." He yanked open the front door, all but ripping it off its hinges, and stalked across the terrace. "Because if I thought you were talking about me, I'd cram a bar of soap so far down your throat, you'd be burping bubbles for the next month."

Cain wanted to get her as far away from the house as he could. The children had seen enough, heard enough. As had the nuns. So with only that big old tropical moon to guide him, and with Cat spitting and snarling behind him, he headed back down the grassy hill they'd climbed only a little while ago.

"Let go of me!"

"Gladly."

Cat didn't just fall on her bottom when he released her. She fell apart. "Damn you, Johnny!" She cried out his name. Cried it out with anger and with anguish. She looked up blindly and cried to the heavens, "Damn you to hell and back, Johnny Brown!" Then she covered her face with her hands and gave in to the grief and bitterness and pain of his betrayal.

Watching her weep, hearing her harsh breaths, Cain burned for her. Yearned for her. He stood clear of her, though, trying to give her a modicum of privacy. Only when her heartbroken sobs had diminished into the hiccuping tremors of catharsis did he drop down beside her.

He didn't touch her. She wasn't ready for that. He sat with one knee raised, an elbow crooked upon it, and the other leg fully extended. Idly, he plucked the longest blade of grass he could find and twirled it in his fingers as he stared out into the jungle just a few yards ahead.

"Tell me." Her voice sounded rusty from so many tears, and moonlight kissed the tormented face she finally turned to him. "No more surprises. No more cover-ups. Just tell me the whole story."

Before, Cain had admired her courage. Now her strength of character, her willingness to confront the worst head-on, awakened a new emotion in him. An emotion that he could not, would not name.

"I only met Johnny twice—once at the end of his first tour, and once at the beginning of his second—so I really don't know the whole story."

"I knew him my entire life, so I can probably fill in the blanks."

He frowned in concern. "You're sure you want to hear this?"

"I need to know." A healthy anger began nibbling at the edges of her hurt. "I'm *entitled* to know."

Diverting his gaze, he delivered the blow in a quiet voice. "Johnny had a Vietnamese 'wife' named Lily."

"'Wife'?" she repeated with forced calm.

"He wasn't alone in that. I mean, it's not the norm or anything, but a lot of guys over here—officers and noncoms alike—have them. They're away from home, they're lonesome, they're afraid."

"They're horny," Cat added bluntly.

Cain bit back a smile. "They're horny."

She studied the stars dusting the sky out beyond the humidity. "Did Lily know that Johnny already had a wife?"

"It was a marriage of convenience, as most of these arrangements are. Lily was a refugee from the mountains with no real job skills, and Johnny was a soldier who needed—"

"Sex," she supplied tartly. "Johnny needed sex."

"It wasn't just sex," he refuted. "Though that was obviously part of it."

"Obviously."

"He needed someone who was there for him day after day, night after night. Someone to hold him when he was sweating with fear and shame and guilt. Someone to tell him that he was doing the right thing even when he was bombing the hell out of their country."

The vehemence in Cain's voice brought Cat's head around. He sounded as if he were speaking from personal experience. Which was preposterous. He was a man on the run. A fugitive from justice. And if Colonel Howard ever got his hands on him, he was a goner.

"Anyway," he went on, "Lily got pregnant just a couple of months before Johnny was slated to go home. She didn't have a family she could go back to because they'd died in a Zippo Raid, so—"

"Zippo Raid?"

"A search-and-destroy mission." He reached in his pocket, pulled out his lighter and flicked it. The flame burned like a blue-and-yellow tongue in the night. "Touch it to a thatched roof, and that's all she wrote."

She flinched at the thought. "That's what Loc meant when he said there were atrocities on both sides of this war."

"War isn't a John Wayne movie, where the good guys always wear white hats and the bad guys black." He snapped the lighter closed and put it away. "It's down and it's dirty and it's mean. On both sides."

She shook her head. "I don't want to hear—"

He ignored her. "They maim or kill your best buddy, you burn them out. You blow them out of the water, they take your new best buddy prisoner. Then they cut off your point man's head and stick it on a pike, so you line up every man, woman and child in the next village you come to and mow 'em all down."

Her shudder was quick and uncontrollable. "That's insane!"

"That's war," he said coldly.

She hugged her knees and, as difficult as it was, tried to put herself in the other woman's place. "And there was Lily, pregnant by a man who was just using her and probably terrified at the thought of being alone again in the—"

"And making noises about going to Johnny's commanding officer—"

"Which could have resulted in a demotion or a court martial."

"So that's when I first met Johnny." Wishing he hadn't left his cigarillos back at the house, Cain began chewing on the blade of grass he'd been playing with. "He'd heard about me from another guy in his squadron—"

"Who'd gotten another girl pregnant?"

"A bar-girl, who didn't want the baby because it would interfere with business."

"So you sent the guy to see *Soeur* Simone—"

"Who agreed to take the baby—"

"And Johnny asked you to make the same arrangement for him."

Cain's laugh was etched in acid. "Asked is hardly the word I'd use."

Cat looked at him over her shoulder. "He threatened you?"

"In a manner of speaking. He pulled the just-between-us-hellions routine on me first. When that didn't work, he let me know he had 'connections' in case I ever needed any spare airplane parts. Then, when I told him where he could stick his spare parts, he tried to put the squeeze on me. Said he'd go all the way to the top to see that the orphanage was shut down for overcrowding—as if he weren't trying to add to the problem—and that *Soeur* Simone was reassigned to someplace like India."

"That doesn't sound like Johnny."

"Desperate men do desperate things."

Cat stared out into that black jungle she'd followed Cain through only hours before. It seemed like days. Years. And now here he was, leading her through an even darker and denser garden of lies.

"I had the feeling you didn't like him, but I couldn't figure out why."

Cain swatted a mosquito that was making a meal of his arm. "Now you know."

"It explains why he was such a basket case when he was home on leave. And why he volunteered for a second tour."

"Lily knew where he lived."

She choked out a weak laugh. "He gave her our address?"

"Guys can do stupid things when they're thinking with their glands instead of their brains."

She shot him a baleful glance. "That sounds like someone who's qualified for the dunce cap himself."

His smile shone wide and white in the moonlight. "Let's just say guilty as charged and leave it at that."

Absently, she scratched her ankle. "So Lily was essentially blackmailing Johnny?"

"Desperate women also do desperate things."

Crickets and geckos filled the silence as Cat mulled over everything that Cain had told her. It was all so unbelievable. She'd known Johnny as long as memory served. And yet it seemed that she hadn't known him at all.

Now she scratched her neck. "And the second time you saw him?"

"He was a gun-shy mannequin who should have been grounded."

"My brother Drew said he told him that he hated the war."

"To turn a phrase—badly——there're no hawks in cockpits or foxholes, either one."

"But he came back because of Lily." And Cat's throat ached at the thought of it.

This time, Cain's laugh was dry as dust. "He came back to cover his own ass."

"When was the baby born?"

"April 2."

"So Johnny died not knowing he'd fathered a son."

"And Lily hemorrhaged to death about an hour after giving birth."

Her eyes slid closed at the horror of it. "Did she ever get to hold her baby?"

"I wasn't there, of course," he said in a subdued tone. "But from what I've heard, I doubt it."

The wind was still and, except for the occasional night bird, the world around them was silent. If they tried, they could pretend there was no war or human tragedy playing out somewhere beyond the trees. No men dying, no women crying and no unwanted babies being born.

But in the here and now, there was a woman struggling to deal with the details of her late husband's betrayal. There was a man who regretted with all his heart that he'd had to reveal them. And there was a baby back at the house who needed a home.

"I trusted him," Cat said quietly. "I always trusted him."

She was ready, Cain thought, cupping a hand under her chin and turning her face to his. "He trusted you, too."

Bitterness rose like bile in her throat. "To stay home and play Betty Crocker while he was screwing around over here?"

"To remember him as a basically decent guy who made a dumb mistake." He dropped his hand. "A mistake he paid for with his life."

Staggered, she stared at him. "Are you defending him now?"

"No. Hell, no." He was just winging it as best he could. "But Johnny and Lily are gone. And you're going back to the world. So who does that leave? Who's the innocent party in all this?"

Cat understood only too well what Cain was trying to say but she refused to acknowledge it. Rankled, she scratched her other ankle until she drew blood. "I don't know about you, but the mosquitoes are eating me alive."

"Speaking of eating . . ." He'd planted the seed, he told himself as he got to his feet. All he could do now was hope it took root. He reached down to give her a hand up. "I'm starving."

"Oh, that's right, you never got your shrimp and rice."

"I got my fill of sharp tongue and cold shoulder, though."

"Shut up, *James*," she said, but totally without venom. No other man had gotten her angry with such regularity . . . and no other man could so readily charm her out of her anger.

He wagged a finger under her nose. "There's only one woman who can call me that with impunity."

"Did you say *immunity*?" she countered archly.

While he groaned at her comeback, their silliness was a refreshing antidote to the serious nature of their earlier conversation.

Her hand still caught in his, they started back to the house. "God, I dread facing *Soeur* Simone."

"Why?"

"You have to ask, after the ass I made of myself?"

That elicited a companionable chuckle. "She's probably already said a rosary on your behalf."

She gave him a gentle elbow in the ribs. "That must make you a candidate for a novena, huh?"

As they crested the hill, laughing, a shrill cry pierced the night. At first, Cat thought it was just a jungle bird. Then a light came on at an upstairs window, throwing its soft glow over the dark lawn, and she could see Sister Simone's silhouette bending over a baby's crib.

"You know the terrible irony in all of this?" She paused in the square of light and peered up at the nursery window with painful intensity. "Johnny grew up without a father. And now his son will grow up without a father or a mother."

"Unless someone adopts him." Cain stopped beside her and slid his hands, palms out, into his back pockets.

"Maybe some nice Vietnamese couple will—"

"Dream on."

The baby was crying in earnest now, his distress reaching deep within Cat to tug at her heart. It was Johnny's baby. She knew it without knowing why. And she could tell by his strenuous protests that something was wrong.

Trying to separate herself from the child and his misery, she cleared her throat and spoke too loudly, "What makes you say that?"

"Take a close look at those kids tomorrow."

But Cat was looking at Cain as though seeing him, really seeing him, for the first time.

"Look at their rounded eyes." His own good one wasn't quite round but it wasn't quite almond-shaped, either. "The shape of their faces. Their complexions." His features were chiseled, his nose aquiline. And his teak-colored skin stretched taut over slashing cheekbones that might have belonged on a warlord. "Hell," he said, stepping away from her so that he was almost one with the night, "some of them even have curly hair."

And as he stood there in the dark speaking so passionately and so fiercely, she began to see the light.

"They're *bui doi*—the 'dust of life'," he bit out over the baby's shrieks. "Who in a country of starving children, a country where the infant mortality rate is almost sixty percent, will take a by-blow of war? No self-respecting Vietnamese couple that I know of." He turned back to her and saw by her dazed expression that she'd made the connection, but he was determined to have his say. "The American people don't know they exist. Might not care even if they did know. So when we lose this war—as we eventually will—and the Communists take over, those kids will either be enslaved or killed."

"You're—" She fumbled for the correct word.

His mouth hooked in a humorless smile. "Amerasian is the term I believe they're using these days."

"James! Catherine!"

As one, they looked up and saw Sister Simone standing at the window holding a small, wriggling body to her shoulder.

"Come quick!" she pleaded over those heart-wrenching cries "The baby is sick!"

"He was fretting at his ear earlier today." Not wanting to wake the other babies who were sleeping in the nursery, Sister Simone had met them at the bottom of the stairs when they came running into the house.

Cain lifted the baby from the nun's arms and carried him into the dining room. Then he pressed his lips to that tiny, furrowed brow. "Well, he's burning up with fever now."

"Take off his clothes," she ordered as she started back upstairs. "I need to take his temperature."

Almost frantic with fear, Cat hovered over Cain as he sat down on one of the chairs and laid the baby on his thighs. She wanted to help but there was nothing for her to do. Already he was stripping the infant, his long, lean fingers making short work of the lightweight sacque and bulky cloth diaper. He was careful to support the delicate neck in his large palm as he undressed the infant.

Cain turned him onto his tummy when Sister Simone returned with a rectal thermometer. The baby howled at this new indignity. Cat would have had to be a pillar of salt not to be moved at the sight of that dark, manly hand smoothing up and down the infant's back to comfort him.

"One hundred and five," the nun said solemnly.

Cat's arms suddenly ached to pick up the baby and comfort him, but Cain beat her to it. He cradled that squirming little body to his broad chest and rocked back and forth, back and forth. She clasped her hands together and asked anxiously, "Is there a doctor we can call? Or a hospital we can take him to?"

"This isn't America, with emergency rooms on every other corner," Cain reminded her pointedly. "This is a country at war. The hospitals are full of the wounded, and the few doctors that are left are all busy treating them. Fortunately, *Soeur* Simone is trained as a nurse."

Cat's respect for the religious woman went up another notch.

"We'll bathe him in lukewarm water to bring his temperature down." The nun turned on her sensible rubber sole and motioned for Cain to follow her.

Half-crazed with panic, Cat trailed them down the hall and into the same bathroom where she'd taken her shower. The baby's skin was mottled under the bright light and his frail arms were flailing like broken wings. His frenzied cries had diminished to pitiable mews.

He's dying, she thought, licking a tear from the corner of her mouth. *My baby is dying . . .*

After Sister Simone filled the sink, Cain submerged the baby. Cat watched with growing dread as he cupped that beautifully rounded head in a gentle hand and began scooping water over the feverish little body. A spasm seized her heart when those trembling rose-petal lips turned blue.

Please, God, she prayed with a mother's fervency, *make my baby well . . . let my baby live . . .*

"Do you still have any of that penicillin I brought you last month?" Cain asked over his shoulder.

"No." Sister Simone switched places with him and nodded approvingly when she saw the baby going flaccid. "Three of the children have been sick since then, and—"

"I've got more, but it's on the boat."

"I'll go get it," Cat said around the lump in her throat.

Cain wheeled away from sink and met her eyes directly. The grim expression on his face reminded her of how he'd looked just before he'd led her into the jungle. At the time she'd been afraid of dying from snakebite or plain old heart failure. But now that tangled wilderness seemed tame by comparison. Now she knew the real meaning of fear. Because now she knew that there was nothing more terrifying than seeing one's child in life-threatening danger.

"I'll go." He reached over the nun's crouched back and touched her cheek with cool, damp fingers. "You stay here and help *Soeur* Simone."

Cat caught his hand before he could retract it and said in a quaking voice, "Be careful."

They shared one last, poignant look before he turned and left the bathroom.

She rolled up her sleeves then and stepped to the sink to relieve Sister Simone.

Where was Cain?

Cat had been walking the floor with the baby for what seemed like hours. His fever was down, thanks to the cool baths, but she could tell by the way he kept batting at his ear that it was still bothering him. She thought he might be getting a tad spoiled from all the attention, too, because every time she tried to lay him down, he started crying again.

Not that she minded. To the contrary, she couldn't believe how right it felt to have him cuddled against her breasts. How wonderful his slight weight felt in her arms. When she'd first picked him up, she'd turned him this way and that in loving inspection. As she'd put his diaper and his clothes back on, she had counted each toe, marveled over each transparent fingernail, smiled at the square jaw he had inherited from his father. She'd even tried but failed to curl that wild tuft of ebony dark hair upon his head.

But after her harrowing experiences of the past two days, she was worn slick.

Sister Simone had put Cat in a first-floor bedroom at the back of the house that the priest from Can Tho used when he came to baptize the babies and give the older children religious instruction. Unlike the nursery upstairs, this room was small and sparsely furnished. It had narrow windows, a padded kneeler for prayer, and a wooden crucifix on the stark white wall. The only thing that looked even remotely comfortable was a double bed with a plain brown spread and two tightly tucked pillows.

Now she eyed the bed longingly, wondering if she dared try to lay the baby down again. He was sucking on his fist and making those sweet little noises that were music to her ears. She smiled poignantly at the sound.

If only Cain were here, everything would be perfect.

She pressed her cheek to the top of the baby's head as she paced the length of the room, wondering what could be keeping him. Had he run into one of the Viet Cong patrols that owned the night? Was he lying hurt and wounded and helpless in the jungle? Had Colonel Howard tracked him down and arrested him?

The grisly possibilities were endless, yet she seemed to think of every conceivable one. She clutched the baby tightly and kissed the downy black hair that hugged his soft scalp. He squirmed, as if he sensed her fear, and began fussing again.

"Ssh, ssh," she crooned. "He'll be back soon."

She wasn't sure at this point just who she was trying to convince—herself or the baby. The waiting was unendurable. But what else could she do? She couldn't take a sick baby outside. And she certainly couldn't leave him alone. Sister Simone had already had a full day taking care of the orphans and had been dead on her feet, so Cat had sent her to bed. She knew the nun would gladly get up if asked, but she had another full day ahead of her tomorrow and she needed her rest.

"*Frère Jacques, Frère Jacques . . .*"

Softly singing the song that her mother used to sing to her, Cat sat down on the edge of the bed and rocked the baby back and forth. He whimpered once, as if he was fighting sleep, then laid his precious little head against her heart. Humming now, she gingerly eased herself back and lowered her own head to the pillow.

Just before she closed her exhausted eyes, she remembered that *Jacques* was French for *James*.

When Cat awoke, Cain was lying on the other side of the bed, facing her, and the baby was tucked between them.

She turned her head on the pillow and blinked rapidly, trying to orient herself in the strange room. It was just before sunrise, and the walls were tinted a faint rose with the encroaching dawn. The air drifting in through the screened window smelled sweet with the mingled perfume of flowers and dew.

Her eyes misted over with emotion when she saw that the baby was sleeping on his tummy. His little rump looked plump and out of proportion to his body because of his diaper. He was snoring softly through slightly parted lips.

As was Cain.

Lying perfectly still now, Cat let her gaze wander up his tanned throat to the proud chin. There was a small scar there—silvered by time—which she hadn't noticed before. His mouth was beautifully shaped, if a bit stern, and the memory of the magic it had worked on hers caused her stomach muscles to contract. She ran her tongue over her own lips, trying to see if she could still taste him—erotic, exotic, narcotic—on them. Caught off guard by a sudden craving to taste him again, she moved on.

Given the risky nature of his business, it was a mystery to her how he'd managed to keep his nose from getting broken. She blessed the fates that had left it straight. The tropical sun, on the other hand, hadn't been quite so kind. It had etched permanent creases around his mouth and eye. Offsetting its harsh effects, the midnight-black hair falling across his forehead made him look younger than his years—boyish, yet every inch a man. That black eye patch only added to his overwhelming masculinity.

She couldn't help but smile when she remembered the first time she'd watched him sleeping. Then she'd considered him nothing more than a mercenary and nothing less than a criminal. A man who didn't care about anyone or anything but making a buck.

Now she knew better. He was tough-minded but tenderhearted. Rough around the edges yet smooth as silk when it came to talking his way out of trouble. He was fighting for what he believed in, although she still wasn't exactly certain what that was, and he was fighting his battle his way.

And he cared as deeply about the orphans as she was beginning to care about him.

Before Cat could fully digest that thought, Cain opened his eye and smiled at her. The lashes he lifted were broom-thick, and the look he gave her was bone-meltingly tender. She swallowed a sudden urge to cry and smiled back.

He mouthed a, "Good morning."

She mouthed one right back.

"Did you get your sleep out?"

She nodded. "You're a real pro when it comes to sneaking in."

His smile widened. "Just call me 'Cool Breeze.'"

They were whispering so as not to disturb the baby. But the baby snuffled and turned his head, telling them that they were tempting fate. So by tacit agreement, they eased out of bed, tucked their pillows around the baby like bolsters to keep him from falling off, then crept out of the room and into the kitchen.

"He woke up?" she asked, her eyes widening in disbelief when she saw the half-empty bottle of clear liquid and the small container of medication sitting on the table.

"I guess he thought it was time for breakfast."

"I feel terrible that I didn't hear him."

He shrugged off her concern and went to the stove to start the coffee. While he was at it, he dropped a couple of pieces of bread in the toaster. "I gave him his penicillin and a little Seven-Up and he went right back to sleep."

"Some mother I'm going to make," Cat muttered in self-recrimination.

Cain wheeled and threw her a heartwarming glance. "You're going to adopt him?"

"If I can get the paperwork done before my visa runs out."

"I'll see if I can speed things up for you."

She scowled. "Legitimately?"

He smiled. "Leave it to me, okay?"

Cat watched Cain pour their coffee. He remembered that she took sugar and he stirred some in before placing the cup of steaming liquid in front of her. Then he retrieved the two slices of toast, slathered them both with butter and passed one to her while sinking his strong white teeth into the other.

The whole scene was so domestic that she suddenly found herself wanting things she could never have. Cozy things, like waking up in the same bed with him every morning for the rest of her life. Simple things, like sharing toast and coffee along with their plans for the day while the children still slept snug and warm and safe. Arousing things, like having him kiss her and caress her in the heat of the night . . .

"Thanks." She looked away before her eyes betrayed the foolish fantasies that were flashing through her head with every heartbeat and bit into her toast.

He leaned back against the counter with his own cup cradled in both hands and let his gaze move restlessly around the room. "We need to leave at full light in order to make it back to Saigon before nightfall."

She suppressed a shudder at the thought of having to retrace her path through the jungle and tried to drown her fears with a sip of coffee. It was hot and sweet. And it gave her time to gather her courage to speak.

"*Soeur* Simone told me that you're an orphan."

"That must have been some conversation."

Cat set down her cup and looked up at him earnestly. "She didn't tell me much. Only that you remembered how it felt to be an orphan. But if it's not too difficult for you to talk about, I'd really like to hear the story from you."

Cain forked his hand through his hair, and she could see that the bruise at his temple was beginning to fade. His rueful expression, though, was evidence that some old wounds never entirely heal. "My father was an American pilot in China—one of the original 'Flying Tigers'—and my mother was the daughter of a Chinese general."

"What was her name?"

"Anna. Anna Lee."

Now she knew where he'd gotten his middle name. "Oh, that's beautiful."

"She was a beautiful woman—inside and out."

Cat watched Cain retreat into himself, as if he were recalling some special childhood memory of the mother he had obviously loved. She wished he would share it with her because she wanted to know as much as she possibly could about the woman who'd given birth to this extraordinary man. Instead, she sipped her coffee and waited for him to return to the present.

"Unfortunately," he continued in a raw voice, "both the American and the Chinese cultures frowned on intermarriage in those days. So my mother 'lost face' with her family and my father was disowned by his when they eloped."

"How awful!"

"It wasn't quite the 'Romeo and Juliet' tragedy you're imagining."

No matter that Cain was stoic about it, Cat was steamed enough for the both of them. "But they loved each other."

"That they did." He took another sip of coffee before he went on. "They fled to America—to California—just before the Japanese overran China, and I was born on—of all things—Pearl Harbor Day. Then, while my father was in the Pacific fighting the 'Yellow Peril,' my mother and I were interned in one of the concentration camps the government had set up to 'protect' its precious *Mayflower* descendants from enemy aliens."

"That sounds dangerously close to what the Germans were doing to the Jews at the time."

"Except we were in America, not Europe."

She pushed her coffee away, sickened to the core now by what he was telling her. "And your mother was Chinese, not—"

Bitterness curled the edges of his mouth. "My mother had yellow skin and slanted eyes, and in the home of the free and the land of the bigoted, that was enough to render her a threat to democracy."

"Your father must have been furious."

"That's putting it mildly."

She frowned. "Yet he went on to fight and die in Korea."

His eye turned to gray iron. "He was a soldier. Flying B-52s was his job."

"Is he buried in California?"

"They never recovered his body."

She managed to keep the pain from showing on her face, but her throat worked convulsively. "And your mother—"

"Died a broken woman when I was eleven," he supplied shortly.

From the bedroom came the whimpering sound of the baby waking.

Cat sprang to her feet, having heard all she could stand. "I'll get him."

"He'll need another dose of his medicine."

She canted her head. "How much should I give him?"

"I'll show you." Cain set his cup down and picked up the penicillin container.

By the time Sister Simone came downstairs, trailed by a dozen sleepy-eyed children, the baby was wearing a dry diaper. He'd also been medicated and fed. Propped up against a pillow and gnawing on his fist, in fact, he looked as contented as a little Buddha.

The nun eyed Cain's bulging backpack containing a sheet, extra diapers and clean sacques and bottles of formula sitting on the bed. A square of mosquito netting lay atop the pack. Then she looked at Cat, who had changed back into her pantyhose, sandals and the black pajamas one of the other nuns had thoughtfully laundered for her.

"You're leaving."

"Yes."

Cain stooped to pick up a little girl with tightly curled brown hair who had lifted her arms to him. He settled her on his hip and she laid her head trustingly on his shoulder. It was all Cat could do not to cry when several of the other children raised their arms in supplication. They were starving—not for food, but for affection. And as sweet and caring as the nuns were, there simply weren't enough loving arms and empty laps to go around.

"I unloaded the boat last night." He gently patted the little girl's back as he spoke to Sister Simone. "The powdered milk and the rest of your supplies are hidden in the roots of that same tree I've used before."

"Our gardener will bring them up to the house." Sister Simone reached down and ruffled the hair of a toddler with round green eyes who was clinging to the skirt of her habit with one hand and sucking the thumb of the other.

Cat's eyes smarted with a fresh batch of tears when Cain set the little girl down and picked up a boy who'd been badly burned—when the orphanage was bombed, perhaps?—and who now carried the scars from his face to his feet.

"I don't know when I'll get back," he said as he bounced the little boy on his hip. "I need to go north again, and—"

"We'll get by," Sister Simone assured him as the little girl turned and raised her thin arms to her in silent appeal.

Her heart on the verge of breaking, Cat knelt and opened her own arms to enfold as many of the other children as she could. She was rewarded for her effort with hugs and kisses and giggles that made her wish she had the means to take all of them with her. But she didn't, and there was no sense in lamenting what could never be.

"Are you ready?"

Cat released the children and looked up at Cain. He was holding the baby now, and as the children stepped back solemnly, she rose and said in a voice that was close to cracking, "I guess so."

He handed her the baby, then bent to kiss Sister Simone on both cheeks.

The nun hugged him fiercely, then turned and smiled down at the baby. She cupped his little face with a loving hand and whispered, "*Adieu, mon petit ange.*"

"He really is a little angel, isn't he?" Cat replied with maternal pride.

Sister Simone smiled serenely. "He's a miracle in the midst of war."

"I'll write to you—" Cat began.

"*Di-di mau,*" Cain snapped as he slid his arms through the straps of the backpack.

She glanced at him, perplexed. "Excuse me?"

He gave her the polite translation. "Get moving."

Cat forced herself not to look back as she followed Cain to the front door. It was time to take Johnny's baby—no, *her* baby—home. But as she stepped outside and, through shimmering eyes, saw the sun rising against a vivid red sky, she knew the forlorn faces of the children she was leaving behind would haunt her forever.

Chapter

Seventeen

$\mathscr{A}$t the edge of the jungle, Cain arranged the mosquito netting over her head like a bridal veil so that half of it hung down her back. But just before he covered her face, his gaze speared into hers. "Now your only job is to hold on to the baby."

Cat tightened her arms and tried to wipe the thought of what lay ahead of her out of her mind. "I've got him."

She was terrified. He could see it in her white face, her fragile eyes. Yet somehow she'd found the inner strength to still her trembling lips and lift her chin in that characteristic gesture. Thinking only to reassure her that everything would be all right, he bent his head and slanted his mouth over hers.

This kiss wasn't hard and quick like the one he'd given her for luck the evening before. No, this kiss was so tender and so thorough that it drove Cat's fears to the farthest recesses of her mind. Cain's tongue delved deeply into the receptive warmth of her mouth, bathing her body with liquid heat. He didn't physically touch her anywhere else because he was still holding the netting, but he could have been caressing her throat, teasing her nipples, parting the secret folds between her thighs, for she was tingling in all those places.

Instinctively, her hand came up to cradle the baby's head against her breasts. In that moment, with her hand trapped between them, she had the best of both worlds. Her new son. And the man she wished had fathered him.

Cain knew that if he didn't pull back, now, he'd never be able to survive without her. He had no idea how it had happened. How the simple comfort he'd meant to offer had grown into something so huge and primal and hot. As he eased out of the kiss, he only knew that he wanted her in the worst way.

And that it was folly of the highest caliber.

Fighting to regain both his breath and his sanity, he dropped the netting over her face. He told himself that the kiss was a mistake he wouldn't make again as he tied the material securely around her slender waist and tucked the ends up under the knot. But once she was all trussed up, he couldn't resist squeezing her shoulders with his hands and asking her gruffly, "You okay?"

Even though she knew better, Cat blamed the salty perspiration that was trickling down her forehead for making her eyes sting. Maybe it was too soon for her to be attracted to another man. Maybe not. But she had opened her heart to him, urged him to take it, and had felt his own heart racing to accept before he'd ruthlessly snapped his control back in place. Crushed, she angled her chin and forced her lips to curve into a smile. "I'm fine."

It took a vicious twist of will on his part to ignore that wounded look in her eyes behind the veil, the echo of pain in her voice. So what if she made him feel clean and innocent again? Made him forget that there was anything or anyone on the planet except the two of them? So what if she had reached in and clamped a hand on his heart? It wasn't fair to either of them to let this go any farther than it already had. Because the more he wanted her, the more he needed her, the more difficult it would be to let her walk away.

"Let's go." He looped his arms around her and, together, they moved forward.

Cat's second trip through the jungle seemed to go not only smoother but also faster than the first. Oh, there were still vines and roots and creepy things that hissed and slithered and crawled. But she was too busy holding tight to the little miracle in her arms to worry about anything happening to herself. And with Cain at her side, despite the emotional distance he'd put between them, she felt safer than she'd ever felt in her life.

"We're almost there," he said when they reached the river.

She let out a sigh of relief on hearing that. "Thank heavens."

He untied the netting he had wrapped her and the baby in, wadded it into a ball and stuck it in his pocket. Then he scooped her up into his arms and started wading out to the boat. He'd left the ladder hanging from the rail the night before, but she couldn't figure out how they were going to accomplish their reboarding without getting the baby wet.

"Grab the ladder with one hand," he said when her feet were secure on the bottom rung, "then give the baby to me."

As soon as she'd climbed up the ladder and over the rail, she reached down and took the baby from him so he could do the same.

"We did it!" Cat crowed as she covered the baby's face with kisses.

Basking in the attention, he gurgled.

"If you two lovebirds will excuse me . . ." Cain removed the pack from his back, then reached into the purse she was wearing Poncho Villa style and took out the can of mosquito repellent. He walked toward the hatch like he had an army of red ants in his pants. Only it was leeches, not ants, that were worming around in there. "I've got a little problem I need to take care of."

While he was gone, she carried the baby into the wheelhouse to get him out of the sun. He had no fever now and his coloring was so much better than it had been the night before, but he was beginning to fuss and she didn't know whether that meant he needed a clean diaper or he wanted a bottle. She took the sheet out of the backpack and spread it on the floor to change him. Then just to be on the safe side, she fed him.

"I'm new at this mothering stuff, pal," she explained as she lifted the baby to her shoulder and patted his back to burp him. "So you'll just have to put up with me until I learn the ropes."

"Don't you think it's about time you gave him a name?" Cain was standing in the doorway wearing a pair of dry jeans. He was shirtless, but his slicked-back wet hair and smooth jaw told her he'd showered and shaved while he was below.

That made her think of the bra and panties she'd left hanging in the head. And that made her blush. To hide the hot color that was climbing her cheeks, she shifted the baby to the crook of her arm and smiled down at him.

He grinned up at her, but Cat was pretty sure it was just gas. Still, she took the opportunity to waggle his cute little nose and stroke his cheek. "What is this?" Now she was positive he smiled. "Men against women?"

"It's going to be us against the Cong if we don't get a move on." Cain's statement was a grim reminder that all wasn't sweetness and light.

Her face was pinched with anxiety as she looked up at him. "Should I take the baby down to the cabin?"

"Use that sheet to make him a pallet on the floor," he suggested. "Maybe the motion of the boat will rock him to sleep."

"Come on, Horatio." Cat gave the baby a quick squeeze before she handed him up to Cain and got to her feet. She tucked her hair, which was damp with sweat, behind her ears. "It's naptime."

"Horatio?"

"It's only temporary, until I can think of a permanent name."

"Frankly, my dear," Cain said in his best Clark Gable voice, "I think he looks like a Fletcher."

She laughed when the baby grabbed her finger. "How about Flipper?"

"Flipper Brown." He pretended to mull that over, then nodded. "Not bad."

"Isn't he beautiful?" Cat cooed.

"Handsome," Cain corrected.

"And so alert!"

"Coordinated, too."

The baby grinned again, and the two adults standing over him smiled at each other, becoming enmeshed in the illusion that they were proud new parents. That's all it was, though—an illusion. Because the woman had no legal claim on him yet and the man never would.

"Well, I'd better raise the anchor . . ." Cain came to his senses first, his smile vanishing like smoke as he relinquished the baby.

Cat took him and, clutching his tiny body tightly, backed out of the wheelhouse. "I'll go below and make him . . ."

"Don't forget the sheet."

"Oh"—she stooped to scoop it up—"right."

He stepped around her. "I'll open the hatch doors for you."

"Yes . . . thanks." Cat started down the first step, but the sheet she'd carelessly thrown over her shoulder had somehow gotten coiled around one of her ankles.

"Don't fall." Cain caught her arm to steady her, his firm touch scorching her skin through the thin cotton sleeve of her pajamas.

But he was too late. She'd already fallen. Not down the hatch, of course, but it was almost as devastating as if she had. Because she'd fallen in love with him. And it had literally knocked the wind out of her.

"No . . ." She looked up into his worried gray gaze with a helpless mixture of wonder and despair. "I won't fall."

Wrenching her arm from his grasp then, she fled down to the cabin as if an entire company of Viet Cong guerrillas was hot on her heels.

Cain was just lighting a cigarillo when he heard Cat come topside. He took a drag, then blew a plume of smoke toward the wheelhouse ceiling. Thunderheads were building in the north, presaging a stormy night in Saigon, but here the sun still beamed hot and brilliant in the sky. And ahead, the river was calm and as gently curved as the woman who was making her way across the deck.

He'd been tempted, so damn tempted, to take her up on that baby-I'm-yours look he'd seen in her eyes right before she'd run down the stairs. Had, in fact, felt his heart tumbling headlong after her. It was something that had never happened to him before. And it surprised the hell out of him.

Not the lust. Hell, he'd been in let's-get-it-on lust with plenty of women over the years. Sex without strings—that had always been his specialty. He wasn't proud of it. Neither was he bragging about it. That was simply the way the world had turned.

No, it wasn't the lust but rather the love he felt for this one special, spunky woman that had struck him like a bolt out of the blue and left him reeling. Which in his line of work wasn't just dumb. It was deadly. Because a man who lost himself to emotion was in serious danger of losing his life.

So now, he parked the slim cigar in the corner of his mouth and flicked her a smile over his shoulder. "Is Flipper asleep?"

Cat had taken the coward's way out, hiding in the cabin and using the baby as an excuse not to have to face the man. Emotions had poured through her—sweet and confusing and sad—as she'd tried to come to terms with her feelings. Despite what Johnny had done, she knew she would always care for him in a special way. He'd been her first love, the boy to whom she'd given her heart when she was but a girl.

But what she felt for Cain was different. It encompassed her entire being. She loved him as a woman should love a man—intellectually, spiritually and physically. The fact that it was a love without hope of a future made it no less genuine. It simply spurred her determination to make the most of the few days they had left to them. Because those few days would have to last her a lifetime.

So now, she took a deep breath and answered the question he'd asked her as she stepped in beside him. "Finally."

He shot her a glance, then tucked his tongue firmly in his cheek. "You look a little frazzled."

She blew her sweat-soaked hair out of her eyes. "Don't start any trouble, and there won't be any trouble."

He snapped her a crisp salute. "Yes, ma'am."

Cat tried to laugh, but couldn't quite manage it. Her heart had fluttered into her throat and swelled. She laid her hand on his arm and looked up at him. "Thank you, Cain." Her voice went husky with emotion. "Thank you for my son."

Fucking war, he thought on a sudden burst of fury. He gunned the throttle when what he really wanted to do was turn this old tub around and head for the South China Sea. Take Cat someplace safe and secluded and solely their own. A peaceful place where he could kiss her and savor the taste of her mouth, the silk-soft texture of her skin for the rest of his days. He wanted nothing more than to breathe in the life of her, the gentle compassion wrapped in courage, the grace of her body against his. And he wanted nothing less than all of her for all time.

Because that was impossible, because he was already committed to a cause that was sacred to him, he focused his attention on the river that was carrying them back to Saigon. "You'll make a good mother, Cat."

It wasn't simply the compliment, but the confident way he paid it that touched her deeply. At the same time, though, she sensed him pulling back on every level. She dropped her hand before she made a fool of herself. Again.

"He really is a sweet baby. And just a touch stubborn."

"I take it he didn't want to go down for his nap?"

"Not at first. So I gave him a bath in the galley sink, which he loved. Then I gave him his medicine, which he hated." With a half-laugh, she lifted her hair off her hot neck. "And then I had to rock him and sing to him until—"

"He's making up for lost time."

Seeing his jaw square reminded her that he was a man who'd been through hell as a boy. He'd survived, though it tore at her heart to think of the scars he must carry on his soul. Losing his parents was bad enough. But as a student teacher, she'd seen how cruel children could be. How they formed little cliques and, often simply echoing sentiments they'd heard at home, made fun of other children who were somehow different from them.

Cat knew the slurs Cain must have been subjected to. Words like "chink," or much worse, that would have been intolerable to a boy who loved his mother and was proud of his heritage. She knew too that he'd probably had to study harder, run faster, jump higher, work longer just to keep pace with his "pure-bred" peers.

Pained, not only for him but also for any child who had to suffer those kinds of taunts, she looked away. She stared out the window and toward the shore, where a grove of twisted banana and coconut trees reminded her that this was a country at war. "May I ask you something?"

"Shoot." He heard their rolling thunder before he saw them—a flight of jets, their silver bellies reflecting the sun, the bombs they carried hanging slim and dark from their wings—and it all came back to him in a flash. The soaring sense of freedom in conquering the heavens. The electric buzz of terror while dropping ordinance in 45 degree dives with the black puffs of flak and automatic gunfire thickening the air around him. The almost sexual thrill of flying into the face of death and surviving.

Cat waited until the deafening whine of the planes' engines faded into a dull roar. While she waited, she watched a woman and a scrawny boy in a rice paddy stop working and stare up at those birds of the Apocalypse. She couldn't see their eyes, of course, but she imagined they were pools of fear. When the woman put a succoring arm around the boy's shoulders, she thought of the baby sleeping peacefully below. And she wondered who would have comforted him if she hadn't come along.

"How many of these children would you say there are?" she asked as the jets' contrails drifted behind them like lazy carnival streamers in the air.

"From this war, tens of thousands." Cain uttered a sound that could have passed for a laugh, though it was far from jovial. "Since 1945—who knows?—probably hundreds of thousands."

She turned back to him, shocked, and tilted her head. "That many?"

"Soldiers always leave children behind, in every army." He took another drag on his cigarillo. "Confining it to Asia now, have you ever stopped to think how many children the American occupation of Japan and South Korea have produced?"

271

She hadn't, of course. "I wonder why I've never read anything about it."

"No one's bothered to write the story. And an ugly story it is, too." A muscle flicked in his jaw. "In Japan, for instance, those children are called *Half* and are ostracized for their Caucasian or black features by a society that prides itself on its ethnic purity."

"How sad."

"It's even more complex in Korea. They respect Americans, almost all of whom have mixed blood, but they don't respect Amerasians. So the kids, who are branded *twi ki*—half-breed—face a lifetime of discrimination, unemployment, and even exclusion from marriage."

"In other words," Cat deduced, "they treat the children like criminals when their only 'crime' was being born."

"What you have to understand," Cain explained, "is that paternity, family name, means everything in Confucian societies. It's the father who enrolls the child in school, bringing along the family birthright. Later the missing name means the child is excluded from the family trade, which is handed down by the father or paternal uncles. Because Amerasian children must retain their mother's name, they have no family rights."

"Their mothers must be devastated."

"Most of them are outcasts themselves for having consorted with the enemy."

"And the American fathers of these children?"

"Some of them really want to marry the women but can't get permission. Others don't even know they've sired a child. And still others just don't give a damn."

She thought a moment. "Do the people at the Pentagon or in Congress know this is happening?"

"They don't want to know," he said in a derisive tone.

"Why not?"

"Because in addition to the politicians having to admit that we got into this war for all the wrong reasons and the generals having to admit that we're losing it for all the right reasons, they'd have to assume responsibility for the kids that resulted from it."

"What about the commanders on site?"

He snorted. "Half of them have hootch-girls themselves."

"Hootch-girls?" Cat's confusion made a blank of her face.

Cain's think-about-it look told her he was talking about women like Lily.

"I wonder if Colonel Howard has a hootch-girl?" she murmured.

Spotting a fishing boat along the shoreline, he cut his speed to avoid rocking it. "Ol' Pencil-Dick is too busy trying to track me down to worry about women."

"Pencil-Dick?" She barely conquered the laugh that sprang to her lips. "Now who's calling names?"

His white teeth grinned around his cigarillo without a hint of apology. "And that's a nice one."

Frowning now, she got back to the subject under discussion. "What about the commanders who don't have hootch-girls?"

"They believe . . ." His smile faded. "Well, it's a pretty gross old military adage."

"I'm a big girl," she said flatly.

"They believe that a man who won't fuck won't fight."

She watched the smoke from his cigarillo haze, then vanish. "I'm still surprised the media hasn't picked up on this."

"They're so focused on their own agenda—which mainly consists of making war on our warriors—that they've yet to notice the boom in babies with round eyes and wavy hair."

Cat tilted her head, considering. "What if someone called it to their attention?"

"Front page news, maybe." Cain hailed an old couple on a sampan going in the opposite direction, then swiped his sweaty face with the back of his hand. "Would you mind getting me a beer the next time you go below? I'm wringing wet."

"No, of course not. I need to check on the baby, anyway." As she stepped out of the wheelhouse, she drew a breath that lay heavily in her lungs. "Gosh, it's really gotten humid."

"Storm's coming," he said, and put the pedal to the metal, hoping to make port before it broke.

They didn't make it.

When the first patrol boat came plowing through the murky water and pulled alongside them, less than a mile from the Port of Saigon, Cain didn't give it much thought. He simply figured it was heading for the naval base on up the river and that the small chop had thrown it off-course. But when the second and third boats moved in like armored geese to complete the V formation, he knew that this was his own personal welcoming party.

Lightning blazed in the cloud-bruised sky as he eased back on the throttle and, ever watchful, started looking for a way out. Thunder boomed, loud as a shot across his bow, when the patrol boats slowed right along with him. At the same time a fourth boat pulled in behind him, blocking that exit.

Despite the adrenaline that was boiling through him, urging him to make a break, there was only one thought in Cain's mind now—how to keep Cat and the baby from getting caught in the net that had been cast for him.

It had been the busiest afternoon of Cat's life. She'd sterilized bottles and nipples, slapped sandwiches together for lunch and scrubbed a couple of dirty diapers. Leaving her hair wet after the quick shower she'd managed to squeeze in, she'd put on her dry underwear and those black pajamas—for the last time, she hoped—before she'd fed and changed the baby. Then, when the boat slowed, she'd wrapped him in his blanket and brought him topside, believing they were about to dock.

But now, squinting against the patrol boats' searchlight eyes that suddenly glared in through the wheelhouse glass, she held his tiny body closely to her breasts and turned blindly to Cain. "What's going on?"

"If I'm not mistaken, we're being busted." And he knew exactly how it had come about, too. He'd broken radio silence only once this entire trip—to let Tiny know what time they'd be pulling into port and to ask him to have Loc meet them so he could take Cat and the baby back to the hotel. But it was obvious that someone else had patched in to the transmission.

"Busted?" With a panicked sound in her throat, she looked up at the sky and saw three helicopters, rotors twirling, hovering overhead like a band of avenging angels. "Busted for what?"

He pointed toward the dock. "Ask Colonel Howard."

She turned her head in disbelief. "Colonel Howard?"

"James Lee Cain, it is my duty to place you under arrest!" the familiar voice barked at him through a bullhorn.

Her eyes widened with horror as lightning streaked across the sky, illuminating Colonel Howard's figure on the dock. He was wearing a regulation trench coat that was buttoned to the throat, and his free hand was hidden in a pocket. Four military policemen in shiny black helmets and fatigues flanked him, Galils at port arms with their right hands on their holstered .45s.

The patrol boat on the starboard side bumped up against Cain's. Once it made fast, the other boats backed off. Then the helicopters rose over the water one by one and, blades *thwap-thwap-thwapping*, were gone.

The baby, startled as much by the noise and the lights as by how tightly Cat was squeezing him, let out a lusty wail. She relaxed her hold and reminded herself to stay calm. It wasn't going to do anybody any good if she freaked out.

But she gaped at Cain, incredulous, when he idled the motor. "What are you doing?"

"I'm turning myself in." If he'd been alone, Cain would have made a run for it. He had the room, now that the patrol was down to one boat, and God knew he had enough horse- and firepower to either leave both Howard and his merry band of MPs in his wake or to go out with a bang. But he wasn't alone. He had a helpless baby and the woman he loved to think about. And right now, their safety was more important to him than saving his own skin.

"No!" The fierceness in Cat's voice surprised her. Cain, too. She saw it in the sharp, sideways jerk of his chin. Felt it in the searing gaze he turned on her. "You can't do it." Tears stung her eyes, but she refused to shed them. "Howard hates you. I saw it on his face the day I went to talk to him. He doesn't just want to lock you up. If he has his way, they'll hang—"

"Yes, Cat." He tempered the finality of his statement by lifting a tear off her lashes. He looked at it, and then at the baby before giving her a bittersweet smile. "It's for the best."

His words struck her chest like heavy stones. She wanted to scream and cry, fall on her knees and beg him not to give up so easily. But to what avail? He'd already made up his mind. And the three linebacker-sized navy crewmen now boarding the boat had their weapons cocked and locked. Their expressions just begged him to give them an excuse to shoot.

"Freeze!" the beefiest of the three demanded as Cain stepped out of the wheelhouse.

He stood so motionlessly he might have been made of ice.

"Your gun."

Trying without success to soothe the baby, Cat watched helplessly as Cain reached in his waistband and withdrew his .45.

The sailor stepped closer to take it. "And the knife."

He removed it from the sheath at his belt and passed it over.

"Now put your hands over your head."

After the second crewman grabbed the arms he raised in surrender and roughly drew them behind him, the first clamped a pair of handcuffs on him. While they were doing that, the third stepped around him and into the wheelhouse, then gunned the throttle and swung the bow to port.

Cain growled deep in his throat when, with a weeping of metal on wood, the driver carelessly scraped the side of the boat against the dock. "Watch it, you stupid sonofa—"

The seaman who'd handcuffed him now backhanded him across the mouth.

Cain's head snapped around, following the impetus behind the blow. To Cat's horror, the corner of his lip was dripping blood. But even shackled in steel, he was still a dangerous man. Still a street fighter. He bared his teeth, braced his weight on his right foot and kicked his left one upward, catching the sailor who'd hit him under the chin and sending him stumbling backward.

The second sailor sprang into action, punching Cain first in the stomach and then in the face with his fist.

"Stop it!" Cat's voice cracked with hysteria when he drew his sidearm and raised the butt of it to hit him on the back of the head. Heedless of the automatic weapons pointed at her, she confronted Cain's assailant. "You've hurt him enough!"

The seaman hesitated, then dropped his hand.

Cain fell to his knees with a grimace and a grunt.

The baby was crying so strenuously that Cat was afraid he was going to make himself sick again. Even though her own body was racked with sobs, she lifted him to her shoulder and crooned mindlessly to get him to stop. The breeze had picked up, and she adjusted the blanket over his head with a shaking hand.

"We'll take over from here." Colonel Howard stepped onto the boat, accompanied by the four MPs but minus the bullhorn. He slid his other hand into his pocket as he adjusted his stance to accommodate the slight sway at the dock.

"Yes, sir." The crewman whose careless "driving" had caused the contretemps in the first place holstered the pistol he'd been holding to Cain's temple, saluted Howard, then signaled the other two that they'd been dismissed.

"Remind me to add resisting arrest to the other charges we'll be filing against him," Howard ordered after the sailors had returned to their own boat.

"Yes, sir." The MP who'd moved forward to take the navy crewman's place now stood over Cain with the muzzle of his .45 set against the base of his skull.

Though Colonel Howard's eyes were flat and his face expressionless, Cat sensed a menace bordering on madness behind the smooth mask he turned to her. He ignored the baby, whose wails had subsided into whimpers, as he gave her the once-over. The black peasant pajamas she was wearing seemed to take him aback. But only for a second. Recovering, he shook his head in disgust.

"You disgrace your husband's memory, Mrs. Brown," he said contemptuously.

When Cain started to surge to his feet, the MP holding the gun to his head cocked the trigger and he wisely remained on his knees.

Her lashes barely flickering, Cat met the officer's gaze and raised her chin unashamedly. "I see you're still letting other people fight your battles for you, Colonel Howard."

Howard's eyes narrowed, and she braced herself for the slap she felt certain was coming as a result of her insubordinate remark. But he kept his hands in his pockets and spoke to Cain, gloating. "Thought you could outsmart me, didn't you, gook?"

Cat gasped in outrage at the nasty epithet.

"Thought you could sneak up river to peddle your drugs and our guns—"

"No," she contradicted him. "That's not what happened. He took me—"

"Frisk him," Howard ordered the MP to his right, ignoring her.

The MP, who didn't look to be a day over eighteen but wore the stripes of a sergeant, glanced uncertainly at him, then at Cain. "He's already surrendered his gun and his knife, sir."

A mocking sneer curled Howard's thin mouth. "You telling me you trust this traitor not to be carrying a concealed weapon? Or to have another knife strapped to his leg? Maybe even a universal key in his pocket that would unlock the handcuffs?"

"No, sir." The MP said it as though he had a mouth full of ashes.

"Frisk him," Howard commanded again in a cold voice.

"Yes, sir."

While obviously wary of Cain's booted feet, two of the MPs dragged him to a standing position while the third kept him covered and the young sergeant did a thorough job of patting him down.

"He's clean, sir."

Suspicion snaked up Cat's spine when Howard jerked his head toward the warehouse. "Take them both inside while I search the boat."

Why was he going to search the boat alone? she wondered. Especially when he had military policemen with him who were trained to do just that sort of thing. Shudders rippled through her, one after another, as she remembered the conversation she'd had with him—was it really only a three days ago?—in his office. And the innocent question she'd asked him at the time.

It all made sense to her now. He was setting Cain up. At her suggestion, no less! And if she wasn't mistaken, he had the evidence—

"You might want to shackle his legs, too," Howard added as the MPs rudely yanked Cain toward the dock. "Just in case he's thinking of putting on another martial arts demonstration."

"What have you got in your pockets, Colonel Howard?" Cat was positive now that this was a sting operation, and that the proof of it lay deep in those very pockets he was guarding so assiduously.

For the first time since he'd boarded the boat, Howard's eyes truly sparked. Then he doused his anger with a smile that was both thin and brief. "My hands."

Cat didn't believe him, but before she could refute him the skies opened up and rain lashed at her face. Because she didn't want the baby to get wet, she bowed her head over his and made a mad dash across the deck. The MP who'd questioned Howard about frisking Cain a second time considerately gave her a hand up and escorted her into the warehouse.

Inside, Tiny had been relieved of his shotgun and relegated to his desk. But he hadn't lost either his smile or his sense of timing. The first thing she heard when she ducked in out of the rain was his transistor radio, its volume turned down lower than the last time but still loud enough for her to hear the Animals screaming at the top of their lungs,

"*We gotta get outta this place . . .*"

The MP who had ushered her inside took up a post at the door while the other three stood guard over Cain. When Cat first saw him, she gasped. His hands were cuffed to a steel beam that ran from floor to ceiling and his legs were in irons. His lip had stopped bleeding but had begun to swell, and there was a new bruise forming on the side of his face—the result of the blow he'd taken on the boat.

She started toward him, but he warned her with a slight shake of his head to stay where she was. How long they waited, frozen in that terrible tableau, she couldn't begin to guess. All she knew was that everything that mattered to her—Cain's life, the baby's future—depended on her being right about what Colonel Howard was doing.

There was only one way to find out, she realized, and that was to catch him in the act. Her decision made, she turned back to the door. But the young MP who was guarding it stretched his arm in front of her, barring her way.

"You have to stay here," he said.

Thinking fast, she gave the MP a chagrined look. "Stupid me, I left the baby's diapers and bottles on the boat."

He glanced down at the baby and smiled, then up at her and shook his head remonstratively. "You shouldn't take him out in that rain, ma'am."

"Then you hold him."

"Me?"

"I need to get his medicine, too." The baby had calmed down, bless his heart, but Cat was a veritable bundle of nerves. "See, he has an ear infection—"

He nodded in understanding. "My little brother used to get them, and we'd have to warm towels for him to lay his head on."

She knew she had him then. "And it's almost time for him to take his penicillin again . . ." Before the MP knew what hit him, he was holding the baby and she was rushing out the door, into the teeth of the storm, assuring him over her shoulder, "I'll be right back."

A rain-drenched Cat found Colonel Howard tearing the main cabin apart with divine vengeance. He was so absorbed in emptying the pantry, flinging paper plates and sugar cubes atop the pile of stuff he'd pulled out of the other cabinets, that he hadn't heard her racing across the deck and down the hatch. It sickened her to see the mess he was making, especially knowing the way Cain kept things in such ship-shape order. Pushing her sopping hair out of her eyes, she stood on the bottom step and watched him for a moment in the light from the lantern he'd hung at the porthole.

Then, taking a deep breath, she entered. "What are you looking for?"

Howard spun, obviously startled to see her. "I ordered you to stay in the warehouse."

"I came back to get this." Feigning calm, she bent down and picked the backpack off the floor by one of the straps. "And to ask you if you have a search warrant."

His eyes narrowed nastily in the flickering light. "I don't need one."

"Why not?"

"For one thing, we're in a combat zone—"

"Cain is a civilian."

"Rules of procedure are different when the enemy—be it the Viet Cong or a traitor—threatens." Smiling snidely, he reached into his pocket and pulled out a half-dozen plastic vials filled with a powdery white substance that could only be one thing. "And for another, I've already found enough of what I'm looking for to throw the book at him."

Heroin, Cat realized dully as she stared down at the vials in his hand. She suffered not a scintilla of doubt about where it had come from because she trusted Cain. Implicitly. The problem was, she had no proof that Howard had planted it. All she had to go on was instinct. It was that same instinct, though, that had led her half way around the world to find her son. Now it gave her the courage to raise her gaze and call the officer's bluff.

"Where did you find that?" she demanded.

A flicker of annoyance marred Howard's features. "What difference does it make?"

"For one thing," she said, mocking him, "I've been with Cain around the clock these last couple of days so I know for a fact that he doesn't do drugs."

Howard glowered at her. "He just sells them to our troops."

"And for another," she continued blandly, "I've been in every nook and cranny of this cabin, and I've never seen anything even remotely resembling heroin."

He thought hard, and then darted a glance at the drawer under the bunk. "That's because you didn't look in there."

"That's where you're wrong." Her own gaze went to the drawer. It was still closed, so she assumed that he hadn't tossed it yet. Which meant he hadn't found the cigarettes that Cain kept there for bargaining purposes, either. She looked back at Howard then. "I put the baby—my *husband's* baby—to bed in there."

His hard face went slack. "Your husband's baby?"

"Yes." Cat was flying blind now, fighting against panic as she tried to think and talk at the same time. "You see, he had a Vietnamese 'wife' who—"

"A hootch-girl," he said scornfully.

"Call her what you will," she countered, "but Lily gave birth to Johnny's son less than a week after he was shot down, and then she hemorrhaged to death herself a couple of hours later."

"Your husband's infidelity is your problem, Mrs. Brown." Howard put the plastic vials back in his coat pocket and made to step around her. "My only concern is seeing Cain tried and hanged for smuggling heroin."

Cat paled at the venom in his voice, but refused to move out of his way. The crucial moment was at hand, and her chest hurt from repressing her mounting anxiety. Still, the man had to be stopped before he destroyed Cain.

She stared up at him, unblinking, as she played her trump card. "Before you leave, Colonel Howard, I want to let you know that I'm planning to attend the press briefing with the baby tomorrow afternoon."

That stopped him in his tracks. "What?"

"You heard me."

"Why?"

"Because I think it's time the American people know what's going on over here. That you and the other commanders are not only ignoring mixed-blood babies like my husband's, but that you're perfectly willing to abandon them to the communists when we lose this damned war."

His eyes darkened ominously. "Are you threatening me, Mrs. Brown?"

"Not at all, Colonel Howard," she said with delicate irony. "I'm simply promising you that by the time I'm done, those 'Five O'Clock Follies' you so despise will have turned into an *opéra bouffe*. And that I will have named you personally as one of the principal obstacles to these babies being acknowledged and granted U.S. citizenship."

He took a step backwards, almost tripping over the bamboo throw rug that lay in the middle of the floor. They both knew that what she was saying wasn't entirely true. He wasn't the ultimate authority where the babies' fates were concerned. The blame for that lay at the doorstep of his superiors, who, by turning a blind eye to the problem, were complicity encouraging it. But if this got out, somebody would have to take the fall. And judging by his expression, Howard knew exactly who that somebody was.

"You're planning to frame me," he accused.

"Kind of like you're planning to frame Cain," she agreed.

Cat couldn't believe that she had so boldly admitted her intention. Howard looked back at her through stricken eyes. Then he lowered them guiltily and swallowed hard, visibly struggling to compose himself.

When he looked up again, the lines in his face seemed deeper, the set of his mouth even tighter than normal. She almost felt sorry for him. He was fighting two wars—one against the North Vietnamese army and one against the growing scourge of drug use by his own troops—and he was losing on both fronts.

"Cain's a traitor, goddammit." The way he pushed the words through his clenched teeth told her that he was convinced of that.

"Then charge him with treason and be done with it." Cat slid her arms through the straps of the backpack and started up the hatch. On the second step, though, she stopped and turned back to make one final point. Her knees were shaking but her voice was calm. "My father landed on Omaha Beach on D-Day, Colonel Howard, so I grew up with a great deal of respect for what America's military can do when it has right as well as might on its side. I'd hate to go home believing otherwise."

When she went up on the rain-slick deck, the storm had abated and the wind had died down. The clouds thinned and a melon ball of moon cast a shimmering light on the water. Singsong voices and the eerie, almost Elizabethan music of a recorder rippled from one of the hundreds of huts that lined the Saigon River.

As she crossed the dock, Cat told herself that she'd done all she could do. That it was up to Colonel Howard now to either press his phony drug charge against Cain or to drop it entirely. Forcibly curving her lips into a smile, she opened the warehouse door. But her eyes swam with emotion when she saw the young MP playing peek-a-boo with the baby.

"Thank you, Sergeant," she said, extending her arms. "I'll take him now."

Colonel Howard swept into the warehouse shortly after her. Squaring his shoulders in a perfect brace, he shot Cain a look. A renegade to the bitter end, Cain straightened and eyed him right back.

Howard blinked first, and shifted his attention to Cat.

Cradling the baby, she angled her head and met his gaze.

"Let him go," he ordered the MPs as he unbuttoned his trench coat, two-fingered a cigarette from the pack in his shirt pocket and lit it with the Zippo he carried in his other hand.

"Sir?" the sergeant at the door said in disbelief.

"You heard me." Howard drew smoke in deeply and exhaled through his nose. "He's clean."

Cat released the breath she'd just realized she was holding as the MPs scrambled to remove the handcuffs and leg irons from Cain. She glanced at Tiny, whose gold front tooth shone like a small sun in his wide, white smile. Out of the corner of her eye, she saw Loc coming toward them and knew they were almost home free.

She relaxed too soon, however.

There was a mean gleam in Howard's eyes when she looked back at him. "I presume you're planning to take the baby home with you, Mrs. Brown."

"Yes. I want to adopt him."

"He'll need a passport and an exit permit."

She nodded. "I'll make application at the American Embassy tomorrow."

"No." He smiled a cold smile at her. "My secretary will meet you at the ticket counter at Tan Son Nhut at eight o'clock in the morning with all the paperwork you'll need. That way, you can catch the first plane to Hong Kong. From there, it's a direct flight to Hawaii."

Cat was so stunned by his statement that it took her breath away. So this was the price she would pay for confronting him. In order to assure that she didn't attend the press briefing tomorrow afternoon, Howard was getting rid of her by putting her on a plane in the morning.

Tears flooded her eyes, but she sniffed them away lest he mistakenly think she regretted the stand she'd taken. She drew a ragged breath and clutched the baby even closer to her. "I'll be there, Colonel Howard."

"Does the baby have a name?" he asked her then.

"John." Cat smiled over at Cain through her tears. "John Lee Brown."

Chapter
Eighteen

"Would you like a cup of tea?"

"Uh, sure."

Cat turned toward the kitchen. "If you'd rather have a beer—"

"No," Cain said with a quick shake of his head. "Tea's fine."

Everything in the living room seemed to mark time as she turned back toward the rattan sofa. It seemed ludicrous, after all they'd been through together, that they were suddenly so uneasy with each other. But there was an undeniable awkwardness between them now that the baby was asleep and they were essentially alone in the guest house.

Perched on the edge of the sofa and praying that she could pour the fragrant tea without spilling, Cat reached for the porcelain pot that was sitting on a lacquered tray in front of her. At the same time she found herself grasping at conversational straws. "It was really nice of Loc to let us stay here tonight."

"Like he said, you'll be safer here than in the hotel, what with the sporadic fighting that's still going on in downtown Saigon." Cain sat on the opposite end of the sofa with his knees spread wide and his large hand dwarfing the delicate cup she'd passed him. "Plus, it's closer to the airport."

"Yes." She was revisited by a bittersweet pang at the reminder of the long trip she still faced, but she carefully hid it behind a polite smile. "There is that."

Another silence fell between them, this one slightly more tense than the last, as they drank the steaming tea that had been steeping in the pot.

Loc had hustled them out of the warehouse before Colonel Howard could change his mind again about arresting Cain. Then, with Cat and John Lee in the Tempest and Cain following on his motorcycle, Loc had driven north and west of the city, not stopping until they'd reached the cream-colored colonial house where he lived with his wife and their four children. A loud *BOOM* in the distance, followed by the distinct *pop, pop, pop* of small-arms fire had confirmed his prediction of another night of fighting in the streets of Saigon when Cat had gotten out of the car.

Seeing how upset she was, Loc had ushered them into the house to meet his family—a first for Cain—and his wife, Ngo, had shyly invited them to share their evening meal. Cat had never been in a Vietnamese home and was fascinated to learn that it was decorated with traditionally dark, deeply carved furniture. Two altars held brass incense burners and offerings of fruit and flowers to their ancestors, to the spirits of great men of the past, and to Buddha.

After dinner, their host had led them out to the guest house where Cat and the baby would spend the night. Cain had unloaded the luggage that Kim had kept for her from the trunk of the Tempest while Loc went back to the main house to get her watch. He'd returned with it and with the tea tray Ngo had prepared for them, as well as the news that they needed to leave for the airport no later than seven-fifteen in the morning. Then he'd bid them goodnight and had discreetly withdrawn so that they could say goodbye in private.

But saying goodbye was proving more difficult than either of them had anticipated.

They'd started out easily enough. Cain had offered to bathe John Lee while Cat repacked her carry-on bag with the bottles and diapers and clean saques she would need for him during their long trip home. Love, enormous waves of it, had rushed through her when he'd come out of the bathroom with the baby diapered and dressed, and she'd wanted to cry when he'd placed the sweet-smelling bundle in her arms. Determined not to fall apart at this late date, she'd thanked him and turned away a little too quickly.

Her cool voice had baffled him, especially after he'd seen the warmth in her eyes. Time to shake her hand, wish her luck and hit the road, he'd told himself. And yet he'd stayed, feeling terribly intrusive but reluctant to just up and leave her so abruptly.

But he was beginning to think that staying had been a big mistake.

After John Lee was fed and medicated and fast asleep in the crib that Ngo had considerately placed in the spare bedroom, Cat had gone into her room to change out of the black pajamas Cain had given her. She'd come out looking like the All-American girl again, with her hair falling neatly to her shoulders and her simple green shift hemmed just above the knees, and he'd gone back to feeling like the rebellious mongrel of his boyhood. Still, even as he'd wondered how he was going to get out of here gracefully, without any recriminations on either side, he'd delayed his departure once again by stubbing out his half-smoked cigarillo and accepting that cup of tea he really didn't want.

Now there they were, sitting on opposite ends of the sofa and trying to ignore the electricity that had been building between them almost from the beginning, while the gaps in their conversation grew increasingly longer and their time together grew ever shorter.

"That meal Ngo fixed for us was delicious," Cat said, having decided that the silence was more unbearable than stilted conversation.

He nodded affably. "She's a great cook."

The thudding of artillery fire had her glancing anxiously toward the front door. "What was that fish sauce called again?"

"*Nvoc mam.*" Then, seeing how distraught she was, he hastened to assure her, "Those are our guns, by the way."

"Oh, good." Somewhat relieved, she looked back at him. "It was really pungent."

His confused gaze riveted on her face. "What?"

"The fish sauce."

"That's because it's made from peppers."

She raised a brow then and gave him that familiar smirk. "You finally got your shrimp."

He met the teasing light in her eyes with a crooked smile. "Yeah, I finally got my shrimp."

Having exhausted her supply of small talk, Cat looked around the living room of the guest house, which was a miniature replica of Loc and Ngo's house. She'd already told Cain about her tête-à-tête with Colonel Howard in the main cabin. And had listened in mute astonishment when he'd confessed that he had a cache of captured AK-47s in the hold—weapons, he was quick to add, that he would give to those American soldiers in the field whose regulation M-16s often failed to function for lack of oil.

She studied the tea in her cup, as if reading the leaves at the bottom. "How's your lip?"

"Much better, thanks to that salve Ngo gave me to put on it after I washed up."

"That's good." Giving him a vapid smile, she reached for the pot. "More tea?"

"No, thanks." The jets roaring over the house almost drowned out his answer. "I've still got some."

Cat nodded and retracted her hand. The teapot was in keeping with their surroundings. When she had admired its exquisite painting, Loc had explained that the various symbols were actually a map for happiness. The bearded sage was for longevity, he'd pointed out. A lady bearing a peach was for prosperity. The child meant many descendants. A dish with a duck was for good food, and a deer for good luck

But the happiest sign of all, he'd pointed out, was the red bat. While she already knew that red was considered a lucky color, she didn't understand that business about the bat. It's because the bat sleeps with his head down and his feet high, he'd said. He's truly relaxed and has no worries at all. Eat red bat meat, he'd encouraged her in all seriousness, and see what it will do for you!

As the silence dragged out, Cain drained his teacup and set it aside. "Well, it's getting late, and you've got an early flight tomorrow . . ."

"Don't go," Cat said with sudden urgency. Her heart was hammering so hard that she wondered it didn't beat its way out of her chest. Yet she held his gaze unwaveringly. "Please. Stay."

He eased back against the cushions and studied her face in the lamp-light. She looked so beautiful, so delicate, so fragile. She was all of those things, yet she was also the toughest, most determined woman he'd ever met. And when she got on that plane tomorrow morning, she would be taking a piece of his heart with her.

"If I stay," he warned her in a raspy voice, "I'm going to make love with you."

She sensed the disciplined strength and resolute will of the man who had already changed her life forever. He was a hero who saw beyond the blood to ultimate justice. He was also the outlaw who'd stolen her heart. And she couldn't let him leave without first creating memories of love that would have to last her a lifetime.

"Then stay," she said simply, and her smile promised him paradise in the midst of this hellacious war.

Her heartbeat thickened when he moved closer to her. She met him halfway, tilting her face up as his mouth came down hard on hers. The passion that exploded between them was instantaneous. Knowing this one night was all they would ever have, neither of them held anything back.

Cain's strong hands delved into her sunburst hair while Cat's arms slid under his and around his back. She kneaded the rippling muscles beneath his shirt, remembering only too well how tan and sleek they'd looked beneath the tropical sun. He released her mouth from the inflaming kiss and dipped his head lower to nuzzle her neck. Her skin was soft and smooth and smelled ever so slightly of Dove soap. For the rest of his life, be it measured in hours or days or years, he would associate that scent with her.

"Touch me," she whispered, shuddering with longing as his searching lips found the sensitive spot at the crook of her neck.

"Where?" he asked, his breath warm and moist against her ear.

"Here." She boldly took his hands in hers and placed them over her breasts. Then she closed her eyes and lost herself in the sensations his stroking fingers and soothing palms elicited.

"Let's go to bed, Cat." He could feel his pulse racing against time and an eternity without her as he rose and pulled her to her feet.

"Yes." She felt like a volcano, ready to erupt, and she wanted nothing more than to be joined with him when the tremors came.

In the moonlit shadows of the bedroom, which was dominated by a four-poster lacquer bed, he slowed things down as if he wanted to savor every last second allotted to them. He tilted her head back, his hand firm on her neck, and she found herself waiting, almost breathless, for his next kiss. The lazily rotating blades of the ceiling fan stirred the heady fragrance of plumeria that wafted in through the open window from the garden beyond. A cricket chirping in the night for its mate seemed to echo her own heartbeat.

And then he was kissing her eyelids, her temples, her cheeks, tasting every tiny patch of her silken flesh. His lips even feathered over the tip of her nose. She felt dreamy, as if none of this was real, and yet she had never wanted so intensely as she did now. Hungry for more, she rose up on tiptoe, drew his head down and guided his mouth to hers.

Giving a low growl, he took the initiative from her. He fused their mouths together and sent his tongue deep, penetrating her mouth and saturating her with desire. The rich male taste of him coated her throat. The things he murmured made her tummy quiver in anticipation. The scent of him, a mixture of musk and the indigo night, caused her knees to go weak.

She made a languid noise, reveling in the carnality of his kiss and letting her tongue dance lightly around his. He continued to kiss her ravenously as he crushed her to the burning length of his body. Her breasts were flattened against his chest and his erection nudged the cleft of her thighs. Exulting in the obvious strength of his desire, she ground her middle against it.

The power of her need for this man, a man she barely knew and would probably never see again, surprised her. But oh, it felt so right. And all that made her woman told her that what was to follow would truly be an act of love.

Cain grasped the skirt of her shift and worked it up to her waist. "How am I supposed to get you out of this damn thing?"

Smiling, Cat wriggled out of his arms and turned her back on him. "Try the zipper."

"Oh," he said on a sheepish laugh, "good thinking."

He eased the zipper all the way down to her slender waist, kissing the shadowed discovery of her shoulder blades and the slender column of her spine. When his lips moved up to her ear lobe, and then behind it, the night air cooled the flushed skin of her back. His deft fingers unhooked her bra, so that he could peel it and her dress and her panties off in one fluid motion. Standing before him, clad only in the tropical moonlight, she allowed herself the satisfaction of hearing him groan with desire.

"I knew you were beautiful," he said hoarsely, looking at the wanton picture she made with her hair-tumbled head thrown back and her skin gleaming camellia white in the dim light. "But I didn't know you were perfect."

"Your turn," she whispered coquettishly, and reached for the hem of his T-shirt.

"Not yet," he temporized, and cupped her breasts in his callused palms.

Her knees nearly buckled when he brushed his thumbs over her nipples. Like torpid buds released by springtime, they burst into feverish flower for him. She gripped his forearms to keep from falling. Then she gasped in ecstasy when he bent his head to kiss them each in turn, applying a piercingly sweet sucking action that she felt all the way down to her toes.

"Now," he said huskily, and gently lowered her to the bed.

Prickles of heat shot through her as she watched him pull his T-shirt over his head and toss it aside. Her breathing grew ragged when he removed his jeans and she saw his erection, hard and huge with arousal. She shocked herself when she raised up on one elbow and reached out to stroke him and read his secret contours.

Groaning, Cain wrapped his fingers around her wrist and whispered fiercely, "Stop, or it'll be over before it begins."

"We can't have that, can we?" All enchantress now, Cat fell back and stretched her arms over her head, arching her breasts upward in tender offering.

His hair shone blue-black in the moonlight as he bent his head and circled her pert nipples with his tongue, causing her back to bow. "No," he said, smiling wolfishly up at her then, "we sure can't."

As their lips bonded again, her hands began to have their own cravings. She caressed his taut buttocks and sinewy back. Her fingers found the ridges of scars old and new and followed them with healing tenderness. Then, giving into an urge she couldn't fathom, she gently sank her nails into his meaty shoulders.

Her blood swam when he deepened the kiss, sending little crackles of excitement surging up her spine. His tongue stroked and pressed, searching out the shapes and spaces of her mouth. Her fingers lifted to his head and threaded themselves through the thick hair that fell like wild black rain over his forehead.

She parted her thighs and felt his fierce passion graze their sensitive insides. Her tummy quickened when the heat of him nudged the heart of her. A shudder seized her then, sponsored as much by his tender torment as by the fact that there could be no future for them. And though it pained her to acknowledge it, she seized the moment with a smile.

"Love me, Cain," she murmured, raising her hips and moving against him.

The hell of it was, he did. He loved her, but he couldn't afford to tell her. Couldn't risk cracking the shell of numbness that kept him going. So he showed her. He rose above her and slowly buried himself within her snug, moist sheath. Ecstasy shimmied through him when she said his name, then whispered it again against his lips.

His body was starved; hers was the feast. But even as the need for release clawed at him, he was mindful that this was all he could offer her. His strokes were long and smooth, which only heightened the eroticism and prolonged the pleasure.

"Cain." Her breath burned her lungs. "It's never . . . Not like this. Cain."

"Look at me, Cat." He sipped at the glad tear that slipped down her glowing cheek.

Their gazes met in the moonlight. Their mouths melded with a fervor that kissed their souls. Their bodies moved in an age-old rhythm that felt miraculously new as the love which neither dared voice culminated in a brilliant, shimmering climax.

A soft, mewling sound woke her. She opened one eye, saw that it was still dark, and wondered what on earth that—

The baby!

Cat opened both eyes and blinked rapidly, trying to orient herself in the strange room. Then she slipped carefully out of bed, not wanting to disturb Cain, and tiptoed out of her bedroom and into John Lee's.

The crib was empty!

Her breath slicing at her throat and her heart thundering fearfully against her eardrums, Cat spun and started back to her bedroom to wake Cain.

Another voice, this one deeper than the first, drew her toward the living room. She stopped in the doorway, her eyes misting over with high emotion when she saw the huge, naked man walking the floor with her baby draped over his broad shoulder.

Cain was singing to John Lee in a soft undertone. The tune was vaguely familiar to Cat but she couldn't make out the words. She cocked her head and listened closely. Then she clapped her hand over her mouth to keep from laughing out loud when she recognized the mellow rendition of "The Purple People Eater."

He turned, his raven hair disheveled upon his brow, and held a silencing finger against his lips when he saw her standing there. She trailed him into the temporary nursery and watched him lay John Lee on his tummy in the crib. The baby gave one little squeak of protest at being put down before falling into the innocent sleep of a child.

"You've got a real mother's ear," Cat said when they were back in her room.

Cain shrugged nonchalantly. "A man who lives on the edge learns to sleep light."

She looked up at him, startled by the reminder that he was returning to the war while she was going back to the world. It was all she could do not to beg him to come with her. Her father would be glad to help him with his legal problems, she was sure of it. Especially after everything he'd done for her and the baby.

But he would never willingly leave the nuns and the orphans. She was as certain of that as she was of her own name. And if he *did* agree to desert them, she knew, he wouldn't be the man she loved.

"That was some lullaby," she said in a wry tone.

His smile shone whitely in the moonlight. "John Lee enjoyed it."

"Well, a one-eyed, one-eared, flying purple people eater is liable to give him nightmares."

"You're right. Maybe I should've started him out on the Big Bopper."

"He's a little young for 'Chantilly Lace'."

"All right, you think of someone."

She pursed her lips. "The Beatles."

"*Catherine, ma belle',*" he crooned in a nasally French accent.

Laughter tickled her throat. "Fats Domino."

"Now you're talking." He pulled her tight against him, placed his mouth next to her ear and began singing, "*I found my thrill . . . boom-boom-boom-boom, boom-boom-boom-boom . . .*"

She tipped her head back. "'Blueberry Hill' hardly qualifies as a cradlesong."

"This isn't for John Lee." His breath blew warm against her face. "It's for me."

"Oh, well, in that case . . ." Caught up in his inspired silliness in spite of herself, Cat wrapped her arms around his neck, laid her head in the curve of his shoulder, and let Cain draw her into his rhythm.

"*The moon stood still . . . boom-boom-boom-boom, boom-boom-boom-boom . . .*"

It was the craziest thing she'd ever done, dancing naked in the dark with a man who was supplying both the words and the music. It was also the most sensual. His body, solid against hers, made her heart flutter. The hair on his chest teased her breasts, and his hard thighs slid along hers. His hand, pressed to the small of her back, marked her as his for all time.

At song's end, he touched his lips to her forehead in a brief kiss and asked huskily, "Any other requests?"

"Yes." Smiling up into his lean face, she reached down and found him hard and ready for her. "Encore."

Cat took one last look around the guest house to make sure she wasn't forgetting anything. In her bedroom, she smiled gently with remembrance. Cain had left sometime before dawn, while she was sleeping, but they had already said goodbye.

It was easier this way, she acknowledged as she pressed a soft kiss into John Lee's downy black hair. She wasn't sure where he'd gone, but she remembered him telling Sister Simone that he needed to go north. And she thought it was smart of him to leave Saigon before Colonel Howard could set another trap for him. But how she'd hated waking up this morning without him!

They'd had more than one encore, as it turned out. Their passions had been quick to ignite each time one touched the other, and the heat of their movements had echoed the heat of the night. They had dozed in between, lying indolently among the tangled sheets.

Cat had been married, but she'd never experienced anything like the intimacies she'd shared with Cain. There'd been no rules, no restraints as they'd plumbed the depths of a more voluptuous sensuality than she'd ever dreamed possible. He'd touched her with astonishing familiarity, his hands and tongue taking liberties that had had left her weak and spent. Shy at first, and then emboldened by his encouraging murmurs, she'd kissed her way down his stomach, and then lower, delighting in both his ragged breathing and the knowledge that she could leave him as drained and relaxed as she.

She'd been awakened from a deep, dreamless sleep by a knock on the front door a little after six. It was Ngo, carrying a tray full of traditional breakfast foods—small meat dumplings to dip in that hot fish sauce, fried pork sausage, and a shrimp paste that looked like a paté. Everything was artfully arranged and smelled heavenly, but she hadn't had much of an appetite. Not wanting to insult her lovely hostess, however, she had thrown on a floral-printed skirt and plain white blouse and eaten a few bites of each dish before going to dress and feed the baby.

"I'm ready," she told Loc now as she returned to the living room.

Nodding briskly, he handed her a package wrapped in several layers of tissue paper before he picked up her suitcases. "For you."

"What is it?" she asked him.

"The teapot." At the front door, he turned back and gave her a rare smile. "It's my wife's and my hope that you will teach your son to honor his Vietnamese as well as his American ancestors. We are an ancient and proud people, a peaceful people at heart, but we are fighting to be free of the communists just as your forebears fought to be free of the English."

"I'll learn all I can," she promised him in a quavering voice. "And then I'll teach John Lee."

Before she left the house, she took a moment to tuck the painted china teapot into the carry-on bag holding John Lee's things so she would have it with her at all times during her long trip home. The heat and humidity slapped at her face like wet hands as she stepped outside. She could still hear shooting in the distance as she settled into the back seat of the car with the baby.

Cat had sworn to herself that she wouldn't look back. What good would it do? Cain was well on his way north by now, and her plane was leaving in less than an hour. But as Loc put the Tempest in gear and pulled away from the curb, she glanced over her shoulder and said a spiritual goodbye to the small house where she had spent the most wonderful night of her life.

Then, telling herself that what was past was past, she turned her stinging eyes to the front and, hugging the baby tightly, began focusing on the future.

Pandemonium reigned outside the terminal at Tan Son Nhut, with taxis and trucks carrying everything from humans to crates of chickens rattling past. Loc parked behind an old school bus, and got out to unload her luggage from the trunk. A skycap of sorts with a brown face and the last of her piasters in his pocket carried the suitcases inside.

"Thank you." With her arms full of baby and purse and diaper bag, Cat couldn't give Loc a hug. So she leaned over kissed his leathery cheek. "For everything."

His face worked with emotion, and for a moment she was afraid he was going to cry. Then he pulled himself together, bowing his head and closing his eyes just as he had the first time she'd met him. "Be proud that you are an American."

"I am," she said, and blinked away tears.

"And know that no matter what others say, your husband died for a noble cause."

The thudding of harassment and interdiction fire sounded beyond the chain link fence that surrounded the airport.

"Be careful," she managed to choke out, then turned and hurried into the busy terminal.

As Colonel Howard had promised, Kim met her at the ticket counter with John Lee's passport and exit permit. She also had a certified copy of the baby's birth certificate that she had already filed with the American Embassy on her way to the airport. Cat checked it over, then lifted her confused gaze to the girl's pretty face.

"The birth certificate lists me as the mother," she pointed out.

Kim's lips curved in a complacent smile. "Colonel Howard said it would be easier for you to take him into the United States that way."

Concern crimped Cat's brow. "But I haven't adopted him yet."

"Adoption in Vietnam by an alien could take months," Kim explained. "Maybe even a year."

The word "alien" left a bitter taste in Cat's mouth. As did the knowledge that a certain officer was once again manipulating the law to suit his own purposes. "So Colonel Howard decided to smooth the way."

"The plane to Hong Kong is boarding, Mrs. Brown," the ticket agent said then.

Kim extended her arms. "May I hold him?"

"Of course," Cat said, and passed a blanket-bundled John Lee over.

But she had to look away when an emotional Kim partially unwrapped the baby and kissed his elbow in parting. Then she whispered something to him in Vietnamese—goodbye—perhaps—before she rewrapped him and handed him back. She lowered her head then, her hair falling like a black velvet curtain across her sweet-sad face. "You see what I meant when I said that Cain was an honorable man."

"Will you do something for me?" Cat asked quietly.

The girl raised her head and looked at her quizzically.

"Love him twice as much for me."

Kim's dark, almond-shaped eyes shimmered with tears as she nodded in understanding. Then, murmuring something about having to get to the office, she straightened her narrow shoulders, turned on her spiky high heel and ran toward the door.

The ticket agent pointed in the opposite direction. "That way, Mrs. Brown."

Her vision growing misty at the edges, Cat followed the crowd to her gate. As she crossed the tarmac, a planeload of American replacements marched past her, double-timing their way toward the military buses that would take them to the in-country processing station. Each of them was wearing khaki and carrying a duffel bag on his shoulder. And all of them looked so young, so innocent—more like boys playing soldier than men going to war—that she felt fear clutch at her heart. How many of these cherub warriors would survive to return home?

Numb with grief for those unknown mothers and wives still to receive a chaplain's call and a curtly worded telegram, she climbed the steps of the plane. In the front were the officers, all creased and pressed and playing gin rummy with each other or with their aides; in the rear were the enlisted men, smelling of hair tonic and after-shave and making plans for R & R in Hong Kong; in the middle were the civilians.

The flight was only half full, which meant that Cat had no seatmates.

And that suited her just fine. She was no mood for company or idle chitchat, either one.

A stewardess with teased blond hair and a full makeup job offered to hold John Lee while she slid into her window seat, stowed his diaper bag under the seat in front of her and buckled up.

"What is it?" she asked as she handed him back.

Cat tensed at the question, thinking of how Cain had been treated because of his heritage. "A baby."

The stewardess rolled eyes as blue as the shadow that decorated their lids. "I mean is it a boy or a girl?"

"Oh." Cat's lips relaxed into a smile. "A boy."

"It's kind of hard to tell when they're so little."

"Let's get this show on the road!" an enlisted man two rows back hollered.

"We'll be airborne in a few minutes," the stewardess told Cat. "If you need me for something—"

"*I* need you for something," that same GI chimed in.

Hoots and catcalls rewarded his clever statement.

"You sure you wouldn't rather trade that boy for a girl?" the stewardess asked, sotto voce, before she left to finish her pre-flight duties.

"I'm sure," Cat said softly but firmly.

Once the doors were closed, the captain's voice came over the intercom to inform the passengers that they were ready to take off.

At the stewardess's suggestion, she gave the baby a bottle he really didn't want to help keep his ears clear when the cabin pressure changed. Then she laid her head back and swallowed thickly as the plane taxied along the runway. Within minutes, they were airborne.

She was going home, but she was leaving her heart in Saigon.

When she removed the bottle from a sleeping John Lee's mouth, Cat saw a silvery tear glistening on his little cheek. She used her thumb to brush it away. Only to realize that it wasn't his, but hers.

Unbeknownst to her, it matched the single tear trickling down the lean, darkly bewhiskered cheek of the man who was sitting astride his motorcycle in the shadows of the hanger, watching her fly away from him.

Chapter

Nineteen

KANSAS CITY, MISSOURI; 1973

*I*n your opinion, Mrs. Brown," the reporter queried, "what should the government do about all the Amerasian children our troops have so cavalierly abandoned over three-plus decades?"

Cat folded her hands on the table in front of her, casting a surreptitious glance at her watch as she did so. The statement she'd prepared for the press conference was still in her purse. Instead of reading it, as she'd originally planned, she had instead spoken from the heart, giving a capsulized rendition of the plight of America's forgotten progeny of war. She had even quoted Cain, though not by name, as she described the lifetime of discrimination and poverty they faced in ethnically pure societies that considered such children less than dirt. Then she had opened the floor to questions.

Which might have been a mistake.

The reception room was thronged with reporters, cameras and recording equipment. Politicians from the city to the federal level, figuring this was an opportunity to do a little glad-handing and maybe garner some favorable publicity in the process, were strategically scattered throughout the audience. There were also representatives from several veterans' groups as well as a number of interested citizens who had read about today's event in the newspaper.

Normally Cat would have been delighted to draw a crowd of this size.

But the air-conditioning in the room that had been provided by the Alameda Plaza Hotel was on the fritz and the early June heat was so stifling that peoples' tongues—hers included—were practically hanging out. Plus, this was taking longer than she had expected it would. She needed to pick up John Lee shortly at the YMCA, where he was practicing with his T-ball team, then swing by the grocery store on their way home. And after dinner, she wanted to run by her parents' house to see her mother, who'd had her first radiation treatment today following her radical mastectomy four weeks ago.

She looked down either side of the conference table—first at the frowning military men who sat to her right, and then at the beaming civilians on her left. Finally, she gave the television reporter who'd posed the question a cool smile and spoke into the microphone that sat in front of her. "To be honest, I wouldn't necessarily characterize it as cavalier."

"But—"

"On the other hand," she continued firmly, "I do think that we as a nation have a responsibility toward these children. They are, after all, the living legacy of our presence in Asia. The real victims, if you will, of our three wars on that continent. And I believe we owe them at least as much as we do the thousands of political refugees from Indochina on whom we're now spending millions of dollars."

"Owe them what?" the reporter followed up.

Cat paused to take a drink of water and to gather her thoughts. As one of the regional spokespersons for Americans for International Aid, which, among other things, worked to facilitate reunions between the American soldiers who had fought in Vietnam and their Amerasian offspring, she walked a fine line. For one thing, she was a volunteer, not a paid staff person. And for another, she worked both sides of the political aisle on legislation that was being considered, so she had to be careful to keep her personal views from spilling over into her answers.

She set her glass back on the table and idly scanned the crowd that had turned out in honor of the reunion between a local veteran and the Vietnamese wife and daughter he'd had to leave behind when he'd finished his stint. He'd promised faithfully that he would return for them just as soon as he could. But the fates had conspired against him. After the Paris Peace Accords ending U.S. involvement in Vietnam were signed in late January and the American ground troops pulled out in March, followed by the return of the "last known prisoners of war," there was no going back.

AIA had worked diligently to bring the small family together again. Their reward had come a little over an hour ago, in an empty office behind the conference room, when the soldier had enfolded his wife and daughter in his arms after their year-long separation. Even his parents, who'd been rather dubious about their son's choice of a spouse, had literally melted when their new little granddaughter had taken her first toddling steps toward them. Once everyone's eyes were dried, the doors to the conference room had been thrown open, the audience invited in, and the serviceman had given a short but moving speech thanking everyone who had helped him get his family back.

Now, Cat felt her heart skid to a jarring halt when her gaze lit on a tall man in Air Force blues who was standing in the shadows in the back of the room. She couldn't see his face because of the cameras that were still popping like fireworks, the microphones that were being held up to catch the panel members' answers and the reporters' hands that were waving in the air. But there was something hauntingly familiar about him . . . something that caused her senses to come tingling to life . . . something that reminded her of Cain.

Which was ridiculous, since he was wearing a uniform.

Thinking her eyes were simply playing tricks on her, she turned her attention back to the reporter who had asked her what the government owed the children under discussion. She couldn't divorce herself entirely from the issue, of course. John Lee was such a happy, loving little boy that she couldn't imagine her life without him. He was also a daily reminder of the orphans at *Sacré Coeur*—many fathered by American soldiers, some scarred, others sick, all without hope of a loving family—and the nuns who had put their own lives in jeopardy to care for them. All she could do was continue to call the public's attention to their plight and pray they would eventually demand that their children be brought home.

"Let me answer your question this way," she began. "Because many of these children are American citizens by virtue of the fact that their fathers married their mothers in legal ceremonies"—she looked pointedly at the couple to her left then—"I believe that Congress should pass the special bill that's being introduced which exempts them from the current two-year residency requirement."

"And if the bill doesn't pass?"

Now she focused on her congressman, a rather pompous fellow with white hair and a florid face who was sitting in the second row of the audience. "Then they should provide the funds to bring the children here—to live in foster homes, perhaps—so that they can fulfill the residency requirement."

"That's a lot of money, Mrs. Brown," one of the newspaper reporters challenged her. "Especially for a country that's already spent something like a hundred-and-ten billion dollars and lost over fifty thousand men . . . not to mention the war."

Cat glanced down at her folded hands again before she answered. She didn't wear her wedding ring anymore, but she could still see it on her finger, as shiny and new as the happily-ever-after dreams that that God-awful conflict had destroyed. Then she met the reporter's gaze head-on.

"Yes, it is a lot of money," she agreed. "And I know the American public is tired of hearing about the war. Frankly, I get tired of hearing about it sometimes. I get tired of talking about it, too." She lifted her chin defiantly higher. "But I believe we have a moral responsibility to those who carry half our features, half our blood and who bear all the terrible consequences of being *Half*."

A smattering of applause broke out in the audience when she finished. She pushed the damp bangs of her shag-cut hair out of her eyes and sat back in her chair, more grateful than words could say that the next question was directed to one of the military officers instead of to her. Listening with only half an ear to the question he'd been asked and was now answering, she let her gaze stray to the back of the room again.

But the man she was looking for was gone.

Cat emerged from her reverie to find that she'd shredded a whole head of lettuce when she only needed half. Disgusted with herself, she opened the drawer beside the sink and reached for a plastic bag. She'd been in this painful, bittersweet state since the press conference that afternoon, and she blamed it—unfairly—on the man who'd made her think of Cain.

These head-trips, while growing fewer and farther between, weren't all that uncommon. In fact, she'd taken quite a number of them over the past five years. She would see a stranger, usually from behind, whose dark hair or devil's laugh reminded her of him, and her heart would do the old hanky-panky. Then the stranger would turn around, as if he sensed her staring at him, and she would turn away, embarrassed to realize that she was.

Five years was a long time to carry a torch. Too long, perhaps, for what might have been—on Cain's part, at least—nothing more than a pleasurable but ultimately inconsequential escape from the war. On Cat's part, though, the flame had never been extinguished. That one night of love had illuminated her soul. And it was that golden light, still burning bright, that had sustained her all this time.

Shaking off her malaise, she scooped the lettuce she planned to use into a serving bowl and put the rest in the plastic bag for another meal. She had better things to do than to stand there daydreaming about what might have happened if they had met in another time and place. That was fantasy, pure and simple, and fantasy didn't put food on the table. Or sit up with a sick child all night or drive a preschool carpool in the mornings. She was a single mother now, just as she'd once been a "single" wife. And while there was no denying that John Lee pined for a father, that he deserved a father, she had yet to meet a man who deserved to have his picture share space with the portrait of Johnny on his chest of drawers.

"Dinner's ready!" she called into the living room of the small shirt-waist-style bungalow she'd bought four years ago, after Johnny's status was officially changed from a presumed finding of death to killed in action. His body had never been recovered, so there'd been no flag-draped casket to give her closure. But at her parents' urging, she'd held a private memorial service for him.

That service had marked a watershed in her life. She'd moved out of her parents' house, where she'd been living with John Lee while she finished earning her teaching degree, and had used half of Johnny's insurance money to make a down payment on a home of their own. The other half she had placed in trust for John Lee. He wouldn't need it to pay for his college education. Those expenses would be met by the death benefits of a father he would never know. Still, with interest, it would amount to a tidy gift when he graduated.

Sighing in exasperation when her son failed to answer her earlier summons, she called again, "John Lee!"

"Just a minute," he replied with the typical reluctance of a five-year-old who was thoroughly engrossed in a "Deputy Dawg" cartoon.

Ordinarily, Cat would have waited until the program was over before giving him an ultimatum. After all, it was summertime and the living was supposed to be easy. But she was anxious to see how her mother was doing after her radiation treatment today, so she didn't hesitate to hurry him along. "I mean it, young man. Turn off that TV right this minute and wash your hands."

"All right." He sounded so put upon that she had to smile.

Cat set the lettuce on the kitchen table, between bowls of chopped tomatoes and shredded cheese, then went to the old gas stove to dish up the simmering hamburger meat. The elderly couple she'd bought the house from had kept it immaculate on the outside but hadn't done much to the inside since the Truman administration. She'd been remodeling and redecorating as her teacher's salary permitted ever since John Lee and she had moved in. Their bedrooms and the living and dining rooms were done, so her big project for the summer was to strip the white-painted kitchen cabinets and refinish them to their original oak. Come winter, she planned to repaper the walls and replace the ugly linoleum floor with one of those new no-wax floors. Eventually she hoped to be able to afford switching from steam heat to a central air-conditioning system.

"Oh, good, tacos!" John Lee raced in, resembling a manic elf in his red T-shirt, denim shorts and high-top tennis shoes. His skin was golden, his cheeks were rosy, and his grin revealed a space recently vacated by a front tooth. He was such an adorable boy, with thick black bangs hanging straight across his forehead and dark, sparkling eyes that were slightly tilted at the corners, that she tended to forget that he was not a child of her own body. She simply thought of him as a gift from God.

"Not so fast, buster." Cat caught him around the waist before he could slide into his chair. She nuzzled his neck, which caused him to squirm and giggle, before she set him down and demanded, "Let me see your hands."

"Mo-om . . ." He stretched the protest into two syllables as he hid the chubby little hands in question behind his back. "I was just watching TV."

"And petting Tiger." She'd allowed him to adopt the skinny, scruffy yellow-striped kitten after his preschool class had visited the animal shelter. He'd come home in tears, having overheard one of the workers there say that it was slated to be "put to sleep" soon. Now, after a few months of tender, loving care, the pitiful little fuzzball was well on its way to becoming a fat, sleek house cat.

"You brushed him yesterday," he rebutted, setting that square jaw he'd inherited from his father in a stubborn line.

Cat pointed a don't-argue-with-me finger at the half-bath off the kitchen.

John Lee, recognizing that he'd lost the battle, headed in that direction to wash his hands.

The doorbell rang just as they were finally sitting down to dinner.

"I'll get it!" John Lee jumped up from the table and hit for the front door.

"Remember, we're going to Grandma and Grandpa's this evening." Cat assumed it was his best friend David, who lived next door, wanting to know if he could come out and play when he was finished eating.

The deep male voice that answered John Lee's piping "Hi" proved her assumption wrong. Irritated to think it was probably one of those door-to-door salesmen, who seemed to have a real knack for catching their potential customers in the middle of a meal or a bath or a nap, she got up and followed her son to the foyer. The summer sun was behind the man, so as she approached she could only see his silhouette on the other side of the screen door.

John Lee, who never met a stranger, was talking the poor guy's leg off. "My dad was a soldier too, but he died in the war. I wasn't borned when he died, but my mom said he was a hero. She said all soldiers are heroes because they help keep us free. I'm going to be a pilot someday, just like my dad, but my mom said I gotta go to college first. In September I'm going to kindergarten." He shrugged, pulling both shoulders up beneath his ears and holding his hands, palms up, out to his sides. "I can tell time and I already know how to read *Goodnight Moon*, so I don't know what they're gonna teach me. But at least I won't have to go to the baby-sitter—"

"John Lee—" Cat began as she stepped up behind him and peered out the wire mesh at the man who was patiently listening to her son's prattle.

Time stopped for her as her precocious son continued chattering. "My Grandma's sick—she's got cancer—and my Grandpa's really sad. But he told her doctor she's gonna fight it just like she fought the Germans in World War Two. He said 'Once a warrior, always a warrior.' And then he started crying."

Looking at the man on the other side of the screen, Cat wiped sweaty palms on her ragged cut-offs and moistened suddenly dry lips. His black hair was short now, almost white-walled on the sides, and his face was even more finely chiseled than she recalled. The lines that etched the corner of his eye and the grooves that bracketed his sensuous mouth had deepened, giving his looks a provocatively seasoned edge.

More astonishing yet was his attire. Today there were no jeans or T-shirts or mud-caked boots. He wore Air Force blues with a bright slash of ribbons across his broad chest and shoes that had obviously been spit-shined.

Still, she would have recognized him anywhere.

"What happened to your eye?" John Lee asked with a child's blunt curiosity. "Did you lose it in the war? Is that why you have to wear that patch? My Uncle Drew didn't go to the war. He went to Canada, and he can't come home 'cause he's afraid they'll arrest him. My Aunt Mary—she's gonna be a lawyer like my Grandpa—said he was a coward. But my Grandma said he did what he thought was—"

"That's enough," Cat admonished her son.

"Well, it's the truth," he insisted obstinately.

"Cain." As she breathed his name, memories of a river of fire, rice paddies and a rain-freshened night in Saigon rushed back at her. She bit her lip, every emotion inside her coalescing and focusing on his rank. "Or should I say Major Cain?"

"You cut your hair," he said in that dark velvet voice she still heard in her dreams.

Of all that she had thought he might say if they ever met again, this was the last thing she had expected. But then, he'd always done the unexpected. Her eyes met his through the thin mesh. "So did you."

"I'll explain later," he promised.

"I'll hold you to that," she assured him.

"Do you like tacos?" John Lee asked. "My mom makes the best tacos in the world. She piles on cheese and lettuce and tomatoes, but she doesn't put onions on 'em 'cause I hate onions."

Cain chuckled at the expression of supreme distaste the boy made, then bent down and whispered conspiratorially, "I hate onions, too."

John Lee looked up appealingly at Cat. "Can he stay and eat with us, Mom? Please? We've got plenty of shells."

In turn, she glanced uncertainly at Cain.

He grinned. "I love tacos."

"I like your parents."

"They like you, too."

Cat and Cain were sitting on her patio. It was a perfect summer night. A full silver moon shone down upon them and countless stars swirled across the heavens. Fireflies danced in the darkened yard as the brass wind chimes hanging on a hook near the back door tinkled musically in the sultry breeze.

John Lee was spending the night, as he did almost every Friday, with his grandparents. He'd done a lot of his growing up in and around their house, and he always slept in Drew and Johnny's old bedroom, which had been redecorated just for him. Cat had been worried that it would be too much for her mother, but both Mike and Anne-Marie had insisted that they wanted to stay in as normal a routine as possible for as long as possible during her bout with breast cancer.

So tomorrow, her father and her son would have their regular boys' day out. Instead of going to the Lake of the Ozarks and taking the boat out to their "secret" fishing cove, as they often did on Saturdays, they were planning to have breakfast at a pancake house and then head for a batting cage where John Lee could work on his swing. Cain had been invited to accompany them, and he'd accepted with alacrity.

"When your mother put her hand on my arm and thanked me for her grandson . . ." His indrawn breath was sharp and serrated with emotion. "I almost lost it."

"They love him so much, both of them." Remembering the tender moment, she blinked to keep her tears at bay. "With Drew gone and Johnny dead, John Lee is like a second chance for them."

Cain reached for his cigarillo, glowing red in the ashtray that was sitting on the small wrought iron table between them. He dragged on it deeply before he exhaled, blowing a stream of smoke from his nostrils. As a concession to the heat, he'd taken off his uniform jacket, unbuttoned his collar and rolled up his shirtsleeves.

"We all need a second chance now and then," he said quietly.

Cat picked up her glass of iced tea and took a sip. While she'd gotten over the initial shock of seeing him standing at her door, they still had a lot of ground to cover. Five years' worth, to be exact. She decided to work backward, starting with today.

"That was you at the press conference this afternoon, wasn't it?"

"Yes."

"Why did you leave before it was over?" Despite the heavy hammering of her heart, she strove to keep her tone light as she looked over at him.

For an interminable moment, she thought he wasn't going to answer her. He stared up at the sky, as though he were lost in the past or hadn't heard her question. Then, lifting the beer he'd been nursing, he took a long swallow. Finally, as though he'd just fought some violent inner battle with himself—and lost—he glanced at her nakedly.

"Because I wasn't sure you'd want to see me again."

"You thought I might regret"—she caught herself before she could say "making love with you" and amended it to—"what happened between us?"

"People sometimes do things in the heat of the moment that they could kick themselves for later," he said in a ragged voice.

After dinner, Cat had changed out of her baggy T-shirt and denim cut-offs into a sleeveless blouse and a pair of linen shorts. Now she extended her bare legs and smiled at him. "Do you see any bruises?"

"Not there." Cain crushed out his cigarillo, then leaned over to brush a gentle finger across her cheek. The faint shadows beneath her beautiful hazel eyes spoke of the strain she'd been under. "But here . . . I see them here."

"I'm worried about my mother."

"Your father told me you're really close to her."

Even as she nodded, Cat kept her gaze locked on his. "And I'm still waiting for that explanation you promised me."

He owed her that, Cain reminded himself as he reached for his beer. Maybe he owed it to himself, too. He'd never known the kind of peace that he'd found so briefly in her arms. Her love had salved the wounds in his soul, had been an oasis of calm in the chaos of war, and he'd felt that a vital part of him was lost when she left Vietnam. The only way to get it back, he decided now, was to give her as much of the truth as he could.

"It's a long story."

And still she didn't waver. "I'm not going anywhere."

"I joined the Air Force the day I graduated from high school." The softness, but not the rawness, was gone from his voice as he recalled the patriotic young man who'd been determined to avenge his father's death.

"Vietnam wasn't even a blip on America's radar screen back then. We'd been aiding and advising the South Vietnamese Army for years. We'd even had a couple of casualties, killed by guerrillas at Bienhoa. But we were more concerned about Cuba than Southeast Asia."

"After President Kennedy forced the Soviets to withdraw their missiles from there, Johnny decided he wanted to go to the Air Force Academy."

"He graduated from the Academy?"

"No." Her eyes glimmered in the dark. "His grades weren't good enough."

His mouth crooked ruefully. "Well, at least I'm not competing with a genius as well as a ghost."

Cat suppressed the sudden, ecstatic hope that beat in her breast as she held his gaze. Johnny was the past, and it remained to be seen whether Cain was the future. Still, she wanted to set the record straight. Just in case.

"You aren't competing with anyone," she said softly.

Cain studied her face in the starlight, remembering it flushed with passion. After all the wild oats he'd sown, it was probably wrong and certainly selfish of him to feel relieved that there was no one else in her life. But there it was, a knot of tension slowly relaxing inside his gut.

"Neither are you," he said gruffly.

She took another sip of tea and then got back to the subject at hand. "When did you go to Vietnam?"

"In February 1965." He watched fireflies winking in the dark as he remembered the gung-ho kid who was going to kick Ho Chi Minh's butt up between his shoulders. "Just in time for Operation Rolling Thunder— the sustained American bombing of North Vietnam."

"I graduated from high school that June."

"Well, while you were marching down the aisle to 'Pomp and Circumstance,' I was crawling around in the jungle wondering what hit me."

Cat's blood chilled. "You were shot down?"

Cain's fingers flexed as if working a control stick. "I was going in to bomb a group of boxcars parked off a railroad. The weather was clear. I was right on target. Then I looked out and saw a SAM—"

"A SAM?"

"Surface-to-Air Missile." He stared into near space. "It went over me, thank God, but the explosion shook me up pretty bad. Anyway, I dropped my ordinance and knocked out the boxcars. I was climbing back up to ten-thousand feet, thinking I was home free, when the second SAM hit me."

Tears gleamed in her eyes beneath the silver of the stars. "You must have been terrified."

"Actually, I was dizzy."

"Dizzy?"

Just talking about it, Cain could feel the plane spinning sickeningly toward the ground. Could smell the choking smoke spreading toward the cockpit. Even with his eye closed, he could still see treetops swirling up to meet him. He took a deep breath, trying to control the hot fear that even now, eight years later, made him break out in a cold sweat.

Watching him, Cat realized that he was suffering a flashback. She'd seen it happen with other Vietnam vets. They would stop in the middle of a sentence and look around, disoriented for a moment, struggling with some nightmare image that still haunted them. The only thing to do, she'd learned, was to wait it out and, when they were ready, let them talk it out.

"Vertigo," he said shakily, gripping the neck of his beer bottle as if seeking a handhold. "I got a goddamn case of vertigo. I managed to bail out though a side window and the plane hit the ground before I did. It was blowing up on the way. The details get fuzzier from there. My face was bleeding and I'd been shot in the side—on my way down, I suppose. I was about half-crazy from the pain, but I had enough sense to ditch my parachute. I hid in the roots of a tree. Lord only knows how long I laid there. All night, I think. I just know I was determined not to let Charlie take me prisoner. Or mutilate my body."

He paused, features pinched, as he recalled darkness becoming light and hope replacing despair. "A day, maybe two days later, I made it out of the jungle. One of our patrols found me and called in a chopper. The doctors at the evac hospital did what they could—saved my life, but couldn't save my eye. And then they rotated me out to Japan."

Cat had been sitting there silently as Cain spoke. Now she thought of Johnny, her first love, her husband and the father of her child. Hot tears streamed down her cheeks as she looked up at the star-studded sky, praying to God that his had been a swift death. That he hadn't experienced more than a few cataclysmic seconds of pain and shock and fear before being enveloped in that eternal blackness. It was too horrible to contemplate otherwise.

"I was finished as a pilot." Cain relaxed his grip on the bottle, but his face was grief made flesh. "I wasn't finished with the war, though. While I was laying in that hospital bed in Japan, I started wondering how many other downed pilots were out there in the jungle and who was searching for them. Then I got to thinking about my father. What if he'd survived only to die at the hands of the Koreans? Or in a POW camp? That's when I decided to go DIA."

Cat blotted her burning eyes with the back of her hand. "DIA?"

"Defense Intelligence Agency."

"You were a spy?" she asked with sudden comprehension.

For security reasons, there were questions Cain still couldn't answer. But this wasn't one of them. "In a manner of speaking."

"Didn't that put you at even greater risk of being captured? Or killed?"

"What did I have to lose at that point? There was no one at home waiting for me. Hell, the Air Force was my home. And all those pilots—Johnny included—were my brothers."

She clenched her hands together in her lap. "That was why you didn't encourage me to believe that he was alive, isn't it?"

"Based on the information I had at the time," he confirmed, "I was fairly certain he died when his plane went down."

"They never recovered his remains," she said in a small voice.

"That's the real shame of this war," he replied bitterly. "The ultimate betrayal, really. Americans leaving their fighting men to die in captivity."

"But all our prisoners were returned in—"

His scoff cut her off. "Last I heard, there were at least 300 POWs still being held in Hanoi."

She gaped at him in disbelief. "Three hundred?"

"And that doesn't count the two thousand or so still reported as missing in action."

"Why isn't the media reporting this?"

"To be fair about it, some of them are. But they're voices in the wilderness of a media elite who would rather deride those who served as either stupid or evil, and therefore deserving of their fate."

Her sigh echoed his. She'd read the lies and exaggerations about those who'd fought in Vietnam. The repeated misrepresentations of American soldiers' actions—that they'd gone around shooting pregnant women and their unborn children for instance—seemed to have become conventional wisdom. Granted, a few GIs had done some gruesome things. The My Lai massacre, in which the entire population of a small village was lined up and gunned down, was certainly evidence of that. But the majority of veterans who'd been under attack on the battlefield had served both bravely and honorably.

"They should be brought home," she said sadly. "All of them. The living and the dead."

"That's why I'm making the Air Force my career." His announcement caught her off-guard.

"You're a lifer?"

"Those men are our sons and fathers, our brothers and best friends." He rolled his shoulders. Shifted restlessly in his chair. "I want to help bring them back. Repatriate the living and return the dead to their families for a proper burial."

Cat mulled it all over for a moment, then shook her head in confusion. "I don't get it."

"What?"

"If you were working for the military, why was Colonel Howard so convinced that you were a traitor?"

"That's the dirty little secret about undercover work," Cain explained. "The military buries your file when you take off the uniform. Then if you're caught, they've got plausible deniability."

"Did Tiny know what you were doing?"

"I think he had a pretty good idea, but he didn't press me on it."

"How about Loc and Ngo and Kim? And Sister Simone. Did they know?"

"The truth is, I tried to keep everyone in the dark. It was safer that way. For all of us."

"Well, you sure fooled me," she said in a sudden fit of temper.

He stared at her, surprised. "You sound angry."

Angry didn't begin to describe it. "Well, how would you feel if you'd spent five years thinking the person you loved was a traitor?"

He sat up straight, his eye glittering with wonder. "You love me?"

"Yes, damn you, I—" She broke off, realizing what she'd just said, and looked at him with misapprehension.

Cain reached over and caught her hand before she could retract her statement. "I love you too, Cat."

"This is ridiculous," she grumbled, trying to wrest free of his grasp.

He tightened his hold. "Why do you say that?"

"Because we hardly know each other."

"That's where you're wrong. We know each other very well. Not just in the Biblical sense, either," he added when he saw the protest forming on her lips. "I know, for instance, that you're one of the most courageous women I've ever met."

"You, on the other hand, are one of the sneakiest men I've ever met," she shot back.

He ignored that for the moment. "I know that you're beautiful—not only on the outside, but on the inside, where it really counts."

"Now that you've cut your hair, you're not so bad yourself," she said grudgingly.

That old pirate's grin revisited his lips. "I know that you can give as good as you get."

She snorted. "A real sweet talking guy, aren't you?"

"I also know that you're hell on wheels in bed."

Now she made a sound like steam escaping from a funnel. "In case you haven't noticed, my neighbors' windows are open and they can probably hear every word we're—"

"Lastly, I know that you're a good mother—a wonderful mother, in fact—to John Lee." He brought her hand to his cheek, held it there while he looked deeply into her eyes. "And I know that I'd like to make a family with you."

He had her there. She felt the pressure building in her chest. Her voice caught emotionally. "Oh . . . you . . ."

"Don't cry, Cat." Still holding her hand, Cain rose and pulled her to her feet. "Please, don't cry."

"I'm not," she sniffed, and swiped at her brimming eyes with the back of her free hand.

"Okay, then," he murmured huskily. "Don't laugh."

Even as a smile curved her lips at that, she felt tears well in her eyes again. She took a step back, tugging him toward the house. "Let's go inside."

"I didn't come here to pick up where we left off," he said, standing his ground. "I came here to see if we could start over." He lifted their joined hands to his lips. "To tell you that I'm tired of being a loner." He kissed her knuckles one by one. "I came here to tell you that I need you in my life. That I want you. That I love you." He lowered his voice to an urgent whisper. " I came here to ask you to marry me."

Her head seemed to be floating somewhere above her shoulders. "This is all happening so fast."

"I don't report for six weeks, so—"

"Report where?"

"Washington."

"As in Washington, D.C.?"

He nodded affirmatively. "I'll work at headquarters. In intelligence."

Fear formed a bubble in her throat. "That means you could be called overseas again."

"All servicemen live with that possibility."

"Their wives, too."

Cain watched the play of expression on her face. Saw the pain that another man, before his time, had put there. Then he said what needed to be said. "Whether I'm at home or abroad, I'll never give you reason to doubt me, Cat. I swear it on my mother's grave."

She believed him. With all her heart, she believed him. "Six weeks." She blew out a breath. "That sure doesn't leave me much time to plan a wedding."

"You'll marry me?"

"On one condition," she said, and watched his smile slide away from his face.

"What's that?"

"No more secrets between us."

He frowned. "There may be times when I can't tell you where I'm going or when I'm coming back."

"I'm not talking about your work."

Cain tensed, knowing now exactly what she was talking about. "It's ugly."

"I'll be the judge of that." Cat reached up and removed the eye patch.

He stood there, his heart thudding with dread, as she silently studied the scarred and empty socket for what felt like the longest moment of his life.

"No," she said, her sorrow at the sacrifice he'd made so that others might live supplanted by a swelling of pride that this heroic man had chosen her to love. "It's not ugly." She lifted her hand and cupped his cheek. Drew his head down until their mouths were but a breath apart. Just before their lips met, she whispered, "It's a badge of honor."

Chapter Twenty

VIENNA, VIRGINIA; APRIL 30, 1975

Sitting alone on the sofa, the saltine she'd been nibbling on to fend off her nausea turning to dust in her mouth, Cat was fixated on the fall of Saigon that was being broadcast on the late-night news special.

Giving silent thanks that John Lee was already asleep, she reached for the remote and changed the channel. Only to see a sobbing Vietnamese mother, her face a portrait of fear and grief, holding her baby out and staring intently into the camera as if to say, "Please take my child." In the background, rockets and mortars were exploding and people were racing through the streets, screaming hysterically.

She should turn off the television right now, she told herself. Give her parents a call and ask how her mother was doing. Or go to bed and read the book of baby names that she'd checked out of the library today.

Instead, she flipped back to the first channel and watched through moist eyes as clouds of tear gas billowed up from the top of the six-floor U.S. Embassy building. Her pulse pounded in time to the gunfire rattling randomly in the streets below the building. She could almost taste the fear of the Marines who'd been serving as security guards and were now stranded on the rooftop. Her heart went out to the frenzied mobs of Vietnamese people—many of whom had worked for the Americans during the war—who were storming the embassy compound, trying to flee the Communist tanks that were slamming into the city.

Oh, God, Cat thought, her blood suddenly shivering to ice in her veins, was this the field assignment that Cain had gone on?

She strongly suspected it was. His "business trips," as they referred to them for John Lee's benefit, had been few and far between in the almost two years they'd been married. And most of those hadn't lasted more than a couple of days. A week at the most. But one afternoon he'd called her from headquarters to say that he wouldn't be home for dinner that night. That was their pre-arranged signal that he'd been pressed into undercover service again. She'd known better than to ask him where he was going. Or when he was coming back. She'd just told him that she loved him and reminded him to be careful.

That was the last time she'd heard from in almost a month.

Now, she laid her hand over the slight swell of her stomach, suffering a sickening sense of déjà vu as she wondered if she was destined to lose her beloved husband and the father of her unborn child to a war that would not end.

Then her heart soared when she spotted the American helicopter settle down on the embassy's rooftop pad. Green, yellow and red smoke from the signal grenades marked the spot as the marines scrambled aboard the chopper. Finally, blades whirling and smoke swirling, the chopper lifted off. It took a brief, steep plunge, then clawed for altitude before fluttering off toward the horizon and the safety of the U.S. fleet riding offshore in the South China Sea.

It was over, Cat realized, wilting back against the sofa cushion. Or was it? For her, it wouldn't truly be over until Cain came home to her safe and sound. But even then, she wondered, would they still be prisoners of the longest, saddest, baddest war America had ever fought?

John Lee saw him first.

"Mom!" he hollered from the front porch of their red brick Georgian house, where he'd been working on a new model airplane since he'd gotten home from school. "Cain's here! And guess what? He's got a—"

Cat was sitting in the kitchen, drinking weak tea and eating a piece of dry toast to help settle her queasy stomach. She was convinced that her morning sickness—which she usually suffered in the evening—was linked as much to the weather as it was to the hormone changes taking place in her body. When it was sunny, she felt fine. But when it was cloudy, as it had been these past four days, she had trouble keeping food down.

Now, on hearing John Lee's shout, she set her cup on the table, pushed her plate away and scraped her chair back. She was barely four months pregnant, but she was already beginning to feel awkward. Yet her feet were fleet and her arms were aching to embrace her husband, her hero.

She came to an abrupt halt at the door.

Cain was standing on the driveway, holding—

"A baby!" John Lee exclaimed as he dashed across the yard.

"A boy," Cain explained, crouching to show off the blanket-wrapped bundle in his arms.

"Oh, wow!" John Lee was jumping up and down for joy. "He looks just like my baby pictures!"

Cat said nothing as she crossed the yard. She was too caught up in looking at Cain. She'd lain awake too many nights to count, aching to hold him. To have him hold her. Now she drank in the sight of him, absorbing everything about him. His hair was freshly cut, his face smoothly shaved and his uniform neatly pressed. Despite the broad smile he gave her when he looked at her, she could see that his eye was shadowed by memories of what he had recently endured.

"Well," she said as she approached the driveway. "Aren't you full of surprises?"

Still holding the baby, he rose. "His mother thrust him at me through the embassy gates and begged me to take him."

Cat thought of the woman she'd seen on the television screen the other night. She couldn't imagine giving her child into a stranger's keeping. Unless that stranger was James Lee Cain. "She knew a good man when she saw one."

"Guess who else got out?" he asked her then.

"Sister Simone?"

He shook his head negatively. "She'll never leave the orphans. Not even at gun point."

"Well, I know that Tiny's going to law school in Oakland, California."

"Last time I talked to him, he was making straight A's."

She threw up her hands. "Okay, I give up."

"Loc and Ngo and their four children."

Cat's happiness for them was tempered by her worry about another. "And Kim?"

A spasm of sadness crossed Cain's face. "She was killed in a crossfire last year."

"She loved you, you know."

"And I loved her. But after you, only as a friend."

"Can we keep the baby?" Now it was John Lee's turn to beg. "Huh? Can we?"

"That's up to your mother," Cain cautioned as he extended his free arm to draw Cat closer for a kiss.

She moved eagerly into his embrace. His lips were warm, hers welcoming. Glad tears streamed down her cheeks as she breathed in the clean scent of his shirt. As she angled her head to accommodate the gentle thrust of his tongue, she felt a faint fluttering sensation in her mid-section. It was too soon, she was sure of it. Fancifully, though, she wondered if it wasn't her unborn child's way of greeting its father.

The baby he was holding, on the other hand, lay quietly in his arms.

Following their private wedding in the parlor of her parish priest, they had talked about adopting a Vietnamese orphan someday. But this . . . Well, it was strange timing, to say the least. In thinking back to when she first got John Lee, though, Cat realized that Cain was healing his wounds through his children. That after all the death, he desperately needed life.

"Please, Mom," John Lee pleaded as the only parents he'd ever known broke apart.

"I'll take the night feedings," Cain whispered against her tingling lips.

"And I'll change his diapers." John Lee immediately qualified his promise with, "Unless they're dirty."

With her husband's arm around her and her seven-year-old son's eyes shining with hope, how could she refuse? She couldn't. Laughing now, Cat splayed her hand over her stomach and nodded. "I guess we're going to have twins, huh?"

"I love you," Cain said with a tender smile.

"Safe home, Colonel," she replied as she reached for the baby he'd carried halfway around the world.

The baby stared up at her, unblinking, as she cradled him to her breast. His hair and eyes were as dark as John Lee's but his skin was just a shade lighter. A wave of maternal love swept through her as she touched his little button of a nose. His wide but tiny mouth opened in a yawn. Then he lowered his lashes and fell asleep in her arms.

"Michael." She looked at Cain. "For my father."

"A strong name," he agreed. "A survivor's name."

"Let's go call Grandpa," John Lee suggested. "Maybe Grandma will feel well enough to talk on the phone and we can tell her about my new brother, too."

Cat's eyes filled with tears at the mention of mother. Despite heavy doses of radiation, treatments that had left her burned and blistered and scarred, Anne-Marie's cancer had metastasized to the bone. The last X-rays had also shown a suspicious lesion in her right lung. Cat had flown back to Kansas City in February to celebrate her birthday with the woman who'd given her life and to tell her parents in person that they had another grandchild on the way. The news had revived their flagging spirits, and she'd come home to Virginia praying it would give them a reason to keep fighting that damned disease.

"Yes," she agreed now. "Let's go call Grandpa and Grandma."

The sun broke through the clouds and beamed down like a blessing as Cat, holding the baby, and Cain, holding John Lee's hand, started back to the house.

And the darkness of a war that had divided a nation but had brought their family together began to fade.

Epilogue

ARLINGTON NATIONAL CEMETERY; 1998

Six Air Force pallbearers slowly carried the flag-covered coffin of Lieutenant John Brown, Jr. from the black hearse to a spot near a dogwood tree that had been shorn of its leaves by the rising November wind.

Wearing his dress blues, Captain John Lee Brown, Johnny's only surviving relative and a career military officer like the man who had raised him, led the procession to his father's grave. Much to his mother's dismay, he'd gained his air combat experience flying AWACS during Desert Storm. He was now based at Aviano, Italy, and was performing fly-over missions in the troubled Balkans—the same region, ironically, where his grandfather had gone down in World War Two. To his mother's delight, however, he was home on leave for a month. Even better, his fiancé, Gina, had come with him so she could meet his family.

Taking her seat under the tent that had been set up for the mourners, Cat shivered as four F-15s in formation screamed across the sky and the front fighter jet peeled up and away to symbolize the lost soldier. Sitting beside her, Cain sensed her distress. He slipped his arm around her shoulder and drew her close. She leaned on him, as she had for twenty-three years now, and allowed the tears she'd been holding inside her all day to flow freely down her cheeks.

Hearing the jets' thunder, Mike Scanlon thought of an empty room on another continent in another war that had once been filled with love. Anne-Marie had been gone for more than twenty years now, but he wasn't alone. In addition to Cat and Cain and their children, his daughter Mary—a tough-as-nails county prosecutor who was being touted as a possible candidate for Missouri's first woman attorney general in 2000—and her husband sat to his right. To his left were his son Drew, a social worker and an unreconstructed hippie in bifocals and Birkenstocks, and his wife. Along with all the other young men who had fled to Canada to avoid the draft, he'd received amnesty from President Jimmy Carter and had finally returned to the city of his birth.

"First," said the Catholic chaplain who was conducting the ceremony, "let us give all glory to God for bringing John Brown, Jr., an American hero, home at long last."

The box containing a few bones and one tooth had been released for burial following a repatriation ceremony at Travis Air Force Base in California. The remains had undergone rigorous testing, which included taking a DNA sample from John Lee, before being positively identified as Johnny's. A joint U.S.-Laos recovery team had found them almost eighteen months ago.

The man who'd led the search, a highly decorated pilot, a former member of the Defense Intelligence Agency and a retired Brigadier General, was also the husband of the deceased's widow.

As Cain had suspected from the beginning, Johnny had been shot down in the Americans' secret bombing campaign in Laos. For years the Laotian government had refused entry to the various teams that were working to recover the remains of U.S. servicemen in Southeast Asia. Only after economic and political pressures were brought to bear had they finally relented and joined the cooperative effort.

Based on both written reports and eyewitness accounts, the recovery team had narrowed their search to the two main mountain passes—Mu Gia and Ban Karat—between Vietnam and Laos. The area had been thoroughly scavenged when they reached it. But among the items excavated were identifiable parts of a B-52 bomber, pieces of a crewman's flightsuit, and the human bones and tooth that were being buried today. To the team's astonishment, an old man in a nearby village had turned over Johnny's dogtags, which he'd kept as a war souvenir all these years.

As the ceremony drew to a close, the mournfully slow notes of "Taps" rent the cold air. Then seven rifles were fired three times each in a 21-gun salute. Finally, John Lee accepted the triangularly folded American flag that had covered his father's casket. It would go in the same box containing the cassette tapes his parents had exchanged during their marriage, Johnny's dogtags and the Distinguished Flying Cross, Purple Heart and Air Medal with Four Oak Leaf Cluster that he'd been awarded for meritorious achievement during flight.

"Go in peace," the chaplain said to the three generations of warriors sitting before him.

Flanked by Cat and Cain, John Lee stood to greet the crowd that had gathered. Some, like the man in a black POW T-shirt and camouflage pants who said he hadn't known Johnny personally but was a Vietnam vet who thought it important that he pay his respects, were complete strangers. Others were friends.

"I'm so glad you could come," Cat said as she enveloped Ngo in a hug.

Loc shook Cain's hand. "Thank you for helping us gain our freedom."

"Don't thank me." Cain looked out over the endless rows of white headstones that consecrated the ground with such crushing finality. "Thank them."

Loc and Ngo's four children, grown to adulthood now, filed solemnly by.

Mike laid a copy of that old black-and-white picture of John and Charlie and him, taken on John and Kitty's wedding day by Daisy, atop Johnny's casket before he stepped outside the tent to join his family.

"What a waste." Drew gazed at the white crosses that marked the final resting place of so many American soldiers from a completely different perspective than Cain's.

Mike and Drew had long since reconciled their differences and could discuss the Vietnam War with little or no rancor now. But as he stood there beside his son, he suddenly realized that neither he nor Anne-Marie had ever fully disclosed the part she'd played with the French Résistance during World War Two. That they'd never really talked about the fact that while war is awful and sometimes morally iffy, it's not always a wasted effort. Like so many in their generation, they'd simply rolled up their sleeves and gone back to either work or school when they'd come home, letting their actions speak louder than their words.

Figuring better late than never, Mike smiled at Drew. "Did you ever hear about a woman called 'Tiger Lily'?"

Drew frowned. "No."

"Come on," Mike encouraged, canting his head toward the curb, "I'll tell you about her now."

Tears of joy sprang to Cat's eyes when she saw Mike and Drew deep in conversation. She knew that this separate peace between father and son was exactly what Anne-Marie had hoped and prayed for to the bitter end. And that her mother was probably smiling down from heaven at the sight of them, arms draped over each other's shoulders, walking toward the family limousine.

She looked at her husband then and asked, "Where do we go from here?"

Cain's mission was complete, but thanks to those who'd made the supreme sacrifice, his life was far from over. He felt his throat swell with pride as he looked at his three sons—John Lee, the child of his heart if not his blood; Michael, who was in medical school now, and his "twin," James, Jr., who was working on his law degree. Then there was the apple of his eye—his daughter, Anna Marie, named for both Cat's mother and his. She was a senior in high school, smart as a whip and a real beauty to boot.

After sketching an invisible salute to all who'd gone before, he slid his arm around his wife's waist and answered her question with one word. "Home."

About The Author

A former court reporter who's married to a judge, Fran Baker has a great track record for producing top-quality fiction. She is a member of Novelists, Inc., The Authors Studio and the Small Publishers Association of North America. Her next book, *Silken Ties*, is scheduled for release in 1999.

Coming in 1999 . . .

Silken Ties

A NEW NOVEL BY
FRAN BAKER

AND

The Lady and the Champ

A DELPHI BOOKS CLASSIC
BY FRAN BAKER

If you enjoyed *ONCE A WARRIOR*,
order a copy for a relative or friend!

DELPHI BOOKS
P.O. Box 6435
Lee's Summit, MO 64064

I enclose a check or money order (not cash) for $12.95, plus $2.00 to cover postage and handling (MO residents add 85¢) per copy. (Allow 4-6 weeks for delivery.) Please send my book(s) to:

Name:_____

Address: _____

City/State/Zip: _____

Available while they last from Delphi Associates 2000

THE PIONEER DOCTOR IN THE OZARKS WHITE RIVER COUNTRY

A non-fiction account of a country doctor
in the horse-and-buggy days by
Amy Johnson Miller

DELPHI ASSOCIATES 2000
P.O. Box 6435
Lee's Summit, MO 64064

I enclose a check or money order (not cash) for $9.95, plus $2.00 to cover postage and handling (MO residents add 66¢ tax) per copy. (Allow 4-6 weeks for delivery.) Please send my book(s) to:

Name: _____

Address: _____

City/State/Zip: _____